THE COMPANY

THE COMPANY

Sally Spencer

**SEVERN
HOUSE**

First world edition published in Great Britain and the USA in 2021
by Severn House, an imprint of Canongate Books Ltd,
14 High Street, Edinburgh EH1 1TE.

Trade paperback edition first published in Great Britain and the USA in 2022
by Severn House, an imprint of Canongate Books Ltd.

severnhouse.com

British Library Cataloguing-in-Publication Data
A CIP catalogue record for this title is available from the British Library.

ISBN-13: 978-0-7278-9094-8 (cased)
ISBN-13: 978-1-78029-773-6 (trade paper)
ISBN-13: 978-1-4483-0511-7 (e-book)

All Severn House titles are printed on acid-free paper.

Typeset by Palimpsest Book Production Ltd.,
Falkirk, Stirlingshire, Scotland.
Printed and bound in Great Britain by
TJ Books Limited, Padstow, Cornwall.

ONE

The rain, which had dogged us all the way from Bristol, was showing no signs of easing up, and the maddeningly monotonous clicking of the windscreen wipers only served to increase the tension which already filled the air inside the car.

There were five of us in the BMW hire car. In the front sat Edward Conroy, my father, and Tony Conroy, my uncle. Crammed tightly together in the back were myself, my brother John, and Bill Harper, Uncle Tony's executive assistant.

Uncle Tony – red-faced, weightlifter-solid – was driving recklessly, negotiating the narrow country lanes at a speed well in excess of the limit. My father – half a head shorter and far less square – was breathing heavily through his nose, in a way which, I knew from experience, indicated irritation.

'Are you sure this is a shortcut, Tony?' my father asked, looking down at the map which was folded awkwardly on his knee.

'Of course I'm sure!' my uncle snapped. 'We wouldn't be taking it if I wasn't.'

'Well, shortcut or not, we're going to be late,' my father said, not without an element of morbid satisfaction in his voice.

'We *won't* be late!' Uncle Tony replied through gritted teeth, as he pulled hard round a bend. 'We can't bloody *afford* to be late.'

Certainly *he* couldn't, I thought. He had a lot riding personally on the meetings he'd arranged with the potential new clients in Swansea. A good first impression was essential, and a lack of punctuality wouldn't help create one. Nor would those clients be likely to be impressed by the five of us arriving in one vehicle – as if Conroy Enterprises was so strapped for cash that we couldn't afford to hire a second car.

'We should have flown!' my uncle said. 'If we'd chartered a plane, we'd have been there by now.'

And I, seeing an opportunity to get under his skin after all the emotional stress he'd put *me* through, couldn't resist the temptation to say, 'It's no good thinking of what might have been.'

It's no good thinking of what might have been. That was rich – coming, as it did, from someone who had spent a great deal of his life thinking about just that!

We reached a T-junction and Uncle Tony, with barely a glance to the left, wrenched the wheel around to the right.

'For Heaven's sake, Tony!' my father exploded. 'Do you want to get us all killed?'

'I know what I'm doing,' my uncle snapped back.

Bill Harper, who was sandwiched between John and me, reached – with some difficulty – for the leather attaché case which had been resting at his feet. Then, with another clumsy movement, which involved elbowing both of us, he managed to open the case and extract some papers.

'Would you like me to brief you on the first meeting, Mr Conroy?' he asked.

And though there were four Mr Conroys in the car, we all knew he meant Uncle Tony, whom he served with an apparent dogged loyalty which seemed to belong to an earlier generation.

'Brief me?' my uncle said, his eyes glued to the road. 'No, I think I've got everything I need to know.'

I glanced down at my watch. We definitely weren't going to make it. On the one hand I was glad, because, if anyone had been riding for a fall, it was my uncle. On the other hand, I had finally come to accept that my small business, which I had lovingly built up over the years, was no more than a small cog in the mighty Conroy Enterprises machine, and that its future was inextricably tied in with whatever decisions Uncle Tony chose to make for the rest of the company.

'Should be joining the main road again soon,' Uncle Tony grunted as he accelerated along a straight stretch of lane.

And so we would have – if it hadn't been for the truck.

It was a military truck, from the air force base at St Asaph. I know that now.

All I knew then was that a great metal beast had suddenly emerged out of the rain and was heading in our direction.

It should have been a safe enough encounter. The lane was

narrow, but by slowing down, the two vehicles would have been able to crawl cautiously past each other. The driver of the truck *did* slow down – but the BMW hire car carried on as if it had the whole road to itself.

'Put your brakes on, for God's sake!' my father shouted.

'I'm trying to!' my uncle screamed back.

I could hear the sound of his foot, desperately pumping the brake pedal.

I could see the face of the truck driver – gazing down, white with horror, as he drew ever closer.

At my side, I felt Bill Harper start to tense at the same moment as my stomach, without consulting me, began to do somersaults.

We were only yards from the truck now, and it had ceased to look like any kind of vehicle at all, instead transforming itself into the solid metal wall which would crush us on contact.

I thought of reaching across Bill and his bloody attaché case, opening John's door, and pushing my brother out. But even as the plan was forming in my mind, I recognized there would be no time to carry it out.

We had just a split second left.

Only Uncle Tony could save us now.

My uncle had given up trying to bring the car to a halt and was finally taking the only evasive action open to him, which was to steer for the narrow gap between the truck and the high stone wall which bounded the lane. He was a good driver and might actually have made it if he hadn't hit the patch of water on the road.

When I heard the scream of the tyres and felt the car slew to the left, I knew we were doomed.

Panic engulfed me – pure blind panic. We were going to die, a voice screamed in my head. We were all *going to die*. Not of old age. Not of some disease which would slowly eat away at us. We were going to die suddenly – violently – the result of some freak accident!

Through the windscreen, I could see a stone wall ahead of us, oddly angled as we skidded across the lane. Then the wing of the BMW hit the wall with a jarring thud, sending shock waves juddering through the whole vehicle.

'Oh God!' my brother gasped.

And I found myself repeating silently, 'Oh God, oh God, oh God!'

The car was on two wheels now, and we were all sliding towards the right-hand side of the lane. Then it flipped completely over, righted itself and began to roll again. It was like being trapped inside some monstrous fairground amusement which had gone tragically wrong. I was fighting for breath but yet, even in the last few moments, I still clung on to the hope that there might be some way for us to escape our fate.

Then the car slammed hard against the truck – and my universe went black.

There were probably less than two hours between the moment when Grandmother – looking down at her husband's deathbed back in Cheshire – was forced to accept that she was a widow, and the ringing on the doorbell which heralded the dreadful news of more family deaths in South Wales.

The first of these events certainly came as no shock to her. Though Grandfather had been a vigorous man in his time – had built up his business empire almost single-handed – the last few years had not been kind to him, and he had spent the final three swathed in rugs in his favourite armchair, like an under-the-weather child or a sick puppy.

That was where he'd been the last time I had seen him – the day I'd stormed out of the board meeting.

That had been two months ago, in late April, and it had been a pleasantly warm day, despite which a coal fire was blazing away in Grandfather's sitting room, and the whole place was filled with a sticky heat.

'I thought it would be you, Rob,' the old man said.

'What do you mean, Grandfather?'

'I thought that, after the meeting, you'd be the one to come and appeal to me. Your father's far too passive. Always has been. So's your brother. But even when you were a little lad, you showed a different kind of spirit. Well, now you're here, why don't you have your say?'

'You can't gamble with the company like this,' I told him.

A thin smile came to his old lips. 'I'm not doing the gambling. Your uncle Tony is.'

'He couldn't do it without your permission.'

Grandfather nodded weakly. 'No, he couldn't,' he agreed. 'And what if I had withheld that permission? In six months or a year, when I'm no longer around, he'll go ahead anyway. Isn't it better to do it now, while I'm still here to offer advice?'

'The heart of your company – the company that you built up from nothing – is furniture,' I reminded him. 'The haulage business was never more than a handmaiden – a useful adjunct. And now Uncle Tony's planning to move haulage centre stage – and you're just standing by and letting it happen.'

'Yes, I am,' Grandfather said, 'because it's what Tony wants.'

'And what about what I want, Grandfather?' I demanded. 'Doesn't that matter to you at all?'

'Of course it matters. Haven't I always done everything in my power to make you happy?'

I thought of the one time he visited me in the institution, just after the caring yet unsmiling doctors had announced I was ready to be released into the community again, and I, for my part, had been far from sharing their conviction.

I remembered listening as he promised to buy a publishing house for me and wondering which one of us was really the lunatic.

And I felt ashamed.

'You've always been very good to me,' I said contritely.

'When I'm gone, somebody will have to take the decisions,' Grandfather said, 'and – barring accidents – that will be my eldest son, your uncle Tony.'

'It doesn't have to be that way,' I pointed out. 'You could split the company. Let each of us run our own show.'

A sudden fire burned in Grandfather's eyes, as bright as the one in the grate.

'Never!' he said. 'Never! I've spent a lifetime building it up. I'm not about to allow it to fall apart after I've gone.'

'Uncle Tony could bankrupt us.'

My grandfather shook his head. 'I'm not quite as doddering as to let him go ahead if there was much chance of that. Besides,

I've taken risks right from the start. I took a risk with you. It's about time someone else in the family had the responsibility.'

'So there's nothing I can do to persuade you?'

'Nothing.'

The heat had made my trousers stick to my knees, and my throat felt incredibly dry.

I stood up.

'If you'll excuse me, Grandfather, it's rather stuffy in here,' I said. 'I think what I need is a breath of fresh air.'

I walked over to the door.

'Rob!' said a cracked voice behind me.

I turned. 'Yes, Grandfather?'

The old man was clutching tightly on to his stick, and there was a pleading look in his watery eyes. 'You won't stop coming to see me when you're up in the village, will you?' he asked. 'Not because of this?'

'Of course I won't, Grandfather,' I promised him.

I loved him dearly, I thought, as I walked back to my parents' house, but that didn't mean I was blind to the fact that he was a stubborn old man – an anachronism who still thought in terms of family firms in an era of multiple-holding, multinational companies.

Perhaps if Geoff Carson had been a little more flexible back in the early fifties, and if Grandfather's father hadn't died of a broken heart, my talk with him might have gone differently.

But we can't change the past, however much we want to, I told myself as I opened my parents' front gate. All that we can hope is that it does not cast too long a shadow on the present and the future.

I didn't know about the will then, of course – didn't know how Grandfather had used the law to create a tunnel down which the remaining members of the family would be forced to march. Even if I had known, I doubt very much whether I would have been able to imagine the devastating effect it would have in the post-crash world into which I was about to awaken.

TWO

've read that when people first recover consciousness, they have no idea where they are or what has happened to them.

It wasn't like that with me. Looking up at the ceiling I knew immediately both that I was in hospital, and that I was there because of the crash.

I became aware that two people – a man in a white coat and a woman wearing a crisp uniform – were standing beside my bed.

'What's happened to . . . is my brother . . .?' I gasped in a voice which seemed to belong to a semi-strangled frog.

'First things first, old chap,' said the man, in a low reassuring voice. 'Can you tell us your name?'

'I'm Rob Conroy.'

'And do you know what the date is, Rob?'

'It's . . . it's the 24th of June.'

'And the year?'

'1991.'

'Good! Just one more question – can you tell me where you were born?'

I told him I was born in Cheshire – more precisely in a small village outside Northwich – and he nodded as if he were pleased by my performance.

'Well, your mind seems all right, old son, but there's no disputing your body's taken a bit of a battering,' the doctor said. 'You've got three broken ribs, a sprained wrist and a bruised femur, but given what you've been through, it could have been much worse.'

'My brother . . .' I said.

'What you should be doing now is concentrating on building your strength up, and to do that you have to push any thoughts of anything else to the back of your mind,' the doctor told me.

'My brother!' I said as loudly as I could.

The doctor looked at the nurse for guidance, and the nurse gave him a solemn nod.

'I'm sorry to have to tell you this, old chap, but only one other person survived the crash, and he was a man called Bill Harper,' the doctor said.

It is hard, even now, to describe the feelings and emotions I found myself having to deal with in those first few hours of post-crash consciousness.

There was the grief, of course. I had never cared much for Uncle Tony, who was a difficult man to admire (or even respect), and my father had held himself so distant from me that I felt I'd hardly known him. Yet both their deaths left a gap – an unexpectedly aching void – in my life. But worse – far worse – was my sorrow at losing my brother John – dear, gentle John, who had made childhood bearable, and who, in my adult life, had been the one person, apart from Grandfather, I felt I could depend on. I had loved him as much as any brother could, and with his dying, a part of me had died.

Then there was the guilt. Why should I have survived, when my father, uncle and brother had not? I asked myself. And why – and this was even worse – why had I failed to save them? The latter feeling was, I knew even at the time, an irrational one, but it was not unfamiliar – I had felt the same burden descend on me that day, a million years earlier, when Jill's father had phoned and told me in a dead voice that she would not be coming back from Cornwall.

Yet as deep and searing as these emotions were, the grief and guilt still sometimes found themselves being nudged to one side by a disappointment which almost bordered on despair.

Where was Marie? a voice wailed inside my head.

She must have heard about the crash on the television, or from the newspapers, but she had not even bothered to phone me.

I tried to tell myself that I had no right to expect her to make any such effort, because she'd made it quite clear – right from the start – that ours was not to be an intimate relationship. Yet wasn't that just what it had *become*? True, we had never so much as kissed, but not only did we enjoy the same things – we seemed to enjoy them the more because we were sharing them.

And even if she hadn't developed the same feelings for me

as I'd developed for her, wouldn't it have been just common humanity to pick up the phone and find out how I was?

I'd have done as much for a casual acquaintance.

Grief, guilt and disappointment – they rode thunderingly back and forth across my brain as if they were three of my own personal horsemen of the apocalypse. But it was the fourth horseman, even darker than the others, who was the worst of all – and his name was Fear.

I was terrified, you see, that I didn't have the mental resources to cope with all this, and that it would force me over the edge for the second time in my life.

Last time, I'd been discovered in my rooms, stark naked and huddled over the fire I'd started on my desk with the notes for an essay I'd been attempting to write. Next time it could be anything. And if there *was* a next time – if I once more allowed myself to sink into the dark nightmare pool of helplessness – I knew I would drown.

It was mid-afternoon when the nurse told me I should expect a visitor.

'He's a policeman,' she said. 'A chief inspector someone-or-other. He wants to talk to you about the crash, but if you don't feel strong enough, you've only to tell me, and I'll do my level best to keep him away from you.'

'I think I can handle it,' I said.

But as I was dozing off, I did wonder why a chief inspector would concern himself with a simple traffic accident.

Dusk was falling when the policeman finally came to see me. He was a tall, thin man of about my age, with a drooping moustache and a slightly mournful expression. My first impression was that he seemed vaguely familiar – though there was no reason at all why I should know a policeman stationed a couple of hundred miles from my home – but it was not until he stopped, halfway between the door and my bed, to take a bag of boiled sweets out of his pocket, that recognition hit me.

'In the children's home where I was brought up, sweets were only distributed on Saturdays – and then only to those inmates who were deemed to have deserved them,' he once told me.

'They were the currency in our little prison. No, they were more than that – they were the source of power and survival. A Fry's Turkish Delight could make a bully go away. A couple of chunks of Cadbury's Fruit and Nut would be enough to persuade one of the prettier boys to jerk you off, if you were that way inclined. We craved sweets, but we never ate them until they were about to turn musty – because magic should never be needlessly squandered.'

'Owen?' I said. 'Owen Flint?'

He grinned, self-consciously. 'I wasn't sure that you'd remember me.'

I wondered how he ever imagined I'd have been able to forget him. Even though, by the time we went up, Oxford had become a little more egalitarian than it had been, he still stuck out like a sore thumb – a skinny Welsh boy totally lost outside the confines of a charitable institution.

'I thought you were going to be a poet,' I said.

'So did I,' he said, picking up a chair and placing it down next to my bed. 'And maybe I am. Poetry's about imposing order and making sense of the world, and being a copper fulfils at least half of that requirement.'

He unwrapped a boiled sweet and popped it into his mouth. He didn't offer me one – the smirks he had received in college had cured him of that habit.

'You've done well for yourself, Rob,' he continued. 'You're a successful publisher – the man who discovered Andy McBride.'

'Yes, that's me,' I admitted. 'Sometimes I think that's what I'll always be – the man who discovered Andy.'

'You've got a private room and even your own telephone,' he mused. 'Very nice.'

He didn't sound envious at all, but I still felt the need to put him right. 'The only reason I have a private room is because everyone who works for Conroy Enterprises has brilliant health insurance,' I said. 'And the phone isn't mine – it's just an extension.'

Owen Flint crossed one spindly leg over the other. 'You want to tell me what you were doing on my patch, Rob?' he asked.

'We were down here on business.'

Owen used his tongue to transfer the boiled sweet from one hollow cheek to the other. 'Would you care to be more specific?'

'Yesterday we were in Bristol, buying a company called Western Haulage. Today we were supposed to travel up to Swansea.'

'To buy more businesses?'

'No, to persuade some of Western Haulage's more dissatisfied clients in the steel industry that they should stick with the company, now that it's under new management.'

'So publishing isn't the only thing you're interested in? You have your finger in more than one pie?'

I sighed. I didn't want to go into complex explanations, but if Owen was to understand the situation, I didn't see how I could avoid it.

'All the companies – the furniture factories, the hauliers, the garages, the catering firm and the publishing house – are controlled by my grandfather,' I said. 'He set each member of the family up in a different business, but he never lets us forget we're working for him.'

I caught the slight flicker in Flint's eye. I didn't understand it at the time, but I think I do now. He already knew that Grandfather was dead, and it was plain from the way I was talking that I didn't.

'I don't see what advantage there was in having a publisher in on this particular deal,' he said.

'My father and I opposed my uncle's plan to take over Western Haulage,' I explained. 'We thought he was stretching the company's resources too thinly. We thought there was a danger he could bankrupt us all.'

Flint's eyes narrowed, and I reminded myself that he was no longer an uncertain undergraduate, but a chief inspector in the South Wales police. 'How could he bankrupt you all?' he asked.

'In order to raise the money he needed for this deal, he would have to mortgage all the other companies, including Cormorant Publishing.'

'I still don't understand why that necessitated you being on this trip.'

I sighed again. It was so difficult to explain my grandfather's philosophy – and the lifetime I had lived in the shadow of it – in a few words.

'Grandfather agreed to allow the deal with Western Haulage to go through as a way of proclaiming my uncle his heir apparent,' I said. 'But he wanted his other subjects to go along with it, too, and he hoped that by involving us all in this project, it might generate some enthusiasm for the new regime.'

'And did it?'

I shook my head. 'All I care about is Cormorant. Anything which threatens that is an enemy.'

'If I'm not mistaken, there's another director of the company – your cousin Philip,' Flint said.

'How would you know that?' I asked. 'And how can that possibly be relevant to the crash?'

'If you don't mind, sir, I'll ask the questions,' Owen Flint said.

He infused the word 'sir' with humour, as if – as old friends – it was no more than a joke we were sharing, but behind the levity was the weight of determined authority.

'Yes, my cousin Philip is also a director,' I agreed.

'So why wasn't he in on this particular junket?'

I laughed, perhaps a little bitterly. 'Philip didn't need his enthusiasm firing up. As the son of the crown prince, why should he? Besides, someone had to stay behind and manage the shop.'

Flint nodded. 'You were all travelling in one car,' he said, almost as if he were making a casual observation. 'It must have been a bit cramped.'

'It was – but we didn't have much choice.'

'Oh? And why was that?'

'We flew down to Bristol and hired two cars from Bristol Airport. We got a Jag for Uncle Tony and his assistant—'

'Your father didn't take his assistant,' Flint interrupted. 'That would be . . . Mr Paul Taylor . . . wouldn't it?'

Again, I wondered what that had to do with anything, but I was tired by then, and just wanted to get the interview over with as soon as possible.

'Yes, Paul is . . . Paul *was* . . . my father's personal assistant,' I said, 'but he's away on a leave of absence.'

'With all these takeovers going on, it seems a strange time for your dad to allow him to go off on holiday,' Flint said. 'Still, I know nothing about business, do I?' He rustled his bag and pulled out another sweet. 'Anyway, let's get back to the cars. You hired two of them, the Jag for your uncle . . .'

'And the BMW for the rest of us. We stayed the night in the Mountjoy Hotel in Bristol. We knew we had to make an early start this morning, and we all went to bed early.'

At least, my father, brother and I did, I thought. Knowing Uncle Tony, he probably got very drunk and then went off in search of a brassy blonde with flexible morals.

'We went down to the garage at seven o'clock this morning,' I continued. 'That was when we discovered the Jag wouldn't start. We asked the man on duty how long it would take us to get a mechanic, and he said at least an hour. We didn't have time to wait for that, or for the car hire companies to open up, either. So we decided we'd all cram into the BMW.'

Flint nodded again. 'Would it be too painful to describe the crash to me?'

I told him about the narrow country lane and seeing the lorry, and about how the brakes on the BMW failed.

'Have you found out yet *why* the brakes failed?' I asked. 'Was it something to do with the rain?'

A look of indecision crossed Flint's face. 'How strong are you feeling, Rob?' he said.

'I've just lost three members of my family, so I've felt better,' I replied. 'But if there's something you think I ought to know about, then I want to know about it now.'

Flint shrugged. 'If I don't tell you, you'd probably hear it soon enough anyway, from somebody else or on the television,' he said.

'Hear what?' I asked, exasperatedly.

'It wasn't an accident,' Flint said. 'Sometime last night, the handbrake cable was sawn through. Not completely – just far enough so that it would snap eventually. And a hole had been drilled in the hydraulic braking system so that fluid would be lost – slowly initially, then faster. According to the police mechanic, it was a very professional job.'

'You mean it was a deliberate attempt to . . .?' I gasped.

Flint nodded. 'Someone out there must hate one of you very much,' he said.

THREE

There was an early morning nip in the air as Chief Inspector Owen Flint surveyed the large car park which lay hidden beneath the Mountjoy Hotel, Bristol.

'How many cars could you cram into here, Sergeant Matthews?' he asked his bagman, who was standing next to him.

'There are spaces marked out for two hundred and twenty vehicles, sir,' Matthews replied.

Flint frowned. He imagined he would be doing a lot of frowning before this particular investigation was over.

It wasn't like any other case he'd ever been assigned, he would admit to me later, when he told me about the investigation. With most murders, he'd explain, the victim was found where he'd been killed. Even if the body had been moved, it was safe to assume – except in the case of poisonings – that the murderer had been with his victim at the time of death. But here, neither of those things applied. The murders, strictly speaking, had been carried out some hours before the actual deaths, and in a place over sixty miles from the scene of the crime.

There was the sound of footsteps from the other end of the garage, and a man wearing a blue boiler suit appeared.

'I'm Harry Thorpe, the garage supervisor,' he said. 'You wanted to see me.'

'That's right,' Flint agreed. 'Is this garage permanently manned?'

'Does this have anything to do with the Jag the local cops towed away earlier?' Thorpe countered.

'It might,' Flint conceded. Then, with a harsher edge to his voice, he repeated his original question.

'Is it permanently manned? No,' Thorpe said. 'But there's always somebody here between the hours of six in the morning, and ten in the evening.'

'What happens if guests need to use their cars outside those hours – if they've gone out for a late dinner, for example?'

'Guests who tell us they'll be getting back late are given a remote control to open the garage door. They've already been allocated a space of their own, so there's no trouble with the parking.'

'And what do they do once they're inside the garage?'

Thorpe pointed to a set of lift doors. 'That takes them straight up to the lobby.'

'So if guests can get from the garage to the hotel, then anyone inside the hotel could get to the garage,' Flint said. 'Is that right?'

'Yes, you can access the garage from the hotel,' Thorpe admitted. 'But what would be the point? The guests are advised to remove all their valuables, so there's nothing to steal. And if someone wanted to boost a car, they couldn't – because without one of the remote controls, which are very strictly monitored, they wouldn't be able to open the door.' He paused. 'You see what I'm saying? There's no reason at all for anybody to come down here.'

No, there wasn't, Flint agreed silently – unless, of course, they were embarking on what was beginning to look like a very carefully planned homicide.

Lying in bed with nothing to do is hell, especially for someone who has spent years devoting most of his waking hours to his business. I tried to watch the television, but the daytime soaps and quiz shows failed to grip me. I attempted to read, but found my mind constantly wandering back to *her*.

She still hadn't called me! More than twenty-four hours after the accident – which I now knew was not an accident at all – Marie hadn't been able to find the time to pick up the phone and ask me how I was!

Marie O'Hara had first come into my life at a student theatre performance in the grounds of St John's College.

The play was Ibsen's *An Enemy of the People*, and was being performed, so I thought, with rather more dramatic emphasis than the intellectual Norwegian author would have felt comfortable with. Still, it was a pleasant evening to be outdoors, and even a bad theatrical performance seems somewhat better when you have a bowl of strawberries and cream in one hand and a glass of Pimm's No. 1 Cup in the other. So all in all, I had decided, it wasn't a bad way to kill some of the free time which Andy McBride's increasing self-reliance had given me.

It was towards the end of the interval that I noticed Marie. She was chatting to a group of male students and making animated gestures with her right hand, which also held a burning cigarette. What first attracted me to her, I think, was that she didn't look the least like Jill. Perhaps that sounds awful, but it made a lot of sense to me then – and still does. I was terrified, you must understand, that if I ever fell in love again, it would be with a girl who resembled Jill, and worse, that I would try to turn my new love *into* Jill – which wouldn't have been good for either of us.

This girl, then, was as unlike Jill as it was possible to be. Jill had straight blonde hair, hers was reddish and curly. Where Jill had been slender without being flat-chested, Marie was ever so slightly on the heavy side. The eyes were green, not blue. Her nose was larger, and her lips were fuller, than my late fiancée's. I wouldn't have said she was my type, yet I felt an attraction towards her that I'd thought I would never feel again.

She saw me looking at her and smiled encouragingly.

I was at a loss for what to do next.

Should I force myself on to a group of people I didn't know?

Should I wait to see if she detached herself from them – and, if she did, home in on her then?

As it happened, the bell to announce the second half of the play obviated the need for either of these actions.

Back in my seat, I tried to concentrate on Ibsen's dialogue, but to no avail. It was crazy to feel these sudden, unexpected flutterings in my heart, I told myself. I wasn't a kid any more – so I should stop behaving like one. Yet I caught myself looking around the audience, hoping to see that mane of red hair.

She wasn't there. Maybe she had found the first half as tediously overdone as I had and decided to call it a night.

I felt bitterly disappointed. In many ways academic Oxford is little more than a village, yet it is possible to go for months

– or even years – without bumping into someone you know quite well.

So what were my chances of bumping into *her* again? She might not even live in Oxford – might, already, be on the train to London.

Or Bristol.

Or wherever else she'd come from.

It was only when I heard the audience applauding that I realized the play had come to an end. I joined in the applause half-heartedly, then rose heavily to my feet. The girl had unsettled me, had opened old wounds which I'd convinced myself were healed forever. I decided that, instead of going back to my flat, I would call in at the office and catch up with some work.

It was as I got to the main gate that I saw her again. She was leaning against the wall, a fresh cigarette in her hand, and looking towards the Banbury Road.

Waiting for someone? I wondered.

Very probably, I answered myself.

I had determined not to bother her and was already heading down St Giles' when I heard a voice behind me, with just the hint of an Irish accent in it, say, 'Goodnight, Mr Conroy.'

I turned around. She was smiling at me again.

'Do I know you?' I asked.

She shook her head, and her hair cascaded enticingly. 'No, you don't,' she said. 'But then I'm not a famous publisher, am I?'

I laughed, self-deprecatingly. 'Famous? Is that what I am?'

'Maybe famous is too strong a word,' she admitted. 'But you're certainly well-known. You're the sort of person other people point out. "That's Robert Conroy," they say. "He's the one who discovered that new author everyone's talking about".'

I felt my heart sink. So that was what this was all about – another would-be author with a manuscript to peddle.

'You don't happen to be a writer yourself, do you?' I asked – expecting the almost-inevitable reply.

'A writer!' Marie repeated. 'Not a chance. I tried being chained to a desk for a while, and it's not an experience I ever want to repeat.'

I breathed a sigh of relief, then just stood there – like a fool – saying absolutely nothing.

Marie glanced at her watch. 'Well, I suppose I'd better be going.'

'You're not meeting anyone, then?'

'No, I'm not.'

Here's your chance, I told myself. Grab it while it's there.

'You wouldn't let me buy you a drink, would you?' I asked.

'I never drink on an empty stomach,' she told me. 'But if you're game for a meal, I wouldn't say no. But *you* don't get to buy it – we split the bill right down the middle.'

'Whatever you say,' I agreed.

I took her to the Italian restaurant just across the road from the college – and tried not to look too pleased with myself when the waiters greeted me warmly.

It was ridiculous, I thought, to find myself trying to impress this woman I'd only just met.

Yet I really wanted to.

When the menu arrived, she brushed it aside. 'What's the house speciality?' she asked me.

'The clams are very good.'

'Then I'll have them.'

As the waiter left us, she reached into her handbag and took out her cigarettes.

'You smoke a lot,' I said.

'Yes, I do,' she agreed unapologetically. She lit the cigarette and blew the smoke out through her nose. 'Now, bearing in mind that I haven't got a book I'm trying to con you into publishing, why don't you tell me about your work?'

'It's not very interesting,' I said.

'I'm sure that's not true,' she said evenly. 'You aren't the sort of man to waste his time doing something that isn't interesting.'

Perhaps it was her words or perhaps it was her tone, but it opened the floodgates. I told her about my battles with the bookshop chains. I outlined the difficulties of getting my authors on television arts programmes. I described how I'd felt when I read the first exercise book full of Andy McBride's wonderful prose. I talked and talked, and it was not until we had reached the dessert that I really paused for breath.

'Do you have family?' Marie asked.

'You mean a wife?'

She shook her head. 'If I thought you were married, we wouldn't be sitting here now. No, I mean blood relatives. Brothers and sisters? Uncles and aunts?'

'I have a brother . . .' I began, then stopped myself. 'I've been monopolizing the conversation. Why don't you tell me a little about *yourself*?'

'Oh, I'm very boring,' she said.

'I'm quite sure you're not,' I told her, returning her earlier compliment.

She shrugged. 'All right then. I'm the original foundling, adopted when I was a baby by a big-hearted farming family deep in the Irish countryside.' She paused and looked vaguely annoyed with herself. 'I always start like that, you know. As if where I come from is far more important than who I am. And it isn't. Not at all.'

'No, it isn't,' I agreed.

'Anyway I was brought up on the farm, like I said, and attended the local primary school' – she grinned – 'where I shone like the brightest star in the firmament. The headmaster told my parents that it would be a sorry waste if I didn't go to university, so' – another shrug – 'when I was old enough, off I went to Trinity College Dublin.'

'And what did you read?'

'Law.'

'So you're a lawyer now?'

'No. I tried working in a solicitor's office for a couple of years, but it bored me. I'm an outdoors girl – even if the outdoors is only the mean streets of Oxford.'

'Then what do you do?' I asked.

'I keep the town clean,' she said, affecting a New York accent on top of her Irish lilt.

'You mean you're with the cleaning department?'

She laughed. 'No, I'm a private investigator.'

Though I didn't mean it to, my mouth must have fallen open. 'A private investigator?' I repeated.

'It's a dirty job, but somebody's got to do it,' she said, still in character.

'You must be the first female private eye in Britain,' I said.

'Nothing like,' she replied. 'I'm not even the first female private eye in Oxford. There was one here a few years ago, an ex-policewoman who had her office on the Iffley Road, and, by coincidence, she also had red hair.'

(I checked up on it later and found Marie was quite right – so on that matter, at least, she hadn't been lying to me.)

'Don't run away with the idea that what I do is either dangerous or glamorous,' she told me. 'I'm the one who people call on to chase up bad debts and do background credit checks. It's really a long way from the stuff you see on television.'

'Do you enjoy it?'

She gave the matter some thought.

'Most of the time,' she said finally, 'which is probably as much as anyone can say about their work.'

The bill arrived. I paid it with my credit card, and – without any sign of embarrassment – Marie slid some notes across the table.

'That's not necessary,' I said.

'Oh yes, it is,' Marie replied firmly. 'You agreed I could pay half, and a deal is a deal.'

We stood up, climbed the stairs, and were out on the street. It was cooler than it had been earlier, but it was still a pleasant early-summer evening. I stood on the pavement, uncertain of what to do or say next.

'I enjoyed that,' Marie said. 'I really did.'

'Could we do it again, sometime?' I asked tentatively.

She took her time lighting a cigarette and inhaling.

'I think we could become good friends, Robert,' she said finally.

'But . . .?'

'But you have to understand from the outset that friendship is all I want. I'm not looking for any deeper relationship. Not right now.'

'Fine with me,' I said, not quite sure whether I was lying or not.

She reached into her purse and took out a business card. 'You can reach me here,' she said.

'You don't have a home number?' I asked, feeling somewhat snubbed.

She shook her head wonderingly. 'Do you think with the kind of operation I run I can afford a home and an office?' she said. 'I work out of the front room of my flat, and when I need to see a client, it's in his office we meet.' She reached up and kissed me lightly on the cheek. 'Ring me. I mean it.'

And then she was gone, striding rapidly and confidently down St Giles'.

Had it meant nothing to her – that first encounter and what followed it – I asked as I lay in my hospital bed. Was I no more to her than a convenience – someone to be used while he was around, and quickly forgotten when he wasn't? I couldn't believe that of Marie. Yet why hadn't she bloody *phoned*?

The receptionist at the Mountjoy Hotel was young, pretty and much less guarded than the garage supervisor.

'Yes, I was on the graveyard shift the night before last,' she told Flint.

'The graveyard shift?'

'That's what we call the shift between ten at night and six in the morning.'

'Do you call it that because it's so boring?'

'Exactly! Only the night before last it wasn't boring at all, because there was a big party in the Grosvenor Room, so I was kept rather busy.'

'There must have been lots of people in the lobby, then?' Flint said, disappointedly.

The girl smiled. 'At times, there seemed to be literally hundreds of them.'

'But nobody who looked out of place?'

'Out of place?' the receptionist asked, puzzled.

Yes, Flint thought – somebody, for example, carrying a tool kit, and looking as if he were intending to sabotage a BMW's braking system.

'What I mean by out of place is a person who was dressed in a way which suggested he didn't really belong here,' he said aloud.

'Oh, that's so sweet and old-fashioned,' the receptionist said, laughing. 'There *is* no proper way to dress any more. Some of our clients wear designer suits, and some walk around in old jeans with holes in them. As long as they have enough money to pay their bills, nobody cares how they look.'

'Did you notice anyone taking the lift down to the garage?' Flint asked, changing tack.

'You can't see it from the reception desk,' the girl pointed out. 'I must have heard it running a number of times, but I couldn't honestly tell you whether the guests who passed by the desk were going to the lift or to the loo.'

Of course she couldn't, Flint thought. And whoever had used the confusion created by the party as an opportunity to slip down to the garage would have been well aware of that.

The pub was a few doors down from the Mountjoy Hotel. It was called the Crown and Anchor, and the walls were decorated with fishermen's nets and lobster pots.

Flint was at the bar, ordering the drinks, when the call on his mobile phone came through. He listened to what the man on the other end of the line had to say, and then asked a couple of questions. Once the call was over, he paid for the drinks and carried the pint pots across to the table where his sergeant was sitting.

'That was the forensics department of the local constabulary, Sergeant Matthews,' he said, as he placed the glasses on the table. 'The lads at their garage have been over the Jag with a fine-toothed comb. They've come to the conclusion that the reason it wouldn't start yesterday morning was because of a failure in the electrical system.'

'So before he sabotaged the Beemer's brakes, the killer had also worked on the Jag,' Matthews said.

'No, that's the point – he didn't,' Flint told him. 'They're convinced it was a genuine honest-to-goodness breakdown.' He paused. 'And that raises some very interesting possibilities, doesn't it?'

'Does it?' Matthews asked.

'Of course. Look, boyo, we have to assume that the killer knew the whole set-up. He knew where the Conroys had come from, how long they'd be staying in Bristol, and where they were going after that.'

'Why should we assume that?'

'Because if the Conroys had been intending to do nothing more than tootle around the city of Bristol for a couple of days, he'd have found another way to get at them. Do you see where I'm going with this? If the brakes had failed in the city centre, there'd have been a minor collision, and nothing more. But he didn't want them bruised – he wanted them dead – so he had to be aware that the next morning they'd be making a high-speed journey.'

'You're right,' Matthews admitted.

'And we can take it even further than that. If the killer knew where they were going, he also knew who would be in each car, which means—'

'Which means that Tony Conroy and Bill Harper were never intended to be victims, because they were supposed to be in the Jag,' Matthews interrupted.

'And . . .?'

'And the real intended victim might still be alive!'

'That's right,' Flint agreed. 'The murderer might have wanted to kill John or Edward Conroy, but it's equally possible that his target was Rob Conroy.'

'Or he could have wanted to kill all three of them,' Matthews pointed out.

'True,' Flint agreed. 'But how often is it that a . . . that a . . .'

'Is something wrong, sir?' Matthews asked.

'Keep talking,' Flint said. 'Say anything – it doesn't matter what.'

'I'm not sure I understand, sir.'

'Tell me about your Uncle Blodwyn's prize leeks. Or where you went for your summer holidays. Anything at all – as long as it leaves me free to concentrate on something else.'

'I did *have* an Uncle Blodwyn as a matter of fact,' Matthews said, catching on. 'I don't think he grew leeks, though. He was more of a fisherman, and—'

'She knows she's been spotted, and she's leaving,' Flint interrupted.

'Who's leaving?'

'Going through the door now.'

Matthews swivelled round just in time to catch sight of the woman. The most striking thing about her was her mane of red, curly hair. But her figure was worth some attention, too. It was, perhaps, a little too full, but it was definitely very feminine.

'Come on,' Flint said, rising to his feet.

'Where are we going?'

'To have a talk with that young lady.'

Once she had the pub door between herself and them, the woman had obviously put on a spurt, and by the time the two detectives had reached the pavement, she was already climbing into the driver's seat of a black Volkswagen GTI, some distance down the street.

'Damn!' Flint said, as the car fired and pulled away from the kerb. 'Well, at least I've got her licence plate number.'

'I still don't know what's going on, sir,' Matthews told him.

'I thought I was imagining it at first,' Flint said. 'She wasn't in the pub when we arrived, so she must have entered just after us. She was sitting at the bar, and she was watching us.'

'Maybe she's on the game,' Matthews suggested.

Flint shook his head. 'She wasn't that blatant. In fact, she was so subtle I almost didn't notice her. But now I'm sure she's been following us.'

'Why would anyone want to do that?'

'I don't know,' Flint admitted. 'But once we've checked with the licensing authorities in Swansea we might have a better idea.'

If Owen had thought to ring me, of course, I could have told him exactly who his mystery woman was. But I would have had no explanation to offer for her presence in Bristol.

It was to be quite a time before either of us would gain an understanding of that.

FOUR

The knock on the door of my hospital room was tentative – perhaps almost timid.

'Come in,' I said.

The door swung open. I had been expecting to see yet another figure clad in white, come to dispense sympathy and tranquillizers, but instead it was Bill Harper.

'The doctor said it would be all right for me to come and see you,' he said, his voice as tentative as his knock. 'But if you think it would be too much of a strain on you . . .?'

'I'm not all that damaged,' I said more gruffly than I'd intended. 'Take a seat.'

Harper walked slowly across the room, as if he were still in some pain.

'The hospital's just discharged me,' he said, as he lowered himself gingerly on to the chair. 'I'm going back to Cheshire for your grandfather's funeral.'

'What about my . . .?'

'The others can't be buried until the post-mortems have been completed.'

I had a nightmare vision of the doctors cutting my brother open. Then I told myself I was being foolish – the damage had already been done, and the scalpel wasn't going to make it any worse.

'Will you be there for the funeral yourself?' Harper asked.

I shook my head. 'They've insisted I stay here for a couple more days.'

'Probably wise,' Harper said awkwardly. 'You don't want to take any unnecessary chances.' He looked down at his hands. 'The thing is,' he continued in a sudden rush, 'there's something I think you should know before I go. About the crash, I mean.'

'Don't I know enough already?' I asked.

'The thing is,' he repeated, 'I gather you were unconscious

for most of it, but I think that if I told you what happened, it
might make your grief a little easier to bear.'

'A little easier to bear!' I repeated angrily. 'Do you realize
I've just lost almost my entire family?'

'Quite so,' Harper mumbled awkwardly. 'Quite so. I just
wanted to let you know they didn't suffer.'

If he was trying to ease my mental anguish, he was far from
succeeding.

'How can you know?' I demanded. 'How can *anybody* know?'

Harper winced. 'I know your brother died instantly because
I was sitting right next to him.'

And so he had been – cramped between myself and John,
trying to fish documents out of his executive case to brief Uncle
Tony with.

I wondered whether the tight squeeze had been what saved
his life.

'What about my father?' I asked.

Harper's pained expression intensified. 'You've got to imagine
what it was like in there,' he said. 'The car had concertinaed
and there was a strong smell of petrol. I could tell I wasn't that
badly hurt myself, and my only thought was to get everyone
out before the bloody thing caught fire – everyone who was
still alive, I mean, because I'd already checked and found that
John had no pulse.'

I didn't want to hear any more, but I knew that I must.

'Go on,' I croaked.

'I'm talking about seconds passing here. And you have to
remember – *please* – that I was in shock myself. I may not
have done the right thing – but it *felt* right at the time.'

At least he'd done *something*, I thought. At least *he* hadn't
sunk into unconsciousness while his family was dying around
him. And though I knew it was irrational, I was once again
flooded with guilt.

'Nobody's going to blame you for what did or didn't happen,'
I said. 'I'm sure you did your best.'

Harper nodded gratefully. 'Thank you.'

'Tell me the rest,' I said, seeming to gain some strength of
my own from his uncertainty.

'I was going to push you out of the car first' – he turned his head to the right, as if he could actually see me there, wedged between himself and the car door – 'then Mr Conroy – your uncle Tony, I mean – groaned, and it suddenly seemed as if he was the most important person to deal with. You see, it was so hard to think . . .'

'What did you do?'

'I reached forward to unhook his seat belt. My whole body was hurting like hell, but I knew that if I blacked out then, I wouldn't be able to save anybody – even myself. Anyway, I was still struggling with the buckle when your uncle Tony spoke.'

'What did he say?'

'He said, "Don't bother about me. Get Edward out first! For God's sake, get Edward out!" I twisted round towards your father. His head was at a strange, unnatural angle. I felt for a pulse in his neck, and . . . and . . . there wasn't one.'

'What happened next?'

'Your uncle said something like, "Is he going to be alright?" I said, "He's dead," but I don't think he heard me because he looked like he was gone himself. So you see, if your father wasn't killed instantly, it couldn't have been more than a second or two.'

'Thank you for telling me,' I said.

And I meant it. What he had told me had brought a small measure of comfort. I was glad my father and brother hadn't suffered. I took some consolation from the fact that however bad the relationship had been between my father and my uncle, Tony's dying thoughts had been for his brother.

'Then the fire started,' Harper continued, his voice cracking. 'I . . . I can't tell you what it felt like. The front seats were an inferno. There was smoke everywhere. I was choking. I tried to get your door open, and that's when I saw the aircraftmen outside. I don't know how long they'd been there. Like I said, the whole thing must have been over in a few seconds.'

'And it was the aircraftmen who pulled us out?'

Harper nodded. 'They were bloody marvellous. If they hadn't been there, we'd both have been dead.' He stood up again. 'I have to go. My train . . .'

'Of course,' I said. 'Thank you for coming to see me. I know it can't have been easy, living through it all again.'

I watched him walk to the door and listened to his muffled footsteps as they echoed down the hallway. Then, alone once more, I felt my mind drift back to the first time I met him.

It was at one of those garden parties that my brother's wife, Lydia, held regularly during the summer months. Fairy lights were strung between the trees, I remembered, and a four-piece band was playing the sort of unchallenging music that four-piece bands always play at parties like this. Groups of guests bunched together in various parts of the garden, and three hired waiters wended their way skilfully in and out of these clusters, offering the guests drinks, or some of the hors-d'oeuvre which Lydia had had specially delivered by an expensive catering firm based in Manchester.

I didn't know most of the people who'd been invited to the party – now Cormorant Publishing was taking up so much of my time, I rarely got back to the village – but I could tell from the way they dressed and the way they moved that they considered themselves to be part of the local 'smart' set.

My brother John appeared by my side.

'Are you enjoying yourself?' he asked, with just the tiniest hint of anxiety in his voice.

'In my own quiet way, yes.'

'I expect that, in your line of work, you must go to tons of parties like this.'

'Not if I can possibly avoid them,' I told him, and the second the words were out of my mouth, I wished I could have bitten out my tongue. 'I'm not really a party animal,' I added, apologetically. 'When I do go to parties, it's usually for business reasons, so they're no more fun than being in the office.' My brother was obviously waiting for more, and I felt obliged to provide it. 'But I must say that this is one of the best organized parties I've been to in a long time,' I finished.

John smiled gratefully. 'Lydia put a lot of work into it,' he said. 'Her parties are very important to her. She says that given our position in the village, it's almost our *duty* to have parties.'

If I hadn't been talking to my own brother, I might have

laughed at the notion. As it was, I confined myself to saying, 'Well, perhaps she has a point.'

'Yes, she's very strong on duty,' John said. 'She's on all the local committees, you know.'

'No, I didn't know,' I admitted.

'Oh yes,' John said enthusiastically. 'You name it, she's on it – and more often than not, she's the chair. The Church Ladies' Committee, the Council to Preserve Rural England, the Parochial Council . . . Frankly, I don't see where she gets all her energy from.'

'I'm glad you're happy,' I said.

'What about you?' John asked. 'Is there anyone special in your life?'

I thought about Marie O'Hara, the Irish gumshoe. We had seen each other two or three times since our meal in the Italian restaurant, and I enjoyed being with her, but so far it didn't seem to be leading anywhere.

'Well?' my brother asked. '*Have* you got anyone special?'

'Not really,' I said, and then, to change the subject, I asked, 'Is Cousin Philip coming tonight?'

John frowned. 'He's certainly been invited.'

'And what exactly do you mean by that?'

'I . . . err . . . I think he's in a bit of a huff because we brought the outside caterers in.'

I began to see what he meant. Grandfather had finally given Philip his own business – a couple of years after he had bought John his vehicle maintenance company, and long, long after he had acquired Cormorant Publishing for me. Philip was now head of a firm of contract caterers – caterers who, naturally enough, immediately signed an agreement to run the canteens at both Conroy Transport and Conroy Furnishings.

Grandfather's web again!

'The thing is, Lydia didn't really think that Philip's people could handle the job,' John said apologetically. 'I mean, they're fine for providing cheap nourishing lunches – their steak and kidney pie is one of the best I've tasted – but really they're not quite . . .' He trailed off.

'Sophisticated enough to cater for the kind of guest you have here?' I supplied.

'Exactly,' John agreed. 'I'll have a quiet word with him in the morning and explain that no insult was intended. I'm sure he'll see my point of view.'

How like my brother to assume that everyone else was as reasonable as he was himself, I thought. How like him to believe he could always paper over the cracks.

A new man entered the garden, and seeing John there, made an obvious direct beeline for him.

'Thank you for inviting me to your party, Mr Conroy,' he said, pumping John's hand vigorously. 'Don't want to talk business now – neither the time nor the place for it – but if you ring me in the morning, I think we've got a bit of extra work we could put your way.'

He looked at me as if he expected to be introduced, and John obliged.

'This is Rob, my brother. This is Bill Harper, Uncle Tony's new executive assistant.'

Ah yes! Grandfather had noticed that my father was looking tired, and had given him an executive assistant, so now Uncle Tony had to have one, whether he needed it or not.

I stepped back a little to get a better look at my uncle's latest status symbol. Harper was probably only five feet five or five feet six, but he had the square body of a man who has always taken a lot of hearty exercise. He had a broad brow over a pair of darting eyes and a pointed nose. His mouth, I decided, had a ruthless twist to it. In short, though I rarely go on first appearances, I found myself disliking the man.

'It's a pleasure to meet you, Mr Conroy,' Harper said, vigorously shaking my hand. 'I've heard you're quite a powerhouse in the publishing world.'

I found it hard to tolerate such obvious flattery, but it was my brother's party and I was determined to be pleasant.

'You're not from round here, are you, Mr Harper?' I asked.

He shook his head. 'You've got a good ear for accents, Mr Conroy. No, as a matter of fact I was brought up in Stoke-on-Trent. But I've taken to Cheshire like a duck to water.'

John chuckled. 'Bill's a great swimmer,' he said.

'That's right,' Harper agreed. 'I've taken to swimming across the mere – there and back – every evening.'

'That's a fair distance,' I said.

And so it was. The mere lay just beyond the base of the hill on which the village perched. It was large enough to host a sailing club, and swimming across it – and then back again – was no mean feat.

'Do you do it even in winter?' I asked.

Harper laughed, as though I'd been incredibly witty.

'I haven't been here long enough to see what the water's like in winter,' he admitted, 'but no, I don't expect I shall be swimming once the weather turns cold. Still, it's wonderful while it lasts.'

Some more guests were arriving through the garden gate. One of them was Uncle Tony with, inevitably, his latest blonde on his arm.

Bill Harper saw him too. 'If you'll excuse me,' he said, then turned on his heel and headed towards my uncle.

'Like a trained lap dog,' I said.

'What was that?' my brother asked.

'He's running to Uncle Tony like a trained lap dog.'

John laughed, slightly uneasily. 'I do think you're rather hard on him. I've heard he's very good at his job. He's supposed to be going places.'

And perhaps I had been rather hard on him, I thought, lying in my hospital bed. The Bill Harper I had just seen was not the same man I had met at that party. He had displayed neither the famous Harper fawning act, nor his equally obnoxious arrogance.

It had been a kind, considerate, and perhaps even a courageous act to come and tell me about the crash. Was it possible that it had taken a tragedy to bring out his better nature? I suspected that it was.

And in that – as in so many other things – I was to turn out to be hopelessly, stupidly wrong.

FIVE

D usk was almost falling when my solitary musings about both the past and the future were shattered by the harsh sound of a phone bell ringing.

When I picked up the phone, the first thing I heard was a slurping sound which could only have been made by a man sucking a boiled sweet.

'Owen?' I said.

'Yes, it's me,' Flint confirmed. 'I'm just ringing to tell you that I'll be travelling up to Cheshire in the morning.'

'You almost sound as if you're asking my permission,' I replied, though from his tone of voice, I already had my suspicions that this conversation wasn't going to be about Cheshire at all.

'There's a few things I'd like to find out about before I get there,' Flint said, ignoring my implied question, 'but first, I've got some advice I'd like you to listen to.'

'All right,' I agreed.

'Once you're discharged from hospital, you need to be very careful. Don't use your own car – take public transport and taxis. Try to avoid being alone. Never accept any invitations from people you don't have absolute trust in – and even then, it would be best to be on your guard.'

Weighed down as I was by feelings of guilt, grief and disappointment, I had barely thought about the motive behind the murders, but suddenly – like that big RAF truck on that narrow country lane – it loomed up in front of me and could no longer be avoided. Yet even now, the idea that I could be the intended victim seemed insane.

'I'm just a boring old publisher, for God's sake!' I protested. 'Apart from my authors and a few other people in the trade, I hardly see anyone. I've done nothing at all to merit somebody wanting to kill me.'

'And had your brother done anything to merit it?' Owen Flint asked quietly. 'Or your father, for that matter?'

Of course they hadn't! It was ludicrous to suggest that anybody would want to kill any of us.

Yet someone clearly had.

I realized that, though I would have to confront the issue at some point, I simply wasn't strong enough at that moment.

'You wanted to ask me some questions,' I said, seeking a diversion.

'Yes, I did,' Owen Flint agreed. 'And listen, Rob, this won't be two old friends talking – it will be a policeman questioning a man who's somehow got himself involved in a murder case. Do you think you can handle that?'

'Yes,' I said, though I'm not sure I convinced either of us.

'I'll be meeting your family tomorrow, *sir*, and it would be of great value to me if you could fill me in a little on everybody's background,' Flint said.

'I'll do my best, chief inspector,' I promised.

And over the next twenty minutes or so, I told him of Grandfather's rise from near poverty to a modest fortune, of the theatrical Aunt Jane, of Philip, of John's marriage, and other bits of family gossip which came into my head. I was quite open on many points, but I kept in mind the distinction Owen himself had made between old friend and policeman, and – especially in John's case – there were things I held back.

Later, lying alone in the darkness, I wondered what Owen Flint – a man brought up in a harsh, soulless institution at the head of a Welsh valley – would make of the village in which I'd spent much of my childhood.

Would he perhaps find it just a little too pretty – just a little too much like the cosy pictures they used to put on the tops of boxes of expensive chocolates?

I couldn't really blame him if that was his first impression. The village *is* almost absurdly picturesque. The High Street, which climbs a moderately steep hill, is lined with neat Georgian cottages, each with its own perfectly kept garden in front of it. Midway between the edge of the village and the church is the post office/general store, which has managed to survive in the face of supermarket competition and is as much a repository for gossip now as it ever was. At the top of the hill stands the church, a proud Norman fortress with a tower which glares imposingly down on all that surrounds it. There are stocks by the lychgate – a reminder of simpler times, when crime was more easily defined, and punishment far less complex. And across the square from the church is the George and Dragon, a fine old pub which was serving good traditional beer long before that became the general fashion.

Apart from a certain degree of gentrification, the village must have changed very little since the day my grandparents moved there. The house Grandfather bought was down a lane which led off the High Street, and from its windows he had a view of the west side of the church. It was a large building with a heavy slate roof and ivy growing up the walls. There were stables – though he kept no horses. There were servants' quarters – a reminder of the days when village girls considered themselves lucky if they had a 'place' which permitted them to 'live in'.

It was then – and still is now – a magnificent house, and easily the largest in the village. But more importantly, it made a statement – it said that, after years of just getting by, my grandfather had finally arrived.

Neither my father nor my uncle Tony lived in the house with my grandparents for long. They were already in their twenties when they moved in, both involved in the family business, and when they got married it was natural they should want establishments of their own.

My father settled for an ample – though modest – cottage near the village school. My uncle chose a house at the other end of the village, with a marvellous view over the sloping green fields, down to the mere and the sailing club.

I sometimes wonder if the two sons ever saw the symbolism in this physical separation. Did they ever really appreciate the fact that they were a pair of satellites, and that the only thing which connected them was Grandfather – that irresistible force in the very centre of the village?

Perhaps they did. Perhaps their choice of homes was a deliberate declaration of their differences.

We will never know now.

SIX

Whe Owen Flint arrived in Northwich, he was assigned a local man called Inspector Hawkins to shepherd him around.

Hawkins, as I would discover later, was a solid, middle-aged bobby, not given to imaginative leaps of intuition, so it was not surprising that it was the detective from South Wales, not the one from Cheshire, who suggested that they should attend my grandfather's funeral.

It was an impressive turnout, I'm told. Grandfather had been a firm but popular employer, and as well as friends and local dignitaries, each of his tangled web of business holdings sent a number of representatives, so the church was full to bursting.

I am trying to imagine what impression the surviving members of my family made on Owen Flint. He would have seen my grandmother, small and frail, suddenly cast out on to a sea of loneliness after well over half a century of Grandfather's protection. He would have noticed my cousin Philip, thin and blond, with eyes which suggested more sensitivity than his hard soul could ever muster. And he would have seen Lydia, my sister-in-law, with her pageboy haircut covered by a large dark hat, and her pale green eyes hidden behind dark glasses.

Perhaps he asked the unimaginative Inspector Hawkins a few questions.

'Where's Rob Conroy's mother?'

'She died a couple of years ago. Cancer, I think it was. By all accounts, she'd never been very strong.'

'What about Philip Conroy's wife?'

'He doesn't have one. He likes to play the field, just like his father, Tony, did.'

'And Tony's wife – Philip's mother?'

'Oh, she ran away from home years ago, when Philip was no more than a kid.'

This conversation, as I say, is only guesswork on my part.

But one thing I do know for sure. As they were laying my grandfather's coffin in the ground, Owen caught sight of a shock of red hair which he had last seen driving away in a Golf GT in Bristol.

Flint waited by the church gate until most of the mourners had left. One of the last to go was the woman with the red hair, and when she saw Flint standing by the lychgate, she looked straight through him.

The chief inspector bided his time until she had drawn level with him, then said, 'Might I have a word, miss?'

She turned. 'Are you talking to me?'

'Yes. Does that surprise you?'

The woman opened her handbag, took out a packet of cigarettes, and lit one up.

'Does it surprise me?' she said. 'No, I suppose it doesn't. But if we're going to talk, I'd rather do it with a glass of something in my hand. Going to funerals always makes me feel thirsty.'

'There's a pub over there,' Owen Flint said, pointing towards the George and Dragon.

'So there is,' the woman agreed.

They walked across the road and entered the pub by the side door. As he would have expected in a village like this one, the bar was all horse brasses and bare oak beams.

'What would you like to drink?' Owen asked.

Marie glanced at the shelves behind the counter. 'A Bush Mills whiskey with water,' she said. 'Better make it a double – and go easy on the water.'

'So you're not intending to drive any more today?' Owen Flint said.

Marie grimaced. 'I forgot, for a moment, that you were the Filth,' she said. 'Better make it an orange juice.'

Owen ordered a pint of bitter for himself and took the two drinks over to the table where Marie was already lighting a fresh cigarette from the stub of her first.

'I'll tell you what I know, then you can tell me what I *want* to know,' he said. 'Your name's Marie O'Hara, you're a private investigator, and you live in Oxford. Correct?'

Marie smiled. 'I thought I'd pulled off too quickly for you to take my number,' she said. 'Obviously, I was wrong.'

'So my first question is, do you know Rob Conroy?'

Marie took a long drag on her cigarette. 'Yes, I know him.'

'How long? And how well?'

'We've known each other for more than two years.'

'I need more than that,' Flint said.

Marie thought about it.

'We spend a lot of time in each other's company,' she said finally.

'Are you saying you're lovers?'

She shook her head. 'No.'

'It's not a crime, you know.'

'The answer's still no.'

'So you're just good friends?'

'That's right.'

Flint took a thoughtful sip of his pint. 'Why are you here today?' he asked.

'It was Rob's grandfather they were burying. I thought I'd come and pay my respects.'

'Did Rob ask you to come?'

'No, I haven't been in contact with him since the accident.'

'I see,' Flint said meaningfully. 'You haven't been to see him, but you've come to one of his relative's funerals. How well did you know his family?'

'I've never met any of them.'

'Some people would say you're acting rather strangely.'

Marie shrugged. 'Some people have always said that. Some people think I'm completely crazy to be chasing bad debts when I could have a nice comfortable office job.'

'Is that what you were doing in Bristol?' Flint asked. 'Chasing down some bad debts?'

'I was certainly there on behalf of a client,' Marie said evasively.

'And you just happened to be in the area around the Mountjoy Hotel at the same time I was?'

Another shrug. 'I was in Bristol on business, and I thought, on impulse, that I'd go and have a look at the hotel where they

spent the night before the crash. I saw you in the lobby. It was
obvious you were policemen, and highly likely you were investigating the case, so – on impulse again – I followed you to the
pub. Then, when I realized you'd spotted me, I thought it would
save explanations all round if I got out of there as quickly as
possible.'

'Murder investigations are jobs for the police,' Flint warned
her.

'So why aren't you investigating the murder, instead of
wasting your time talking to me?'

'If I find you're getting in my way, Miss O'Hara, I'll stamp
on you,' Flint said. 'Might not be a very nice way to put it, but
that's exactly what I'll do.'

Marie knocked back her orange juice and stood up. 'I'll
remember that,' she said. 'Thanks for the drink.'

Flint's eyes followed her to the door – and they were not the
only ones to do so. She was a very attractive woman, the chief
inspector decided – a very sexy woman.

He wondered if she'd lied when she'd said she wasn't sleeping
with me. And if she hadn't lied, *why* she wasn't sleeping with
me, when all the signs seemed to be that we were very close.

It was a question I'd often asked myself, during so many
long, lonely nights.

SEVEN

During my conversation with Owen Flint the previous
evening, I thought I was giving him a fairly accurate
(though edited) sketch of my family, but as the hours
passed, I began to be more and more dissatisfied with my
performance. What I'd actually given him, it now seemed to
me, was not only sketchy, but flat. It had been like describing
a train by doing no more than listing its destinations and the
times it ran.

My comments on my cousin Philip were a good case in point.
I'd explained all about his mother and his father's girlfriends. I'd

stated – though not fully explained – that I considered him a selfish, thoroughly unlikeable individual. Yet I'd breathed no life into the skeleton I'd presented – I'd failed totally to flesh out the bones. And it would have been such an easy thing to do. To sum up Philip – perhaps to sum up all the grandchildren of Charlie Conroy – I need only have mentioned the incident with the shrew.

Philip and I were six, and my brother John was seven, when it happened. We were all destined for public school, but at that point we attended the local primary, mainly, I think, because that was what Grandfather – who had risen through the ranks in the army – wished us to do.

Our school life wasn't a happy experience. We were the grandsons of Charles Conroy, and the other children, whose fathers worked on farms and in factories, treated us with wariness at best and hostility at worst. The result was that, whether we liked it or not – and even *then* I didn't – we were thrust into each other's company.

That particular summer, we all had a passion for collecting living things. Screw-top jars of caterpillars sat proudly on our bedroom dressers. Baby rabbits, found abandoned in the woods, would be taken home amidst excited talk of watching them grow, even though we probably secretly knew that without their mothers to look after them, they would almost certainly die. When one of us had a budgerigar, the others must have one too. The purchase of a white mouse for one necessitated the same for the remaining two. So it was not surprising that when we were walking the fields one day, and Philip saw the startled shrew break cover from its grassy hiding place, his first instinct was to dive at it.

He caught it neatly between his two cupped hands, then climbed carefully back to his feet. Only when he was standing again did he open the hands a little, for us to see his prize. The shrew was making no attempt to escape. Instead, it was lying on its back and writhing.

'Give it to me,' I said.

'I caught it,' Philip said aggressively. 'It's mine.'

'I only want to look at it,' I told him. 'You can have it back in a minute.'

'Cross your heart and hope to die?'

'Cross my heart and hope to die,' I promised, making the approved gesture with my index finger.

Reluctantly, my cousin transferred the small bundle from his hands to mine. I can still remember how its hot, furry little body felt as it nestled in my palm, can still picture the look of uncomprehending terror on its tiny face.

'I want it back now,' Philip said.

But I hadn't finished with it yet.

'I think you've hurt it,' I told him. 'I think you've broken its back legs.'

'Didn't mean to,' Philip said petulantly.

I knelt down and placed the tiny creature on the ground. It tried to run, but only its front legs were working, so it did no more than paw the ground.

'What are we going to do?' I asked my cousin.

'Don't know,' Philip replied.

'We could take it home with us,' John suggested, speaking for the first time.

I shook my head. 'I think it's like racehorses,' I said. 'I think once their legs are broken, they're finished. We'll have to kill it.'

'We can't!' John said, with a hint of anguish in his voice.

I sighed. My brother may have been the oldest of the three of us, but he was no leader, and I realized it even then.

'We *have* to put it out of its misery,' I told him.

John sighed too, then looked around him, located a large stone, and handed it to Philip.

'All right, you do it,' he said.

Hands firmly by his sides, Philip took a step backwards. 'Why me?' he demanded.

'Because you were the one who hurt it.'

Philip shook his head. 'I'm not doing it. Why don't we just leave it here?'

'Because it's in pain,' I explained.

'Not my fault,' Philip muttered. 'Didn't ask it to be here, did I?'

I looked down at the tiny creature once more, and for a moment, I was tempted to do as my cousin suggested. Then I saw it make another futile attempt to run away and knew I would be doing it no favours.

'Why don't we all do it?' I said.

'You're talking rubbish now,' Philip retorted.

'No, I'm not,' I countered. 'If we all get a stone and hit it at the same time, we'll never know which one of us has killed it.'

I looked up at my brother for support, and he reluctantly nodded. I turned to my cousin, who shrugged his shoulders. 'All right,' he agreed.

The next two stones were more difficult to find than the one John had uncovered, but a couple of minutes search provided us with the instruments of death we needed.

Philip examined my stone, and then the one he was holding in his own hand. 'Mine's bigger than yours,' he complained.

'So what?'

'So you'll be able to say I did it, because I'd got the bigger stone.'

I held mine out. 'We'll swap.'

'OK,' said Philip, as if he was doing me a favour.

We all knelt down beside the shrew.

'I'm going to count to three,' I said, 'and then we'll all hit it. One . . . two . . . three.'

I brought my stone down as hard as I could. My brother did the same and managed to trap two of my fingers between my stone and his. I yelped with pain and jumped back. My fingers were on fire. I stuck them in my mouth and sucked furiously.

'That should fix it,' I heard my cousin say in the background.

Almost forgetting my own agony, I looked down at the tiny, battered body on the ground, and realized that the shrew must have gone through more suffering than I could even begin to imagine.

'It's nearly teatime,' Philip said, almost cheerfully. 'Shall we go home, now?'

'What about him?' John asked, looking down at the shrew.

'What about him?' Philip reiterated. 'He's dead.'

'Shouldn't we bury him or something?'

'Don't talk wet,' Philip said scornfully. 'It won't make any difference to him now.'

'Well, I'm *going* to bury him,' John said, with a more decisive tone in his voice than I think I'd ever heard before. 'I'm going to bury him, and you're going to wait until I've finished.'

He picked the dead shrew up – showing no signs of squeamishness – and walked over to the edge of the field, where there was bare earth. Once there, he laid the small corpse gently on the ground, and using his hands, clawed out a shallow grave. When the burial was over, he stood up and wiped his hands on his short pants.

'Better be getting home,' he said, as if he had put the incident completely behind him.

But he hadn't, because though he tried to hide it, I could see that he was fighting back the tears.

On the way to the village, I thought over the enormity of what I had done. Though I told myself I'd had no choice, I had killed one of God's creatures – for I was sure it was my stone which had struck the lethal blow.

Would the Almighty ever forgive me? I wondered.

Would I ever be able to forgive myself?

I'd felt guilty before, of course – when I'd broken a window in the garden shed, when I'd told a lie about why I was late for school – but this was the first attack of the real thing. It was to be far from the last.

The incident of the shrew, might, I suppose, have brought us closer together. After all, we did share in its extermination, though I am not sure, even to this day, that Philip did actually hit it as John and I had. Yet far from achieving that aim, it seemed to drive us further apart, so that in the end even John gave up trying to hold the gang together. Looking back on it now, I think the reason for the split was that our instincts grasped what we might never have realized on any intellectual level – that our different approaches to the death demonstrated quite clearly that we would never be compatible.

Then again, it may have been much less complicated than that. It may have simply been that, as we approached the village, I noticed that Philip was whistling.

EIGHT

Flint turned off the High Street and walked up the dirt track towards the house which, until three days earlier, Uncle Tony had shared with his son, and which, once the legal formalities were over, would belong to my cousin Philip outright.

A furniture van was parked outside the house, and while two workmen were loading a solid mahogany desk into the back of it, another pair were carrying a smoked glass and tubular steel table towards the front door.

A grey-haired woman – Mrs Roberts, who had been Uncle Tony's housekeeper ever since Aunt Jane disappeared – was supervising the operation and gave him a quizzical look.

'Police,' he said, showing her his warrant card. 'I'd like to talk to Mr Conroy.'

'I'll see if he's up to it,' Mrs Roberts said, and then added, severely, 'Mister Philip's been through a devastating experience, you know.'

But not so devastating that it prevented him from ordering new office furniture, Flint thought, looking at the van.

Mrs Roberts disappeared into the house and re-emerged about a minute later.

'If you'll follow me,' she said.

She led him into the large lounge, which had a picture window with a clear view of the rolling fields and the mere.

Philip had changed out of his mourning suit into an expensive casual jacket and trousers. He was looking out of the window, but as Flint entered the room, he turned around and walked towards him.

They shook hands, then Philip said crisply, 'I have a great deal to get through today, so I'd be grateful if you could make this as brief as possible.'

'Of course,' Flint agreed.

'Take a seat,' Philip said, waving towards the deep leather armchairs. 'Would you like a drink?'

Flint shook his head. 'No, thank you, sir.'

'Is that because you're on duty, because if it is, I can assure you . . .'

'No, it's not because I'm on duty – it's because I don't want a drink,' Flint said.

Philip shrugged, and while Flint was taking his seat, walked over to the drinks cabinet, and poured himself a generous scotch.

'So how can I help you?' he asked, returning to the centre of the room, but not sitting down.

'We could start by you telling me what your whereabouts were on the night before the crash,' Flint said pleasantly.

My cousin coloured. 'Are you accusing me of killing my own father?' he demanded angrily.

'Not at all, sir,' Flint replied. 'I'm just trying to eliminate you from the frame.'

'I was at the office until eight o'clock, as several witnesses will confirm,' Philip said.

'And after that?'

'I came home.'

'Was your housekeeper still here?'

'No, she always leaves at seven o'clock. If I'm planning to eat at home – as I did that night – she leaves me something to heat up in the oven.'

It occurred to Flint that the way he was talking – 'if *I'm* planning to eat at home, she leaves *me* something to heat up' – it was almost as if he'd already written Uncle Tony out of his autobiography.

'So from the time you arrived home, you were alone?' Flint asked.

The smile that came to my cousin's lips was little less than a smirk, Flint told me later.

'No,' Philip said, 'I wasn't alone – I had a woman with me.'

'And what time did she leave?'

Philip's smile broadened. 'The same time most of the women I entertain leave – the next morning.'

Flint took his notebook out of his pocket.

'Might I have her name, sir?' he asked.

'No,' Philip replied firmly. 'You may not.'

'So you're asking me to take your unsubstantiated word that you weren't alone?' Flint asked.

Philip looked uncertain as to whether he should become angry again or play the reasonable man.

'Look, if it becomes absolutely necessary, at some point in your investigation, to give you her name, then I will. But the fact is, she's married,' he said, settling for the latter approach.

'How would you describe your relationship with your cousins?' Owen Flint asked.

'Why should you want to know that?'

'Possibly because I'm trying to find out who killed one of them – and may have wanted to kill the other – and I have to start somewhere.'

Philip nodded. 'My relationship with my cousins isn't – or, in John's case, *wasn't* – what you'd call close.'

'Would you care to be a little more specific?'

'More specific?' Philip repeated. 'What do you mean?'

'"Not close" covers a multitude of sins,' Flint explained. 'I've talked to your cousin Rob, and I got the impression that, in your case, "not close" meant actively hostile.'

Philip reddened again. 'If there is hostility, it's entirely on my cousin's part,' he said.

'And is there any reason for his hostility?'

'No – at least, not any *reasonable* reason. The truth is, my cousin Rob hated the idea that my father and I were about to take over the company. He feared, quite correctly, that we'd make him run Cormorant Publishing more like a business and less like a hobby.'

'I thought he'd made a great success of it,' Flint said.

Philip looked at him suspiciously. 'It hasn't been a complete failure,' he conceded, 'but we're getting a far lower return on our capital out of it than we receive from any other branch of Conroy Enterprises.'

'What about your cousin John? Did he resent you, as well?'

Philip laughed. 'John was never any trouble. He didn't care *who* controlled the company.'

'Do *you* care?' Flint wondered.

'Oh yes, I care,' Philip said, with a sudden fire in his voice.

'I want to run this company as it should be run. I want to double our turnover in the next few years.'

'So you'll be in charge, will you? What about your cousin, Rob? Won't he have a say?'

'He had his own company years before I had mine, you know,' Philip said bitterly. 'Years! Grandfather bought him that publishing house the moment he came out of the loony bin. That was insane in itself.'

'I don't think you've answered my question,' Flint pointed out. 'Will Rob have a say in how the company is run, or won't he?'

The expression on Philip's face told him that my cousin had decided he'd already given away too much.

'Until my grandfather's will is read, we won't know what the actual situation will be,' Philip said.

And Flint was almost sure that he was lying.

Philip had been right about at least one of the things he told Flint – buying the publishing house had seemed almost insane at the time and, but for Andy McBride, might still seem insane today.

I remember the visit during which Grandfather had first floated the idea. It came at the end of my two-year nightmare journey which had started with drugs and electric shocks and gradually evolved into group therapy sessions and weekly meetings with my counsellor.

We were sitting in the institution's garden. The sun was shining with an autumn glow, and the leaves on the beech trees – which only partly hid the high walls – were just turning a soft golden brown.

'I'd have come to see you long before now,' Grandfather said, 'but it seemed to me you were getting plenty of visitors without being bothered by a tiresome old man like me.'

Plenty of visitors! Yes, I supposed that was true.

My parents came to see me once a fortnight. They always tried to put on a cheerful air, but could never quite manage to mask the haunted looks which expressed their real feelings.

The conversation would always follow the same lines, until it became almost a ritual. My father would ask me how I was getting on, and I would tell him I was doing quite well. Then my mother would ask when I was likely to be released.

'I really don't know, Mother,' I'd explain over and over again. 'They don't believe in setting deadlines in this place. They think it puts us under too much pressure.'

'We should never have let you go back to Oxford,' my mother would invariably reply, sniffing slightly. 'It's our fault as much as anybody's that you're in here now.'

And then my father would offer one of his mild rebukes.

'Hush, Elizabeth! There's no point in dwelling on the past, now is there? And it's not such a bad place, is it, son?'

I had to agree with him there. In fact, for much of the time, staying within those walls for the rest of my life held a powerful appeal. After all, I argued to myself, I was safe, and I was nurtured. Why run the risk of going out into the cold hard world again?

My brother John came to see me often, but though the institution was as cheery as any such institution could possibly be, his sensitive soul found it hard to take, and our conversations were always so strained that I think it was a relief to both of us when each visit was finally over.

Even Uncle Tony called in once, though he did not stay for long.

'Got to meet a chap in Chepstow in an hour and a half,' he'd explained, leaving me with the distinct impression that the 'chap' in question would have long blonde hair and a spectacular bosom.

'Yes, I've had a lot of visitors,' I told Grandfather, on the fine autumn day.

'It's a terrible thing, an old man's pride,' Grandfather said, unexpectedly. 'It can even turn a man who's been a straight talker all his life into a complete bullshitter.'

I was shocked to hear him swear, because it was something he had never done.

'What do you mean?' I asked.

'It's not because of all your visitors that I've put off visiting you,' Grandfather said. 'The reason I haven't been was because I wasn't up to it.'

'Why? What's the matter with you?' I asked, alarmed at the

sudden thought that Grandfather wouldn't always be there to lean on whenever I needed to.

'Age is the matter,' he told me. 'There are bits of me that just don't work as well as they used to.' He paused for a moment. 'I hear they're going to be letting you out soon.'

'That's what they tell me,' I said glibly. I laughed. 'It appears that I've come to terms with all my sorrows.'

Grandfather did not join in with my laughter. 'She was a lovely girl, your Jill,' he said seriously, 'and I'd be lying to you if I said I thought you were ever going to get over her completely. But you have to do something with your life, don't you?'

'I suppose so,' I said, though without much conviction.

Grandfather's watery eyes suddenly assumed the sharpness of a young man's. 'Have you ever thought about committing suicide?' he demanded.

'Yes, I have,' I admitted – because I could never lie to Grandfather.

'And how would you go about it?'

'I don't know.'

'If you've thought about it, you'll have thought about how you'd do it,' Grandfather said fiercely.

He was right, of course. 'I'd hang myself,' I said.

Grandfather nodded as though he'd been expecting that answer – though I had no idea why he should have done so.

'It's a man's right to choose to die,' he said. 'But what if you choose to live, instead? What will you do with the rest of your life?'

'I could always do what I planned to do three years ago,' I said. 'Go back and finish my degree, then get a teaching post somewhere.'

'Or you could join the business,' Grandfather suggested.

I shook my head so violently that my teeth chattered. 'If I'm ever going to pull myself back together, it won't be in a furniture factory or as part of a long-distance haulage operation.'

'I never said it would,' Grandfather pointed out mildly.

'Well, then?'

'I've been looking at a small publishing house in Oxford which is up for sale.'

'What does it publish?'

'New poetry. Anthologies of short stories by up-and-coming authors. The occasional novel by an unknown who can't get accepted by one of the big houses. You know the sort of thing.'

Yes, I did.

'It'll never make a profit,' I told the old man.

'It doesn't have to,' Grandfather responded. 'If it gives you a purpose in life, then it'll more than pay its way.'

'How do the others feel about it?'

Grandfather smiled. 'They feel much as you'd expect them to feel. Your father thinks it's a good idea. Your brother's worried it might be too much of a strain on you.'

But that wasn't what I'd meant, and we both knew it. 'What about the other half of the family?' I asked.

Grandfather hesitated for a second. 'Your uncle Tony thinks it's a waste of money – and by his own lights, I have to say he's right. Philip probably shares his view, but he's wise enough to know he hasn't got sufficient clout in the company to really stick his oar in.'

'Well, then . . . if they're against it . . .' I began

'What they think doesn't matter one way or the other,' Grandfather interrupted me. 'That's the advantage of having a company you've got overall control of – you can do what the hell you like. And I'd like to buy this publishing company for you – if you want it.'

Suddenly, I realized that I *did* want it – wanted it desperately. Publishing would satisfy whatever creative instincts I still had left, and since Grandfather wasn't expecting the company to do well, I would have plenty of scope for helping people with genuine talent who weren't getting recognition elsewhere.

And there was one other important factor to be taken into consideration. The publishing house was in Oxford – and Oxford was the demon I would have to confront if I were ever to become whole again. Perhaps I would fail, as I had done so spectacularly the last time, but at least I would be better prepared – more able to spot the signs of an imminent collapse.

'I'll take it,' I said.

My Grandfather grinned. 'I thought you would.'

And, not for the first time, I realized he had been several steps ahead of me throughout the whole conversation.

NINE

The church clock was just striking six as Flint made his way down the narrow lane by the side of the church which led to Grandfather's house. It was an impressive building, he thought – a house which *should* belong to the kind of family patriarch which Charlie Conroy had obviously been.

At the gate, he came to a halt, partly to admire the house from closer to – the wide frontage, the dormer windows in the deep blue slate roof, the archway which offered just a tantalizing glimpse of immaculate gardens beyond – and partly to consider whether calling on the widow so soon after the funeral was an appropriate thing to do.

He had just decided to leave it for another day when the front door opened, and a young woman in a white nurse's uniform appeared.

The nurse walked over to the gate.

'You're the policeman who's come up from darkest Wales, aren't you?' she said, with a smile.

'That's right,' Flint agreed. 'And you'd be . . .?'

'I'd be Jo Torlopp.' She grinned. 'I'm a nurse.'

'I'd guessed that,' Flint said, grinning back.

'I'm also a messenger,' Jo told him. 'Mrs Conroy noticed you standing out here and wondered if the reason was that you wanted to talk to her.'

'That was my intention—' Flint began.

'Because she wants to talk to you,' Jo interrupted, 'or rather, I think she feels the need to talk to someone who's not directly involved in the tragedy.'

'You don't think it would be too much of a strain on her?' Flint asked.

'Well, it's certainly not something I would recommend as a medical practitioner,' Jo Torlopp said frankly. 'But Mrs Conroy has suddenly become *very* independent since her husband died. So if you'd like to follow me . . .'

Grandmother was in her favourite parlour – a room which was small enough to be intimate, yet was crammed with memories of her life with Grandfather. She was sitting in a large armchair which made her look even tinier than she was, and on the coffee table in front of the chair, Flint noticed, was a leather-bound album.

'It's good of you to see me,' he said.

Grandmother indicated the armchair opposite hers. 'Sit down,' she said in a voice which he found was cracked but firm. 'I've asked Josephine to bring us some tea.'

'That's not necessary,' Flint told her.

'Perhaps not for you,' Grandmother told him, 'but it is for me. When you have nothing big to look forward to in the future, it's the anticipation of little things which keep you going – and I've been promising myself a cup of tea for the last half hour.'

Flint nodded, but said nothing.

'Who do you think could have done this terrible thing, chief inspector?' Grandmother asked.

'I've no idea,' Flint admitted. 'But I promise you that I'll work day and night until I find out.'

'I miss them all, you know,' Grandmother said. 'It was such a waste. I can almost accept Charlie's death – he'd had his time and was ready to go. But the others were so young.' She paused. 'I suppose you find it almost comical that I can describe my sons as young, don't you?'

'I never find death comical,' Flint said gravely.

'Yes, I miss them all,' Grandmother said, 'but it's my grandson, John, that I feel the worst about.'

'Why him, especially?'

Grandmother sighed. 'Because he finally seemed to be seeing the light at the end of the tunnel.'

'What do you mean by that?' Flint asked.

'For most of his life, John never really seemed happy, but lately I've noticed a change in him. He was more . . . more at peace with himself.' She opened the leather-bound album. 'Would you like to see some pictures of my family?'

'Very much so,' Flint replied – and meant it.

Grandmother opened the album at the first page and held it out for her visitor. Flint took it and found himself staring at a tall man with intelligent eyes and very short hair, who was dressed in a suit which belonged in the 1940s.

'That was Charlie when he'd just been demobbed from the army,' Grandmother said. 'He didn't *have* to join up at the start of the war, you know. He was thirty-one when Hitler invaded Poland – old enough to have missed it. But he said that he felt it was his duty to go and do his bit.'

'He was a sergeant major, wasn't he?'

'He was a sergeant major at the *end* of the war, but he started out as a *private*. He could have joined the army as an officer – he was an assistant manager in his father's furniture store by then, and that made him officer class – but he wasn't having any of that.' She turned the page to show him a photograph of Grandfather in uniform. 'Do you see that medal? He earned it in North Africa. His unit came under attack and he was wounded – but that still didn't stop him carrying his captain through the desert for two days.'

'He must have been a remarkable man,' Flint said.

'He was,' Grandmother agreed. 'It's a funny thing, war, isn't it? You think it's over once the peace is signed, but it never is. It changes people.'

'How did it change your husband?'

'He said it had taught him the value of the chain of command. There could only be one boss, and you had to make sure everyone knew who that was. He'd been so easy-going before the war. He'd have been quite happy working for his father and Mr Carson . . .'

'Mr Carson?'

'That was the name of his father's partner.'

Jo Torlopp arrived with the tea tray and poured two cups. Flint took his with three sugars.

'Will there be anything else, Mrs Conroy?' the nurse asked.

'No, thank you,' Grandmother replied, but when Jo Torlopp had almost reached the door, she changed her mind, and said, 'You could bring me the box.'

The nurse turned around, a troubled look starting to form on her face.

'Which box?' she asked.

'You know very well which one I mean – the polished wooden one that Charlie always kept in his study.'

The nurse's troubled expression deepened. 'I'm not sure that's such a good idea.'

'Well, I am,' Grandmother said firmly.

'It might upset you.'

'For heaven's sake, girl, he was Charlie's father, not mine,' Grandmother said exasperatedly. 'Go and fetch the box.'

For a moment it looked as if the nurse might continue to argue, then she turned and left the room in a manner which indicated that whilst she was going to do as she'd been told, she very much disapproved.

'As I was saying,' Grandmother said to Flint, 'the way Charlie was before the war, he'd have been quite happy working for his father and Mr Carson until they both retired, then he'd have taken over himself. But when he came back from Africa, he was full of plans.'

'Plans for what – moving into furniture manufacture?'

'No, not at first. Initially, all he wanted to do was to modernize the store. "It used to be enough to keep things just as they'd always been," he'd say, "but now it's a question of expand or die. We need new premises – somewhere light and airy. And we need to get ready to diversify, because once rationing is over, people will want to get rid of some of that money that's been burning a hole in their pockets." His father would have gone along with it, but Mr Carson wouldn't listen, and so, in the end, nothing was done. He got so annoyed about it. "No chain of command, Sarah, that's the problem," he'd say to me.'

Jo Torlopp re-entered the room carrying a polished wooden box large enough to contain duelling pistols. She laid it on the coffee table next to the photograph album, then left without saying a word.

Unexpectedly, Grandmother chuckled. 'I think Josephine finds this rather macabre,' she said. 'But it wasn't macabre to my Charlie – he saw it as nothing more than a reminder.'

'Of what?' Flint asked.

'We'll come to that in good time,' Grandmother told him. She took a sip of her tea. 'By 1950, Conroy and Carson were losing a lot of their business to the big new department stores,' she continued. 'By 1951, not even my Charlie could do anything to stop the rot, and they had to call the receivers in. His father took it very hard. He'd put his whole life into that shop, and now he had nothing. He was ashamed and humiliated. He didn't even want to show his face on the street.'

'I can well imagine it,' Flint said.

'I don't think you can,' Grandmother said, with just an edge of rebuke in her words. 'I don't think any of us can.' She hesitated. 'The day after the business officially went broke, Charlie went round to his parents' house to see how his father was. There was a fog that day – a real pea-souper. Even the trolley buses had stopped running. He found his mother in a real state. She'd heard her husband get up in the middle of the night, but she thought he was just going to make himself a cup of tea and went back to sleep. But when she woke up again, in the morning, she was alone – and his side of the bed was cold.'

Flint nodded, guessing the rest of the story. 'Where did they find him?'

'Charlie's father was a keen gardener, and Charlie thought that maybe he'd gone down to the potting shed, to make sure the weather hadn't damaged any of his plants. Like I said, there was a thick fog, and he was picking his way carefully down the path when he saw something hanging from the apple tree. At first, he thought it was a sack – though why anyone should hang a sack from the tree, he couldn't imagine – but as he got closer he could see it was too big for that.'

'It was his father,' Flint said.

Grandmother nodded. 'His feet were no more than two inches off the ground. "Imagine being so full of despair that you'd get up in the middle of the night and hang yourself," Charlie said to me. "No man should die alone, eaten up by defeat. If we'd expanded the store like I wanted to, this would never have happened".'

Grandmother leant forward and reached out to the shiny wooden box. She had some difficulty flicking back the brass catches which held it closed, but Flint, sensing his intervention would not be welcomed, made no effort to help her.

Finally, it was open, and Grandmother lifted the lid. The box was lined with purple velvet cloth which, over the years, had faded. In the centre of the box lay a six-inch piece of rope.

'This is part of the rope my father-in-law used to hang himself with,' Grandmother said. 'I don't know how Charlie managed to lay his hands on it – I'm told all evidence belongs to the police – but he was a determined man, and he usually succeeded in getting his own way.'

'He kept it in his study, you say?'

'That's right. It was on his desk. And whenever people put pressure on him to delegate more, he'd open the box and look at the rope.' Grandmother closed the box again. 'Charlie didn't really blame Mr Carson for his father's death, you know – he blamed the fact that there was no chain of command.'

'So did your husband start his furniture company right after his father's death?' Flint asked.

'No,' Grandmother said. 'At first he tried to get other jobs in retailing – it was the only trade he knew – but after a couple of weeks he began to see the situation was hopeless. Nobody wanted to employ a man who'd worked for a business which had gone broke. Going into furniture manufacturing was nothing more than an act of desperation.'

'Where did he get the capital from?' Flint wondered aloud.

'He went down to London, to see his old captain, who was an architect and property developer. He didn't mention that he'd saved the captain's life. He didn't have to – the captain brought it up the moment he entered the room. Charlie outlined his ideas. There was a building boom, he said. People were moving out of the slums into new houses. They had more space than they'd ever had before. Children who'd shared bedrooms with brothers or sisters would have a room of their own. All this extra space would need furnishing – but people wouldn't want the dark heavy stuff they'd been used to before the war. Bright and light – that was the key.'

'And the captain loaned him the money?'

'Not immediately. He could see the possibilities, and he suggested they go into partnership. But my Charlie wasn't having any of that – not after what had happened to his father and Mr Carson. In the end, he persuaded the captain to lend him the cash he needed at a proper commercial rate.'

'You're looking tired, Mrs Conroy,' Flint said.

'Yes,' Grandmother agreed. 'It's been a long, hard day.'

The chief inspector stood up. 'I'll see myself out,' he said. He looked down at the photograph album, which was still lying on the coffee table. 'Could I borrow that?'

'Borrow it!' Grandmother asked, alarmed. 'Why should you want to borrow it?'

'I think it will help me to get to know your family better,' Flint said. 'I'll take care of it. I promise.'

'Well, I suppose it will be all right,' Grandmother said, as she reluctantly handed her lifetime of memories over to him.

He was almost at the door when Grandmother said, 'We never told our children – or their children – about what happened to Charlie's father. We've kept it a secret from them all these years. But now Rob and Philip – Rob especially – will have to be told.'

'Why?' Flint asked.

'Because if they don't know what Charlie found hanging in the garden that morning, they'll never understand why he wrote his will the way he did.'

It was as Flint was walking up the lane from my grandparents' house that he noticed two people standing by the stocks in front of the church. He recognized one of them – the broad young man, who he'd last seen in Bridgend hospital – but his companion, a woman of about the same age, was a complete stranger.

The couple were looking down the High Street, as if admiring the view, but there was a certain stiffness about them which didn't look quite natural. It was almost as if they'd struck up a pose to disguise their real purpose for being there, Owen Flint thought.

The chief inspector drew level with them, and Bill Harper seemed to notice him for the first time.

'Ah, Mr Flint! Well met! Well met indeed!' he said with a heartiness which may not have been faked, but certainly sounded as if it was. He lifted his arm and placed it possessively on the woman's shoulder. 'May I introduce my wife – Susan.'

'I'm pleased to meet you, Mrs Harper,' Flint said, but he was thinking, *Just what the bloody hell is going on here?*

'We were just taking a walk around the village,' Harper continued. 'It's something we often do in the early evening.'

Now *that* didn't ring true, Flint told himself. He'd only spoken to Bill Harper once before, but he'd come away with the firm impression that staying late at the office to demonstrate his dedication to his job was much more his style than strolling round the village.

The chief inspector took a closer look at Susan Harper. His initial impression had been that she was pretty – and it was an accurate assessment, as far as it went. Yet although she did have all the right features, conventionally arranged, there was something missing.

It was the eyes that were wrong, he decided. They were deep wells of disappointment. They affected her whole being. And even the way she was standing next to her husband – like a dog which knows it has only been taken for a walk as an excuse to visit the pub – reflected her disillusionment with life.

'Funny running into you like this,' Bill Harper said, 'because I was just wondering if you'd managed to contact Paul Taylor yet.'

He sounded casual – but not quite casual enough.

He's rehearsed this, Flint thought. He's got the whole conversation scripted, and he wants to lead me by the nose. Well, maybe it's time he learned that this particular Taffy chief inspector isn't anybody's dupe.

'Paul Taylor? That name rings a bell, but I couldn't quite say from where,' Flint lied.

Harper looked surprised. 'Paul was Edward Conroy's executive assistant,' he said. 'My oppo, in a manner of speaking.'

And now you're about to have a go at stabbing him in the back, aren't you? Flint guessed.

'Is there any particular reason why it should be of interest to you whether or not I've talked to Mr Taylor?' he asked.

Harper shrugged. 'No, I was just curious. He's been away on a short holiday, you see.' He scratched his nose thoughtfully. 'It did strike me as odd that he should go away just when the biggest deal the Conroys have ever been involved in was going through. But there you are, I'm only an executive assistant myself, and it wasn't really my place to comment.'

'Yes, well, people do odd things every once in a while,' Flint said philosophically. He made a half turn. 'Now if you'll excuse me . . .'

'The thing is,' Bill Harper said hastily, 'I've been wanting to talk to him myself, because, as you can imagine, with four directors dead, there's a great deal of company business that he and I need to deal with. I was expecting to see him at Mr Conroy's funeral – paying due respect to the big chief and all that sort of thing – but there was no sign of him.'

'Perhaps he just doesn't like funerals,' Flint suggested.

'So I rang him at home,' Harper pressed on, 'but there was no reply. Finally, since there seemed to be no other way of contacting him, I motored over to his house to leave a message. His car's not there, and the neighbours say they haven't seen him since he set off on his trip.'

'Perhaps he's staying with friends or relatives,' Flint suggested.

'I don't think he is. I called his parents. They said he normally rings them every couple of days, but they haven't had a peep out of him for a week.'

Enough was enough. 'So because he's disappeared, you're trying to finger him for three murders, are you?' Flint asked.

'Of course not,' Harper said, clearly outraged. 'But I was brought up to cooperate with the police, and I thought this was something that you needed to know.'

And being a devious bastard by nature, he'd had to go all round the houses instead of coming straight to the point, Flint thought. Still, it was a useful piece of information – and there was no point in ignoring the message just because you couldn't stand the messenger.

TEN

The nurses in Bridgend hospital worked on a three-shift system, and the one responsible for my welfare between four in the afternoon and midnight was a pretty blonde girl called Lucy Cavendish. Lucy was in her last year of nursing, having finally set the date to marry her young man, who was making steady progress up the career ladder in Lloyd's Bank. She liked going to the theatre – though only to see musicals – playing tennis and visiting stately homes. When I occasionally – and accidentally – let what she would consider 'bad' language slip into my conversation, she always looked suitably shocked.

It was Lucy who brought the news that while I'd been taking my afternoon nap, someone had called the hospital and asked about me.

Marie! my soul screamed.

'Was it . . . was it a woman?' I asked.

Lucy shook her head regretfully. 'No, I'm afraid it was a man – a Mr McBride. He's down at the railway station. He wanted to know if you were allowed visitors.'

That was typical of the man, I thought fondly. Anyone else would have established what the visiting hours were before travelling all the way from Oxford, but Andy had never been good at long-term planning.

'Is he *the* Andy McBride?' Lucy asked. 'You know – the one who wrote' – she coloured slightly – 'the one who wrote *Gobshite*?'

'Yes, he's *the* Andy McBride,' I admitted.

'But I love it!' Lucy gasped. 'I mean, I don't normally read that sort of book, but it was so . . . so . . .'

'So sweeping?' I suggested. 'So poetic?'

'It gave me goosebumps,' Lucy said. She cleared her throat. 'Anyway, we told him he could see you, and he's taking a taxi right up here. I hope that's all right.'

'It's fine,' I assured her, remembering a time when, if Andy had had the money for a taxi in his pocket, he would have chosen to spend it on something else much more fundamental to his existence.

I remembered something else, too – the moment I'd seen the first extract of what would eventually turn out to be *Gobshite*, but to me would always be simply THE BOOK.

I'd received it one warm June morning six years earlier, sandwiched between two lots of new manuscripts. It was in a cheap exercise book and was written in pencil. There was no title – no author's name on the front cover. The handwriting was erratic, sometimes degenerating into printing, and often very difficult to decipher. I'd almost thrown it straight into the bin, then, guiltily, I'd told myself that if someone had bothered to write it, the least I could do was make an effort to read the first page.

By the end of the second paragraph, I was hooked. It was written in a vernacular style and told of a Glasgow boyhood in the fifties. The author, I guessed, had not had much more than a rudimentary education, but he was a natural writer. I could smell the bonfires which he described burning on the old bomb sites. I could feel the thrill of the chase when the writer and his friends went hunting wild cats. My bowels turned to water as I stood, side by side, with the writer's gang as it confronted its rivals. Then I reached the last page – and on the final line, the manuscript ended mid-sentence.

I walked out of my office, the exercise book still in my hand, and went over to reception. 'Where did *this* come from, Janet?' I asked.

'I'd never have bothered you with it, but you did say you wanted to see *everything* which came into the office,' my secretary answered defensively.

'Yes, yes,' I agreed impatiently. 'But where did this particular piece of "everything" come from?'

'I found it in the letter box.'

'In an envelope?'

'No, just as you see it now.'

So I had received the freshest bit of writing I'd read in years, and I had no idea what its source was. I went back into my office to think things over. Perhaps when he sent the next extract, the author would include his address. Or perhaps there wouldn't be another extract at all. There was nothing to do but wait. I picked up the next manuscript and noted with dismay that I could count seven clichés in the opening paragraph.

Time passed, and more exercise books kept appearing, irregularly, on the mat. The manuscript – although that was a polite word for it – had grown to fifty thousand words, and had reached the point at which the unknown author had been released from prison, and decided that it was time to leave the city of his birth and explore the wider world. He had hitchhiked down to Carlisle, and from there to Manchester. He had been intending to travel all the way to London, but had got drunk one night in Oxford and, waking up on a bench, stinking of his own vomit, had decided that since life was brutish everywhere, he might as well stay where he was.

It was after I'd come to the end of that notebook that I decided not to wait for the next, but instead to go out and find the author.

The door opened, and Andy walked into the hospital room. He was wearing a car coat, check shirt, jeans and combat boots – all of them clean, all of them reasonably expensive. I anxiously examined his face for signs that he'd been drinking, then breathed a sigh of relief when I found none.

'I'd ha' been here sooner, but I was outta the country when it happened,' Andy said. 'I was on a book tour of Australia.'

I smiled. 'I know you were,' I said. 'I sent you on it.'

Andy nodded. 'O' course ye did. Anyway, I caught the first flight back . . .'

'You shouldn't have done that,' I said.

'You're a loon if you think I'm gonna stay away when you might need me,' Andy said. 'Listen, Rob, I'm hellish sorry aboot what happened, an' if there's anythin' I can do . . .'

'You can tell me about the tour,' I said. 'Did it go well?'

'Na' bad,' Andy said. 'They're awright, them Aussies. I get on well with them.'

'Why wouldn't you?' I asked. 'You're all right yourself.'

Since the notebooks had been delivered by hand, it was very likely that the man who had written them still lived in Oxford, and since he was a habitual criminal with a serious drink problem, there didn't seem much point in asking after him at the Randolph Hotel. If I was to find him anywhere, I decided, it would be at the Salvation Army Citadel at the end of Littlegate Street – a stone's throw from my office.

I felt as if I were stalking a frightened animal – one so timid that even the slightest wrong move on my part would send my quarry scurrying for the undergrowth, never to reappear. So I trod cautiously, exercising a patience which, knowing my own nature, surprised me. Each morning, including the weekends, I would tour the city centre, studying the dropouts, searching for a clue which might tell me that one of them was my mysterious writer.

Many of the residents of the Citadel congregated, for reasons known only to themselves, around the Carfax Tower area. There they would sit, wearing overcoats tied up with string even on the hottest day, and drink their cider or cheap wine. By nine o'clock in the morning, they were already drunk. By nine thirty, many of them were insensible. It was a depressing quest I had set myself, but I felt compelled to find the man who had somehow managed to make sense out of the meaningless journey which was his life.

It was during the third week of my search that I found my man. Andy was sitting on a bench in St Giles, his exercise book on his knee, a pencil held in his grubby hand. There was a bottle of Strongbow cider at his feet, and after writing a few words, he would gaze longingly at it. Then, by what was obviously a supreme effort of will, he would return to the page and force out another sentence.

I watched him for over ten minutes before I plucked up the nerve to approach him, and when I did, the only words which came to my mind were, 'Thank you!'

The derelict looked up. He was probably my age, but he looked older – or at least, worse. He was a broad man, but had clearly let his body go to seed. He had sandy hair with strands of white in it. His eyes were bloodshot, his cheekbones full of broken veins. His nose had obviously been smashed at some time and reset badly. The teeth in his wide mouth were mostly rotten.

'Wha' did ye say?' he demanded belligerently.

'Thank you,' I repeated. 'Thank you for writing such a wonderful book.'

For a moment, I thought he would deny that he had, then he shook his head and said, 'I wasna sure that anybody was readin' the bloody thing.'

'But you kept writing, anyway.'

'It didna seem like I had any choice.'

I held out my hand. 'Robert Conroy.'

Andy had hesitated for a moment, just looking at the hand, before he finally shook it. 'Andy McBride.'

'I want to publish your book,' I told him. 'I can't pay you as much as some of the other publishing houses might offer, but I can assure you that I really do care about it.'

Andy reached down for the bottle of Strongbow and took a deep swig. 'It isna finished,' he said, wiping his mouth on his sleeve.

'I know that. I'm prepared to wait until it is.'

A look of anguish came into Andy's bloodshot eyes. 'I don' know if it'll *ever* be finished,' he moaned. 'It gets harder all the time. The drink's the problem. I canna hold off it for as long as I used to.'

He took another gulp from his bottle. Already I was starting to notice the change in him. Another few minutes, and he would have no idea where he was, let alone what our conversation had been about.

'If you want help, I'll give it to you,' I promised.

'Help? What kinda help?'

'I'll rent somewhere for you to live. Probably only a bedsit, but it should be an improvement on the Citadel.'

Andy shook his head. 'Wouldna do nae good. Doesna matter where I am. Like I told you, the drink's the problem.'

'If medical treatment will help, I'll pay for it,' I said. 'And if you need to go to Alcoholics Anonymous, I'll go there with you.'

Andy's eyes narrowed suspiciously. 'What's the catch?' he asked.

'No catch. I just want you to be in a position to finish your book so I can publish it.'

McBride shook his head. 'There just hasta be more to it than that.'

'Maybe there is,' I agreed. 'I hit a low a few years ago, and perhaps I'd still be there now if my grandfather hadn't stepped in and helped me.'

McBride took his third swallow of cider. The bottle was nearly half-empty, and he was swaying from side to side. 'The only thing ma granddad ever give *me* was the back o' his hand,' he said.

'Let me do for you what my grandfather did for me,' I pleaded.

Andy looked down at his exercise book. 'Canna even see the words nae more,' he slurred. 'Just a loada squiggles.'

'You can come through this thing if you really want to,' I said.

McBride screwed up his eyes, as if he were having difficulties focussing. 'Go away!' he said.

'Please think about what I've just said.'

'Go away afore I turn nasty and hurt ye.'

It was laughable even to suggest that in his condition he could do me any harm, but I left anyway. There didn't seem to be much else I *could* do, now that the writer I'd spoken to a few minutes earlier had transformed himself into just another drunkard.

I went looking for Andy McBride again the next morning, but he was neither at St Giles nor in any of the other places where the residents of the Citadel gathered. I repeated the procedure the following day, and the day after that, but I had no success.

In spite of my best efforts, I told myself, I'd done what I feared I'd do, and frightened McBride off. The man could have gone anywhere – perhaps to London, as he'd originally intended, perhaps back to Glasgow. There would be no more exercise books dropping through Cormorant's letterbox. I had lost Andy McBride, and all I was left with was an incomplete work of near-genius.

It was more than two weeks after our encounter on St Giles that Janet rang through to my office to say, agitatedly, that we had an unwelcome visitor at reception who insisted on seeing me.

'What's the matter with him?' I asked.

'He's . . .' Janet lowered her voice. 'Well, he's a tramp.'

I sprang from my chair and rushed down the corridor. Janet was sitting at her desk, glaring up at Andy McBride. The tramp-writer was wearing the same clothes he'd had on the last time I'd seen him, but his face and hands were looking considerably cleaner.

McBride seemed to find my appearance on the scene embarrassing, even though meeting me again was the purpose of his visit.

'Ye said . . . ye said if I wanted help . . .' he mumbled, staring down at the ground.

'Come into my office and we can talk about it, Mr McBride,' I said.

He followed me into the office and sat down in the chair I offered him. He didn't look comfortable. 'Aboot what ye said yesterday—' he began.

'It wasn't yesterday,' I interrupted. 'It was two weeks ago.'

Andy shook his head, as if trying to clear it of muzzy thoughts.

'I sometimes lose tracka time,' he admitted. 'Anyway, what ye said . . .'

'I meant it.'

'Ye'll rent me a bedsit?'

'Yes, and I'll give you a small living allowance while you finish the book.'

'I nearly didna come,' McBride said. 'Even when I waz halfway up the stairs, I didna know if I waz gonna make it.'

'I'm glad you did.'

'Thing is, where I am now, I've got no further to fall,' McBride said. 'An' there's a kinda comfort in that – a kinda security. But what ye're offerin' me is a chance, an' I'm bloody terrified I might blow it.'

'We're *all* terrified we might blow it,' I told him, thinking of all the nights I had lain awake worrying about my own delicate mental balance. 'And I can't tell you that *you* won't. But just think of the rewards if you *don't* blow it.'

McBride's lower lip quivered, and the sight of the big Glaswegian on the point of crying almost made me want to burst into tears, too.

I reached across my desk and put my hand on his shoulder. 'You can handle it, Andy,' I said. 'We'll handle it together.'

McBride nodded. 'Maybes I can a' that,' he agreed. 'When do I start?'

I picked up the phone. 'Janet, put me through to one of those estate agents on the Cowley Road. No, it doesn't matter which.' I turned my attention back to Andy McBride. 'You've already started,' I said.

*　　*　　*

We very quickly fell into a pattern. I would pick Andy up from his bedsit every morning and take him to the office. Once there, he would go straight to the desk I'd made available for him. Sometimes he would write, sometimes he would just gaze at the wall, but all the time he would be fighting his craving for a drink. The two of us would have lunch together, then after the day's work we would usually go for a long walk, followed by dinner. To close the evening, I would drive Andy home, making sure that we arrived at his door after the pubs and off licences had closed. And twice a week, on Tuesday and Friday, we attended meetings of the Oxford branch of Alcoholics Anonymous.

It was an exhausting process, but a rewarding one, too. Andy had a fund of stories to tell and, now that he was sober, a genuine interest in what was going on around him. I had originally thought that he would eventually produce just the one marvellous book he had in him, but now I began to let myself hope that perhaps there might be others to follow it.

The days grew into weeks, the weeks into months, and still Andy steered clear of the drink. It was a great feat of courage – a marvellous transformation – and when I left Oxford to attend my brother's wedding, I was confident that even without my presence Andy would be able to stay on the wagon.

'I'm thinkin' o' tryin' to get inta university to study lit'rature,' Andy McBride told me in the hospital room in Bridgend. 'What do ye think?'

'It's a good idea,' I replied. 'Most writers claim they've benefited from studying the works of other people.'

'But d'ye think I'd get in?' Andy asked worriedly. 'I have'na got much in the way of formal qualifications.'

I laughed. 'Give them a couple of years, and *Gobshite* will be on the university's syllabus,' I said. 'So I don't imagine they'll have any difficulty admitting you as a student.'

Andy checked his watch. 'I'd better be goin' if I'm to get back to Oxford tonight,' he said, standing up. 'I'll come down an' see ye again soon.'

'Don't bother,' I told him. 'They're discharging me tomorrow.'

'So ye'll be comin' home yerself?'

Even the thought of returning to Oxford made my stomach churn.

'No,' I said. 'Not for a while, anyway.'

Andy gave me a strange look. 'It's not like you to stay away from your work. Wha's the problem?'

The problem? The problem was that Marie was in Oxford – Marie, the woman who hadn't even bothered to ring me to see how I was feeling.

How would I face her when we next met? Should I act as if I hadn't noticed her lack of concern? Or should I, with a towering anger, demand to know how she could have been so callous? Did I even have the choice? Was I enough in control of myself to guide my own actions?

'It's her, isna it?' Andy said. 'She's the problem.'

'It's her,' I admitted.

He shook his head wonderingly. 'I dunna know why you bother wi' her,' he said. 'The woman does nothin' but play games with ye.'

I sighed. 'It's not as simple as that.'

'Isna it?' Andy countered. 'Ye've bin seein' her for two years, an' she'll not let ye do so much as hold her hand.'

'We agreed at the start that we'd be no more than friends,' I said hotly.

'You mean she *told* ye that ye'd be no more than friends. But she's more than that to you, isn't she?'

'Maybe,' I said – because I didn't want to admit to the truth, but I couldn't tell an outright lie, either.

'She must know how ye feel – an' if she canna feel the same way herself, then she should do the decent thing an' stop seein' ye.'

I felt as if a red hot iron had been plunged into my gut, burning through flesh, melting the fat, because while the thought of not seeing Marie again was terrifying, there was at least a part of me which recognized that Andy was right – that she should have done the decent thing and stopped seeing me.

'An' then there's that flat o' hers,' he said, leaving me no time to recover my strength.

We had had this particular discussion countless times before. 'I don't want to talk about it,' I said wearily.

'She's bin roond to your place, but ye've no been roond to hers,' Andy pressed on relentlessly. 'Now why is that?'

'She has a small flat. Part of it is her office. There simply isn't room to entertain,' I said, even though I'd been the first one to raise the question of why she would never let me cross her threshold.

'No room! Tha's bollocks!' Andy retorted. 'She wilna have ye roond because she's got somethin' to hide. But it'd be easy enough to find out what that *somethin'* is,' he continued, lowering his voice, even though there was no one else in the room.

'No!' I said emphatically.

'We'd be in an' oot o' the place in five minutes,' Andy said. 'Christ, I musta broken inta hundreds of flats in my time.'

'It's not right,' I said.

'It's not right tae torment yerself, either. If you had a quick look aroond, it might answer all kinds o' questions.'

'And if we got caught, a three-time offender like you would go straight back to gaol,' I pointed out.

'I'd be willin' tae take the risk if I knew it was helpin' you,' Andy said. 'I owe ye more than I can ever repay.'

I forced a smile on to my face. 'Who's talking bollocks now?' I asked him. 'What I'd really like – what would really make me happy – is for you to go back to Oxford and write me another masterpiece. Will you do that for me?'

'Aye, I will, if that's what ye want,' Andy agreed. 'But if ye ever change yer mind aboot that other thing . . .'

'I won't,' I said, with more certainty than I actually felt.

ELEVEN

Owen Flint told me that he hated hotel rooms. He hated the way the mass-purchased beds were precisely slotted in, he said, so that there was just enough room for the mass-purchased bedside cabinets. He hated the fact that the room next door would probably be a perfect replica of his own room, and that they had probably been laid out in some design office in London. He hated, in other words, the feel of the places, because though they were a hundred times more luxurious than the spartan dormitory he had lived in as a child, they were still institutional. So it was hardly surprising that the moment he had unpacked his small suitcase, he picked up the leather-bound photograph album that Grandmother had lent him, and headed for the bar.

Once there, he ordered a pint of best bitter, and opened the album at random. The first picture he came across was a group photograph, probably taken some time in the late forties when Grandfather was still working in his father's store. Grandfather stood in the centre of the photograph next to Grandmother. The serious expression on his face could almost have been Victorian, Flint thought, had it not been for the slight twist of the mouth which suggested that as well as dispensing authority, he was also capable of great kindness. The children were either side of their parents. The one on the left – my father – had a slightly preoccupied look, as if he lived most of the time in a world of his own. The one on the right – Uncle Tony – seemed very much aware of the real world, and the possibilities it offered for making mischief, and Flint sensed that, the second before the photograph had been taken, Tony had been glancing around the room, assessing his opportunities.

The chief inspector took another sip of his pint, and turned a few pages. The wild boy he'd seen in the previous picture had grown into a broad man. The woman next to him had dark brown hair which spilled in curls over her shoulders. She was wearing a cloak over a low-cut dress. She held a cigarette in her left hand, and underneath the picture, someone had written 'Tony and Jane. Their engagement party'.

So this was Philip's mother – the woman who had run away from home when her son was still a child. Flint found himself wondering what had made her do it, just as he wondered – though he had never plucked up the nerve to find out – what had happened to his own parents. He made a mental note to ask Grandmother about Jane the next time he saw her.

Somehow, examining the photographs seemed to drain him. He'd look at one more, he promised himself, and then he'd call it a night. He turned almost to the back of the album and saw the familiar sight of Magdalene College Bridge. He recognized the people in the picture, too. How could he not! There was me, looking blissfully happy. And there was Jill – beautiful, delicate Jill – with her hand resting on her proud boyfriend's shoulder.

'It's Mr Flint, isn't it?' said a voice to his left.

Flint looked up and saw a pretty blonde woman. For a moment he wondered where he'd seen her before, then realized it was the absence of a uniform which was confusing him.

She was the nurse who had looked after Charles Conroy, and her name was Trollop. No, it was Torlopp.

'Is it your night off, Miss Torlopp?' he asked.

'That's right,' the nurse replied. She hesitated for a second, then said, 'Well, it's been nice meeting you again.'

'Would you like to join me in a drink, Miss Torlopp?' Flint suggested.

The nurse giggled. 'I don't think we'd both fit into just one,' she said, but she pulled out one of the high stools and sat down. 'You're looking at one of Mrs Conroy's photograph albums, I see.'

'That's right,' Flint agreed. 'How is the old lady?'

'If you ask me, it's not all sunk in yet,' the nurse told him. 'But it will. It always does in the end.'

Flint signalled a waiter. 'What would you like to drink, Miss Torlopp?' he asked.

'A white wine, please. And call me Jo.'

The chief inspector placed the order. 'Can I ask you a question, Jo?' he asked, turning back to the woman.

'I'm thirty-one, and what you've heard about the voracious sex drive of nurses is a gross exaggeration,' she said.

Flint smiled. 'No, it wasn't anything like that. I was just wondering, since you've lived in the village for three years, whether you'd fill me in on a few details.'

'What kind of details?'

'Well, let's start with Edward Conroy's executive assistant, Paul Taylor. Do you know him?'

'Not well, but I've talked to him a few times.'

'And what do you make of him?'

'I'd say he was as well matched to Edward Conroy as that lout Bill Harper was to Tony.'

Flint smiled. 'What is it you don't like about Bill Harper?' he asked.

'For all his show of loyalty to Tony Conroy, the only person he's really loyal to is himself. He's the sort of man who'd step on your fingers as you were climbing up the ladder behind him – just because he could. I don't like the way he is with his wife, either. Admittedly, she's not the most spirited woman I've ever met, but that's no reason for treating her like a doormat – and mark my words, one day, that particular worm will turn.'

'And Paul Taylor?' Flint asked.

'He's very quiet and gentle. I don't mean to say that he's effeminate, but there's a softness about him you don't see much nowadays. I would imagine many women would find him appealing.'

'Does he strike you as the irresponsible type?'

Jo Torlopp frowned. 'No, I wouldn't say so. He's got no great spark about him, but I'm sure he's conscientious enough. Why did you ask that?'

'Because he still hasn't returned from his holidays.'

'Do you know, with all that's been going on, I hadn't really thought about that,' Jo Torlopp confessed, with a frown, 'but you're right. You'd have thought he'd have at least *interrupted* his holiday to attend the funeral, wouldn't you?'

'You would indeed,' Flint agreed.

Jo Trollop's frown deepened. 'You don't think he had anything to do with the murders, do you?'

'I think,' Flint said, slowly and carefully, 'that he needs to offer some explanation as to why he's stayed away so long.'

The clock on the wall of my hospital room continued to click relentlessly. The hands crawled around the dial, bringing ever closer the moment of my discharge. I felt just as I had on my last day in the mental institution – as if I was about to be ejected from a world filled with certainty into one full of malevolence and hostility, where – just possibly – there might be someone waiting for his opportunity to kill me. And then,

as I lay there, tossing and turning, I found my thoughts turning
to memories of my brother John.

John, who had started primary school the year before Philip
and myself, and who had endured a full twelve months of
bullying without support or complaint.

John, who had cried that day we killed the shrew.

I felt so close to him, even in death, and yet I could not say
that I'd ever really understood him. Perhaps part of the problem,
I rationalized to myself, was that we'd spent so little time
together since he turned eight. It had always been part of
the plan – part of *Grandfather's* plan – that we should go to the
same prep school as Father and Uncle Tony had attended, but
John failed to reach the required standard in the entrance examination and had to settle for somewhere a little less prestigious.
It hadn't seemed to bother him. Nor had he minded when I
took the examination myself and passed with flying colours.

'I hope Shadwell's a tremendous place,' he told me during
the summer holidays which followed his first year at his new
school. 'But I'm glad I go to Stoners. The chaps are marvellous,
and we have no end of fun.'

Somehow, I always found it hard to imagine John having
fun. He was so serious, so responsible, so . . . so introspective.
Only occasionally did he show any sign of expressing emotion
– like the time he first told me about Lydia.

It was at the summer board meeting of 1984 that my grandfather
announced Conroy Enterprises' latest acquisition.

'The company's called Mid-Cheshire Mechanical,' he told
us. 'They do contract maintenance for a number of haulage
firms in the area. From now on, they'll be doing ours as well.
I'm putting John in as managing director.'

I glanced across the table at my brother, who appeared to be
slightly uncomfortable at being the centre of attention. He hadn't
changed much over the years, I thought. At twenty-eight he still
looked like the earnest boy who'd tried to make Philip and me
like each other, though it must already have been plain to
everyone else that we'd never get along. Still, it was undoubt-
edly true that his appearance would stand him in good stead in
a business which was often conducted by cowboys.

'You won't get any padded bills from me,' his serious expression would tell his clients. 'I won't charge you for an expensive repair when a cheap one would do just as well. What you'll get is exactly what you pay for.'

Grandfather took out the heavy brass pocket watch, which was the only thing *his* father had been in a position to leave him, and squinted at the face. 'We'll take a twenty-minute break,' he said. 'There'll be coffee and biscuits on offer in the entertainment suite.'

The entertainment suite was located next to the boardroom, and our gatherings in it were the part of these meetings I most disliked, because the simple fact was that, although I felt obliged to talk to my uncle and cousin, we really had very little to say to each other. On this occasion, however, Philip seemed eager to talk, and steered me away from the rest of the group.

'How's the publishing business going?' he asked.

'It's going quite well,' I told him.

Philip nodded as though, even if he had asked the question, he wasn't very interested in the answer.

'Saw that writer – what's his name? Geoffrey Caldwell – on the box the other night.'

'Oh yes?'

'He was talking about his life. He said he'd had his manuscript turned down by half a dozen publishers before he sent it to Cormorant. Were you the one who spotted it?'

'As a matter of fact, I was,' I admitted.

'That was pretty smart of you.'

I smiled, self-deprecatingly. 'It's a very good book,' I said. 'And it wasn't so much that I was smart as that the other publishers were stupid.'

'People on the box are always mentioning you,' Philip said, with an edge of bitterness creeping into his voice. 'Always saying how you gave them their start.'

'I've been lucky,' I said. 'Most publishers have to show the sort of profit their shareholders demand, but Grandfather made it plain from the start that wasn't strictly necessary with CP. So I can take chances other publishers daren't. And sometimes they pay off.'

It was clear from the expression on my cousin's face that he was no longer listening to me. 'Four years,' he said, almost to himself.

'I beg your pardon?'

'You've had that company four years, haven't you?'

'About that.'

'And here I am, a couple of months older than you, still working for my father.' He put his hand on my shoulder. 'You've got more influence with Grandfather than the rest of us,' he said.

'Have I?'

'Yes. I don't understand the reason, but you have. That's why I want you to do me a favour.'

'What kind of favour?' I asked cautiously.

'Talk to him. Persuade him it's time I had a company of my own, too.'

'I'll try,' I promised, 'but I'm not sure it will do any good. Grandfather's always been very much his own man. Besides, it's a question of waiting for a suitable opportunity to arise. This new company's ideal for John, and that's why Grandfather has put him in charge of it. And when he sees one which is right for you, you can be certain he'll buy it. All you have to do is be a little patient.'

I'd been trying to be diplomatic, but I'd obviously failed. Philip's face clouded over, and it was clear that he was having great difficulty containing his rage.

'Maybe I should have a nervous breakdown,' he said bitterly. 'Yes, that's it. Have a nervous breakdown tomorrow, and Grandfather will give me my own company the day after.'

'It's not as simple as that,' I protested, starting to get angry myself. 'I was in therapy for two long, painful years.'

But I was wasting my breath. Having delivered his barb, Philip turned on his heel and marched back into the boardroom.

After the meeting broke up, John said he felt like a drive, and asked me if I'd go with him. I didn't really fancy the idea, to be honest, but he seemed so keen on it that I agreed. And so it was that I found myself sitting in the passenger seat of John's Audi, watching the familiar countryside – which no longer seemed to be a part of me – flash by.

'Are you pleased with your promotion?' I asked my brother. John shrugged. 'I suppose so.'

'You don't *sound* very enthusiastic. Philip would kill for his own company.'

'I'm not Philip,' John said.

'And thank God for that,' I agreed. 'I don't think I could handle someone like him for a brother.'

'So how are things in Oxford?' John asked me.

I started telling him about the business in general, then began to focus in on what was becoming a growing obsession – THE BOOK.

'A new chunk of it turns up roughly every six months,' I told him. 'Always in an exercise book. Always written in pencil. I must have forty thousand words of it by now – he's reached the point where he's in prison for burglary – but I still have no more idea who he is then I had when I received the first extract.'

'Hmm,' my brother said, changing gear as we approached a bend in the road.

'Of course, the most exciting part was when he was an amateur vampire in Transylvania,' I said.

'Yes, that must be interesting,' John commented.

'You're not really listening to me, are you?' I asked sharply.

'What? Of course I am?'

'Then what was the last thing I said?'

'You . . . uh . . . keep getting exercise books full of brilliant stuff dropped through your letterbox.'

'That's what I said about five minutes ago,' I agreed. 'But what have I been talking about since then?'

'I'm sorry, Rob,' my brother said. 'You're right – I wasn't listening. I've got something on my mind.'

'I rather thought you had. Is it the new job?'

'No. Nothing like that.'

'Well, out with it, then.'

'I've met a girl,' John said in a rush, and looking across at him, I could almost have sworn he was blushing.

'A girl!' I repeated, trying to hide my smile – because I really *did* find it funny.

I assumed, of course, that in the time since I'd left Cheshire,

he had been out with women, but now we had come down to
actual cases, I found some difficulty in picturing it. The problem
was that John, in my mind, was in some ways still a teenager
– and I couldn't help associating him with all the fumbling and
sweating which most teenagers go through on their first few dates.

'Her name's Lydia,' John said, sounding slightly aggrieved,
as if he could read my thoughts.

'Oh yes?' I replied neutrally, not wanting to cut him off, yet
not wishing to be intrusive either.

But I needn't have worried about him falling silent. The
floodgates had opened, and everything which had been on his
mind came spilling out.

'She's twenty-four,' he told me. 'I met her at the village fête
last summer. We talked for a while. She . . . I didn't think she
was really interested in me. I mean, I've got a pretty ham-fisted
approach to girls. But she asked me for my telephone number,
and a couple of weeks later she rang me. We've been seeing
quite a lot of each other since then.'

This time, however much I tried, I could not hold back a
grin.

'And have you taken her home for Sunday tea, so she could
meet Mum and Dad?' I asked.

'No,' John confessed. 'I will, when the time's right. But I
thought *you* might like to meet her first.'

I wondered if my suffering, and my modest success, had
automatically promoted me – in his mind – to the role of older
brother. But it wasn't that. Even when we were kids, he'd looked
to me for guidance, rather than the other way around.

'I'd be honoured to meet her,' I told him. 'When can we
arrange it?'

John released an involuntary sigh of relief.

'I've booked a table at a country pub in Lower Peover for
tonight,' he said. 'Just the three of us unless . . . unless there's
somebody you'd like to take.'

'No,' I said, trying not to sound too sad, 'there's nobody who
I'd like to take. But won't it be a little awkward if . . .'

'Not at all, Rob. Not at all,' John said, as much to reassure
himself as to answer me.

*   *   *

The pub-restaurant John had selected was just off the main road, and since my brother had to go into Warrington to pick Lydia up, it was agreed that we should travel separately. Though he left home before me, I arrived first, and after parking my Ford Granada on the asphalt behind the pub, I went into the bar and ordered a pint.

It was a pleasant place in which to have a drink, full of old oak beams made black with age, and copper bedpans which could almost be mistaken for the genuine article.

As I sipped my pint, I found myself thinking about my encounter with my cousin Philip. He wanted his own company badly enough to kill for it, I'd said, and though that had clearly been an exaggeration, I didn't think I had ever seen a man with as much frustrated ambition as Philip seemed to have. I tried to feel sorry for him, but found that I couldn't. Absence is supposed to make the heart grow fonder, but the enmity which had existed between us as children had not been lessened one jot by our separation.

Turning my mind to more pleasant subjects, I began to think about my brother John. It was comical the way he had gone about this courtship business, I told myself. He'd been seeing the woman for nearly a year, yet he'd kept it a secret from our parents.

Even tonight, he had told them some cock and bull story about how he and I were going out for a drink together, to talk over old times. What was he afraid of? That our mother and father would disapprove? He was twenty-eight years old and managing director of his own company, for God's sake!

The main door of the pub swung open, John entered, and I got my first look at the woman he had been meeting clandestinely since the summer fête. She was not what I'd expected. For openers, she looked considerably younger than the twenty-four John had told me she was. And whereas I'd been half expecting some busty blonde, she was quite the opposite – a slim brunette.

John saw me and waved like a man who needed someone to throw him a life belt. Then he pointed me out to the woman, took her by the arm, and led her towards me.

As she got closer, I was able to get a better look at Lydia.

She had short hair, which was styled in what might have been called a pixie cut. Her eyes were green, her nose slim, and her mouth – I thought – perhaps a little tight. She was wearing a tailored suit which clung to her boyish figure.

I don't want to make her sound unattractive – I noticed that several men in the room were following her with their eyes – but she was certainly not a woman who would ever have attracted me.

They reached the bar, and John slapped me warmly on the shoulder.

'Rob, this is Lydia,' he said, in a voice which sounded over-jovial. 'Lydia, this is Robbie.'

We shook hands. 'Pleased to meet you,' I said.

'The feeling's mutual,' Lydia replied.

There was something unnatural about the whole situation and, from experience, I knew where that feeling came from. We were sizing each other up, accepting that we could be either allies or enemies, and not sure yet which it was going to be. I'd got exactly the same feeling when I'd first met Jill's father.

'Have you checked that they've reserved us a table?' John asked, with just a hint of panic in his voice.

'It was the first thing I did when I came in,' I assured him.

'Good.' My brother wiped his hand across his forehead. 'Then let's go and eat, shall we?'

We walked through to the dining room, and the waiter showed us to our table. By contrivance or accident – I'm not sure which – I found myself sitting directly opposite Lydia.

'John's told me so much about you,' she said.

So much of *what* about me? I wondered.

Had he told her that I'd lost the only woman I was ever going to love? Had he mentioned the fact I'd had a mental collapse, and been institutionalized for over two years?

'John talks too much,' I said.

Lydia giggled. 'I know he does. I'm always telling him that. But he's so proud of having a famous brother that sometimes he just can't help himself.'

I was still not quite confident enough about my present situation to feel secure about my past, and I breathed a secret sigh of relief that John seemed to have given his girlfriend an edited version of my life story.

'So you met at our village fête,' I said.

'That's right,' Lydia agreed.

'And what happy chance took you from the metropolis of Warrington to a rustic little village like ours?' I asked, thinking even as I spoke the words how patronising I sounded.

But if Lydia noticed my tone, she gave no indication of it.

'I suppose it was a feeling of nostalgia that took me there,' she said. 'I was brought up in a small village in Lancashire, and the fête always used to be one of the high spots of our year.'

'Do your parents still live in Lancashire?' I asked.

'What is this?' my brother asked, in a mock-light, semi-concerned tone. 'An interrogation?'

'If I've said something wrong—' I began.

'No,' Lydia interrupted. 'No, you haven't.' She reached across the table and touched my brother's hand. 'John's just trying to protect me, that's all. He's got this idea of me as a delicate flower, but I'm tough as old boots really.'

'Still, if you'd rather not talk about it . . .' I said.

'I don't mind. Really! My parents are dead.'

'Oh, I'm so sorry!'

Lydia shook her head. 'No need to be. They died when I was very young. It was a plane crash – their first holiday alone together for years. I was brought up by a maiden aunt. Then, when I was eighteen, she died too. And I moved to Warrington to work in a building society.'

'I see,' I said, unable to think of a more appropriate response. 'And do you like your work?'

'Hate it,' Lydia said, matter-of-factly. 'But we all have to do something to put food on the table, don't we? Actually, if my father had managed his money better, I wouldn't have had to work at all. He was quite well off when he got married – and Mother brought something into the marriage, too – but it seems that he had this terrible weakness for the horses.' She paused. 'Anyway, you were asking me about the fête.'

'So I was,' I agreed.

'I hadn't been there for more than a few minutes when I saw

John,' Lydia said. She looked up affectionately at my brother's square jaw. 'Saw him – and knew that he was the man for me.'

John laughed uncomfortably. 'It wasn't like that at all,' he said. 'Once I'd seen *you*, you didn't have a chance.'

Lydia squeezed his arm. 'If that's what you want to believe, you go right on believing it,' she said. She winked at me. 'It's always wise to leave your man with a few of his illusions, isn't it?'

'I suppose it must be,' I agreed. 'Shall we order the wine?'

Later that night, lying in the same bed I had occupied as a child, I did my best to put the evening in perspective.

My brother, it seemed to me, was absolutely besotted with Lydia – but how did she feel about him?

I wasn't sure. She certainly acted as if she were in love with him, but was it any more than an act?

Wasn't there a danger, I asked myself, that I might fall into the same trap as Martin Barnes – the man who should have become my father-in-law – had? He had hated me initially, and it was only later – when it became obvious to him that I really did love Jill – that his attitude started to change. Wasn't it possible, therefore, that because I was so fond of my brother, I would automatically become suspicious of any woman he became attached to? And wasn't there a further danger that I was comparing Lydia to Jill – a comparison in which any other woman in the world would come second?

I heard the church clock strike two, and realized that though it seemed only minutes since I'd got into bed, I must have been lying there for well over an hour – which could only mean that the problem of my brother had been bothering me more than I was prepared to admit.

Why was I worrying? I asked myself.

The relationship might well be over in six months.

It *could* be over tomorrow.

But what if it wasn't? What if John decided to marry the girl?

Well, for all I knew, she might turn out to be an excellent wife. And if she didn't, it wasn't as if we were still living in the 1950s – divorces were both quick and clean now.

Of course, a failed marriage would hurt a sensitive soul like John, but then, I thought with an uncharacteristic edge of brutality in my mind, we all have to take knocks in this life.

The old church clock stuck three, and I finally began to feel sleepy. I plumped up my pillows and settled down for the night.

John wouldn't marry her, I told myself as I closed my eyes. Though for very different reasons, he was as much a confirmed bachelor as I was.

I was still half-telling myself that as I drove up north for his wedding, twelve months later.

TWELVE

It was just after nine o'clock in the morning when Owen Flint dropped in on the village store for his morning's ration of sugared sweets. After some thought, he chose a bag of Nuttall's Mintos (with two tubes of Spangles as back-up), then set off up the High Street in the general direction of my brother's house.

As he walked, he turned his mind to thoughts of Paul Taylor. There might be a perfectly simple explanation for the executive assistant's disappearance, he told himself, but he distrusted coincidences, which was why he'd already put out feelers to every police force in the country.

At the top of the hill, he turned left along Church Street, following it until he reached the dirt track which went by the name of Smithy Lane. If he hadn't been told that my brother's house was halfway down the track, facing the bowling green, he'd never have guessed that was where John lived, because he'd formed the impression of him as a diffident man, and the last thing this house suggested was diffidence. It was not quite as big as Grandfather's house, he thought, but it was close enough – and that made it the second largest house in the village.

Flint knocked on the front door, and though – given his

experience with other Conroy gatekeepers – he was expecting the knock to be answered by some kind of servant, it was, in fact, Lydia herself who appeared at the door.

'Do come in, chief inspector,' she said in a tone that Flint would later describe as 'gracious hostess'.

Flint's initial impression of the large hallway was that it had been expensively furnished, and that it would have looked perfectly at home in the glossy pages of a magazine like *Country Life*. The living room gave him the same impression – it, too, was *right* rather than *personal*.

None of this surprised him, though what *did* come as a surprise was Lydia's appearance. At the funeral, in her widow's weeds, she had looked flat-chested and almost boyish. Now, dressed casually – or at least, as casually as anyone can while wearing expensive cashmere – it was clear that she was pleasingly rounded in all the right places.

'It was good of you to find the time to see me,' he said. 'This can't be easy for you.'

'No, it isn't,' Lydia admitted. 'But it has to be done.' She gestured that he should sit down. 'Can I get you a drink? Tea? Coffee?'

'I'm fine,' Flint said.

He sat down, and unlike my cousin Philip in a similar situation, Lydia sat down, too.

'I suppose the first thing I should ask you, Mrs Conroy, is if your husband had any enemies.'

Lydia laughed in a way which Flint thought managed to be simultaneously gentle and slightly scornful.

'If you'd known John in life, you wouldn't have felt the need to ask that question,' she said. 'He was – how can I put it? – a completely harmless person.'

'He was a businessman,' Flint pointed out. 'He must have rubbed some people up the wrong way.'

Another small laugh.

'John wasn't a businessman in any sense you'd recognize. His grandfather bought his company for him, and most of the business he did was with other branches of Conroy's.'

'Did he ever talk to you about having disagreements with any of his employees?'

Lydia shook her head. 'He didn't talk much about his work at all. I expect he didn't think it would interest me.'

The phone on the table next to Lydia's chair rang.

'Will you excuse me for a moment?' she asked.

'Of course,' Flint agreed.

Lydia picked up the phone.

'Margaret,' she said, 'how kind of you to call,' Lydia said. She covered the mouthpiece with her hand and turned towards Flint. 'Margaret Wilson. We serve on several committees together. It shouldn't take long.'

'I'm in no great hurry,' Flint told her.

'What's that?' Lydia said into the phone. 'Temporary leave of absence . . . No, thank you, there'll be no need for that . . . I know you're perfectly capable of taking the chair, and it's very sweet of you to offer, but quite frankly, I think it will be best for me to keep busy . . . The autumn garden party? No, that will be going ahead as usual. We can't let our personal grief stand in the way of raising money for those poor little orphans . . . Well, that's settled then. I'll see you soon.' She slammed down the phone. 'The bitch!' she almost screamed.

'I beg your pardon,' Flint said.

'She's wanted to be the chair of the fundraising committee for years,' Lydia said, calming down somewhat, 'and with me in mourning, she sees this as the ideal opportunity to snatch it away from me. Honestly, if I thought she'd be any good at it, I'd let her have it. Lord knows, the last thing I want at the moment is to sit through endless meetings.'

'How did you and your husband get on?' Flint asked.

'What's that supposed to mean?'

'I should have thought it was plain enough.'

'Are you insinuating that I might be behind John's murder?' Lydia demanded.

'It wouldn't be the first time a wife had killed her husband, but no, that's not what I'm saying,' Flint said calmly, before popping a Nuttall's Minto into his mouth. 'Try to understand my position, Mrs Conroy. I'm looking for a motive here, and the more I can learn about the victims – what they were like as individuals, and how they related to other people – the better the chance I have of uncovering that motive. Clearly, then, anything and everything I learn might be of value. And *that's* why I asked you about your marriage.'

Lydia nodded, somewhat mollified. 'Neither John nor I were what you'd call passionate people,' she said. 'The earth certainly didn't move every time we looked at one another, but we *did* love each other.'

'I have to ask you this,' Flint said apologetically. 'Did your husband, as far as you know, ever have an affair?'

'I think I can promise you that he never looked at another woman after he married me.'

Flint coughed awkwardly. 'And what about yourself?'

'What about me?'

'Did you have an affair?'

'Certainly not!' Lydia said, with just a hint of conventional outrage returning to her voice. 'I wouldn't even consider risking my position in this village for the sake of a few cheap thrills.'

'You say your husband has no enemies – is the same true of his brother, Rob? Is he the sort of man likely to work anyone up into a homicidal rage?'

'I'm sure a few of his rivals in publishing hate him,' Lydia said. 'That would only be natural, especially after he was named Independent Publisher of the Year two years running. But that's just speculation on my part, because I can't honestly say I've seen enough of him to form a real opinion.'

'I see,' Flint said, noncommittally.

'He hardly ever comes to the village,' Lydia amplified. 'Oh, he's put in the odd appearance at the family parties – because that's what old Charlie wanted, and by and large what old Charlie wanted, he got – but apart from that we rarely got together.'

Flint smiled. 'You didn't like the family parties much, did you, Mrs Conroy?' he asked.

Lydia waved her hands in a gesture of dismissal. 'Oh, I suppose they went as well as could be expected, considering they were made up of a group of people who had nothing much in common apart from blood ties.'

'Tell me about Philip Conroy,' Flint suggested.

'There's nothing to say, except that he's spent his whole life trying to be a bigger playboy than his father.'

'And what about your father-in-law, Edward Conroy?'

'We didn't have a lot to talk about – I like to entertain a great deal, and he was a solitary soul by nature, especially after his wife died – but I certainly never argued with him, and I don't think anyone else did, either.'

Flint stood up. 'I'll not take up any more of your time, Mrs Conroy, and don't bother getting up, because I'll see myself out.' He walked to the lounge door, then suddenly swung round. 'Were you here in the village the night before your husband died?'

'No, I wasn't.'

'Then where were you?'

'I was at a health farm. It's part of my regular routine. I go for the full treatment twice a year.'

'Do you always go to the same one?'

'No, I like to vary it.'

'And where was the one you were staying at the night before the crash?'

'It's called the Middleton Health Spa. It's outside Bath.'

'In other words, it was very close to where your husband spent his last night alive.'

'Don't you think that hasn't crossed my mind, too?' Lydia said with some emotion. 'Can you appreciate how dreadful it is to realize that, instead of him spending his last few hours alone, I could have been with him?'

'Yes, it must be a very hard cross for you to bear,' Flint said. 'Thank you for your time, Mrs Conroy.'

As he walked down the lane that led back to the village, Flint took out his phone and dialled Sergeant Matthews' number.

'How are things going at your end, Matthews?' he asked, when the sergeant picked up.

'There's very little to report, sir,' the sergeant admitted. 'We've got the results of the post-mortems, and there were traces of alcohol in Tony Conroy's system, but – according to the doc – not enough to impair his driving. Other than that, there's nothing worth commenting on – no trace of poison, no evidence of serious illness. It was the crash that killed them, pure and simple.'

'What about the Bristol police?'

'They've made a general appeal for anybody who might have seen something in the garage that night, but there's been no response.'

'John Conroy's wife says she spent the night before the crash at the Middleton Health Spa, near Bath,' Flint said. 'I want you to drive down there and find out if she did.'

'Do you suspect her?' Matthews asked.

'I suspect no one – and everyone,' Flint said, in an Inspector Clouseau voice. 'No, she's not a prime suspect – she doesn't look particularly devastated, but everyone reacts differently to death – but then again, we'd look complete bloody idiots if she did turn out to be the murderer, and we hadn't even tested out her alibi.'

'That's true enough,' Matthews agreed.

If I had really been the murderer's intended victim, I thought as my train slowed down to enter Warrington railway station, then I was safer in Cheshire than I would have been in Oxford, where it was likely that my unknown enemy lived. But was I *really* safe anywhere? The killer had managed to reach us in Bristol, why should the village I'd been brought up in present him with any insurmountable difficulties? The only sensible course would be to go into hiding – but I had too many questions needing an answer to even contemplate that.

The train journey up had done my injured body no good at all, and when I put a little weight on my left leg as I walked towards the ticket barrier, shooting pains travelled from my knee up to my hip.

I stepped out into the forecourt. Once upon a time, either my father or my brother would have been waiting for me, but now they were both dead, and I hailed a taxi.

The trip to the village was just over eight miles. The first part of it was through the outskirts of the town. Then, after we had crossed the Manchester Ship Canal and passed by the golf course, we were in open countryside, and I found myself thinking of a summer day just like this one – though an eternity ago – when Jill paid her one and only visit to the village.

* * *

It had been the long vac at the end of our first year – and though we didn't know it, our *last* year – at college. We'd agreed that she should spend some time with her own parents before she met mine. When we made the arrangement, it had seemed perfectly reasonable, but the second I was back in the village, I found myself wishing the weeks would melt away so I could get my ordeal over.

And an *ordeal* was what I expected it to be, because I had no idea what Jill would think of my family, and I fretted, as I tried to perceive them through the eyes of an outsider.

The closer her visit drew, the more I worried about her reactions. I told myself I was being stupid – if she married anyone, it would be me, not the family – yet I couldn't suppress the fear that her meeting *them* would cause her to see *me* in a new light.

The day finally arrived. I picked Jill up from Warrington railway station and drove her back to the village along the country lanes in which the hedgerows were a glorious summer green, and young birds, celebrating their new mastery over life, swooped joyously in the sky above.

'Are you always this nervous behind the wheel?' asked Jill, who had never seen me on anything but a bicycle before.

'I'm not nervous,' I said, surprised. 'Why would you think I was?'

She smiled. 'Oh, I don't know – probably the fact that you're driving so slowly.'

And I realized that she was right – I *was* driving slowly.

I was behind the wheel of my uncle's Jaguar X-J.

'Take it,' he'd urged me. 'You'll soon learn, Rob, that nothing impresses the totty like a big powerful machine being put through its paces.'

And maybe I would have put it through its paces with anyone else as my passenger, but Jill was different. I didn't want to impress her. I wanted, with every ounce of my being, to protect her and keep her safe – to lay down my own life for her, if that was what it took.

We had tea with my parents – who were as shy and withdrawn as usual – then walked down the narrow street which led to

the church, and from there down the hill to my grandparents'
house.

It was Grandmother who answered the door. 'So you're Jill,'
she said. 'Well, you're even prettier than I imagined you'd be.'

I grinned at my girlfriend's discomfort, but, in fact, I was
feeling vaguely uneasy because, though I told myself I
was being irrational, I had my strongest misgivings about Jill
meeting my grandfather.

The problem was that I'd come to value the old man's opinion
over the years. And now I was frightened that he might disapprove of Jill. Or more to the point – if I'm being honest – I
was afraid he'd spot in her some fatal flaw which I had previously overlooked.

Grandmother made us a second tea – despite our protests
that we'd already eaten – and out of politeness we had to make
a show of picking at it as we sat in the lounge and talked. The
conversation flowed freely, but most of it passed between Jill
and my grandfather. I had never realized before what a good
listener Grandfather really was, nor how interested he could be
in the answers. He treated Jill as if she were the most important
person in the world, which of course – to me – she was.

When it was finally time to go, Grandfather hoisted himself
slowly to his feet and gave Jill a kiss. 'It's been a delight to
meet you,' he said, 'and you're welcome to visit us any time.'

'I'd like that,' Jill told him, and from the sideways glances
they both gave me, I knew the meeting had been a great success.

Afterwards – when it was all over – I looked back on the two
weeks Jill stayed with us as the golden period of my life. The
weather helped – it was one of those idyllic summers which is
not too hot and not too cold, when the air smells so fresh and
the breezes are caressingly gentle. But it was Jill who made
those days for me, just as I knew she would make my life for
me. We walked in the woods. We swam in the mere. Sometimes
we seemed to be continually talking, and at others we said
nothing much at all. It didn't matter what we did, or where we
went. We were together, and that was the only important thing.

At the end of her holiday, I delivered her to the same station
from which I had picked her up just two, brief, wonderful weeks

before. We didn't speak much in the car. We were both, I think, contemplating the future – the short-term one before the university year began again, and the longer one which stretched into the vague distance.

The short-term future was very clearly laid out. I was to work for my father for a few weeks, to compensate somewhat for the cost of putting me through an expensive education. Jill, for her part, had accepted a job supervising under-privileged kids on an adventure holiday in Cornwall.

But after that? In the long term? That seemed clearly laid out, too. Though we had not discussed it, we both understood that as soon as we had completed our degrees, we would get married. And though we would not have children right away, they would be the perfect seal on the love we felt for each other.

I parked my father's modest Allegro in front of the station and took Jill's case out of the boot.

'I can handle it, Robbie,' she told me.

I laughed. 'But I don't want you to handle it. I'll carry it for you.'

'I want to say goodbye now,' she told me, and I could see the tears forming in her eyes. 'No long, drawn-out farewells. Just a clean break.'

'But only for a few weeks,' I reminded her.

'Yes,' she agreed. 'Only for a few weeks.'

We kissed, and though both of us were reluctant to let go, she finally broke away.

'I'm glad you've struck out on your own,' she said seriously.

'What do you mean?'

'I'm glad you're doing an English degree. I'm glad you want to become an academic.'

I smiled. 'What made you say that just now?'

She gave a shrug. 'I don't know. Maybe it's just . . . Your family's not the right place for you, Robbie.'

I should have been expecting that, I suppose – I had been expecting it before she arrived – but the two idyllic weeks we'd spent together had lulled me into a false sense of security.

'You don't like them,' I said, sounding almost hurt.

'It's not that,' she protested. 'Your grandparents are lovely.'

'What about my parents?'

'I don't feel I really got to know them,' Jill admitted. 'They mean well, but maybe because your mother isn't in the best of health, they live in their own little world – very much a nation of two.'

Jill wasn't wrong, I thought. My mother's health had started to deteriorate when John and I were very small, and my father, who loved her as much as she loved him, had focussed most of his emotional concern on her.

It wasn't that he never showed his two sons any affection, but, as Jill had said, so much of it was being absorbed by Mother that he very rarely had much to spread around. In a way, I suppose, my mother and father abdicated from parenthood with my mother's first illness, and it was Grandmother and Grandfather who took up the slack.

'I like John, too,' Jill continued. 'He's a little strange, partly, I think, because he can't really accept himself for who he really is, but he's got a good heart and he'd die for you, without a second's hesitation.'

'I'd do the same for him,' I said.

'I know you would,' Jill agreed. 'And then there's the other side of the family. You couldn't call your uncle Tony a bad man – he's more of a naughty schoolboy. And even Philip could turn out all right if he really decided to make the effort.'

How well she'd summed them up, I thought. Yet still – and totally unexpectedly – there was enough of the tribal instinct in me to bridle at anything which might sound remotely like criticism.

'So what's the problem?' I asked, more belligerently than I'd intended.

'The problem is the situation,' Jill said. 'You're all trapped in your grandfather's net, and that can't be healthy – even for him.' She glanced down at her watch. 'I'd better go, or I'll miss my train.'

A sudden fear swept over me – gripped me tightly with its iron claws, dug its icy cold nails deep into my very soul.

'Don't go!' I said.

'What do you mean?' Jill asked.

'Don't get on that train,' I pleaded.

'I have to. I'm expected in Cornwall in the morning.'

'To hell with Cornwall! Stay here!'

She shook her head. 'The children are depending on me, so I have to go.' She broke out into a smile. 'I tell you what, why don't you come with me? We can always use an extra pair of hands, and I'm sure the organizers can find you a tent from somewhere.'

'I'd like to,' I said, 'but . . .'

'But what?'

'I've promised Grandfather I'll work for the company for a few weeks.'

'He's still trying to reel you in, isn't he?' Jill demanded. 'He thinks that if you get a taste for the business, you'll drop the idea of being a don, doesn't he?'

'It's not like that,' I protested. 'He encouraged me to go to university.'

'He values education,' Jill retorted, 'but he doesn't set much store by independence.' There was the sound of an approaching train in the distance. She turned her head towards it. 'I'd better go.'

I half-expected her to kiss me once more, but instead she picked up her suitcase and headed for the entrance. Watching her retreating back, I willed her to turn around, and just before the point at which she would have disappeared from sight, she finally did.

'I love you,' I told her.

'I love you, too,' she replied. 'I always will.'

How often, I wonder, have I relived that scene in my mind? A hundred times?

A thousand?

Perhaps neither of those guesses is anywhere near accurate.

Perhaps, at some level, it is never *out* of my mind.

That long, lingering kiss.

The way she swung the heavy suitcase, as if, in some way, that would make it seem lighter.

The almost hesitant way she turned for that final declaration of love.

There's more.

The image of the train I secretly watched pull out of the station, knowing that she was inside it – and that it was taking her away from me.

The walk back to the car park, on legs which felt as if they had turned into lead.

The slow drive home to the family which my beloved Jill thought fed upon itself.

And all the time there was a voice in the corner of my brain whispering the same message over and over and over again.

'*You should have gone with her. You should have gone with her.*'

It was a rasping voice, one which fell somewhere between sympathy and malicious glee – and it has never gone away.

THIRTEEN

It was bright and early in the morning, on the day after I had arrived back in the village, when Owen Flint turned up at the headquarters of Mid-Cheshire Maintenance, the company that Grandfather had bought for my brother John.

It was an impressive set-up, he thought. The garage itself was both clean and orderly, and a dozen or so men in smart overalls were working purposefully on various vehicles. Whatever else could be said about John, he thought, it seemed he'd known how to run a business.

The chief inspector met Sam Weatherspoon, the foreman, in the office which overlooked the main work area and, like the rest of the installation, seemed to him to have been designed for efficiency.

'What was John Conroy like as a boss?' Flint asked, noting as he spoke that, though the foreman was probably no older than thirty-five, he was already combing his hair in a way which showed he was worried about a bald spot.

'He was a good boss,' Weatherspoon said. 'Quiet, but firm, that was Mr Conroy. You always knew where you were with him. We're going to miss him.'

'I was talking to his wife yesterday . . .' Flint began.

'Oh, her!' the foreman snorted.

'I take it you don't get on,' the chief inspector said mildly.

'Putting it simply, she's a right proper bitch. She tried to get me fired once, you know.'

'And why would she have done that?'

Weatherspoon pulled a packet of Benson and Hedges out of his overalls and offered them to Flint. The chief inspector shook his head and reached into his pocket for his reserve supply of Bassett's Liquorice Allsorts.

'It was like this,' Weatherspoon said, inhaling the smoke from his cigarette greedily. 'She's always had her own car serviced here. Well, she's – she was – the boss's wife, so we've always given her priority over all our other jobs, even if we've got a rush on. You'd have thought that would be enough to satisfy anybody, wouldn't you? But it wouldn't do for Madam.'

'Why wouldn't it do for her?'

'Because she expects miracles – that's why. Look, this one time, she brought her car in because the gears were slipping. I took it for a quick spin, and it was obvious to me that the clutch was buggered. "So put a new one in," she told me – like I was too stupid to work that out for myself. "I'll do it as soon as I can get my hands on one," I promised. She asked me how long that would be, and I said probably a couple of days. Well, that didn't please her at all. Then she spotted one of the company's cars we were working on. "Take the clutch out of that, and put it in my car," she said.'

'Same model?' Flint asked.

'Was it hell as like. The company provides its reps with Fords, and Madam's was a Volvo. She needs a big car for her horsebox, you see.'

'Rides, does she?'

'Oh yes, she's very big in the local hunt – or so they tell me. Anyway, I tried explaining to her that the clutch from the Ford just wouldn't work – but she wasn't interested in explanations. "You're the grease monkey," she said. "Find some way to make it work." I told her it was impossible, and she marched right into Mr Conroy's office and demanded he gave me my cards on the spot. Of course, he wouldn't do it.' Weatherspoon

chuckled. 'She was so furious with him that I bet he had to do
without his "bit of the other" for at least a week.'

'And now she's probably your boss,' Flint said. 'That doesn't
exactly bode well for you, does it?'

'She'll never be the boss,' Weatherspoon said. 'I don't know
exactly what plans old Charlie Conroy had for the business
when he passed on, but I *do* know he'll never have let control
fall into the hands of anybody who wasn't a blood relative. So
either Rob Conroy will be in charge or his cousin, Philip, will
– or maybe it might even be both of them.'

'So who do you think will actually be *running* Mid-Cheshire
Maintenance?' Flint asked.

'I expect that will be me,' Weatherspoon told him.

'Will it indeed?' Flint said musingly. 'That'll be a bit of a
promotion for you, won't it?'

'It'll mean more work,' Weatherspoon said, 'but I don't think
it will mean more pay – especially if *Philip* Conroy is chairman
of the board.'

'Let's get back to the question I'd intended to ask when we
started discussing Lydia Conroy,' Flint suggested. 'Did John
Conroy have any business rivals?'

'Hang about – are you asking me if one of the other garage
owners might have bumped him off?' Weatherspoon asked.

'If that's the way you want to interpret the question,' Flint
said neutrally.

'There's a few other garages round here do contract work,'
Weatherspoon said, 'but they're not real rivals. None of them
is anywhere near big enough to handle the volume of work we
do, you see. Anyway, if somebody wanted to steal all our business off us, there are better and quicker ways of doing that than
by killing poor Mr Conroy.'

'Like what, for example?

'They might burn the place down.'

'And all the Conroys would have to do is rebuild it.'

'True, but that would take at least a month, even working at
full pelt. And our customers couldn't wait for a month, because
they've got obligations to *their* customers, so they'd be forced
to take their business elsewhere. And once you've lost a customer
in this trade, you very rarely get him back.'

Yes, it all made sense, Flint thought, discarding the maintenance business as a possible motive for murder.

'Now we've ruled out business rivals, can you think of anyone else who wouldn't shed tears if they heard John Conroy had died?' he asked.

Weatherspoon shook his head emphatically.

'Not really.'

'Did he have any habits which might have got him into trouble?'

'No. Mr Conroy didn't gamble, not even in the garage's Grand National sweepstake. And as far as I know, he never chased other women.'

'Boozing?'

'He drank, but only in moderation.'

'He must have knocked back a few when he was entertaining,' Flint pointed out. 'And as I understand it, he entertained a great deal.'

'It was his wife who did the entertaining. And even at the parties, when everybody else was supping champagne cocktails like they were going out of style, Mr Conroy never had more than a couple of beers – at least, that was true of the party I went to.'

'*You* were invited to one of the parties?' Flint asked incredulously.

'Yes, it was well before the incident of the clutch, but it's still amazing, isn't it? Imagine me – a humble mechanic – rubbing shoulders with the *crème de la crème* of local society. The reason I was invited, I think, was that I was partially responsible for landing a big contract, and it was Mr Conroy's way of showing his appreciation.'

'Did you enjoy it?'

'Not really,' Weatherspoon admitted. 'But the point is, neither did he. We were both like fish out of water.'

'So you can't think of anybody who'd wish him harm,' Flint said, summing it up.

'No, I don't often say this about people, but he was a lovely man,' Weatherspoon replied.

I had called on Grandmother soon after arriving in the village, but Jo Torlopp told me the old lady was exhausted, so it was not until around ten o'clock the next morning when I finally got to see her. She did not look as bad as I'd feared, but I knew that inside she was almost destroyed. Yet even in the midst of her grief, she did not fail to look at me with the questioning expression which all the family had in their eyes after not seeing me for some time – the expression which said, 'How's he doing? Is he close to cracking up again?'

'I've been thinking about your father,' she said. 'And about John, and your uncle Tony. I've been trying to work out what terrible thing one of them could have done to make someone hate him enough to want to kill him.'

'You'd be far better off leaving that kind of thing to the police,' I replied gently.

'I can't imagine Edward would – or could – do anything terrible. Or that anybody would notice if he did.'

'Grandmother . . .'

'Let's be honest,' my grandmother said, 'your father wasn't a man who stuck out in a crowd, was he?'

'No, he wasn't.'

'I don't think I could even describe him very clearly to someone who didn't know him. He wasn't tall and he wasn't short. He wasn't ugly, but you couldn't exactly have called him handsome, either. I know he loved you two boys, but I'm willing to wager he never put it into words.'

'Not to me, anyway,' I admitted.

'No, he hardly ever showed his emotions,' my grandmother continued, 'though I did once catch him crying over the Verdi "Requiem".'

I could believe that. He was like John in that respect – they both kept things bottled up.

'Uncle Tony was quite different, though, wasn't he?' I said, attempting to shift her away from a subject which I was already finding uncomfortable.

'Oh yes,' Grandmother agreed. 'While your father was doing his homework, Tony would be out scrumping apples from other people's orchards – even though we had plenty of our own. Do you know that on his fifteenth birthday he was summonsed for riding a motorcycle without a license?'

'No, I didn't,' I confessed.

'It would have mortified your father, but your uncle Tony treated it like a badge of honour.'

'Have you seen Philip?' I asked.

'Yes. He was at your grandfather's funeral.'

'I mean, has he been round here to see you?'

'He's been very busy,' Grandmother said defensively.

'I'm sure he has been,' I agreed, but I was thinking, The bastard! The selfish little swine.

'You've always been too hard on your cousin,' my grandmother said, reading my thoughts. 'He didn't have it easy when he was growing up. Do you remember his mother?'

Did I remember Aunt Jane? Yes, I thought I did, though my memory was only an impressionistic – and possibly romanticized – recollection of a woman seen through the eyes of a child.

Aunt Jane was tall and quite thin. Her complexion had been almost unnaturally pale, though I assume now that was as a result of her make-up.

She had been a struggling actress before she married Uncle Tony and, once she was established in the village, she threw herself into all the local amateur dramatic productions with an energy which left the rest of the cast exhausted.

'They used to fight a lot, her and your uncle,' my grandmother said.

I didn't need reminding of that. Everyone in the village was aware of their stupendous rows – of the screaming and the flying crockery.

'Why doesn't his father do something about it?' I can imagine the neighbours muttering after one of these rows had kept them awake well into the night. 'I mean, it isn't as if Charlie Conroy keeps his nose out of anything else the lad does.'

But that just shows a fundamental misunderstanding of what made Grandfather tick. He was the boss in his own house – as Grandmother freely acknowledged – and Tony was the boss of his, so if he got himself into a mess, he was the one who should deal with it.

'Of course, it was different while she was pregnant – and even for a while after she gave birth to Philip,' Grandmother said. 'While she was carrying, you'd see your uncle Tony

walking round the village with Jane on his arm, anxiously
looking for any small potholes she might step into. In the pub,
he'd be constantly adjusting the cushion at the back of her seat
and asking her every five minutes if there was anything she
needed. People who saw them smiled and said that perhaps
the marriage wasn't such a bad thing after all. And you should
have seen them with Philip. Talk about proud parents! They
couldn't wait to show him off to the whole world.'

'It didn't last though, did it?' I asked.

Grandmother sighed. 'No, it didn't last. Jane wasn't so much
being the proud parent as she was acting the *role* of one. I'm
not saying she didn't believe it herself – a good actress always
tries to immerse herself in her part – but she couldn't have been
entirely genuine, or she'd never have behaved the way she did
later.'

I was amazed to hear my grandmother talking like that –
amazed that she even *could*. While Grandfather had been alive,
she'd been no more than a passive adjunct to him. Now he was
dead she seemed to have acquired an intelligent, analytical
personality of her own.

'Don't be so surprised,' she said, reading my thoughts again.
'I've always had it in me – it's just that it never seemed to be
of much use before.'

'Tell me more about Aunt Jane,' I said, to mask my own
confusion.

'The trouble started again around the time Philip had his
first birthday,' my grandmother continued. 'I don't know why.
Maybe it was a symptom of post-natal depression. Or perhaps
it was the sight of the growing child which made Jane realize
that she was growing older, too, and that if she was ever to
achieve her ambitions, she'd better get on with it. Whatever
the reason, she calmly announced the fact that she'd applied
for a job backstage at one of the Manchester theatres, and had
been accepted.'

'Uncle Tony couldn't have been very pleased.'

'He wasn't. He said her job was to stay at home and look
after the baby, and she said that there were plenty of licensed
childminders far better equipped to do the job than she was.
He pointed out it would probably cost them more to pay the

childminder than she'd be earning in the theatre, and she said, so what, they could easily afford it.'

Which, of course, they could – because whatever else had been lacking in the family, we'd always had plenty of money.

'But he let her take the job in the end, didn't he?' I asked.

'What choice did he have? If he'd thrown her out of the house, there would have been a custody battle, and he'd have ended up losing Philip. Anyway, he gave into her, and soon she was completely wrapped up in this job of hers. She was only paid to work a forty-hour week, yet the theatre made so many demands on her time, that she was almost never at home. That poor little baby started to think that the girl they paid to look after him was his mother. And even when she *was* home, she never seemed to have any time for Philip. It was always theatre, theatre, theatre with her.'

'How did Uncle Tony take it?'

'He hated what she was doing, but had more or less learned to live with it. Then your Aunt Jane made her next demand. She wanted to go on tour. She'd got a small part in one of the plays they were doing, and she was sure it was going to lead on to bigger things. Of course, the pay wasn't much – certainly not enough to live on – but if your uncle would give her a few pounds a week . . . Well, your uncle Tony put his foot down. He wasn't going to pay to have her missing for months at a time, he said. If she insisted on going on tour, she could pay for herself.'

'And she couldn't, could she?'

'No. In her own right, she didn't have two ha'pennies to rub together, so she was forced to miss her big chance. Perhaps Tony hoped that with more free time on her hands, she'd devote a little of it to her son, but if he did, he must have been sadly disappointed. As far as Jane was concerned, Philip was a part of her life which was over. She'd carried him in her body for nine months, she'd fed him and changed him for a year, and now he was on his own. Your uncle Tony did his best to fill the gap, it was a rare day indeed when he wasn't seen pushing the expensive pram around the village – but it just wasn't the same. Well, things went on like that for several years, then . . .'

'I know what happened next,' I said.

'Do you, indeed?' my grandmother asked. 'But you were only a child at the time.'

Yes, I was only a child, but I'd been old enough to both witness and understand the last dramatic act in the Jane–Tony saga.

I think I must have been around five and a half when it was played out.

Uncle Tony and Aunt Jane had been invited round to our house for drinks – an invitation which, I suppose, was one of my father's guilt-ridden attempts to get on better terms with a brother he had very little in common with.

My mother – who was not a well woman, even then – had, by an almost superhuman effort, spent most of the day helping our housekeeper to produce a dazzling array of canapés, which were now spread out sumptuously on the coffee tables in the living room.

My uncle and aunt were due to arrive at seven thirty, and John and I had been informed that we could stay up to greet them, but then we would have to go straight to bed. So we sat around in our dressing gowns and pyjamas and waited.

And waited.

Time passed. My mother glanced anxiously at my father. 'I think it's time the children were climbing the wooden hills to Bedfordshire,' she said.

'A few more minutes,' my father pleaded. 'After all, it is family.'

I was drowsy by the time the front doorbell finally rang, but I heard my mother say, 'Well, better late than never, I suppose. I just hope the snacks haven't all dried out.'

Rubbing my eyes, I accompanied my father and older brother to the door. We were halfway up the hall when the bell rang again, as if my uncle and aunt, having kept us waiting so long, were now impatient to be admitted.

When my father opened the door, I saw that only Uncle Tony was standing there. He had one arm resting on the wall, and there was a glazed look in his eyes.

'Are you alone?' my father asked.

'Damned right,' my uncle slurred in response.

'Is Jane not well?'

'I've absolutely no idea.'

I became aware of my mother standing behind us in the hall.

'It's time you boys went up to bed,' she said.

'But we haven't said hello to Uncle Tony yet,' I protested.

'Now!' my mother insisted.

John turned and headed for the stairs, and I reluctantly followed. But that didn't mean I wasn't listening to everything which was going on behind me.

'Is anything wrong?' my father asked my uncle.

'Wrong?' Uncle Tony repeated. 'Far from it. That woman's been a cross I've had to carry for more years than I care to remember. And now she's been lifted off my back.'

'Meaning what?' my father asked.

'Meaning she's gone.'

'Gone?'

'Yes! Gone! Absconded! Disappeared into thin air!'

My brother and I had climbed the stairs and reached the landing. Though we were now invisible to those below us, we could still clearly hear what was going on.

I stopped.

'We should go to bed,' John whispered. 'That's what Mummy said.'

'Well, I want to listen,' I hissed back.

'We could get into trouble.'

'I don't care!'

'Well, I do.'

'So go to bed.'

'I *will!*'

With one ear, I listened to the sound of my brother's carpet-slippered feet walking along the landing, the click of his bedroom door, and the sigh of his bedsprings as he lay down. But the other ear was directed firmly towards the hallway.

'When did this happen?' my mother was asking, with evident concern in her voice.

'This morning,' my uncle Tony told her. 'Jane and I haven't had sex for over a year.'

'Really, Tony,' my mother said, with obvious embarrassment.

'Not for over a year,' my uncle said emphatically. 'So there didn't seem much point in sharing the same bed anymore.'

'I don't think this is helping,' my mother told him.

'The point is that when I woke up this morning, she wasn't anywhere around the house,' my uncle continued. 'I didn't think anything of it at first – the idle bitch rarely emerges before lunchtime anyway. But when I got home from the office, she still wasn't in evidence, so I went up to her room to see if she was all right. Her wardrobe and dressing table were empty. There was no sign of the suitcases she'd bought for that ridiculous tour that I refused to let her go on. She'd clearly done a moonlight flit.'

'Did she leave a note?' my mother asked.

My uncle laughed bitterly. 'A note? Her? Oh, that would have been far too considerate.'

'I'm so sorry, Tony,' my father said.

'Are you?' Uncle Tony asked belligerently. 'Well, I'm not. I'm well shot of her, if the truth be told. Christ, she's made my life a misery – and she's been no good for the boy. Well, now she's gone, he and I will finally be able to get on with our lives.'

'Why don't you come inside and have a little something to eat, Tony?' my mother suggested.

'No thanks. Now I've broken the good news, I think I'll be going.'

'There are loads of snacks on the table, and you need *something* to line your stomach with,' my mother insisted. 'Besides, I'm not sure you should be alone tonight.'

My uncle sighed. 'All right, maybe I'll come in for a few minutes,' he conceded.

There was the sound of footsteps, and the voices began to grow faint.

'I expect you'll find someone else in time,' I heard my mother say.

'Never!' Uncle Tony replied emphatically. 'Once bitten, twice shy. That's going to be my motto from now on.'

To a child as I was then, it seemed an impossibly long time before I saw Uncle Tony with a woman again, but looking back, I don't suppose it could have been more than a few months. She was a busty blonde, and though I can't remember her name, I do know she was introduced to me as 'Auntie

Something-or-other'. If I thought she was going to replace Aunt Jane, I was wrong. She was soon replaced by 'Auntie Something-else', then by a third, and a fourth, until it was plain even to John, Philip and me what was going on.

'You're thinking of all your uncle's women, aren't you?' my grandmother said, surprising me again.

'Yes, I am,' I admitted.

'Well think about this, as well,' Grandmother instructed me. 'Philip might have had all those big expensive toys you were never given, and he might have been allowed to stay up long after you went to bed – but he never had a mother like you did.'

'You're right,' I said humbly.

Grandmother narrowed her watery old eyes and gave me a look which seemed to pierce right through to my soul. 'If you tried being easier on other people,' she said, 'you might just find yourself able to go easier on yourself.'

On my way back to the house which had been my parents' home but now, I supposed, belonged to me, I found myself thinking about Aunt Jane again.

Where had she gone, and what had she done?

As a child – knowing of her ambitions – I'd kept expecting to see her suddenly pop up on some television show or other, but she never did.

Uncle Tony had said she'd disappeared into thin air, and that was exactly what *had* happened. There were no phone calls. No letters. Not even a postcard from some provincial rep, or a greeting card at Christmas. Tony and Philip never spoke of her, and so, in their company, neither did we. After a few years it was almost possible to believe that she had never existed – that Philip was some obnoxious fairy child who had landed, miraculously, on Uncle Tony's doorstep.

But people rarely vanish so completely. Though I never saw Aunt Jane again, the spectre of her existence did visit the village shortly after the car crash, while I was still lying in my hospital bed – but even if I'd been there at the time, I doubt I would have recognized it for what it was.

FOURTEEN

The Middleton Health Spa – the place where my sister-in-law Lydia claimed to have spent the night before her husband died – was, Sergeant Matthews discovered, a spacious late-Georgian building, surrounded by extensive landscaped grounds, and located in an almost ideal rural setting. High railings surrounded the property, but the big double gates at the edge of the driveway were open, and the gap they revealed was wide enough to drive a couple of tanks through.

The person he had gone there to talk to was called Ellen Bannister. She was an attractive woman in her late twenties, and as Matthews studied her across the table of the small conference room which had been allocated for his use, he decided that she had intelligent eyes and would probably be a good witness.

He switched on his tape recorder. 'What's the security like in this place, Miss Bannister?' he asked.

'What exactly do you mean by that?'

'How easy is it for people to come and go?'

'In the daytime, it's very easy indeed. You see, Middleton's not so much a spa as a luxury hotel which offers top class spa facilities. And the health club has dozens of associate members who aren't even staying at the hotel. So there's loads of people arriving and leaving at all times during the day.'

'What happens at night, when the spa has closed down?'

'At night, things are controlled much more tightly. For a start, all entrances and exits are locked – except for the fire doors, of course.'

'So it would still be possible to get out through one of the fire doors?'

Miss Bannister shook her head. 'Not without setting off the alarms, and I don't remember that ever happening in the three years I've worked here.'

'Could anybody get out of one of the windows?'

'Why would they want to do that?'

Well, for example, they might want to slip out and commit a murder, Matthews thought.

But aloud, all he said was, 'I don't know – but let's just say they did.'

'None of the windows open,' Miss Bannister said. She pointed to a grill, near the top of the wall. 'The entire spa is air-conditioned.'

'What other security is there?'

'There's always a man patrolling the grounds. We've had some trouble with vandals, you see. And, of course, the main gate is locked.'

'What happens if one of the guests decides that he or she would like to go off for a night on the town?'

Miss Bannister grinned. 'Not many of them do. It's too many nights on the town that have brought them to Middleton in the first place.'

'But if they do?' Matthews persisted.

'They come and see me – or whoever else is on duty at the main desk – and I buzz to let them out.'

So it looked as if there would have been no way for Lydia Conroy to get to Bristol the night before the crash, he thought.

Unless, of course, she had already left before the security measures were put in place!

'Let's get on to Mrs Conroy, now,' Matthews said. 'Do you remember her?'

Miss Bannister nodded emphatically. 'Oh yes, I remember her all right. I'd have remembered her even if the police hadn't turned up.'

'The police?'

'We normally only do a single shift, but sometimes things go wrong – staff get sick, et cetera, et cetera – and we have to double up, which is why I was still here when the uniformed sergeant and a woman PC came to the front desk and asked to see Mrs Conroy, because they had some bad news to break to her,' Miss Bannister explained.

Yes, it made sense they would have been there, Matthews thought. The South Wales police would have contacted the Cheshire police, who would have spoken to someone in the Conroy family. Then the Cheshire police would have contacted the Somerset police.

'You told me you'd have remembered her even if the police hadn't appeared on the scene,' he said. 'Was there any particular reason for that?'

'Yes, there was,' Miss Bannister replied. 'She was one of those people who really go out of their way to make themselves unpleasant to the staff. You know the sort. If everything isn't just as they want it, precisely *when* they want it, they're screaming that the hotel is nothing but a disgrace.'

'She was the same with the mechanics at Mid-Cheshire Maintenance,' Flint would tell Matthews later. 'She seems to have the gift of spreading sunshine wherever she goes.'

'People like her expect you to be at their beck and call twenty-four hours a day,' Miss Bannister continued. 'Of course,' she conceded, 'we do offer that service in our brochure, but most of our clients have more consideration than to take advantage of it.'

'But Mrs Conroy wasn't like most of your clients?'

'Indeed, she wasn't,' Miss Bannister agreed. 'There wasn't a night when she didn't call up room service. Coffee was what she always wanted. Usually at about three o'clock in the morning. She said she couldn't sleep. Well, there's no wonder she couldn't sleep if she was drinking coffee at three o'clock in the morning, now is there?'

'And who took it to her?'

'Me. You see, there's only a skeleton staff on at night – just the receptionist and the security guard. So if anybody calls down for anything, I'm the one who has to fix it.'

'Do you remember serving her coffee the night before she left?'

'Oh yes.'

'You seem pretty sure of yourself.'

'As I said, I served her *every* single night of her stay,' Miss Bannister said. 'Besides, with the police coming to see her the next day, it sort of stuck in my mind.'

'Can you remember exactly what happened?'

Miss Bannister closed her eyes. 'I was sitting at my desk. I glanced at the clock and I saw it was nearly three o'clock, and

I thought to myself it was about time the Witch Lady from Room Thirty-Seven rang. And I'd no sooner thought it than the phone *did* ring.'

'And what did she say?'

'What she always said. "I can't sleep. I want a pot of coffee right away." No please or thank you, mind you, just an order – and me with a diploma in hotel management!'

'So what did you do?'

'Made the coffee and took it up to her.'

'Did you see her?'

Miss Bannister shook her head. 'When I knocked on the door, she said, "Come in." She was in the bathroom. She usually was. She probably considered she would be lowering herself to be in the same room as the hired help.'

Matthews chuckled.

'It's no joke,' Miss Bannister said. 'You haven't met her – she really is like that.'

'I'll take your word for it,' Matthews said. 'Carry on.'

'I put the tray down on the table, and I said, "I've brought your coffee, Mrs Conroy," and she said, "All right, you can go now." So I went.'

'And you're sure it was her?'

'Oh yes. I'd recognize that voice of hers anywhere. I've always found it grating.'

Well, even if she hadn't actually been seen, that seemed about as tight an alibi as anyone could hope for, Matthews thought.

I walked slowly down Church Street, giving my injured leg the regular exercise which the doctor had advised.

I'd been a coward to think of staying away from Oxford, I thought, because however things turned out between Marie and me, I should at least have the guts to handle them face-to-face.

I reached the church and saw Owen Flint. The skinny Welshman was standing with one foot on the stocks, gazing pensively down the High Street. When he saw me, he smiled – but I knew him well enough to detect the underlying level of worry below that smile.

'Is something the matter?' I asked.

'I was hoping they'd keep you in hospital a while longer,' he admitted.

'And why should you hope that?'

'Because you'd be safe in hospital. Even the most determined killer would be unlikely to risk committing a murder with so many potential witnesses around.'

'Why should I be his target?' I asked.

'Why should your father or your brother have been his target?' Flint countered. 'How long are you going to be here in the village?'

'I'm planning to leave this afternoon, as soon as the will's been read,' I told him.

Owen gave me a quizzical look. 'That would be your *grandfather's* will, would it?'

'Yes.'

'You sounded surprised I asked the question.'

'I was,' I admitted.

'Yet there are two other wills to be read – your father's will and your uncle Tony's.'

Despite myself, I grinned ruefully. 'That's the kind of family I was brought up in,' I said. 'If you talked about the dog, you meant Grandfather's red setter. If it was any other dog, you said Tony's bull terrier or Edward's Labrador.'

'What do you expect the will to say?'

'I've no idea.'

'And aren't you even curious?'

'As long as I keep control of Cormorant Publishing, I couldn't care about anything else.'

'And you think you will?'

I shrugged. 'Grandfather knew how much I cared about Cormorant.'

'He might well have done, but he was prepared to let your uncle mortgage it,' Owen Flint pointed out.

That thought had been nagging away at my mind, too. There were times when I saw it as a complete betrayal, but I wasn't about to speak ill of the old man to anyone else, not even an old friend like Owen.

'So where will you be going when you leave here?' Flint asked. 'Back to Oxford?'

'That's right.'

Owen looked troubled again. 'I'll get on to the local coppers and ask them if they'll keep an eye on you,' he said. 'They can't provide round-the-clock protection – they don't have the manpower for that – but perhaps the fact that there's a uniform around some of the time will be enough to deter anybody who wants to harm you.'

I thought of trying to resolve my problems with Marie under the watchful eye of an Oxford flatfoot.

'I don't need police protection,' I said.

'I think you do,' Owen countered.

'I'm not important enough to have enemies,' I told him. 'I'm just a humble publisher.'

Owen laughed. 'A humble publisher who just happens to publish Andy McBride,' he said.

'I don't have the *opportunity* to make enemies,' I protested. 'I work most of the time, and even when I'm not working, the only people I see are Andy McBride and . . . and . . .'

'And Marie O'Hara,' Owen supplied.

'How do you know about her?' I asked, shocked.

'I'm a policeman investigating three murders and two attempted murders,' Flint said. 'Marie O'Hara is part of your life, and that makes her part of my investigation.'

'I don't think she is,' I said.

'You don't think she's part of my investigation?'

'I don't think she's part of my life. There was a time . . . but I really don't want to talk about it now, Owen.'

'Have you been out with many girls since Jill?' Flint asked.

And from the tone of his voice I could tell that the policeman in him had temporarily receded, and I was talking to my old college friend.

'Well?' he said.

'There haven't been *any*.'

Owen shook his head sadly, then checked his watch. 'The pub's just opened,' he said. 'Do you fancy a pint?'

I shrugged. 'Why not?'

We were the first customers of the day. We ordered our drinks and took them over to a table by the window.

'You should have someone special in your life, you know,

Rob,' Owen said. 'People like you aren't meant to be alone.'

'What about you?' I asked, pulling the famous Rob Conroy trick of changing the subject whenever it got vaguely uncomfortable.

'I grew up surrounded by other kids,' Owen said. 'When I first got my rooms in Oxford, I couldn't believe how much space there was. It terrified me. But it's remarkable how quickly you can get used to things. I don't want to share my space with anyone, Rob. I *like* being alone.'

Perhaps it was his obvious candour which made me say, 'I'm *never* alone. I've always got my guilt to keep me company.'

'Guilt?' he repeated. 'What have you got to feel guilty about?'

'The first week Jill was working in Cornwall, she took the kids out canoeing on the river,' I said. 'The second week, she was involved with pony trekking. It wasn't until the third week that she went abseiling. So you see, I had plenty of time to do something.'

'You're not making a lot of sense, boyo,' Owen Flint told me.

'I asked her not to go, but she said she had to – and suggested I went with her. I told her I couldn't, because I'd agreed to work for Grandfather, but if I had gone, I'd have been there that second day of abseiling, when her harness broke halfway down the cliff and . . .' I shuddered. 'And she plunged backwards to her terrible, frightening death.'

'But it was an accident, wasn't it?'

'Yes,' I said heavily. 'It was an accident. They say harnesses sometimes break, however careful you are about checking the equipment. But it shouldn't have happened to my Jill!'

'The harness would have broken whether or not you were there,' Owen said quietly.

'I once read a science fiction story about a group of big game hunters who time-travelled back to pre-history,' I told him. 'The only dinosaurs they killed were the ones which were due to die that second anyway, so nothing would be changed. Then one of the hunters stepped off the safe path and crushed a leaf. A single leaf! When they got back to their own time the world had changed so much they hardly recognized it.'

'I understand what you're saying but . . .'

'If I'd gone with her, like she wanted me to, everything would have been different. We might have had a few too many drinks the night before, so she'd have cried off the abseiling. We might have stopped to talk for a minute or two, and some other poor bugger would have ended up with the faulty harness. A thousand things could have happened which would have meant that Jill hadn't died. And she gave me the choice. "Come with me," she said. But I wouldn't listen.'

'You're being too hard on yourself,' Owen said sympathetically.

'Perhaps I'd agree with you if it was only an isolated incident, but I'm always running away from things – evading my responsibilities.'

'You didn't run away from Andy McBride,' Owen pointed out in my defence.

'No,' I agreed. 'I didn't run away from a stranger I met on the street. But I ran away from my brother.'

'What's that you say?' Owen Flint asked, and in an instant he was the policeman once more.

'I have this feeling deep down inside me that there was some way I could have stopped this whole bloody tragedy from happening.'

'Would you like to elaborate on that?'

'I can't. As I said, it's just a feeling. But it's a very strong one. I believe that at some point in the last few years I could have said something, or done something, which would have meant that John would still be alive now.' I laughed. 'Of course, it's well known that I'm a mental case, so if I were you, I'd take absolutely no notice of anything I say.'

Owen didn't join in my laughter, or even show any signs of pity. 'If you get anything more definite on this feeling of yours, come and see me right away,' he said.

FIFTEEN

For several days before the crash, I had been carrying around a heavy secret which belonged to my brother – as well as others – and now, as I stood in front of the austere Norman church, I found myself wondering if I should have revealed it to Chief Inspector Flint, who sometimes slipped back into the role of my old friend Owen.

It was not an easy question to answer. On the one hand, anything I told the police might help them to track my brother's killer down. On the other, it was hard to see how this particular piece of information could be of any use to them at all – and having done little enough for my brother in his life, I was determined not to do anything now which might turn him into a posthumous figure of fun.

The dead are always entitled to retain their dignity, I told myself – my brother more than most. And if I could somehow manage to drag out from the recesses of my mind the one crucial fact – the one essential element – which had been nagging at my brain since I returned to the village, then perhaps there would be no need to expose the secret which John had been at such pains to hide.

I let my eyes climb the high church tower and thought of John's wedding day.

If the weather can be taken as an omen of things to come, then, on that particular morning, it looked as if the marriage of my brother, John Conroy, to Miss Lydia Hornby Smythe, was off to a marvellous start.

Looking out of my bedroom window, I could see that the sky was a perfect blue, without a trace of cloud. And when I opened that window and breathed in, the outside air had that balmy feel to it which can only be found in England – and even then, rarely. It was going to be a terrific day, and I hoped from the bottom of my heart that John and Lydia would have a wonderful life together.

I walked over to the wardrobe and inspected my morning suit. The alterations my tailor had made had ensured that it fitted perfectly, I thought, but should he have had to make them at all? I was still far enough away from my thirtieth birthday not to be concerned about it, yet I was already acquiring a middle-aged spread.

When I got back to Oxford, I would start to take regular exercise, I decided. But even as I made the promise to myself, I knew I would never keep it. The desk which greeted me on my return would be piled high. There was Andy McBride's book to nursemaid into its final form. There was an American tour to organize for one of my authors who had just started to make a name for himself over in the States. There was a book of poems from new writers, which would sink without trace if I didn't mobilize my media contacts. There was . . .

There were so many things, and the second I returned to my office, I would be completely immersed in my work again.

Someone was knocking softly – almost hesitantly – on my door.

'Come in,' I said.

The door opened, and my brother walked into the room. We had had a quiet drink together the night before, but from the way he looked at that moment, it would have been possible to believe he was suffering from the effects of a full-blown stag night hangover.

'Have you got a minute?' John asked.

'Of course.'

My brother sat down on the bed. It creaked under his bulk. For a few seconds, he was silent, but when he did speak, his words came out in a rush – as if he were afraid that if he didn't get them out then, he would *never* get them out.

'I think this whole thing is a mistake,' he said.

Was this nothing more than normal pre-wedding nerves, I asked myself, or was it something much more fundamental?

'What makes you think it's a mistake?' I asked, picking my way cautiously.

John shrugged his powerful shoulders. 'I just . . . I just don't think it's going to work out, that's all.'

'But you must have a reason,' I pressed him. 'Has Lydia

done something or said something which has led you to believe—'

'This isn't about *Lydia*,' John interrupted, almost angrily. 'It's about me. I'm not sure I'm the marrying kind.'

'Who is?' I asked. 'I don't think marriage is the natural state for most people – yet we feel incomplete without it.'

John smiled weakly. 'Do you feel incomplete?'

It wasn't something I wanted to analyse.

Not then.

Not ever.

'I'd have married Jill, if she'd lived,' I said, side-stepping the question.

'Maybe that's my problem,' my brother told me. 'I saw you with Jill, and I've seen myself with Lydia. And it's simply not the same.'

I felt a heavy weight resting on my shoulders. With just a few words, I could destroy this marriage – and I was not sure whether that would the right thing, or the wrong thing, to do.

'Do you love Lydia?' I asked.

'Yes,' my brother replied. 'Yes, I really think I do.'

'Then stop comparing yourself and Lydia to Jill and me,' I said. 'Every relationship's different. Look at Mum and Dad. They're an odd couple in so many ways, yet you can't deny the fact that they've been perfectly – if quietly – happy together for over thirty years.'

John nodded. 'You're right,' he agreed. He stood up. 'Thank you, Little Brother.'

'I'm only doing my job as best man,' I said.

But I wondered how good a job I'd *really* done.

I found my father sitting alone at the breakfast table.

'Everything under control?' he asked, in the mild tone he habitually used.

'Seems to be,' I said, mentally brushing aside John's moment of panic.

'Err . . . there's something you should know before we go to the church,' my father told me.

'Yes?'

'The seating arrangements will be a little unconventional. It would be best if you pretended not to notice it.'

I felt the back of my neck start to prickle.

'In what way will they be unconventional?' I asked.

My father shrugged awkwardly. 'Well, as you probably know, it's normal on these occasions for the bride's family to sit on one side of the aisle and the groom's family on the other. That won't be happening today.'

The prickle at the back of my neck was almost becoming an itch.

'And why's that?' I asked.

'As you know, Lydia's an orphan.'

'So?'

'Well, it . . . err . . . it would be rather uncomfortable for everyone present if one side of the church was conspicuously empty.'

'But why should it be empty? Even if she hasn't got family, there are her friends to consider.'

My father shifted in his chair. 'She's . . . From what she said to me, she sees this marriage as a new start.'

'So you're telling me that *no one* from her side is coming to the wedding?' I asked incredulously.

'There may be one or two people,' my father said. 'Lydia was a little vague about it when I asked her. But certainly none of the wedding presents which have been arriving at the house all week seem to have come from anyone other than our friends and relatives.'

'Do you know *anything at all* about the woman who's about to become your daughter-in-law?' I demanded.

'Not a great deal, no,' my father admitted.

'And haven't you even tried to find out?'

My father put his hands – locked together – on the table. It was almost as if he were praying.

'John's an adult . . .' he began.

'But even so . . .'

'. . . and therefore perfectly capable of taking his own decisions. Besides . . .'

'Besides what?'

'I'm so relieved that John is getting married at all.'

Because I wasn't, I assumed. Because at least one of his sons was prepared to make the effort to continue the family name.

'I still think you should have done some checking up on her background,' I said sulkily.

'And I think *you* shouldn't be so wrapped up in your own miseries that you fail to notice what's going on in other people's lives,' my father replied.

It was perhaps the harshest thing he ever said to me, and it hit me like a slap in the face.

Was he telling me that I was the one who should have checked up on Lydia? Or that I should try to see things more from his point of view?

I had no idea. All I *did* know was that, whatever was behind the rebuke, I'd probably deserved it.

I hung my head in shame. 'What do you want me to do?' I asked.

'I want you to give your brother all the support he needs – both now and in the future,' my father said. 'That's all any of us can do.'

Yes, I thought, even Grandfather couldn't do more than that.

The service went without a hitch. John was splendid in his morning dress. Lydia, in her white bridal gown, looked everything a blushing bride should be. They both proclaimed their vows with a clarity and sincerity which had at least a couple of our female relatives sniffing into their handkerchiefs.

Then, for better or worse, it was all over. As we posed outside the church for the inevitable wedding photographs, I took a quick, sideways glance at my brother. John was looking considerably happier than he had earlier that morning, so perhaps he'd been suffering from no more than pre-marital nerves after all.

As soon as the reception was over, John and Lydia were flying to Greece for a fortnight's honeymoon.

And after that?

After that, they would naturally be returning to the village – and moving into the house on Smithy Lane which Grandfather had bought them as a wedding present.

'You're all too close,' I could almost hear my darling Jill whispering in my ear as I stood next to my brother and grinned

for the camera, *'That's the trouble with your family – you're all far too close.'*

Yet we weren't – at least, not in the conventional way. Some families shared their joys and sorrows, their triumphs and defeats. All we shared was a common home village and an interlocking web of companies which Grandfather had spun around us as skilfully as any spider could have done.

Once the photographer was satisfied he had captured the moment forever, we all trooped down the short slope to Grandfather's house, where a marquee had been erected for the reception.

Inside, standing under the canvas roof, I looked around at all my relatives. There were my parents, holding hands as if they both needed the support. There was Grandfather, looking every inch the patrician he actually was, and Grandmother, who had lived her life so much in his shadow that she hardly seemed to cast one of her own.

There was my uncle Tony with his latest girlfriend on his arm. She seemed quite young, and it occurred to me that the older he got, the younger his women seemed to be getting.

Did Uncle Tony ever wonder about what happened to the wife who left him to pursue her acting dreams? I asked myself.

Then again, did he actually *need* to wonder? True, he never talked about her, but wasn't it perfectly possible he'd known all along where she was, and perhaps even sent her money to help her out? After all, why shouldn't he have? She'd certainly done him a great favour, because in abandoning him in the way she had, she'd left him in sole charge of the son he so obviously adored.

Philip, the son in question, was standing by the entrance to the marquee. His left hand held a glass of champagne, and his right arm was resting on the bare shoulder of a very pretty blonde girl. He caught me looking at him and winked lasciviously.

I turned away. I loved my brother dearly and had been happy to serve as his best man, but there was no denying the fact that I would be glad when this whole show was over, and I could get back to my safe, busy office in Oxford.

I felt a tap on my back and turned to find Philip standing

there. From the look in his eyes, it was obvious he'd started celebrating long before the actual service began.

'So what do you think of young Enid?' he asked me, slightly slurring his words.

'Enid? Is that what the girl you're with is called?'

'They're all called Enid,' Philip replied, contemptuously. 'Can't, for the life of me, remember what the real name of this particular Enid is, but I'm sure it'll come to me again when I need it to.' He swayed a little. 'Anyway, I noticed *you* couldn't take your eyes off her.'

'That's rather an exaggeration,' I said mildly – because the last thing I wanted was a scene at my brother's wedding. 'I may have glanced at her, but you were the one who got most of my attention. You're looking well.'

I wasn't lying. He'd been rather pasty as a child, but he'd grown out of it, and was now a healthy young man.

'I've only just met this Enid, but I'll have her before the night is out – just see if I don't,' Philip boasted. He sniggered. 'Even if I don't get all the way, I'll probably have more luck than your John will.'

'And just exactly what do you mean by that, Philip?' I asked, my voice hardening.

My cousin's mouth dropped open in a look of comical amazement. 'You don't know, do you?' he said. 'You really don't know.'

'Know what?' I demanded. 'Is this something to do with Lydia?'

Philip laughed. 'Well, bugger me,' he said. 'And I always thought you were the smartest out of the three of us.'

'If you're aware of something which might hurt John, you should tell me about it right now,' I said.

'You never did like me much, did you, Rob?' my cousin slurred.

'We're not talking about you and me,' I told him. 'It's my brother that I'm concerned about now.'

'Well, I've never liked you much, either,' Philip continued, as if I hadn't spoken. 'And I'll tell you something else. I wouldn't lift a finger – not one little finger – to help either you *or* your brother.'

He was so obviously drunk that I should have let it all wash over me, yet despite my best intentions, my head began to pound and I found I had clenched my fist.

'Now you listen to me . . .' I began.

There was suddenly a new person standing between us – a man in his mid-twenties.

'Mr Conroy,' he said, addressing me. 'I don't think we've met before. I'm Paul Taylor, your father's new executive assistant. I wonder if you could spare me a few moments.'

And almost before I knew what was happening, he had one hand on my shoulder and another on my elbow and was steering me away from Philip.

We came to a halt near the buffet table.

'So what do you want to see me about, Mr Taylor?' I asked.

Taylor grinned. 'Nothing really,' he admitted. 'It's just that in another two or three seconds, you'd have taken a swing at your cousin. And I really didn't think that was a good idea.'

He was right, of course, on both counts. I would have knocked Philip down – and it *wouldn't* have been a good idea.

I took a proper look at my rescuer. Paul Taylor was tall and slim. He had silky blond hair which touched lightly on his collar, and his eyes were a very deep blue. The overall impression was one of gentleness – perhaps even weakness – but there'd been nothing weak about the way he had stepped in and saved me from myself.

'How long have you been working as my father's assistant, Mr Taylor?' I asked.

'Not long,' Paul told me. 'A matter of weeks – long enough to know that your cousin likes to cause trouble. What was he trying this time?'

'It doesn't matter,' I said.

Paul Taylor nodded, but that didn't mean he was prepared to leave the matter there.

'If you asked me to guess, I'd say he was speculating about how long your brother's marriage is going to last,' he said.

Which, I supposed, was close enough.

'How long do *you* think it's going to last?' I asked.

Paul shrugged. 'Who can say how long any marriage is going to last these days? It could be for a lifetime. It could be over in a matter of weeks. Only time will tell. But I am convinced that your brother wants it to work.'

I liked Paul Taylor, I decided. Despite his soft appearance, he seemed a stable, decisive young man, and I was pleased that he would be working beside my father.

'Let's get a drink?' I suggested.

'I'd love to,' Paul replied, 'but I rather think the big boss would like a word with you.'

I turned around, and saw that Grandfather was indeed signalling me to go over to him.

'Maybe we can have a drink later,' I said to Paul

'I'll be around,' he promised.

I made my way over to where Grandfather was standing. The old man was, I noted, leaning much more heavily on his stick than he would have done a couple of years earlier.

'How are you, Grandfather?' I asked.

'What was that all about?' he replied.

'I was just talking to my father's new executive . . .'

'That's not what I mean – and you know it.'

So he had not missed the exchange with Philip. I supposed I shouldn't have been surprised. The old man rarely missed anything.

'Philip was drunk, and because he was drunk, he was rude,' I said. 'There was nothing more to it than that.'

'Your cousin hasn't had it easy,' Grandfather said.

'Hasn't had it easy?' I repeated, incredulously – and determined not to be intimidated even if it *was* Grandfather I was talking to. 'He's had it all on a plate. He got his own brand-new car on his seventeenth birthday.'

'I'm not talking about *things*,' Grandfather said. 'I'm talking about *feelings*. Oh, your uncle Tony did his best for him – I'll not deny that – but there's no substitute in this world for a mother. I used to watch the way young Philip acted towards those women who your uncle would bring home. He desperately wanted affection from them, and sometimes they'd give it – but then Tony would get bored with the woman and trade her in for a new model, and Philip would be left alone again.'

'Even if he did have a rough time when he was growing up, it still doesn't excuse the way he's acting now,' I said.

'I love all my family, whatever their faults,' Grandfather said softly, 'and you're not without a few big faults of your own, you know.'

A bit below the belt, I thought – but if anybody had the right to take a low punch, it was Grandfather.

'I know I'm far from perfect,' I admitted.

'I love you all,' Grandfather repeated, 'and I want you all to get on together. And you're going to have to learn how to do that quickly – because if you don't, there'll be a civil war that nobody can win after I've gone.'

I laughed. 'Civil War!'

Because the idea was ludicrous – each of us would inherit enough to live comfortably for the rest of our lives, and without Grandfather as the focal point of the family, we would simply drift apart.

'I'm being serious,' the old man said sharply. 'The company matters to me – I've put my life into it – and knowing me as well as you do, you should already have worked out what that will mean.'

But I hadn't – though, God knows, I should have.

I wondered later, as I was driving back to Oxford after the wedding, which it was that Grandfather cared most about – the family or the company.

It probably wasn't that simple, I decided, because for him the family *was* the company, and the company *was* the family.

We were all a part of his plan – each one of us a piece of the jigsaw which comprised his elaborate vision. And even if Jill hadn't died – even if I hadn't had my nervous breakdown – I would have ended up working for him eventually, because he would have piled offer on top of offer, until eventually he made one that I couldn't refuse.

As I changed gear, my thoughts shifted from my grandfather to my brother. I should have asked him more about Lydia's background before I started to give him advice on whether he should or should not marry her. Perhaps I should even have done a little investigating of my own. Yet my father didn't seem concerned – or if he was, he had a very *different* concern from my own.

Another gear change, and I was thinking about Philip. What exactly had he meant at the reception? Did he really know something I didn't? Had he been snooping around and uncovered a dark secret in Lydia's past – a secret he was now taking malicious glee in hiding from the rest of us?

Then I saw a signpost which announced that it was now a mere fifty miles to the city of Oxford, and my thoughts – I'm ashamed to admit – turned to the mountain of work which would inevitably have built up on my desk during my absence and would be demanding my immediate attention.

Six years had passed since that wedding – hardly a moment in the existence of the forbidding church I was standing in front of now, but a fair chunk of a human life. And still I had no answer to the questions I had raised with myself back then.

But that didn't seem so important anymore, because as intriguing as they were, they didn't seem to me to be the *right* questions – the questions which might have helped me to save my brother's life. Those questions lay buried even deeper in the sludge at the bottom of my mind and would have to be painfully and painstakingly dredged out.

I checked my watch. I was not due at Philip's house for the reading of Grandfather's will for another half hour, and though I knew it was probably a mistake to have too much to drink before lunch, I went back into the George and Dragon, and ordered myself another pint.

SIXTEEN

I had expected Cousin Philip's car to be parked next to his house, but the space it usually occupied was empty. I wondered, briefly, if he'd forgotten we were due to hear Grandfather's will in less than half an hour – but knowing my cousin as I did, that didn't seem likely.

I walked on to the end of the dirt track and looked down the steep slope at the path which led across the fields and down to the mere. A week earlier, it would have been a simple enough matter for me to follow that path myself, I thought, but since the crash, everything had become more complicated, and my injured leg was already sending out signals that I had probably overdone things that morning.

There was the sound of a car engine behind me, and turning, I saw that my cousin's Audi had just rounded the bend. I took a step forwards and felt a stab of pain in my leg. It didn't bother me much – I could handle *physical* pain.

Philip stepped nimbly out of his car. He was wearing a very smart business suit and carrying an expensive executive briefcase.

'You're lucky I made it on time,' he said crisply, by way of greeting. 'I just managed to get the last First Class seat available, and even so, my plane only landed three quarters of an hour ago.'

'You've been away?' I asked.

'You don't normally take a plane unless you're intending to go somewhere,' Philip replied. He took out his keys and opened the door. 'Let's go through to my study.'

I followed him down the hallway and into the high-tech office which, in Uncle Tony's day, had been full of antique furniture and over-stuffed sofas. I accepted my cousin's invitation to take a seat – one of a pair of chrome and leather ones in front of his desk – but turned down his offer of a drink.

Philip poured himself a generous glass of scotch, then sat down on the other side of the desk.

'Yes, I've been away,' he said, about as pleasantly as he ever got with me. 'As a matter of fact, I've been down to Swansea.'

'Swansea?' I repeated stupidly. 'Why did you go to Swansea?'

My cousin sighed, his moment of amiability obviously over.

'Did you suffer brain damage as well as everything else?' he asked. '*You* were going to Swansea when you had the crash. Do you remember *why* you were going? Remember the deals you were trying to close.'

'Oh yes,' I agreed, though after all I'd been through, the idea of closing deals now was as unreal to me as the thought of walking on Mars would have been.

'Well, aren't you at least going to ask me how all it went?' Philip said.

'How did it go?' I said, dully.

A complacent smile came to my cousin's face. 'All signed and sealed. I've saved the company.'

'Congratulations,' I said, and though I knew that meant he had also saved Cormorant Publishing, I still found it hard – at that precise moment – to raise much enthusiasm.

'Yes, it was rather clever of me,' Philip said, 'though I must admit, the crash helped.'

I had no idea what he was talking about.

'The crash?' I repeated. 'You're saying that *helped*?'

'Of course. You remember the customers had their doubts about giving their business to us?'

'I know your father was rather concerned the deal might not go through.'

'And he was quite right to be. After the way they'd been treated by Western Haulage, the people in Swansea were very dubious about continuing to use it, even under new management. But, you see, the crash changed everything. The customers couldn't really fail to give us a chance to prove ourselves after such a family tragedy. No one likes to kick a man when he's down.'

How could he talk like this? I wondered. How could he speak about the deaths of three members of our family as if it were no more than a business negotiating tactic?

'Look, I'm as devastated about what's happened as you are,' my cousin said, reading my expression. 'But someone has to take charge. The company is Grandfather's legacy, and by maintaining it, I'm honouring his memory. And let's not forget all our employees. There are several hundred people who depend on Conroy's to keep a roof over their heads and food on the table – and we have a responsibility to them, too.'

In a way, I supposed, he was right. No, I corrected myself, he was *completely* right whichever angle I looked at it from. But I just wished he wasn't taking such obvious pleasure from being the young tycoon.

Philip glanced down at his Rolex. 'The solicitor should arrive any minute now.'

'Are we expecting anyone else?'

'Anyone else? What do you mean?'

'Are we the only two people who are supposed to be here for the reading of Grandfather's will?'

'Yes – it's just you and me, Cousin – Grandmother isn't up to it.'

There should have been the whole family there for the reading, I thought – Father, John and Uncle Tony – but now Philip and I were the only men left. It was not a comforting thought.

'Do you know what's *in* the will?' I asked.

'In general terms,' my cousin said airily. 'But we still have to have the details spelled out.'

There was a knock on the door.

'That's probably the solicitor now,' I said.

'Yes, that'll be the old fool, all right,' my cousin agreed. 'And for once, he's on time.'

My cousin went to the door and returned with Mr Gryce, the family solicitor. Gryce was a short man with bandy legs and a bald shiny head. He dressed in durable suits which looked as if they dated from the 1950s, and had been my family's solicitor for as long as I could remember.

After we'd all shaken hands and Philip had resumed his seat, the solicitor coughed and said, 'If you don't mind, I'd prefer to sit at that side of the table, Mr Conroy.'

'And what if I do mind?' Philip asked.

Then, realizing how petulant he must sound – and how inappropriate such behaviour was for a dynamic young tycoon – he walked around the desk and took the seat next to mine.

Mr Gryce opened his briefcase and spread his legal papers over the pristine surface of Philip's desk.

'The will is quite a short one,' the old man said. 'Most of your grandfather's personal fortune was placed in family trust funds long before he died. The rest of it had already been signed over to your grandmother for her use during the rest of her natural life.'

'We know all that,' Philip interrupted.

The solicitor gave my cousin a disapproving look, but Philip was either so tense – or so excited – that I don't think he even noticed it.

'So what the will mainly concerns itself with is the voting shares in Conroy Enterprises, which have absolutely no monetary value, and merely establish who has the right to take the decisions which will affect the entire company,' the solicitor continued. 'Until his death, all these shares were held by your grandfather. His will specifies that they can never be sold, nor can they be divided into smaller blocks and distributed amongst other members of the family. Strictly speaking, I suppose, it could be said that your grandfather hasn't *left* the shares to anyone. He has merely bestowed stewardship of them on to one person, until, by a mechanism I will outline later, that same stewardship will be passed on to another.'

And that person had to be me, I realized with horror, because, if only by a few months, I was the oldest surviving member of the Conroy family.

I didn't want it – I really didn't want it – but neither did I want to commit Grandfather's legacy to Philip's hands.

I glanced at my cousin. His thoughts must surely have been running along the same lines as mine, so he must have realized by now that what he wanted most in the world was about to be snatched away from him – and yet he seemed so confident.

He knew what was in the will, I realized – and knew, furthermore, that it was not as straightforward as it first appeared.

'Had he lived, the shares would have gone to Mr Antony Conroy, as the eldest son,' Gryce said. 'In fact, strictly speaking, they already had, because your grandfather died before the crash, so it can be said that for an hour or so – though he didn't know it himself – the shares were his.'

'And now they're mine,' Philip exclaimed.

'Yes,' Gryce admitted, 'but only because Mr Edward Conroy died, too.'

'What do you mean?' Philip demanded.

'The Conroys are not the Royal Family, though you sometimes act as if you thought they were,' Gryce said, with a malicious grin, 'so there is no divine right of succession. If Edward had not been in the car, the shares would have gone to him as the second son, and when he died, they would have gone to his son, Rob. As it is, they will still go to Rob if you die before you have an heir who has attained the age of thirty-five.'

'There's no danger of that,' Philip said.

'Really?' the solicitor asked. 'I was under the impression you weren't married.'

'I'm not,' Philip said, 'but I've got a real incentive to get hitched now, haven't I?'

The solicitor had gone, and Philip stood at the big picture window, looking out towards the mere. 'There'll have to be some changes made,' he said in the off-hand manner he had so quickly developed.

'Changes?'

He turned around, but did not look me fully in the eyes.

'Yes. Changes. In Cormorant Publishing. I'm afraid you're simply not making full use of its potential as an income generator.'

'Andy McBride's book was a number one bestseller,' I reminded him.

'Yes, but you can't live on the strength of that forever,' my cousin countered. 'You need to diversify.'

'Into what?'

Philip waved his hand impatiently. 'Into the mass market, of course. Look, I shouldn't need to be telling you any of this. You're the one with the experience in the business, for God's sake. You should already know what needs to be done.'

'Since I seem to be being particularly stupid on this occasion, would you care to spell it out for me?' I asked my cousin.

'For a start, you could bring out a series of books which would appeal to dowdy housewives. You know the sort of thing I mean – the ones which have pictures of gooey-eyed women and dark handsome men on the front cover. Then there's the men's market.'

'The men's market?'

'You invent a private eye who gets laid a lot. Call him – I don't know – Dick Hard. Then you commission a series of desperate hacks to churn out stories about him for practically nothing. Bloody hell, man, it's almost pure profit.'

So my worst fears over Cormorant were all coming true.

'You want me to publish sentimental romantic crap and soft-core pornography?' I said.

'If that's what you want to call it. I'd prefer to see it as

producing the kinds of books that the public – the *real* public,
rather than the few trendy left-wing intellectuals you seem to
be interested in – actually want to read.'

'I won't do it,' I said firmly.

Philip smiled. 'Let's settle this democratically,' he suggested.
'My voting shares in Conroy Enterprises are in favour of
dumbing down Cormorant a little. What are your voting shares
in favour of?'

'You know I don't have any.'

'That's right!' Philip said. 'So it looks like you'll have to do
exactly what I say – because from now on, my opinion is the
only one that really counts for anything.'

There was enough tension in the air for us both to start
slightly when the phone suddenly rang.

'You answer it,' Philip ordered me. 'And unless it's urgent,
say I'm in a meeting.'

I picked the phone and recited the number.

'Is that Rob?' asked a vaguely familiar voice on the other
end.

'Yes,' I said. 'Who am I speaking to?'

'Bill Harper. Is Philip there?'

'Yes, he is.'

'And has the will been read?'

I remembered Harper's visit to my sick room in Bridgend
Hospital. How sensitive and considerate he'd been – how gently
he'd told me the story of how my family had died. I'd thought
at the time how tragedy had changed him, but the change – if
there had been one – had certainly not lasted. If anything, he
was worse than ever, with the natural arrogance he'd taken
trouble to mask in the past now completely unleashed and
running free.

'I said, has the will been read?' Harper repeated.

'Yes it has – not that that's anything to do with you.'

'Put Philip on,' Harper said, ignoring the implied rebuke.
'Tell him it's very important.'

It would have been childish – something Philip might have
done – to make him say please before I did as he'd asked, and
instead I just handed the phone over to my cousin.

'Yes?' Philip said in his best executive voice. 'The will? . . .

Yes, I do know the terms now. They're pretty much as I'd been led to believe . . . What? . . . Is that some kind of sick joke? . . . Yes, yes, I can see what that means.'

He stood up and walked as far away from the desk as the telephone cord would allow.

'What?' he asked in almost a whisper. 'But that's outrageous . . . No, I won't do it! . . . I . . . Yes, yes, I understand.'

When he returned the telephone to the desk, I noticed that his hands were trembling, and his face was as white as a corpse's.

'That was Bill Harper,' he said.

'I know.'

'There's . . . there's been some trouble at the furniture factory. There's talk of a strike.'

But it didn't seem to me as if that was what the conversation had been about at all.

My cousin put his hands up and covered his face.

'I really don't need the aggravation at a time like this,' he mumbled, 'so I suppose I'll just have to give in to their demands.'

He took his hands away again, and I saw that he appeared, by a tremendous effort of will, to have calmed down a little.

'We were talking about Cormorant Publishing before Bill's call, weren't we?' he asked.

'Yes, we were.'

'That's all you want? If I leave you alone to run it as you see fit, you'll be perfectly happy?'

'Yes.'

Philip took a deep breath. 'Then it's yours.'

I couldn't *quite* believe what I was hearing.

'I'll have complete independence?' I asked.

'Absolutely. Of course, I'll expect you to make a profit, just as I'll expect all our other divisions to, but other than that, you'll get no interference from me.'

'What's the catch?' I asked.

'No catch.'

'Five minutes ago, you were talking about turning the company upside down, now suddenly you're prepared to leave it just as it is. What's made you change your mind?'

'That phone call,' Philip said. 'It made me realize that Bill and I have quite enough on our hands without worrying about some tuppenny-ha'penny little company down in Oxford.'

'You and Bill?' I repeated incredulously. 'Are you still talking about Bill *Harper*?'

'That's right. I'm making him joint managing director. Didn't I mention that earlier?'

'But he's not much more than a kid!' I protested.

'He's only a few years younger than we are. And he's certainly older than you were when you took over Cormorant Publishing.'

'That was different,' I protested. 'Cormorant wasn't expected to make any money.'

'But it did,' Philip pointed out. 'And what makes you think that Bill has any less business sense than you have?'

'I know you've been under a lot of pressure in all sorts of ways, but don't rush into anything without thinking it through properly,' I pleaded. 'The organization you've inherited is a very complex one. You need help at the top level – but not from Bill Harper. Draw on the experience of the people who've already been working for us for years at a high level of decision taking – who have a proven track record. I'm not saying it's a bad idea to have a joint managing director, but the person you pick should be one of our existing senior staff.'

'It's going to be Bill,' Philip said stubbornly. 'And as that old fool Gryce pointed out less than half an hour ago, there's absolutely nothing that you can do about it.'

SEVENTEEN

The tall thin figure didn't move as I made my way slowly – and occasionally, painfully – up the hill, but I was almost certain that he was watching me every step of the way.

What did Owen Flint fear? I wondered.

That the maniac who had already killed three members of

my family would suddenly leap out of the shadows and attack me with a machete?

That I was already in the sights of a sniper's rifle?

If that was the case, there was very little that Owen – standing by the stocks outside the church – could do to protect me.

When I had almost reached the church, he stepped forward.

'Just coming back from the reading of the will, are you?' he asked.

'That's right,' I agreed.

'Any surprises?'

'No,' I lied, not wanting to go into details of Grandfather's final – if complicated – testament. 'I'm still in charge of Cormorant Publishing, and that's all I've ever wanted.'

'Can you spare me five minutes, Rob?' Owen asked, popping a bright purple boiled sweet into his mouth.

'You can walk up to the house with me, if you like,' I said, 'but I'm going back to Oxford, and as soon as the taxi I've ordered arrives, I have to leave.'

Owen looked worried. 'Do you *really* have to go back to Oxford, Rob?' he asked. 'Couldn't your business do without you for a few more days?'

Yes, it probably could. But my need to see Marie – to find out what kind of future lay ahead of me – *couldn't* wait.

'There are things I can't put off,' I said – avoiding explanations again.

'Well, if you insist on going, at least let me ring the Oxford police and make them aware of your situation,' Owen said.

I shook my head. 'Perhaps later I'll ask for your protection, but now isn't the time.'

We turned up Church Street. The air was mild, and the sunlight made the village look particularly delightful, but I couldn't wait to get back to my cramped office in Oxford.

'I've got my lad Matthews down in the Bristol area at the moment,' Owen said, 'and the thought occurred to me that while he's down there, he might as well have a word with this bloke that Conroy Enterprises bought Western Haulage from. His name's Morgan, isn't it?'

'That's right,' I agreed. 'Hugh Morgan.'

'And you've met him, have you?'

'Oh yes, I've met him all right. Twice!'

'So why don't you give me a quick rundown on what he's like?' Owen suggested.

The first time Hugh Morgan and I met, it had been in my office at Cormorant Publishing.

'He hasn't got an appointment, but he's prepared to wait until you're free,' Janet said over the intercom. 'He says he doesn't mind waiting all day, if that's what it'll take.'

'And what exactly does he want?

'He won't say, except to assure me that he's not a writer or in any way connected with publishing. But he does say it's a very private and personal matter which can only be communicated to you.'

I walked to the window which looked out on reception and lifted one of the blind slats. The man standing by Janet's desk was around fifty, stocky, and had large hands. His hair was brown, and his suit, though not new, was well, if painstaking, pressed. He looked everything that a solid, respectable, middle-aged man should be – and I was intrigued to know what business he thought he could possibly have with the publisher of a shocking book like *Gobshite*.

I returned to my desk and consulted my appointments' book.

'I've got some calls to make, but I can see him briefly in about half an hour,' I told Janet.

The first thing Hugh Morgan did when he entered my office was to cut off my apology for keeping him waiting midstream and say that it was very good of me to see him at all.

Up close, he confirmed the impression I'd had of him from a distance, except that what I *hadn't* been able to see through the slats was that he had the greenest and most candid eyes that I'd ever encountered.

'Do please take a seat, Mr Morgan,' I said, indicating the one in front of my desk.

He sat down gingerly, as if he was afraid he would break the chair, and even when it took his weight without protest, he seemed far from comfortable.

'So how can I help you, Mr Morgan?' I asked.

'I thought I'd come to you since you was the publisher of the family,' Hugh Morgan said.

I frowned. 'My secretary told me that you'd assured her you weren't an author.'

'And so I'm not,' Morgan said hastily. 'The fact is, I'm just a plain working man.'

'Then . . .?'

'Look at where you work, Mr Conroy,' he said, gesturing with one of his big hands at the bookshelves behind me. 'You love books, don't you?'

'Yes,' I admitted. 'I do.'

'And you're not just in this business for the money you can make out of it, are you?'

'No,' I agreed.

'And neither am I in my business just for the money *I* can make,' Morgan said. 'Oh, don't get me wrong, I like some of the things it can buy me, but things aren't really important at the end of the day – it's the satisfaction of a job well done that counts.'

'What's your point?' I asked.

'I'm not an educated man, Mr Conroy,' Morgan said earnestly. 'I'm not even a creative man – at least not in the way you are. But I've built my business up from nothing, and now they're trying to take it away from me.'

'I'm afraid I'm not following you.'

'You know about Western Haulage' – he pointed a large thumb at his chest – 'that's me.'

I was beginning to get the picture.

'I understand your company's in some kind of trouble, and that your shareholders are eager to sell,' I said.

Morgan twisted awkwardly in his seat. 'Oh, we've had trouble,' he admitted. 'But none of it's been of our making.'

'You'd better explain,' I told him.

'We've been losing contracts to people who seem willing to carry goods for less than cost,' he said. 'And that's only the start. Some of my best drivers have been lured away for fabulous wages that I could never even think of paying. We've had a fire in one of our depots which the police think was started deliberately. And a score of other things have gone wrong recently which never should have.'

'And who do you think is behind all this trouble?' I asked cautiously.

'It's not for me to say,' Morgan replied.

'Isn't it?' I stood up. 'Then I can't see much point in continuing this meeting.'

Morgan shifted uncomfortably in his seat.

'Look, Mr Conroy,' he said, 'I don't want to go around accusing people without proof – that's not my way – but there's only one company that's goin' to benefit from my misfortunes, and that's Conroy Transport.'

Was it possible that Uncle Tony would have used such dirty tricks? I wondered.

Would he actually have gone to the extreme of sanctioning arson?

Under normal circumstances, I would have said no. But these were *not* normal circumstances. The acquisition of Western Haulage was to be a feather in my uncle's cap – the springboard that would launch him to the dizzy heights of chairman of the board. And that might – just *might* – have been enough to push him into taking shortcuts.

I sat down again.

'I can see what you're thinking, Mr Conroy,' Morgan said. 'It's not nice to have to face the possibility that one of your own family could do anything like that. And I'd never have laid the burden on you – honest I wouldn't – if I hadn't been so desperate.'

'What exactly do you want me to do?' I asked, the note of caution still in my voice.

'Talk to your uncle. You're good with words in a way I never could be. You should be able to persuade him that what he's done is wrong.'

'And what if he says he has no idea what I'm talking about?'

Morgan reached into his pocket, pulled out a folded sheet of paper, smoothed it on the desk, and handed it to me. I opened it, and saw it was a list of names and telephone numbers.

'All these people have worked with me at one time or another,' he said, 'and they're all respectable pillars of the community. Ring them up. Ask them if I've been telling the truth, or if it's just a pack of lies I've been feeding you. And when you've heard enough to see things from my point of view, well, then, you can get in touch with your uncle.'

'I'm not making any promises . . .' I said.

'But you will give a few of them a ring?' he asked, anxiously.

'Yes, I'll certainly do that,' I agreed.

Morgan stood up and held out his hand. 'That's all I ask, Mr Conroy,' he said. 'That's all I ask.'

After he had left me, I sat quietly at my desk for several minutes, deep in thought.

If what Hugh Morgan had said really was true – and after talking to him, I was almost certain it was – confronting Uncle Tony would be a complete waste of time.

But Grandfather was a different matter. He had always been a hard-headed businessman, but he had never been an unscrupulous one. If he learned that Uncle Tony had been using dirty tricks, he wouldn't allow the takeover to go through.

Thus, at one stroke, I would accomplish two things – I would save a decent, hard-working man from losing his lifetime's dream, and I would protect Cormorant Publishing, which I loved almost as much (so I imagined) as I would love my own child.

'Did you do as Morgan suggested?' Owen Flint asked me.

'I was on the point of picking up the phone when I had an idea,' I said. 'I asked myself why I should let my fingers do the walking when I could leave the work to someone who was a specialist in the trade.'

'That someone would be your "friend" Miss Marie O'Hara, would it?' Flint asked.

'That's right,' I agreed. 'I called her to say I was faxing the telephone numbers Morgan had given me, and we agreed we'd meet later, so she could tell me what she'd found out.'

I met Oxford's prettiest private eye in a pub called the Head of the River, at seven o'clock that same evening. The place was packed, as usual, with a combination of students, tourists and locals, but after I'd bought the drinks, we managed to grab a corner table.

'Did you find time to make those phone calls for me?' I asked.

Marie took a deep drag on her cigarette. 'Yes, I did. A couple of them, anyway.'

There was a strange note to her voice that I didn't quite like.

'Is something the matter?' I asked.

'No – nothing much, anyway.' Marie stubbed her cigarette in the ashtray, and immediately took a fresh one out of the packet. 'It's just that I'm not happy conducting this investigation by phone.'

I chuckled. 'I'd scarcely go so far as to call it an "investigation". It's just a few inquiries.'

Marie did not seem to share my amusement. 'I'd like to go to Wales for a couple of days and see some of these people. Will you pay my expenses?'

'I suppose so,' I said. 'But is that really necessary? Hugh Morgan's gone to all the trouble of providing you with the telephone numbers. Shouldn't that be enough for you?'

'I'd feel a lot happier if I could talk to some of these people face-to-face,' Marie said stubbornly.

'I don't see what they could tell you in person that they couldn't say over the phone.'

Marie's lips curled, and I knew she was about to do her hard-boiled PI impersonation.

'Listen, Buster,' she said, 'you don't tell me how to be a private dick, and I won't tell you how to sell books.'

I laughed, and this time she joined in.

'All right,' I said. 'If it's a paid holiday in sunny Wales you want, it's a paid holiday in sunny Wales you'll get.'

'You won't regret it,' Marie said enigmatically.

She drove up to Wales on Tuesday morning, and though I tried to ring her several times that day – and several times on Wednesday and Thursday – she wasn't picking up.

By Friday I was really starting to miss her. And yet that was only four days, I reminded myself. What would it be like if I didn't see or hear from her for a month?

Or a year?

Or ever again?

The prospect was too awful to contemplate.

She called me just after I'd arrived at my office the following Monday morning.

'When did you get back?' I asked.

'Last night.'

And she hadn't even called me!

'I've been trying to contact you all week,' I said, trying not to sound too aggrieved.

'I switch my mobile phone off when I'm working,' she said, without a hint of an apology. 'Can you make some time for me this morning?'

'Is it important?' I asked – suddenly, for some insane reason of my own, playing hard to get.

'Yes, I think you might consider it important,' she said, in measured tones. 'I've certainly found out some things I think you ought to know.'

'Like what?'

'I never divulge the result of my investigations over the phone.'

I glanced down at my appointments' book.

'I can fit you in at eleven,' I said.

'Good enough,' she agreed.

When Marie arrived at my office, she was wearing a business suit which somehow managed to combine efficiency and aggression, and her normally wild hair was held in place by clips. In fact, she didn't look like *my* Marie at all.

'You'll get my written report tomorrow, Mr Conroy,' she said, 'but I thought you'd appreciate a verbal one now.'

'*Mr Conroy?*' I repeated. 'You haven't called me Mr Conroy since that night outside St John's College.'

'You've never been my client before,' she said briskly. 'Listen, Rob, tonight we can go back to normal, but at the moment, you're the one who's paying the bill. And,' she added with a smile which showed me just a flash of the Marie I knew, 'it *is* quite a bill I'll be putting in.'

I sighed, theatrically. 'OK, let's have your report, *Miss O'Hara.*'

'By the time I'd finished ringing up the first few of the numbers you gave me, I wasn't quite happy,' Marie said. 'Oh, on the surface, the people sounded plausible enough, but something – an investigator's instinct if you like – told me they weren't quite kosher. That's why I had to go to Wales and see for myself.'

'And what did you find out?'

Marie took her notebook out of her pocket. 'When I spoke to Mr Clifford Davies at West Wales Plastics over the phone, he told me he had a factory which employed a hundred and fifty workers.'

'And he doesn't?'

'No such factory was listed in the directory of companies, and when I got to Swansea, I found out why. West Wales Plastics' sole asset is a crummy one-roomed office which it shares with a firm selling novelty sex goods and another which deals in practical jokes. The sole proprietor and employee of these three companies is Mr Clifford Davies. There's a whole list of similar shady operators on Hugh Morgan's list. I can tell you about all of them now, if you want me to – or you can wait for my written report.'

'I'll wait for your written report,' I said. 'What else did you find out?'

'After I'd discovered that Mr Morgan's character witnesses weren't totally reliable, I took a closer look at Mr Morgan himself. When you met him, how did he strike you?'

I shrugged. 'Honest. Reliable.'

'He's a con man, and he really did the business on you,' Marie said cuttingly. 'He's gone bankrupt at least three times, and each time he seems to have done much better out of the disaster than his partners did. If he's been losing drivers, it's only because he pays the lowest union rate – and even less than that if he thinks he can get away with it. And that's only the start. The police can't prove it, but they strongly suspect he's been moving stolen goods . . .'

'How did you find that out?'

'You don't want to know. They also suspect that he's arranged to have other companies' lorries stolen, then cannibalized them for the parts which will keep his own fleet on the road. As to the fire, it's a pretty good bet that he started it himself – he was certainly overinsured.'

'So why did he come to me?' I asked.

'I don't know for sure, but if I had to make a guess, I'd say he probably wanted to stay in the business a little longer, so he could continue milking his partners right up to the point at which the official receiver was called in,' Marie said. 'He must have known it was a long shot that you could persuade your uncle to change his mind . . .'

'He never wanted me to go to my uncle,' I said, suddenly realizing just how much Morgan had manipulated me. 'It's true he asked me to talk to Tony, but it was my grandfather who he'd targeted all along. If I'd been able to convince the old man that his son had been up to dirty tricks in order to get what he wanted, Grandfather would have called the whole deal off.'

'There you are then,' Marie said. 'He can't have been sure he'd even have the slightest chance until he actually *met* you, but once he had, his hopes must have risen considerably, because he knew a mug when he saw one.'

'Thanks very much,' I said.

'It's not your fault,' replied Marie, the emotionless private investigator. 'Morgan's a professional, which means that you were way out of your depth. He took you in completely, and if you'd talked to the man at West Wales Plastics, why wouldn't he have done the same?'

I had to admit she was right.

'You've done a good job,' I told her.

'Then why are you looking so down in the mouth?'

Why?

Because my one chance of thwarting Uncle Tony's plans had just gone out of the window.

Because now I knew that the takeover of Western Haulage would be good for its investors, there was simply nothing more that I could do to stop the deal going through.

Owen Flint and I had reached the front door of the house, which was now mine, but in which I had no intention of ever living.

I checked my watch. 'The taxi should be here in a couple of minutes,' I said. 'I need to go inside and pick up my bag.'

'You shouldn't be carrying it yourself – not in your

condition,' Owen said. 'Tell me where it is, and I'll bring it down for you.'

We entered the house. Four of us had lived here once, and three of them – three gentle human beings – were gone forever, whilst I, the least worthy of the quartet, remained. It took a huge effort on my part not to scream until my lungs collapsed.

'The suitcase?' Owen said.

'It's upstairs – second bedroom on the left.'

'Right-ho,' Owen said. 'I won't be a tick.' He put his foot on the first stair, then turned around. 'You told me you'd met Hugh Morgan twice, didn't you? When was the second time?'

'When the five of us went down to Bristol to sign the contract with Western Haulage,' I told him.

The two hire cars – the Jag and the BMW – were waiting for us at Bristol Airport. It came as no surprise to anyone when Tony announced that he had earmarked the Jaguar for himself, nor when he added that Bill would ride with him, and the rest of us could follow in the BMW. The writing had *already* been on the wall before that, but Uncle Tony, being the man he was, just couldn't resist the temptation to heavily underline it.

We drove straight from the airport to the headquarters of Western Haulage, which was located in Patchway. It was a single-storied brick building that wouldn't have impressed anyone, but from the number of lorries parked around it, it was clear that the company had the capacity to handle a lot of business – even if it wasn't doing so at the moment.

We were met at the door by our lawyer and led into what passed for a boardroom. There were five men already sitting around the table – Hugh Morgan and his four partners.

Morgan seemed a very different man to the one who had visited me in my office in Oxford a few weeks earlier. The suit he was wearing was much sharper. His movements were more self-assured. The hands, which had looked so huge when he was playing the role of an honest working man, had now shrunk to normal size.

But most of all, it was the eyes that I noticed. The frankness and lack of guile which filled them in Oxford had been replaced by the cunning look of a man who could go bankrupt three times, and still find people willing to invest in him.

The four partners were a complete contrast. All of them wore expressions which hovered somewhere between apprehension and relief. I guessed – and I suspect I was right – that they had each invested their life savings in a business which Morgan had convinced them would make their fortunes – and that now they were pleased to get out with rather less than they had put in.

The deal had been concluded by complex negotiations beforehand, and the signing was just a formality. The papers were passed around the table, and I signed after my father, thinking as I did so that, as long as Uncle Tony had Grandfather's permission to use the voting stock as he wished, my signature – and those of all the other directors – was about as much use as a rubber sword.

The signing over, Morgan stood up and walked over to the drinks cabinet. 'What'll you all have?' he asked, as he made the smooth transition from hard-headed businessman into jovial host.

One of his partners – one rather, of his now *ex*-partners – rose from his seat. 'Err . . . if it's all the same to you, I think I'll pass on the drinks,' he said. 'I've got things to do.'

The other partners made similar excuses, but what they really meant was that they wanted Morgan out of their lives – and daren't risk being near him any longer than was absolutely necessary, in case he took the opportunity to con them into putting what capital they'd managed to salvage into something else.

Uncle Tony had no such scruples. This was his crowning moment, and he really didn't care who he shared it with.

We stayed there drinking for around half an hour, with Uncle Tony and Hugh Morgan doing most of the talking, and my side of the family just feeling awkward.

Finally, Uncle Tony slapped Morgan on the back and said that much as he would like to stay longer, we had important business meetings the next day, as he, Hugh – ho! ho! – could well appreciate.

Morgan replied that yes – ho! ho! – he imagined we had.

It was as we were moving towards the door that Morgan, still jovial, put a restraining hand on my shoulder. 'Could we have a word in private, Mr Conroy?' he asked.

'Why not?' I replied.

Why not indeed? I had nothing to fear from this man. And if our private conversation unsettled Uncle Tony even for a second, well, so much the better.

Morgan led me into his office – which was little more than a cupboard – next to the boardroom.

'Like it?' he asked.

'It's not what I would have chosen for myself,' I said.

Morgan grinned. 'I know you wouldn't. I've been to your office in Oxford, don't forget. But this is what the punters like to see. They're not going to invest their money in a company where the boss lavishes money on himself, now are they? They think if you work in an office that even a rat would turn its nose up at, you must be looking after their cash. That's the thing about punters.'

'What is?'

'They're stupid. And every night, while I'm driving my old banger back out to my big house in the country – which has two Mercs parked in the garage – I laugh myself silly about them.'

'What exactly was it that you want to talk to me about, Mr Morgan?' I asked coolly.

'Hugh,' Morgan said. 'Please call me Hugh.'

'What exactly was it that you want to talk to me about, *Hugh*?'

'I'm just curious,' Morgan admitted. 'I thought I did a pretty good job on you when I came down to Oxford.'

'A brilliant job,' I confessed.

'So the fact that you *didn't* talk to your uncle—'

'My grandfather, you mean,' I interrupted.

Morgan grinned again. 'Yeah, that's right, your grandfather,' he conceded. 'Charlie Conroy – one of the old school, upright and honest, with his hands firmly on the purse strings.'

'You've done your research,' I said.

'In my line of business, you have to do your research,' Morgan told me. 'It's the only real working capital you've got. Anyway, as I was saying, when I left you that day, I had you marked out as a bloke who'd do just what I wanted him to do. So where did I go wrong? How did I manage to misread the signs?'

'I didn't call those numbers you gave me myself,' I said.

'So what *did* you do?'

'I hired a private detective.'

Morgan shook his head as if, once I'd said it, the answer was obvious.

'And he saw right through the little network I'd set up to con you,' he mused.

'She,' I corrected him. 'But yes, that's right. She did.'

'That was smart,' Morgan said. 'Smarter than I'd ever have given you credit for.'

But it wasn't really. If I hadn't known Marie, and wanted to put work her way, I'd have fallen into the trap – just as he'd intended I should.

Now he'd learned what he wanted to know, Morgan dropped all pretence. The eyes, which had been genial before, turned to ice. The jaw, which had suggested bonhomie, jutted aggressively forward.

'You could have bought me another six months, Mr Conroy,' he said. 'I could have done a lot with another six months.'

'You mean that you could have stolen more of your partners' money?' I said.

'I mean that I could have transferred more assets,' Morgan replied. He raised his right arm and pointed his index finger at my chest. 'By being too clever, you've cost me money. I don't forget things like that easily.'

'You're about the lowest form of life there is,' I told him. 'I don't care whether you forget or not.'

'Oh, but you will,' he said, starting to show signs of anger. 'You definitely will – because I'll find a way to pay you back. It might be tomorrow, or it might take years, but I'll find a way.'

The taxi which was to take me to Warrington had arrived, and my case was already sitting in the boot.

'Why didn't you tell me about this conversation you had with Morgan before?' demanded Owen Flint, who was holding the back door of the cab open for me.

I bent over to climb into the back seat and felt a pain shoot through my bruised ribs.

'I didn't think it was worth mentioning,' I said.

Owen Flint sighed. 'A man makes a direct threat against you, and a few hours later someone sabotages the brakes of the car you'll be riding in the next day – and you don't think that's worth mentioning?'

I eased my body on to the seat. 'When Morgan said he'd find a way to pay me back, he wasn't talking about physical violence,' I told Flint. 'He's a con man, not a thug.'

'That's your opinion of him, is it?'

'Yes, that's my opinion of him.'

'You read him completely wrong once, didn't you?' Flint asked.

'Yes, but . . .'

'So how do you know that you didn't make the same mistake a second time?'

EIGHTEEN

I called Marie several times on the train journey down to Oxford, twice in the taxi from the railway station to my flat, and once before (and once after) the pre-cooked meal which I heated up in the oven, and then left largely uneaten. Each time, I got a recorded message telling me to speak after the beep.

It was the same story the following morning – I rang from my office, and a voice with a gentle Irish lilt to it said, 'I'm not available at the moment, but if you'll leave your number, I'll call you back.'

Except that she hadn't!

It seemed an eternity since the crash in that Welsh country lane, and I hadn't spoken to her once.

There was a pile of work on my desk. I promised myself I'd make a considerable dent in my correspondence before I rang Marie again, but even as I was making the promise, I half-knew I'd never keep it, and after fifteen minutes, I abandoned the pretence.

I stepped into the outer office. Janet gave me a quizzical look.

'I'm going out,' I told her. 'I don't know when I'll be back, but it probably won't be at least until late afternoon.'

She glanced down at her diary. 'Do you have an outside appointment I don't know about?' she asked, with a hint of stern disapproval in her voice.

I shook my head. 'I don't seem to be able to concentrate on work this morning. I thought a breath of fresh air might do me good.'

I put my hand in my pocket and felt my fingers brush against my mobile phone. If I took it with me, Janet would be ringing me with an enquiry from a book chain (or from the printers or from one of my authors) before I even reached the end of the street. On the other hand, if I didn't take it with me, and Marie called . . .

Marie wasn't going to call!

I placed the phone on Janet's desk.

'Look after this for me,' I said.

'And if anyone wants to reach you . . .?'

'They'll just have to wait until I'm reachable, won't they?' I said, more harshly than I'd intended.

Janet looked concerned. 'Are you all right?' she asked.

No, I wanted to say, I'm not all right. My brother and father are dead. I'm in danger of losing my sanity – again. And there's a strong chance that a homicidal maniac is stalking me. All of which I could probably handle if the only woman I really cared about would show just a little concern for me.

But I was still enough of Edward Conroy's son – and John Conroy's brother – not to tell her any of that, and instead, I said, 'I'm fine. It's just that I'm finding it a little difficult to settle into work again so soon after the crash.'

My secretary's eyes moistened. 'I'm so sorry, Rob,' she said. 'You must be going through hell.'

I'd asked her many times to call me by my first name, but she never had, and the fact that she'd finally chosen to at that moment, both touched and terrified me.

'Thank you. I'll . . . I'll see you later,' I said, limping to the door.

*   *   *

As I stood on the pavement, looking up at the converted Victorian house in which Marie lived, I wondered, perhaps for the thousandth time, why I had never been invited inside.

What was it she was hiding behind the door of her flat that she didn't want me to see?

What secret could be so dark that she was not prepared to share it with someone who had become her closest friend – and wished to be a great deal more?

I walked up the path. There were six bell pushes by the side of the front door. I pressed the one which had Marie O'Hara printed neatly on a card beside it.

I waited for about half a minute, and when there was no response, I rang again.

Nothing!

The third time I pressed the bell, I kept my finger on it. I could hear the ringing sound coming from inside the house and, though I knew it would make no difference, I pressed even harder.

A first-floor window flew open, and a young woman with a towel wrapped around her head looked angrily down at me.

'I'm *trying* to wash my bloody hair!' she said.

'I'm sorry to disturb you,' I said apologetically, 'but I really need to see Marie.'

'She's not here,' the woman said, and then, as if further clarification were necessary, she added, 'she's gone away.'

'Where's she gone?'

'Are you a client?' the woman asked.

'No, I'm a friend.'

'She didn't say where was going, but she left straight after she'd heard on the news that someone she knew had been injured in a car crash in South Wales. She seemed quite upset about it, so maybe that's where she went.'

If she had been upset, she hadn't been upset *enough* to come and see me, as Andy McBride had done, I thought bitterly. She hadn't even been upset enough to ring – so it couldn't have been anything more than coincidence that she left Oxford just after the crash.

'If she does come back, could you say Rob Conroy called, and would like to hear from her?' I asked.

In an ideal world, the woman would have said, 'Oh, you're Rob – she never stops talking about you.'

In the miserable world where I existed, she simply said, 'Bob Conway – right.'

'Rob *Conroy*,' I said, with some emphasis.

'Got it,' she told me. 'Do you mind if I get back to washing my hair now?'

'No,' I said. 'Sorry to disturb you.'

As I walked away, head bowed, I thought again about Andy McBride's offer. It would be so easy for the two of us to break into the empty flat and find out just what the big secret was.

But Marie would be bound to guess it was me, and even if she didn't, I knew I'd have to confess. Then our relationship – if we still had one – would be well and truly over.

Detective Sergeant Matthews had been forewarned by Flint (who had been forewarned by me) that Hugh Morgan was a crook, but what he had not been prepared for was to find out just how *successful* a crook the man was.

'Morgan's country house isn't quite a stately home, but it's pretty damn close to it,' he'd tell Flint, when they eventually met up in Cheshire, after the next murder. 'You could lose my little semi-detached in a corner of its stable block.'

It was just as Matthews was parking in front of the not-quite stately home that Morgan emerged through the front door. He was dressed in a heavy tweed jacket, cravat and cavalry twill trousers, as befitted a country squire, but there was nothing of the rural gentleman in the way he slammed the palm of his hand down on the roof of the sergeant's Escort, nor in the way he leant down to the open window and said, 'I don't care what you're selling, because whatever it is, I'm not buying – so you can just piss off.'

'I'm not selling anything,' Matthews said, producing his warrant card from his shirt pocket.

Morgan stepped back, as if the car roof had suddenly given him an electric shock, and Matthews seized the opportunity to open his door and climb out.

The two men stood facing each other.

'I'm not saying anything until I've seen my lawyer,' Morgan said.

After a number of false starts in the previous couple of days, Matthews felt as if he were suddenly hitting pay dirt.

'Now why should you suddenly feel the need to talk to your lawyer, Mr Morgan?' he asked. 'Got something to hide, have we?'

Morgan started slightly, as if he'd been anticipating the question but still couldn't quite hide the impact it had on him.

'No comment,' he said.

'Come on, Mr Morgan,' Matthews coaxed. 'Ever since you heard the news that the men you'd just sold your business to had been murdered, you must surely have been expecting a visit from the South Wales police.'

And almost as if by magic, the tension, which had shrouded Morgan like a suit of armour, seemed to melt away.

'Is that what this is all about?' he asked. 'The bloody car crash?'

'What else *could* it be about?'

Disconcertingly, Morgan laughed. 'Do you mean to say that the reason you're here is because you suspect *me* of killing them?' he asked. 'Now that's not just funny – it's bloody hilarious!'

'You did threaten Robert Conroy,' Matthews pointed out.

'No, I didn't,' Morgan countered, 'but if I *had* done, I'd have made sure there were no witnesses around, so it would only be his word against mine. And murder simply isn't my style. When I pay somebody back for what they've done to me, I like them still to be around, so I can look into their eyes, and see just how much they're suffering.'

'Where were you the night before the crash?' Matthews asked.

Morgan grinned. 'There was a big do at my lodge in Bristol. After it was over, a few of us carried on drinking. We didn't split up until about five o'clock in the morning, then I called a taxi to take me home.'

'It's a long way to go by taxi,' Matthews mused. 'It must have been expensive.'

'I can afford it,' Morgan told him.

'What was the name of the taxi company?' Matthews asked,

expecting – or perhaps merely hoping – that the other man would say that he didn't really remember.

'It was the Downs' Motor Service,' Morgan replied, without hesitation. 'They're the ones I always use. I have a monthly account with them, so they'll have the trip logged to me.'

'And these people you were with – I expect they'll be able to provide you with an alibi, will they?'

Morgan's grin widened. 'Yes, they will, but I'm not sure you'll believe them.'

'And what makes you think that?'

'Well, quite frankly, and just between ourselves, most of them are very dodgy characters.'

'Dodgy characters?' Matthews repeated, and then cursed himself as he realized that in this unwitting double act of theirs, Morgan was using him as his straight man.

'Very dodgy,' the con artist repeated with relish. 'If I remember rightly, there were two city councillors and a couple of police chief superintendents at our little gathering.'

'Just because you didn't do the job yourself, doesn't mean you couldn't have paid someone else to do it,' Matthews countered, rattled.

Morgan shook his head.

'You young coppers,' he said, with some disgust. 'You're always charging in headlong, without getting your facts straight first. If I conducted any of my businesses the way that you conduct your investigations, I'd still be living in a grubby little house in the back streets of Cardiff.'

'Why don't you tell me what the facts are?' Matthews challenged.

'Like I said, I'm a businessman—'

'You mean, you're a con man,' Matthews interrupted.

'You're not the first person to call me that,' Morgan said, unconcerned. 'It should offend me, I suppose, but then I think of how much money I've got sitting in the bank, and somehow your opinion of me doesn't seem to matter much anymore.' He reached into his jacket, took out a box of small cigars, and lit one up. 'The point is,' he continued, 'what I am *not* is a gangster. I don't surround myself with a team of heavies. I do know a few ex-criminals, but none who've been inside for committing crimes involving violence. So even if I wanted somebody to carry out a murder for me, I wouldn't know where to start looking.'

The problem is, Matthews thought, I believe him.

And then he reminded himself that getting people to believe in him was Morgan's stock-in-trade.

The con man made great show of looking at his gold Rolex.

'I think I've given you quite enough of my valuable time,' he said. 'My final advice to you is to talk to the local fuzz. They'll tell you the same as I've told you. Murder just isn't my style.'

Watching him turn around and walk back towards the house, Matthews felt weighed down by failure. He'd had the man on the ropes at the beginning – he was sure he had – and mentioning the murders should have been enough to force him to his knees.

Yet it hadn't been.

Instead it had seemed to offer him an escape.

So just what *had* Morgan been worried about? Just what guilty secret was he hiding?

Matthews had no idea, nor did Flint – and when the chief inspector told me about it, I didn't know either.

And so it was that Morgan's secret would *remain* secret, until, that is, someone who had more street smarts than the rest of us combined eventually worked it out.

I had approached the whole of the night's operation with logic and forethought. I'd hired a car, rather than use my own, because I needed to be in a vehicle that Marie wouldn't recognize. I'd chosen the Renault 19, because it gave my gammy leg more room than my Ford Granada would have done. And I'd remembered to bring a bottle of water and some sandwiches with me.

Yet my principal thought, as I sat there in the midnight darkness outside Marie's house, was not how clever I'd been, but how stupid.

There were any number of reasons why she might not be in Oxford – she could have gone to visit her family in Ireland, or be working on a case.

So what were the chances that her disappearance was explained by the fact that she was so frightened of meeting me that she would only sneak back to her own flat under the cover of darkness, and leave again at the crack of dawn? The answer, obviously, was practically no chance at all.

Yet there I was – watching and waiting – because when you're desperate, *practically no chance* still seems like pretty good odds.

Sitting alone, in the enclosed world of my rental car, I found myself thinking about the first night we met. At the time, I'd been too grateful it had happened to worry about *why* it had happened, but now – for the first time – I saw just how set up I'd been.

She'd said she knew my name because my name was well-known – but it wasn't, not outside that tiny circle which is the publishing world.

I'd offered to buy her a drink, and she'd insisted on a meal – because that would ensure we spent more time together.

But why had she done it?

If she'd been looking for a friend, why hadn't she chosen someone she'd already met, rather than selecting a complete stranger?

And if she'd wanted me for my body, why hadn't she taken advantage of the numerous opportunities which had been offered to her over the previous two years? God knows, I wouldn't have pushed her away.

So why had she picked me up? And even more important, what had made her decide to drop me so completely now?

I thought of Andy McBride's offer again. We could be in and out of the flat in five minutes, he'd promised me. Five minutes! Three hundred seconds! In that short space of time, I just might be able to resolve all the questions and worries which were eating away at my brain.

I sighed and checked my watch. It was a quarter past three. I would give it till five, then go home and grab a couple of hours' sleep before setting off for work.

NINETEEN

I t was another chocolate-box-pretty morning in the village, and the church clock was just striking ten as Detective Chief Inspector Flint walked up the High Street toward the church.

He had just reached the stocks when the tranquillity of the morning was suddenly shattered by the sound of a powerful car engine being heavily revved. He turned in the direction of the noise and saw a black Jaguar X-JS roaring up behind him.

He recognized the driver immediately, and was not the least surprised when the man brought the shiny new machine to a halt in front of the stocks.

'That's a nice vehicle,' Flint said. 'It's very nice indeed. Had it long, have you?'

Bill Harper shook his head. 'I only took delivery of it last night, as a matter of fact.'

'You must have a very optimistic nature, Mr Harper,' Flint commented.

'Optimistic nature? I'm not sure I'm following you.'

'I'm sure this is a very suitable car for a joint managing director . . .'

'Yes, you have to keep up appearances when you're a serious player in the business world.'

'. . . but I would have thought it was well beyond the reach of a mere executive assistant. Yet that's what you must have been when you ordered it – and at that time, the possibility of making the leap that you have, in fact, made, must have seemed very remote.'

Bill Harper laughed uneasily. 'Oh, I see what you're getting at. The Jag wasn't ordered for me at all. It was going to be Tony Conroy's new company car. But he doesn't need it now, does he? And so it's mine.'

'There are some people who could fall into a shit heap and

come up smelling of roses,' Flint said dryly. 'So what are you doing in the village at this time of the morning, Mr Harper? Just showing off your new wheels?'

'No, of course not – that would be totally irresponsible. The fact is, I needed to talk to you, and at the police station, they told me that this was where I'd find you.'

'And what would you like to talk to me *about*?' Flint wondered.

'Are you still looking for Paul Taylor?' Harper asked.

More than just looking for him, Flint thought. There was a general alert out. But the search lacked both the intensity and the urgency – not to mention the resources – which would have been devoted to it if the object of the search had been a missing child, because Taylor *wasn't* a child – and anyway, they simply didn't have enough on him to warrant that sort of operation.

'I asked you if you were still looking for him,' Harper repeated, in a tone which said he didn't like to be kept waiting, especially by a man who probably earned a quarter of the salary he was now pulling in.

'I don't see how it's any business of yours, sir,' Flint said, 'but I believe it's fairly common knowledge that we'd appreciate the opportunity of having a few words with Mr Taylor.'

'You haven't really answered my question, you know,' Bill Harper pointed out.

'No, I haven't, have I?' Flint agreed.

For a moment, it looked as if Harper would slide his new toy into gear and drive away. Then, though he gave Flint a look which showed both anger at him as a man and disappointment in him as a chief inspector, he seemed to decide not to abort his mission.

'The reason I was asking about the search is that I think Paul Taylor might be much more involved in this case than you seem to imagine,' he said. 'I also think that you should extend your search – if indeed, since you seem to be so cagey about it, you're actually conducting one – to the continent.'

'Are you telling me that you know for certain he's done a runner?' Flint demanded.

Harper smiled smugly. 'Let us just say that I consider it a very distinct possibility.'

'Based on what?'

Bill Harper ran his hands lovingly over the leather-covered steering wheel of his new car.

'It was something that one of my accountants came up with, which set me on the trail,' he said.

One of *my* accountants, Flint repeated silently. Only a few days earlier, Harper had been nothing more than an executive assistant, but now he was talking as if he had built up Conroy Enterprises single-handed.

'And what, exactly, did this accountant of *yours* find?' he asked.

'Both Paul and I have drawing rights on the company's current account,' Harper explained. 'It's a necessary mechanism for the smooth running of the business, because there are circumstances when one of us needs to make a large cash payment and—'

'There are times when *I'd* really enjoy a nice leisurely trip round the houses, sir,' Flint interrupted him, 'but right now I'm investigating a murder case, and I really would be grateful if you'd come straight to the point.'

Just for an instant, the expression on Harper's face was of a man who was not as confident and self-assured as he appeared to be. But it didn't last. He was a joint managing director of a large and expanding business now. He didn't need to feel intimidated by a mere policeman.

'A couple of hours after the crash, Paul Taylor made a substantial withdrawal from that account,' he said.

He waited for Flint to ask him how much.

'How much?' Flint said.

'Twenty thousand pounds – which is the largest amount either us can withdraw without it being countersigned by one of the directors. But what is even more significant – at least to me – is *where* he drew it out. Can you guess which bank he used, Mr Flint?'

You bastard! Flint thought. You cocky, smug bastard. I'd like to shake you until your teeth rattled.

'He wouldn't have withdrawn the money from a branch of a bank in Bristol, would he, Mr Harper?' he asked levelly.

Harper nodded. 'That's right. In fact it was the branch closest to Temple Meads railway station.'

Having gone down to the village store to replenish his stock of sweets – and settled on a mixed mint selection and a bag of chocolate éclairs – Flint wondered what he should do next.

'The problem was, Rob,' he would tell me later, 'I knew in my gut that the roots of the murder lay buried in either the village or Oxford, but I hadn't got a bloody clue where to start digging. And that meant that instead of making things happen, I was forced to hang around, like a spare prick at a wedding, and hope that when something *did* happen, I'd notice it.'

As he walked back towards the church, he found himself thinking about Paul Taylor again.

Could the case really be as simple as Bill Harper had implied it was? Could Paul Taylor have travelled down to Bristol, sneaked into the garage, sabotaged the brakes of the BMW, then taken the money and run?

Why should he have done that?

What could have motivated him to arrange three murders?

He didn't look, on the face of it, to have any reason to want the Conroys dead. Unless, of course, my father had treated him so badly that he wanted his revenge at any cost.

But even that didn't make sense, firstly because from what Flint had learned of my father, he didn't seem to have been the kind of man who could arouse such passion. And secondly, everyone – including the admirable and practical Jo Torlopp – had said Taylor was a gentle man, who wouldn't hurt a fly. Besides, if Taylor *had* wanted to kill him, it would surely have been simple enough to arrange an accident in the village.

Flint reached the pump house next to the pub and wondered where he should go next. Turn to the right, and he would soon reach the home of the late Charles Conroy, the founder of the empire. Turn left, and he would eventually arrive at my sister-in-law's house. For no particular reason, he decided to go left.

Paul Taylor ... Paul Taylor ... Paul Taylor ... Paul-bloody-Taylor.

The name kept running through his brain, matching the rhythm of his footfalls.

The man was supposed to be trying to make a name for himself in business, yet he had asked for – and been granted – a leave of absence just when the company was on the verge of making the most important deal in its history. Why should he have done that? And perhaps even more to the point, whatever had possessed my father to give his permission?

Flint was less than a hundred yards away from my sister-in-law's house when he noticed the black Golf GTI parked outside.

Now that was interesting, he thought – indeed, it could almost be said to be fascinating. Just what the bloody hell was *she* doing back in the village?

Flint reached into his pocket and popped a glacier mint in his mouth. It might be some time before she came out, but he was perfectly prepared to wait.

It was, in fact, less than ten minutes before Lydia's front door opened, the red-haired woman stepped out, and somebody – probably Lydia – closed the door behind her.

Marie walked halfway down the path, stopped to light a cigarette, and saw Flint.

'She wouldn't let me smoke inside,' she said disgustedly. 'Too house-proud.'

'What exactly are you doing here, Miss O'Hara?' the chief inspector asked.

Marie took a deep drag of her cigarette and blew the smoke out through her nostrils.

'What *exactly* am I doing here?' she repeated. 'I'm visiting.'

'I may be wrong, but when we spoke at Charles Conroy's funeral, didn't you tell me that you didn't know any of the family?' Flint asked.

'That's right,' Marie agreed.

'So am I to take it that the nature of your visit to Mrs Conroy was not social?'

Marie sighed. 'You can take it any way you want, Mr Flint.'

'If it wasn't social, it was business,' the chief inspector said doggedly. 'And your business is private investigation. So what I have to ask myself is what Mrs Conroy would need a private detective for.'

He paused, giving Marie time to speak, but she said nothing. 'This wouldn't be connected with the murders by any chance, would it, Miss O'Hara?' he continued.

'If I didn't come to see Mrs Conroy on business, then your question's meaningless,' Marie said, choosing her words with extreme care. 'And if I did come to see her on business, then exactly what we discussed is protected by client confidentiality.'

'I've warned you before, you should be careful not to get mixed up in a police investigation, Miss O'Hara,' Flint said sternly. 'You could lose your licence. You could even go to prison.'

Marie took her keys out of her handbag and unlocked the driver's door of the Golf.

'We must have another drink some time, chief inspector,' she said. 'I owe you one.'

'You like to live dangerously, don't you?' Flint asked. 'You drive a fast car, you smoke too many cigarettes—'

'And you, chief inspector, are rotting your teeth with all those sweets you guzzle,' Marie interrupted him. 'I'll see you around.'

Then she put her key in the ignition and fired up the engine. As she pulled away, the back wheels of her car threw up cinders and small stones.

Flint watched her drive off down the lane at a speed he knew was solely designed to provoke him.

What the hell had she been to see Lydia about? he wondered.

Whatever it was, he doubted very much whether my sister-in-law herself would tell him.

TWENTY

The Georgian carriage clock on my desk – a gift from Andy McBride, which, he assured me, he had paid for 'wi' real money' – said it was a quarter past ten in the morning. I shifted uncomfortably in my chair. Spending the entire night cramped in a car outside Marie's flat had done my injured leg no good at all, and my eyes prickled from lack of sleep.

I picked up a manuscript, already dog-eared from passing through the hands of a dozen publishers, and started to read. It was only when I got to the bottom of the third page that I realized that though my eyes had passed over the words, my brain had received no message at all, and I couldn't even begin to guess what the book was about.

I pushed the manuscript aside and turned my thoughts instead to my brother. His death had become an obsession with me, not only because I missed him, but also because I still believed – perhaps even more strongly now than ever – that there had been some point in the past when the chain of events which led to the crash could have been broken – and that I should have been the one to break it.

I found my exhausted mind wandering back to the day of the board meeting at which I'd been told that my beloved publishing house was to be put at risk for no other reason than to enable my uncle to increase the size of his own personal empire.

I'd stormed out of that meeting and – after I'd failed to persuade Grandfather to reverse his decision – I'd gone back to my father's house, where I was just on the point of pouring myself a very stiff drink when the phone rang.

It was John.

'I thought we might go out for a drink tonight,' he suggested.

'I'm not sure I'm in the mood,' I told him.

'Not in the mood for a drink?' John asked, with mock incredulity. 'I'm willing to bet you've already got one in your hand.'

Despite myself, I laughed.

'Nearly right,' I said. 'Another five minutes, and I'd have been halfway down the world's strongest gin and tonic.'

'Save it for later,' my brother told me. 'I'll pick you up at eight.'

'Will Lydia be coming?' I asked.

'She'd like to,' John said, unconvincingly, 'but she's got another one of her blessed committee meetings to attend. So it'll only be the two of us – just like old times.'

John arrived at exactly eight o'clock. He looked as calm and placid as he normally did, but as I climbed into the passenger seat, I could sense a hidden tension.

'Since you've brought the car, I'm assuming we're not going to the George and Dragon,' I said.

John nodded. 'I'd rather like to get out of the village for a couple of hours, if you don't mind. I thought we could drive over to that little pub in Lower Peover.'

'The one where I first met Lydia?'

'That's right.'

'Why there?' I asked.

'No particular reason,' John replied – and I could tell he was lying.

It was a fifteen-minute drive to the pub, and during the journey, though I got the distinct impression John had something he was bursting to tell me, he said nothing. Even when we were sitting down, with pints in front of us on a copper-topped table, my brother still seemed unwilling to come out with what was on his mind, and it was me who broke the silence.

'What happened after I left the meeting?' I asked.

John shrugged. 'Not much. Uncle Tony said that unless there were any questions, we could consider the business of the day over. Then he told us where to pick up our briefing folders. I've got yours in the boot of the car, if you want it.'

'I don't.'

'That's up to you, Little Brother.' John picked up his pint. In his massive hand, it looked more like a half. 'You didn't do yourself any good by storming out of the meeting like that, you know.'

'It made no difference whether I left or whether I stayed,' I told him. 'My opinion didn't matter. Uncle Tony had it all neatly sewn up before any of us even entered the room.'

'True,' John agreed.

'I can't believe you're taking this all so calmly,' I told him. 'This acquisition is dicey. We're probably over-extending ourselves. The company could quite easily go to the wall, you know.'

John smiled, softly. 'And what if it did go bankrupt? Where would that leave us? Out on the streets with our begging bowls?'

I forced myself to smile back. 'Not quite that,' I conceded.

'Nothing *like* that,' John said. 'Grandfather's a smart man. There's enough private family money, outside the company, for us all to live in modest affluence for the rest of our lives.'

'So what?' I said exasperatedly. 'Doesn't it bother you that you might lose your business?'

'I enjoy my work,' John said, 'but it's certainly not the obsession with me that yours is with you. Perhaps that's because when you've got someone to love, business doesn't really seem that important anymore.'

I remembered John's moment of panic on the morning of his wedding, and the doubts I had entertained myself about Lydia as a suitable partner for my brother. Well, we seemed to have both been wrong – thank God! She wouldn't have done for me – I could never have stomached all her committees and her social gatherings – but if she made John happy that was all that mattered.

But was he right in what he'd implied about me? Was my obsession with Cormorant Publishing only there because I had a great void in my life to fill? If Marie could bring herself to feel for me as I felt for her, would I be spending quite so much time in the office? And would I really care as much as I did about the success of the people I had under contract?

I was experiencing an emotion which was entirely new to me. I found myself envying my brother his happiness – and wishing I could trade places with him.

'You're not listening to me, are you, Rob?' John asked, piercing my bubble of moody introspection.

I jumped slightly. 'Sorry, I was a million miles away for a minute. What did you say?'

John smiled again, but this time there was a sad edge to it.

'It doesn't matter,' he said.

'It does,' I insisted. 'It really does. If something's important to you, then it's important to me, too.'

My brother's smile became more self-conscious.

'I don't think I'd have the nerve to tell you a second time,' he said. 'And anyway, you'll find out soon enough, as it is.'

'Find out what?'

'Something you should have known a long time ago.'

'Don't play games with me,' I said.

'I'm not,' he replied earnestly. 'I'm through with games, and

I'm through with pretending. For the first time in my life, I think I'm actually facing reality.'

'Then tell me about it!' I insisted.

Instead, John had stood up.

'I'll get you another pint,' he said. 'But since I'm driving, I think I'd better switch to orange juice.'

I was still at my desk, my leg still aching, my eyelids drooping – but suddenly my brain was wide awake, because what my sleepy thoughts had drifted into was precisely the thing my active mind had been trying – and failing – to pin down.

This was it!

That conversation in the pub had been just like the conversation I'd had with Jill in front of Warrington railway station, as she set off for Cornwall. It had been the point at which – if I'd been sharper, or cleverer, or more sensitive or . . . or I don't know what – I could have broken the chain.

I rang for black coffee and tried to order my thoughts. It was clear to me now that in that minute or so in which I'd been musing about myself and the great black hole in my own life, John was telling me something vitally important about his. And I'd let him down!

I raised the question of the company again, on the way back to the village.

'Your problem,' I told my brother, 'is that you think Uncle Tony and Philip are going to leave you alone to run your own little empire. But they won't, you know. Uncle Tony will want to show everyone who's boss. And as for Philip – well, every slight that he thinks he received when we were kids will be paid back a hundredfold. You just see how you'll like running your maintenance business with Philip sticking his nose in it every five minutes. See how you'll like going to him and asking permission before you take the smallest decision.'

'It won't be like that,' John said confidently.

I laughed bitterly. 'Do you really think you can fight them off? Do you imagine, even for one second, that you've enough clout of your own to prevent Philip from taking malicious pleasure in turning you into nothing more than a glorified office boy?'

'I'm sure he'd like to do that, but it isn't going to happen.'

I slammed my hand down – hard – on the dashboard.

'Oh, for God's sake, John, grow up!' I said. 'You told me earlier for the first time in your life, you're facing reality – but you're not! You're living in Cloud Cuckoo Land.'

'And the reason it won't happen,' my brother continued calmly, 'is that I won't be around to be turned into anything.'

'And what, exactly, do you mean by that?'

'I mean that I'm resigning. I'm going to let someone else run MCM.'

His words came as a shock. I'd always been the restless one. I was the one who'd made the decision to go to university, instead of joining the family business. It was John, not me, who'd inherited our father's placidity – and it was almost inconceivable to think of him cutting loose.

'When do you plan to make the break?' I asked.

'As soon as Grandfather dies.'

Another shock.

'But he could last for years and years,' I said.

John shook his head. 'You've not been here. You've not seen how frail he really is. He makes an effort for your benefit, because you're never here for long, but he can't keep it up all the time. He'll be lucky – very lucky – if he lasts till Christmas.'

'But if he does hold on longer?'

'Then I'll just have to grit my teeth and bear it, won't I?'

'Why?' I asked. 'What's so important about staying on until he's gone?'

'I don't want to hurt him,' John said simply.

'And you think that leaving the company will hurt him?'

'Perhaps a little – but that's not what I'm talking about.'

'Then what *are* you talking about?'

My brother turned towards me. I couldn't see his face in the darkness, yet it was almost as if he could see me. Worse, it was almost as if he could see right through the skin and the bone into my inner self.

'You really don't know, do you?' he asked. 'I thought for a while that you did and were pretending not to. But you really don't know.'

'Know what?' I asked impatiently.

John shook his head. 'You can be really thick sometimes.'

'Can I?'

'Yes, you can,' my brother said. 'But let's get off the subject,' he continued, and from the tone of his voice I could tell he was smiling. 'Let's talk about where I plan to go when I resign.'

'All right,' I agreed.

'There's this little Greek island. Thira, it's called. Lydia and I went there on our honeymoon, and we both fell in love with it. It's so peaceful – so unspoiled. You don't need a sports car or a deep freezer there. If you want to go down to the market, you walk. And the fish you buy is fresh from the sea.'

'And you think you could be happy there?' I asked.

'I *know* we could be happy there,' John murmured, as if he could already taste the salt air and feel the Mediterranean sun on his back. 'Very, very happy.'

The church clock was just striking twelve as John pulled up in front of our father's house.

I opened the passenger door and climbed out. 'Do you want to come in for a nightcap?' I asked.

My brother shook his head. 'It's late, and I've got a lot to do tomorrow. I think I'll go straight to bed.'

I wished him good night, then watched as he reversed out of the driveway. The thought that I hadn't listened to what he'd had to say earlier was preying on my mind, which was perhaps why I was careless, and dropped my keys.

They fell into the flower bed which ran along the edge of the path, and though there was an almost full moon that night, I couldn't see them from where I was standing.

'Bloody idiot!' I rebuked myself, squatting down and running my hand over the damp soil between the plants.

It only took a couple of seconds to locate the keys, and as I was straightening up again, I heard the sound of my brother's car coming to a stop.

I walked back to the gate. To get home, John should have turned right at the end of School Lane, but instead he had parked just on the corner of it.

What the hell was he playing at? I wondered.

The sound of the car door slamming cut through the quiet night air, and I saw my brother striding towards the High Street.

Perhaps he'd decided that taking a walk might help him think through whatever he'd tried to tell me in the pub.

And perhaps, now we were back in the village where we'd both grown up – and where *he*, at least, felt secure – he might give me a second chance to listen to what he had to say.

I slipped my keys back into my pocket and set off in pursuit.

By the time I reached the church, there was no sign of him or anyone else. I was faced with two choices – I could either assume he'd followed the High Street down to the steep hill which led on to the main road, or I could gamble on him having taken the small lane which led to Grandfather's house. I chose the latter, but two minutes' investigation was enough to convince me I'd made the wrong decision.

Very well then, I thought, I'd see if I could catch up with him on the High Street.

John wasn't to be found there, either, nor on any of the small lanes which ran off it.

I saw nothing in the least sinister in his disappearance, but it was certainly frustrating that I appeared to have missed my chance to make amends for my earlier inattention.

I checked my watch. I'd been wandering around for nearly fifteen minutes, and what now seemed most likely was that John had decided simply to leave his car on School Lane for the night and walk home. I took the path to Smithy Lane, wondering if he was still up, and felt like talking.

Through a chink in the drawn curtains of my brother's lounge, I could see a light shining. I strolled up the path, and was almost at the door when, though that chink, I caught sight of something which froze me in my tracks.

The gap wasn't very wide, and it only gave me a partial view of the lounge, but a partial view was enough to see the couple. They were locked in each other's arms, kissing passionately. From both her hair and her general build, the woman was obviously my sister-in-law. But the man who was holding her tightly to him did not have my brother's bulk. He was slimmer than John – much more elegant. And he looked vaguely familiar.

The lovers broke off from their embrace. Lydia walked across the room, out of my line of vision, and I was left looking at the profile of Paul Taylor, my father's executive assistant.

How long had this been going on? I wondered.

And did John know about it?

I thought back to a conversation – or perhaps, more accurately, a confrontation – that I'd had with Philip at John and Lydia's wedding reception.

'I've only just met this Enid,' Philip had said, referring to the girl he'd been chatting up, 'but I'll have her before the night is out – just see if I don't. Even if I don't get all the way, I'll probably have more luck than your John will.'

'And just exactly what do you mean by that, Philip?'

'You don't know, do you? You really don't know.'

'Know what? Is this something to do with Lydia?'

'Well, bugger me. And I always thought you were the smartest out of the three of us.'

And hadn't John used almost the identical words to me on the drive back from the pub?

'You really don't know, do you? I thought for a while that you did and were pretending not to. But you really don't know.'

Both John and Philip had seen something in or about Lydia that had gone completely over my head.

And yet, earlier, in the pub, John had said not just that he loved her, but that his love made all of the other concerns of life seem of no consequence.

Perhaps that was why they had been planning to move to their Greek island. Perhaps they thought that once they were there, Lydia would have the opportunity to become the kind of wife she should be – the kind of wife that John deserved.

Lydia appeared again, and the couple moved across the lounge towards the hallway. Paul was leaving!

I wanted to stay where I was – to confront them, to say that John was the best man I'd ever known, and they were worth less than the dog shit on his shoe.

But I didn't – because if John knew what was going on, and had decided that it was a price worth paying to keep Lydia, then my intervention might do more harm than good.

And so I stepped quickly back across the road and – like a guilty schoolboy – took cover behind one of the plane trees.

The front door opened and I saw Lydia framed in front of the hall light. She glanced quickly up the lane and then down it, but shrouded in darkness as I was, I was confident she couldn't see me. My sister-in-law stepped to one side, and Paul Taylor emerged. After checking the lane for himself, he turned quickly to the right, and headed for the track to the village which I'd come up.

Lydia closed the front door, and I was about to move off myself when I saw the car headlights coming from the opposite direction to the one Paul had taken.

John! It could only be John!

I heard the church clock strike. It was exactly one o'clock.

Was that a coincidence?

Or had it been pre-arranged? Had John deliberately stayed away until one because he knew Paul Taylor would leave just before then?

John drove his car into the garage and entered the house. I waited until the downstairs lights went off, then set off towards home.

Should I tell my brother that I knew what was going on? I thought, as I walked.

Or should I pretend I didn't know – as he seemed to think I'd been pretending all along?

I hadn't made up my mind by the time I reached my father's house and was no closer to a decision as I pulled up in front of my flat in Oxford the next day.

Why hadn't I told Owen Flint any of this? I asked myself, back in my office, as another pain shot through my bad leg.

I hadn't told him because I hadn't thought it was relevant. With divorce so easy nowadays, no one kills for love. I was sure, too, that Lydia knew John well enough to realize that, even though she was the guilty party, he would still make a generous financial settlement – so money couldn't have been the motive, either. And while I couldn't bring my brother back to life, I could at least prevent people from sniggering at his memory by keeping quiet.

That was how I felt the first time I spoke to Flint, and how I continued to feel until I turned on my car radio later that afternoon and heard that the police urgently wanted to talk to Paul Taylor in connection with three murders, and believed him to be somewhere in the Bristol area.

TWENTY-ONE

t was two days later, the coroner having finally released the bodies, that I drove back to Cheshire to attend the funerals of my father, brother and uncle.

The church was full-to-overflowing for the service. Grandmother was not there – Jo Torlopp had ruled that the strain would be too much for her – but the remaining members of my immediate family, my cousin Philip and sister-in-law Lydia, sat on the front pew next to me.

I listened for a while to the eulogies and opened my mouth when the vicar's words required a response from the congregation, but my mind was not really on the service at all. I was not there to remember the dead – my mission was to seek out justice for them.

Lydia and Paul.

Paul and Lydia.

Had they really plotted to kill my brother? It still didn't make sense that they would have – but if they hadn't, why wasn't Paul Taylor there now, saying just how ludicrous the whole idea was?

We all walked solemnly to the graveyard. My mother's grave had been opened to accommodate my father, and two fresh graves had been dug for my brother and my uncle. We listened to the vicar talk about ashes to ashes and dust to dust, we watched as the coffins were slowly and reverently lowered into the holes, we threw a handful of soil on each of the shiny wooden lids. Then, with a collective sigh, we turned our backs and began the process of getting on with the rest of our lives.

I lost Lydia in the crowd, and by the time I had reached the lychgate there was no sign of her. But that didn't matter because I knew where she was going. She would be at Philip's house, to which Philip – the new patrician of the Conroy family – had summoned us all for post-funeral drinks.

When I reached the house, ten minutes later, Philip was at

the door, greeting new arrivals. In his stylish black silk suit, he looked every inch the grieving son. But I was not fooled – there was a lot of his actress mother in my cousin, and he was doing no more than playing the role.

We exchanged what passed for a dignified handshake, and I made my way to the lounge. A number of people were already there, including Lydia. Another early arrival, Bill Harper, was surrounded by several young executives and quite clearly holding court.

I made a beeline for my sister-in-law, but Harper broke away from the group and stepped in my path.

'I've been taking a close look at the whole set-up in Cormorant Publishing,' he said, 'and it seems to me that what we have are some tremendous possibilities for expansion into a wider market.'

It could have been my cousin talking, only a few days earlier – just before he did a complete volte-face after speaking to this same Bill Harper on the phone.

'Do you really think this is the time and place to discuss business?' I asked coldly.

Bill grinned. 'There's never a time or place when you *shouldn't* talk about business,' he said. 'Not if you want to get on. And my impression of you, Rob, is that you're a man who wants to do just that.'

He was intoxicated, I realized – not rolling drunk, but drunk enough to make him shed what little inhibition he still seemed to have left – and my wisest course would be to end the conversation there.

'What do you mean by "*we* have some tremendous possibilities"?' I heard myself say. 'Philip promised me that I'd have complete freedom to run the publishing house the way I wanted to.'

Bill's grin broadened. 'Philip!' he said contemptuously. 'What does Philip know? And what does Philip matter? He was born with a silver spoon in his mouth, and as long as nobody tries to take it away from him, he'll be perfectly happy.'

'I will not tolerate any interference in the way Cormorant Publishing is run,' I said stiffly.

Bill Harper's smile froze, but did not completely disappear.

'I wouldn't be so dogmatic if I were you, Robbie-Boy,' he said. 'You either work *with* me – or you work *against* me. And if you decide to work against me, don't go conning yourself into thinking that you can rely on Philip for support, because you can't. He'll back me over you every single time. And the sooner you learn that, the easier it will be for you.'

'You'll have to excuse me,' I said, taking one step to the side.

I felt his hand on my arm. 'I haven't finished what I was saying yet,' he snarled.

'But I've finished listening,' I countered. 'And if you think I wouldn't dare hit you because this is a wake, you're wrong. It's what my father and brother would want me to do – in fact, I can almost hear them urging me to take a swing at you right now.'

Harper released his grip. 'I'll talk to you later, when you're feeling more rational,' he said, before turning and re-joining his courtiers.

Lydia had been watching the whole exchange – mainly, I think, because she had already been watching *me* – and as I advanced towards her, she smiled and held out her hand.

'It's good to see you, Rob,' she said.

'How are you, Lydia?' I asked, noncommittally.

'Well, as you can imagine, I've been better,' she said. She looked around the room. 'We need to talk, Rob.'

'That's funny,' I told her. 'I was just about to say exactly the same thing to you.'

'In private,' Lydia said, with emphasis.

'Where do you suggest?'

'I don't suppose Philip would mind if we used his study, would he?'

'I shouldn't think so,' I agreed.

As I followed her down the hallway, I was working out the best way to deal with her. My instinct was to grab hold of her and shake her until she told me the truth – but as personally satisfying as that would have been, it wasn't the way to find out what I wanted to know.

We entered the study. When it had been Uncle Tony's work-place, a large, antique roll-top desk had dominated the room.

To the left of it, there'd been bookcases, weighed down by heavy leather-bound volumes which my uncle had never opened. Facing that had been a plain wall which had been covered with nineteenth-century hunting prints, purchased in bulk, I'd always suspected, by an interior designer who specialized in country themes. Now, the old desk had been replaced by an expensive – but functional – chrome and glass desk, the bookcase held glossy company reports, and the hunting prints had been replaced by flow charts and a whiteboard. King Tony – who had reigned ever so briefly – was dead. Long live King Philip!

Lydia sat on the edge of the desk and crossed her legs. Though I didn't want to look at those legs – the very act of looking seemed almost incestuous – I found my eyes drawn momentarily to them.

They were shapely legs, I thought – very feminine – and I wondered how I could ever have thought of her as boyish.

'I wish I'd done more for John,' my sister-in-law said.

'More?' I repeated.

'Yes. I could have worked so much harder than I did at making him really *count* in the village. I should have pushed him to stand for the parish council. He'd have been bound to be elected. I should have been able to persuade him to join the hunt – with my backing, you know, he'd have stood a good chance of being master in a few years.'

'Perhaps that's true,' I said, 'but would he have cared about those things, one way or the other?' I asked.

'But of course he would. Everyone wants a better position in society,' my sister-in-law said fiercely, 'and anyone who says he doesn't is nothing but a liar.'

There was an air of unreality about the way the conversation was going. We didn't need the privacy of Philip's study to discuss Lydia's social aspirations – and we both knew it. Besides, I sensed that if my sister-in-law wasn't exactly fearful of saying what she had led me into the study to say, she was at least extremely apprehensive about it.

'What's really on your mind, Lydia?' I asked.

But she wasn't ready to tell me yet and, reading her uncertainty, I thought it likely that before she took a leap into the dark, she wanted to prepare some soft ground for her landing.

'They're like a pack of hounds out there, baying for blood,' my sister-in-law said.

'Who are?'

'People.'

'That's a rather broad generalization.'

'Maybe it is – but it's still true.' Lydia paused. 'If I tell you a secret, will you promise to keep it to yourself?'

Ah, the *let me tell you a secret* tactic!

I'd done enough negotiating over the years in Cormorant Publishing to recognize how the tactic was expected to work. The first thing it was designed to do was flatter me – I would, after all, have been entrusted with something that the rest of the world was being denied – and draw me into a camp in which Lydia and I were 'us' and everybody else was 'them'. Then, once my defences were breached, she would attempt to slip something through the gap – in this case, I was betting that she would try to make me feel sorry for her, which could have the additional bonus that it just might stop me from probing for any darker secrets which she'd do almost anything to protect.

The tactic wasn't going to work on me, but before any advance could be made in any direction, I had to give her the chance to employ it.

'Please, Rob, it was hard enough for me to pluck up the nerve to ask that question, and your silence is nearly killing me,' Lydia said.

'If what you're going to tell me has anything to do with my brother's death, then I can't keep quiet,' I said. 'If it hasn't, then I promise you I won't tell another living soul.'

'It's nothing to do with John at all,' Lydia assured me. 'Do you remember, when we first met in that sweet little country pub, that I told you my parents had died in a plane crash?'

'Of course I remember.'

'I wasn't telling the whole truth. Mother did die in the crash, but Father wasn't even on the plane. Not that that made much difference in the long run – he couldn't handle Mother being gone, and within a year of her accident, he'd managed to drink himself to death.'

'That's why no one from your past was invited to the

wedding,' I said, with sudden realization. 'You didn't want any of them shooting their mouths off about your father.'

'That's right,' Lydia agreed, looking down at the floor. 'Most people are so mean and narrow minded that they'll look for *any* way to bring you down. If they'd found out my father was an alcoholic, it would have given them just the weapon they needed.'

Her tactic appeared to be working after all – though not in the way she'd intended. I *did* feel sorry for her – sorry that she was so pathetic that she put such a high value on her social life.

She seemed to sense the change in my mood – and to decide to take advantage of it, while it lasted.

'There's something else I want to tell you,' she said, 'something even John didn't know.'

'Go on,' I said.

'I . . . I was having an affair with Paul Taylor.'

I was almost certain that John *had* known. Why else would he have waited until one o'clock, that night we had gone for a drink in Lower Peover, before returning home?

'Did you ever intend to go with John to his Greek island?' I asked.

'Yes.'

'I don't believe you. I can't see you giving up your garden parties and your committees for that kind of life.'

'You're very harsh,' she said.

'Then convince me I'm wrong.'

'You *are* wrong. Of course I would have missed my parties, but it was what John wanted, and after what I'd done to him – even though he didn't know I'd done it – what John wanted was the most important thing in the world to me. And it wouldn't have been too bad – there's an English community of sorts out there, and I'd soon have got them organized.'

'How did Paul Taylor feel about you leaving him? Or hadn't you got around to telling him the news?'

'I'd told him. That's what my trip to the spa hotel near Bath was really all about.'

'Do you want to spell that out for me?' I asked.

'If I'd broken off the affair here – in the village – there was a chance the whole thing would have blown up in our faces, and John would have been humiliated. What Paul and I needed was a few days together, so he could get used to the idea.'

'Is that what he thought was going to happen?'

'Of course not! He thought we were just slipping away for a dirty weekend, during which he might finally be able to persuade me to leave John.'

'*Did* you tell him it was all over?'

'Yes.'

'And how did he take it?'

'Very badly. He said he couldn't imagine a life without me. I tell you honestly, I was afraid he'd go and do something silly.'

'Like kill your husband?'

'Good God, no! But I was worried that he might kill *himself*.'

'You are aware that there's a nationwide police hunt for him, aren't you?' I asked.

'Yes, I heard it on the radio – but they're only looking for him because they want him to help them with their inquiries.'

'That's code for saying he's their number one suspect.'

Lydia looked as shocked as if I'd just slapped her in the face. 'But they can't possibly think that!' she protested.

'Were you with him on the night before the murder?'

Lydia shook her head 'No. I was where I was supposed to be – at the health farm.'

'So isn't it possible that he decided that if he couldn't have you, John couldn't either? Isn't there a chance that he drove to Bristol that night, snuck into our hotel and damaged the braking system of the BMW that he could easily have found out John would be driving?'

'No!' Lydia said, bunching her hands into tight little balls. 'No, no, no! You don't know him like I do, Rob. He's a gentle person. He'd never be capable of such violence.'

'That's the beauty of a murder like this one,' I pointed out. 'The killer never gets to see the violence he's caused with his own eyes.'

'Paul's a sensitive soul,' Lydia said stubbornly. 'He wouldn't have had to see the crash to imagine what it was like – and he would never have been able to rob three people of their lives.'

'So if he didn't do it, why has he disappeared?'

Lydia shrugged. 'Who knows how his mind was working? Maybe he couldn't face the fuss, on top of everything else that had happened to him. Maybe he thought he was protecting me.'

'Why would he think that?'

'Oh, you know how people always add up two and two and make five – especially the police. Perhaps he thought that if it became public knowledge that we'd been lovers, Chief Inspector Flint would automatically suspect us.'

'Well, when they find him – and they *will* find him, you know – the truth will come out,' I said. 'And it'll look all the worse for having tried to hide it.'

'You're right,' Lydia said with a sigh. 'Isn't it all such a bloody, bloody mess?'

She was saying just what I might have expected her to say in this situation, but somehow it didn't quite ring true to me.

The simple fact was that she seemed more relaxed than she had a few minutes earlier – and I had no idea why that should be.

I was walking up the High Street when I saw the car coming towards me. It was a black Golf GTI which I'd seen many times before. I recognized the driver, too, because even from a distance the shock of red hair was unmistakable. My perverse nature stopped me from waving or showing any other outward sign of recognition, but the driver had seen me and slowed down to a halt.

'I think we'd better go and have a drink somewhere,' she said to me, through her open window.

We sat facing each other across one of the rough wooden tables outside the George and Dragon – more like adversaries than friends.

'What are you doing here in the village?' I demanded angrily.

'I came to see you,' Marie said.

'Why now?' I asked, my anger cranking up by the second. 'You never bothered to visit me in hospital, so why now?'

Marie lit a cigarette. 'I rang the hospital just after you were admitted,' she said. 'They told me your injuries weren't serious.'

'And you never thought to ask to be put through to me?'

'I've . . . I've had troubles of my own,' Marie stammered, uncharacteristically. 'I couldn't face talking to you just then.'

'What kind of troubles?' I asked harshly – unforgiving. 'An income tax demand? The clutch going on your Golf? I imagine it must have been at least as serious as that for you to neglect me.'

Marie's eyes were reddening. 'There's been a death in my family, too,' she said.

'Who?'

'My father.'

I felt rivers of shame course through my whole body. 'I'm sorry,' I said. 'I didn't know. Was it . . . was it a . . .?'

'A quick death?' she supplied. 'Yes, he didn't suffer for long.'

'At least you've that to be thankful for,' I said inanely.

'I was never really very close to him,' Marie said musingly. 'But in a way that makes it even worse. Now he's gone I keep feeling so . . . so guilty. Do you know what I mean?'

Oh God, did I ever! I felt guilty that I never seemed to be able to protect anyone I loved. That I had survived while my brother and father had died. That, in the middle of her own grieving process, Marie had had the courage to come and try to share mine – only to be treated as if she were nothing more than pond scum.

'Forgive me,' I pleaded.

'It's already forgotten,' she told me, and I didn't think I had ever loved her more than I did at that moment.

'Where are you planning to spend the night?' I asked.

'I booked a room in a hotel in Knutsford,' Marie said.

'But that's miles away! Why don't you cancel it?'

Marie checked her watch.

'It's far too late now. I'll have to pay, whether I use the room or not.'

'So lose the money – or let me pay it,' I said. 'Whichever you prefer.'

'And where would I sleep if it wasn't at the hotel?'

'At my father's house.'

'I don't think so,' Marie said seriously.

'There are five bedrooms,' I pointed out. 'I'll be using one. That leaves four spare.'

She shook her head. 'It's not a good idea.'

'What's the matter?' I asked, trying to hide my annoyance as best I could. '*Why* isn't it a good idea? Do you think I'll burst into your room at three o'clock in the morning, and try to have my wicked way with you? Can't you trust me? Even for one night?'

'Oh, I can trust *you*,' Marie said. 'I've known you long enough to be sure of that.'

'Well, then?'

A strange, crooked smile came to her face. 'What I'm not sure of is just how much I trust myself,' she said. She stood up. 'And now if you'll excuse me, I have to go to the toilet.'

I watched her disappear inside the pub and noted that I was not the only man admiring the view.

Women were an enigma to me, I decided. I didn't understand Marie – and I certainly didn't understand Lydia!

I tried to puzzle out exactly what had gone on during my talk with my sister-in-law. What had she been worried about at the beginning of the conversation? And what had caused her to suddenly relax?

As I saw things now, it was almost as if she'd been more eager to learn what I *didn't* know, rather than find out what I *did*? And in her need to do that, she'd been willing to both confess to her affair *and* place Paul and herself close to the murders.

So just what was the secret she was trying to hide? And what could possibly make it more important than the secrets which – after a show of reluctance – she'd had absolutely no qualms about revealing?

'You look very deep in thought,' said a voice, and looking up I saw that Marie had returned to the table. 'What's on your mind? Is it your brother?'

'No, it isn't,' I replied. 'As I matter of fact, I was thinking about my sister-in-law, Lydia.'

'Ah yes,' Marie said. 'The lady of the manor.'

A sudden thought struck me. 'I've told you quite a lot about her, haven't I?' I asked.

'You've told me quite a lot about *all* your family.'

Yes, I had, hadn't I? I'd fallen completely into the trap

which Jill had warned me about so many years earlier, and if
Marie had listened to what I was saying as keenly as she
seemed to, she probably knew almost as much about the
Conroys as I did.

Yet what did I really know about Lydia? I could talk about
her snobbery and social climbing, but her life before she came
to the village was a complete mystery to me. And how could
I make up my mind about whether or not she'd had anything
to do with my brother's death, when I had no knowledge of
what it was that had moulded her into the person she'd become?

'I may have some more work for you,' I told Marie.

'Investigative work?' Marie answered cautiously.

'That's right.'

'And what would it involve?'

The caution was still there.

'I want you to check into my sister-in-law's background.'

Marie took a packet of cigarettes out of her handbag and lit
one.

'I can't do it,' she said.

'Why not?'

'Because I have all the work I can handle at the moment.'

'So why didn't you say that in the first place, instead of
sitting there and letting me waste my breath?' I asked.

'You're right, that's what I should have done,' Marie agreed.

'Or is it a case of you wanting to find out what specific job
I was offering you before you knew whether you were going
to turn it down?' I probed.

Marie hesitated. 'We're talking as friends here, aren't we,
Rob?' she said finally.

'Of course.'

'And as friends, I would expect you to hear what I'm about
to tell you in confidence.'

'Again, of course.'

'And not to use the information in any way which might
damage me or my business relationships?'

'Why are you speaking all this legalese?' I asked. 'Everything
you've asked goes without saying. You should know that by
now.'

Marie took a long drag of her cigarette.

'All right. The other reason I can't work for you at this particular time is that it would mean I'd be investigating one of my own clients.'

'Lydia!' I exclaimed. 'You're working for Lydia!'

'Yes, I am.'

'Since when?'

'That's not really relevant, is it?'

'And what has she hired you to do?'

Marie shook her head, and her glorious curls wafted gently from side to side. 'You know I can't tell you that,' she said.

'It's something to do with Paul Taylor, isn't it?'

'No comment.'

'There's an ongoing police investigation, for God's sake!' I exploded.

'Then I'll have to tread very carefully, won't I?'

'You could go to gaol. You realize that, don't you?' I reached in my jacket pocket for my cheque book. 'Look, if you want money, you know you only have to ask me.'

Her eyes flashed with real Irish anger.

'If I need money, I'll work for it,' she said. Then a smile crept on to her face. 'Don't worry, Rob. It'll all work out for the best.' She checked her watch. 'It's getting late. Time I was going. Thanks for the drinks.'

She stood up and walked towards her car.

'When will I see you again?' I called after her.

She turned and gave me one last smile. 'I'll be in touch.'

I watched her drive away in a state which was something close to shock. Why, I asked myself, had she agreed to work for Lydia? And even more to the point, what had been Lydia's purpose in hiring her?

As I walked up the path to my late brother's home, I remembered the night I had peered in through a chink in the curtains and seen my sister-in-law locked in the arms of Paul Taylor, and I felt my anger rising again.

I hammered on the door with my fist and heard the sound of high heels clicking on the polished wood hall floor. Then the door swung open and Lydia was standing there. She had changed out of her widow's weeds and was now wearing tan trousers and a yellow blouse which was perhaps a little tight across her firm bosom.

She didn't seem very pleased to see me standing there.

'I've already said all I needed to say to you, and now I'd like some time to come to terms with my loss, Rob,' she said, making no sign of inviting me in. 'I would have thought you'd appreciate that, without having to be told.'

'Did you hire Marie O'Hara?' I demanded.

'Whether or not I hired Miss O'Hara is really none of your business,' Lydia said, speaking slowly and carefully.

'It is if it's anything to do with my brother,' I answered hotly.

Lydia threw back her head and laughed so hard that I almost reached out and slapped her.

'What's so bloody funny?' I shouted.

Lydia calmed down a little. 'You are,' she told me. 'It's funny that, though you're pretending to represent John's interests, that isn't why you're here at all.'

'Isn't it? Then why *am* I here?'

'You're here because of Marie O'Hara. You're doing your big protective man bit, aren't you? And the *reason* you're doing it is because you're in love with her.'

I could have denied it, but I was quite sure that my face had already given me away.

'Yes, I am in love with her,' I admitted.

'And do you think that *she's* in love with you?' my sister-in-law asked nastily. 'Or is her interest in you nothing more than camouflage for her interest in the family as a whole?'

I had not been expecting her to say that – or anything like it – and the whole idea hit me like a bolt of lightning.

'Her interest in the family?' I repeated, to give me time to recover.

'Yes, that's what I said. I've only talked to her on a couple of occasions, but it was perfectly obvious to me, right from the start. You've been seeing her for some time. You must have noticed.'

'I noticed it,' I said reluctantly, because now I thought about it, it was not so much a case of me wanting to talk about the family, but Marie encouraging me to. 'But if she has shown any interest in the Conroys, that may be because we're so different from her own family.'

Lydia laughed again. 'That sounds so weak and feeble that you don't even believe it yourself,' she said.

She was right, of course. It was feeble, and I wondered how I could have gone so long without questioning why Marie seemed to take such an interest in us. But the answer was obvious – I didn't question her because I was frightened of what she might say.

'Do you want to know why *I* think she's so interested?' Lydia asked.

No, something inside me screamed. No, I don't want to hear it at all!

And yet there was a part of me which said it was time – finally – to face the truth.

'By all means tell me your theory, Lydia, if that's what you really want to do,' I said.

'Are you sure you're strong enough? After all, you were in the nuthouse for two whole years the last time you lost a woman.'

She was paying me back for what she thought I'd put her through in Philip's study, I suddenly realized. Now she didn't need anything from me anymore – and I still had no idea what it was she *had* needed me for earlier – she was taking her pound of flesh.

'Come on, let's hear it,' I said – praying that her theory would be so ludicrous that I could just laugh it off.

'I was going to tell you, but now I don't think I will,' Lydia said. 'After all, I worked it out for myself – and I'm not even from the village. It should be *much* easier for you.'

'Why would it be easier for me?'

Lydia shook her head in mock dismay. 'You're a clever man, Rob,' she said. 'In fact you've probably got more brains than the rest of the Conroys combined. But you've never really understood what makes other people tick – and I don't suppose now you ever will.'

It was her parting shot, and with it she turned her back on me and closed the door.

It was only when I was halfway down Smithy Lane that I realized how completely she'd outmanoeuvred me. By skilfully steering the conversation towards my relationship with Marie, Lydia had managed to keep well away from any discussion of what *her* relationship was with Marie – and I'd let her get away with it!

So what was I left with – apart from the ashes of my own failure to take command of the situation?

I knew that Lydia was employing Marie, and I was almost certain that the work was somehow connected with Paul Taylor – but that was about it.

It was then that I had the revelation that brought me to a complete halt.

'You bloody fool, Marie,' I groaned.

Paul Taylor wasn't missing at all – at least, as far as Lydia was concerned. She knew exactly where he was, but she didn't dare contact him herself, in case the police were watching her. So she was using my Marie as a go-between – to deliver messages and keep his spirits up.

'Why, Marie?' I asked the empty lane. 'Why, in God's name, did you ever decide to run such a risk?'

I had to do something to save her from her folly, and the only thing I could think of was to find Paul myself – find him and bribe him not to mention Marie's name when I handed him over to the police.

Yes, that might work. The problem was that I had no idea where to start looking.

I took a deep breath and tried to clear my mind. If I were in Lydia's shoes – if I were doing my best to keep *Marie* out of the hands of the police – where would I choose to hide her?

Not in Bristol or some other large town that neither of us knew our way around, that was for certain. No, to hide her effectively, I would have chosen familiar territory.

Oxfordshire would have been my first thought, but it would have been the police's first thought, too, and it wouldn't take them long to track her down. And once I had eliminated the place where I lived, there was only one possibility left – the place where I *used to* live.

I would hide Marie in Cheshire – and Lydia would be hiding Paul somewhere in Lancashire!

TWENTY-TWO

B y eight o'clock on the morning after the funerals, I had already put a dozen miles between me and the village and was heading north on a desperate mission to save my Marie from her own stupidity.

As I turned on to the M6, I ran through the logic of my argument one more time. If Lydia was hiding Paul, she would have chosen somewhere she knew well – and the place she probably knew best of all was a village in Lancashire where she was brought up.

Of course there might not be any such village, I cautioned myself. She said she came from a Lancashire village, but she could have been lying about that as she seemed to have lied about much else.

But I didn't think it was a lie, because though she mainly spoke with the lazy drawl of the county set, her accent did slip occasionally, revealing traces of the Lancashire twang that she normally kept hidden.

'You're looking for a needle in a haystack,' said a mocking voice in my head. 'Worse than that – you're looking for a specific needle in a stack made up of nothing *but* needles.'

'It's not as bad as that,' I said aloud, to encourage myself.

And it wasn't – quite.

My task would have been considerably easier if I'd known the name of the village, but I didn't, and if one thing was certain, it was that Lydia herself wasn't going to tell me.

The Lancashire telephone directory offered no leads, either. There was not a single listing under the name of Hornby Smythe in it – though since Lydia had told me she was the last surviving member of the family, that fact was hardly surprising.

So given that the obvious avenues were denied to me, I would have to go about things another way. From my study of the ordinance survey map, I had discovered there were seventy-five villages – some almost big enough to be described as small towns, others barely justifying the title of hamlets – within the county boundaries. It would take one hell of a long time to visit them all and conduct the necessary enquiries – perhaps *too* long if the police came up with the same idea as I had – but it seemed to me to offer the only chance I had.

There was no more than a narrow track running along the south end of the mere, which made the journey from the road to the edge of the water – across a ploughed field – somewhat difficult for the police Land Rover, the three patrol cars and the ambulance.

By the time Flint arrived – steering the Ford Escort he'd borrowed from the police car pool along the tracks previously gouged out by the earlier vehicles – the area had been cordoned off, and uniformed constables were posted around the boundary to discourage the sightseer ghouls who were already starting to appear.

Flint got out of the car and walked over to the sergeant who seemed to be in charge.

'Where's the man who found the body?' he asked, showing the sergeant his warrant card.

The other man looked uncertain about how to handle this situation. 'Since you're from another force, sir, I'm not sure I can . . .' he began.

'It's all right, I've got full clearance from your chief super,' Flint assured him.

The sergeant nodded. 'In that case, sir, he's in the Land Rover – him *and* his dog. Do you want me to come with you?'

'No,' Flint said, 'I think I can handle it on my own.'

The man – who looked to be around fifty – was sitting in the passenger seat of the Range Rover, and the dog – a black Labrador – was sprawled contentedly over his knees.

'You're Mr Willets, are you?' Flint asked.

'Yes.'

'And how are you feeling?'

'I was a bit shaken at first,' Willets confessed. 'Well, anybody would be, wouldn't they? But one of the constables gave me a flask of hot sweet tea, and I'm feeling much better now.'

Flint nodded. 'What I'd like you to do, Mr Willets, is tell me the whole story, starting at the beginning. Don't leave anything out, however trivial it might seem. Do you understand?'

'Yes.'

'Off you go, then.'

'I'm a teacher,' Willets said. 'As a matter of the fact, I'm the headmaster of the village primary school.' He paused. 'I don't know why I said that – it's probably of no interest to you at all.'

'Don't go editing yourself on my account,' Flint told him. 'Just say whatever comes into your head.'

'Unless the weather is really terrible, I always bring Lucy down to the mere before school starts. It's her favourite walk, because she gets to splash about in the water.' Willets paused again. 'Have you seen where I found the body?'

'Not yet,' Flint admitted. 'I thought the most important thing was to talk to you, while everything was still fresh in your memory.'

'In that case, if what I'm going to tell you is to make any sense, you'll need to know a little about the physical geography.'

'Fair enough.'

'On most of this side of the mere, the field slopes down to the water, but there are a few points where there's an overhang, so you can't actually see the beach from the path, and those are the points where most courting couples go.'

'Got it,' Flint said.

'So I'm walking along, and Lucy's paddling in the lake, and when she comes up the bank, she's got what looks like a piece of cloth in her hand. I tell her to bring it to me, but, of course, she doesn't. What she wants is for me to chase her, though we both know I've no chance of catching her. But it's early in the morning, and I'm not quite as awake as she is, so I offer her a bribe, instead.'

'A dog biscuit,' Flint guessed.

'A dog biscuit,' Willets confirmed. 'So she drops the bit of cloth at my feet, and I can now see it's a pair of underpants – and not the sort of underpants a lad would wear, but the kind you buy when you've finally decided you're an adult. Anyway, I had a quiet chuckle to myself.'

'Why?'

'Because the fact that he'd taken his underpants off meant that he was down there for sex, and any grown up who has sex on a damp beach, rather than in a comfortable bedroom, is only doing it because he doesn't have any other choice.'

'In other words, he's conducting an extra-marital affair,' Flint said.

'Exactly. And I had this mental picture of him going home and telling his wife he'd had to work late at the office, then taking off his trousers and realizing – at the same time she does – that he's not wearing underpants.'

'When did you realize it was something much more serious than that?' Flint asked.

'Lucy ran down the bank again, and when she came back, she was carrying a shirt in her mouth, and it struck me that while a man might forget to put on his underpants in a post-coital haze, he wasn't going to forget his shirt. So I backtracked a few yards to where the slope was gentler and went down to the beach – and that's when I saw him.'

'Describe what you saw.'

'He was naked, and he was lying in the shallow water, face-down. I grabbed him by the ankles, pulled him out and turned him over. I could see he was dead even before I checked his pulse, but what really shook me was that he wasn't a stranger – he was someone I saw nearly every day.'

I waited patiently in line at the small sub-post office in the village just on the Cumbrian border, and when it came to my turn to be served, I made sure of winning the cooperation of the old woman who ran the store by ordering enough provisions for the bill to come to at least twenty-five pounds.

It was as I was handing over the money over to her that I produced a photograph of Lydia.

'I'm looking for a friend of mine who used to live around here,' I said earnestly. 'I've somehow lost contact with her, but I thought that if I could find some of her relatives, they might be able to give me her address.'

The old woman behind the counter squinted at the picture. 'What's her name?' she asked.

'Lydia,' I said. 'Lydia Hornby Smythe.'

The postmistress sniffed – disapprovingly. 'Pretty posh name for anybody living round here,' she said.

'But does she look familiar?' I persisted.

The old woman examined the picture again, then handed it over to a man with a red face, who was waiting to be served.

'Do you know this girl, Tom?' she asked.

The red-faced man studied the photograph. 'Never seen her in my life,' he said decisively.

'Same here,' the old woman agreed. 'I don't know where this friend of yours comes from, but it's certainly not from these parts.'

I thanked the two of them for their help and left the shop. Back in my car, I put a neat cross through the name of the village on the map and worked out which one I was going to visit next.

I looked at the two plastic bags sitting on the passenger seat, filled with soap and shampoo, tins of baked beans and tubes of shoe polish. I'd have to dump them before I buttered up another shopkeeper by buying a similar amount, but if I did that in the village, I'd only be drawing attention to myself.

And that was the last thing I needed.

I turned the ignition key and slipped the car into gear.

Owen Flint and his sergeant stood at the top of the bank, watching the activity on the beach below. The whole of the area around the mere had been sealed off by police security tape, and in the field which led down to the water, at least two dozen uniformed constables were carrying out a painstakingly careful search for clues. A police frogman had just emerged from the water and was shaking his head, while Inspector Hawkins and the local top brass were talking seriously, close to where the body had been found.

'I see problems,' Owen said, popping an Uncle Joe's Mint Ball into his mouth.

'What kind of problems?' asked Sergeant Matthews, who had arrived in Cheshire only an hour earlier.

'Territorial problems,' Owen replied, after running his tongue around the edge of the black sweet. 'Up to now, the Cheshire police have been quite happy to have us do all the investigating, because the murders took place on our patch. This new death could change everything.'

'No doubt it *is* murder, then, sir?' Matthews asked.

Flint shook his head. 'The police surgeon who examined the corpse says he's got a contusion on the back of his skull as big as a duck's egg. It's too early for him to finally commit himself, but he thinks the murder weapon was a flat piece of metal – possibly an iron bar. So, like I said, the boundaries between us and local coppers are suddenly quite blurred.'

'Isn't it possible that the two cases aren't even connected?' Sergeant Matthews asked.

'They're connected,' Flint replied.

But he didn't feel quite as confident as he sounded. The prime suspect in the killings of Edward, Tony and John Conroy still had to be Paul Taylor, yet wasn't it stretching things just a little too far to argue that Taylor had slipped quietly into the village in the middle of the night, committed another murder, then slipped quietly out again?

'Perhaps Paul Taylor didn't kill the Conroys after all,' Matthews suggested. 'Perhaps none of them was ever the intended victim.'

'Go on,' Flint encouraged.

'Say it was Bill Harper who was intended to die all along, and when he survived the crash, it was just a case of the killer waiting for another opportunity to come along.'

'You're forgetting the fact that the Jaguar in which Bill was supposed to be travelling broke down,' Flint reminded his sergeant. 'That was an act of God. There's no way the killer could have known about it in advance.'

'The boffins in Bristol might have got it wrong,' Matthews said, reluctant to abandon his theory. 'Perhaps the Jaguar *had* been tampered with, and they just didn't notice it.'

'But if the intended victim was Bill Harper, why didn't the killer just interfere with the Jag's brakes and leave the BMW alone?' Flint asked.

The chief inspector glanced down at the top brass conference which was going on below them. Inspector Hawkins had detached himself from the group and was heading in their direction.

'My boss has been on the phone to your boss for the last half hour, and between them, they've decided on a joint operation,' the local policeman said, as he drew level with the two Welsh detectives.

'And who'll be in charge?' Flint asked.

Hawkins grinned. 'They were a little vague about that.'

Yes, that was only to be expected, Flint thought, because this was the kind of investigation that the press might soon start calling 'incompetent' – and neither of their bosses would want to be too closely associated with it once the shit started to fly.

'I'm sure we'll work out some arrangement between us,' he said to Hawkins. 'Would you mind if I finish this little chat with my lad before I bring you up to speed on the way our minds are moving?'

'No problem,' Hawkins assured him.

'So where were we, sergeant?' Flint asked Matthews. 'Oh yes, here's a possibility we've never considered before. What if it wasn't a question of trying to kill just the people in the Jag or the ones in the BMW? What if the killer – for some twisted reason of his own – wanted to get rid of the whole lot of them? He got three of them the first time, now he's added Harper to his list and . . . Jesus!'

And that was when my old friend Owen Flint started to get seriously worried about me.

It must have been just after his discussion with Matthews and Hawkins that Owen Flint made the first call to me. I ignored it, as I ignored the five or six other calls he made in the next hour and, in the end, I switched my mobile phone off.

By early afternoon, I had crossed off four villages from my list and was driving towards the fifth when I heard the news item on my car radio which made my blood run cold.

'In further developments following the murder of Cheshire businessman Bill Harper,' the newsreader said, 'the Cheshire police would like to interview Mr Robert Conroy, whose current whereabouts are unknown. Mr Conroy is believed to be driving a Ford Granada, licence plate number . . .'

My hands were suddenly gripping the steering wheel so tightly that it almost felt as if I would crush it to powder.

Bill Harper was dead!

And the police wanted to talk to me!

Could they really believe that I was involved?

But what they believed or did not believe was an irrelevance. I couldn't afford to be in police custody, even for a day, because, for Marie's sake, I had to find Paul Taylor before they did.

TWENTY-THREE

Susan Harper – Bill Harper's widow – was dressed in jeans and an old sweater. She sat on the edge of the sofa in the living room of her executive-style detached house at the edge of the village, with her arms folded across her chest and her hands clasping her forearms as if to ward off the cold. She looked like a thirteen-year-old kid who'd just been told that her dog had been run over, Flint thought.

'We need to know what your husband was doing down by the mere last night, Mrs Harper,' Inspector Hawkins said.

'He was swimming,' the young woman told him. 'He . . . he really liked to swim.'

'And what time did he go for this swim of his?'

'It was around eleven o'clock. I know that, because the late film was just starting on BBC1.'

'Bloody funny time to go swimming,' Hawkins said.

'He always swam at night. He preferred swimming in the nude, you see, and since he didn't want to offend other people, he left it until after dark.'

'Weren't you worried when he didn't come back?'

'I didn't know he hadn't come back. The film on the television wasn't very good, so I decided to go straight to bed.'

She was lying, Flint thought. But why was she lying? She was no killer – he'd stake his professional reputation on that. She wasn't even someone who'd *conspire* with a killer. So just what was she covering up?

'When he went down to the mere, did you ever go with him, Mrs Harper?' he asked.

Susan Harper shook her head. 'He was quite happy to go on his own, and I don't like getting into cold water.'

'Tell us about your friends,' Hawkins said.

The question seemed to bewilder Susan Harper. 'Well, there's the Conroys . . .' she began.

'I don't mean your husband's business acquaintances,' Hawkins interrupted her, probably not intending to be quite as sharp as he sounded. 'I'm talking about people you saw socially.'

'Perhaps, in this case, that's the same thing,' Flint suggested.

Susan Harper smiled gratefully.

'That's right,' she agreed. 'Bill says . . . Bill *said* . . . that it was always a good thing to mix business with pleasure. That's why, when we entertained, it was always somebody from the company. And when we went out, it was usually because we'd been invited by people Bill worked with.'

'How would you describe his mental state in the last week or so?' Flint asked.

Susan Harper brushed a stray strand of hair away from her eye.

'I'm not quite sure I know what you mean,' she confessed.

I mean, did he feel threatened? Flint thought. Did he act like a man who thought he might get his brains bashed in someday soon?

But he knew he couldn't be as blunt as that with someone in Susan Harper's fragile emotional state.

'Well, for example, he must have been excited about his promotion, mustn't he?' he said – not because he expected her answer to be very revealing, but simply as a way of getting her talking. 'And since it's not every young businessman who goes from being a humble executive assistant to joint managing director in one mighty bound, I should imagine he would have been surprised, too.'

'He wasn't surprised, actually,' Susan Harper said. 'Not at all.'

It was at this point that he felt goosebumps, Flint would tell me later.

'Obviously Bill wasn't surprised when it was *announced*,' he said, 'because Philip Conroy would have told him in advance, but there must have some point at which he said something like, "You'll never guess what position I'm going to be promoted to, Susan".'

'No,' Susan Harper said. 'He never said anything like that. But then, he never discussed business with me anyway. "Men take care of business, and women take care of the home," he'd tell me. He was very old fashioned, in some ways.'

He sounded like a bloody Neanderthal – in *most* ways – Flint thought.

Susan Harper frowned.

She's trying to think of something useful to say, Flint told himself – she may have lied before, but she really wants to help me now.

'There was one occasion when he seemed excited,' Susan said.

'Tell me about it.'

'He rang me up and told me that next year, we'd go to the Caribbean for our holidays. He said that was where all the jet set went. I asked how we could possibly afford it, and he told me not to worry, because we were going to have plenty of money from now on.'

'You say he *rang* you. Where was he ringing you from? Was he in his office?'

'No,' Susan said, 'he was calling from the hospital in Bridgend.'

'How long after the crash would this have been?'

'It was the same day.'

So even before Philip Conroy had become the new boss of Conroy Enterprises, Bill Harper had been confident he'd secured a first-class seat on the gravy train.

How was that possible?

I was tuned into Radio Two, seeking distraction from my predicament in the music that I'd listened to when I was young and still hopeful.

It wasn't working!

I needed more than a few songs from the likes of 10CC and Rod Stewart to make me forget – if only temporarily – that I was a fugitive from justice.

In fact, I was still hyper-aware of my situation. The driver of every car that passed me on the other side of the road seemed to be looking at me strangely, and I found myself continually gazing into my rear-view mirror to see if people in the vehicles behind me were noting down my registration number.

I'd only been on the news once, I told myself, and even then, the announcer hadn't specified where I was, because nobody *knew* where I was. So it was surely unlikely that the whole population of Lancashire had been galvanized into action, and was now determined to hunt me down like a dog. It certainly wouldn't have galvanized me if I'd heard a similar message about someone else. I wouldn't now be spending my time examining the face of every man I saw, and wondering if he was the one the police were looking for.

The petrol gauge on my dashboard showed I was getting very low on juice, and when I saw a country garage with three petrol pumps in its forecourt, I signalled that I was about to pull into it.

'It's only been broadcast once,' I kept repeating as a kind of safety mantra. 'It's only been on the air that one time.'

And then the programme I'd been listening to switched over to the news desk – and the treacherous newsreader said, 'The Cheshire police would like to interview Mr Robert Conroy, whose current whereabouts are unknown. Mr Conroy is believed to be driving a Ford Granada . . .'

I switched off the radio as I pulled on to the forecourt, but there was no guarantee that the same programme wasn't playing in the garage workshop.

I watched as the stocky middle-aged man in grease-streaked overalls made his way leisurely from the workshop to the pumps, and was acutely aware of the fact that he might already have noticed that the number plate of the car was the same as the one which the newsreader on the radio had said was being driven by a wanted man.

An almost overwhelming urge was building up in me to switch on the engine again, hit the accelerator, get the hell out of there, and find somewhere safe to hunker down. But even as I was experiencing the urge, I knew I couldn't allow myself to give way to it, because if I went into hiding, I wouldn't be able to search for Paul Taylor – and if I wasn't looking for him, then there was no point in trying to evade the police any longer.

The attendant gave me barely more than a glance when I asked him to fill the tank, and it was probably his obvious indifference which gave me the courage to produce Lydia's picture – along with my usual line about looking for a very dear old friend – when I was paying him.

'No, I can't say I have seen anybody like that round here,' he told me. 'The name Hornby don't ring no bells with me, neither. But there was a family called Horn*bill* who had a farm on the edge of the moors some years gone, if that's any good to you.'

'No, I don't think it is,' I said.

I took the picture back from him and was sliding it into my wallet when I saw another face from another photograph smiling up at me. I pulled it out and handed it to the attendant.

'How about her?' I asked him.

'You seem to be looking for a lot of girls,' he said suspiciously.

I cursed my own stupidly and clumsiness. If Marie had been after information, she'd have pumped him dry without him even noticing it, but I'd only asked him two questions, and already he was starting to look at me as if I was some kind of pervert.

If I was going to survive on the run, I'd have to do better than this.

'This woman is the other one's sister,' I said.

'She don't look much like her.'

'They're stepsisters – same father, different mother,' I improvised wildly. '*That's* probably why they look so different.'

The attendant nodded, took Marie's picture between his thumb and forefinger, and held it up to the light.

'Thought so,' he said.

'You have seen her?'

'Yes, she's not the kind of girl you easily forget, is she?'

'*When* did you see her?'

'I think it must be two or three days ago. She filled up here just like you did.'

'And you're absolutely certain it was her?'

'Pretty sure. She was driving a black Golf GTI, if I remember rightly. She had a nice smile, and she spoke with an Irish accent.'

There was no doubt about it. It had to be Marie.

I should have been glad to get the conformation that my search was running along the right lines. Instead, I felt my heart sink, because I'd been hoping all along that I'd been wrong about her helping Lydia to hide Paul – and now that hope was gone.

Owen Flint and Inspector Hawkins sat opposite my cousin in the lounge of the big house which overlooked the mere.

'It must have been a great shock for you to hear about Bill Harper's death,' Flint said.

'A great shock,' Philip agreed.

And he did look as if he really *was* shocked, Flint thought. His face was unnaturally pale, and his hands were twitchy.

'Can you think of anyone who might have wanted to hurt him?' Flint asked.

'Might have wanted to hurt him?' Philip repeated, in a hectoring voice. 'That's a nice way of putting it, isn't it? Don't you mean "might have wanted to kill him – might have wanted to smash his head to a pulp"?'

My cousin buried his face in his hands and emitted what may have been a sob.

Flint watched him, unmoved, and when Philip uncovered his face again, he said, 'I hope you feel strong enough to carry on with this interview now, sir, because if you don't . . . well . . .'

'Yes, I feel strong enough,' Philip said, interpreting Flint's words as a threat, just as he'd been intended to. 'Look, I'm sorry. I didn't mean it to come out like that, but, as you can imagine, I'm still rather upset. And in answer to your question, no, I can't think of anyone who would have hated him that much.'

'How did he get on with the people he worked with?'

Philip hesitated for a second before speaking. 'To be perfectly honest with you, chief inspector, he wasn't too popular with some of them – perhaps even with the majority.'

'And why might that be?'

'Bill wasn't the kind of man who suffered fools gladly, and he could be quite direct with anyone he thought wasn't up to the mark. But I certainly can't imagine one of his co-workers disliking him so much that they'd want to murder him.'

'Could I ask you where you were between eleven o'clock last night and one o'clock this morning, sir?' Flint asked.

'Are you saying that *I* killed him?' Philip demanded.

'No, sir,' Flint said mildly. 'I'd just like to know where you were at one o'clock this morning.'

'I was in bed.'

'Alone?'

'Yes.'

'From what you told me the last time we talked, that's a rare occurrence indeed,' Flint said. 'It's a great pity that, for once, you seem to have given your Casanova complex a rest.'

'I should be the last person you suspect, for God's sake,' Philip said. 'I was Bill's boss! I gave him his big break only a few days ago. Why should I want to kill him?'

'Yes, I've been wondering about that myself,' Flint said.

'I beg your pardon!'

'I was wondering why you'd given him such a big promotion. And what's even more puzzling is that Mrs Harper said he seemed to know about it long before it was official.'

'Bill always knew I had big plans for him,' Philip said. 'He must have guessed that with the death of three of the directors, there'd be a major role for him to play in the firm.'

'What I'm still not clear about is *why* you had big plans for him,' Flint said musingly. 'I mean, by your own account, he was a fairly abrasive character, and he certainly didn't have any experience of running a large organization like Conroy Enterprises.'

'Bill was an achiever. I admire that. Besides, I knew I could trust him, because as long as I was boss he'd give me his total loyalty – and he'd let me know about those who didn't.'

'So he was going to be your spy within the company, was he?' Flint asked. 'Your nark?'

'He was going to be my joint managing director, and share the burden with me,' Philip said coldly.

'One other question, Mr Conroy,' Flint said. 'I accept it is perfectly reasonable that you don't have an alibi for last night, but you *do* have an alibi for the night someone sabotaged the braking systems of the car in which your father met his death, don't you?'

'That's right, I do,' Philip agreed. 'As I told you before, that night I *was* with a woman.'

'But you won't give us her name.'

Philip sighed. 'You really should take a few notes down to help you remember things, you know. The "Enid" I was with that night happened to be married, and I see no reason for causing her any grief if I don't have to. And I *don't* have to, do I?'

'No, you don't have to – not for the moment, anyway,' Flint said, 'but we may reach a point in the investigation at which you'll wish you'd been more cooperative.'

'I'm perfectly innocent of any wrongdoing, but the next time we talk, I think I'm going to insist that my lawyer is present,' Philip said.

'That's certainly your right,' Flint told Philip. He stood up. 'You stay right where you are, Mr Conroy. Inspector Hawkins and I will see ourselves out.'

Flint and Hawkins parted company on the High Street. Hawkins planned to go back to police headquarters and write a couple of reports which just might keep his superiors at bay. Flint, for his part, had decided that what he needed most in the world was a drink.

Owen was still worrying about me as he walked up the hill to the pub. He tried to phone me, but I, of course, was not answering.

As he got closer to the pub, he saw a woman sitting on the stocks, and realized that it was Susan Harper. He would have liked to have ignored her – gone straight into the pub and ordered a foaming pint of Tetley's Best Bitter – but it had never been his way to run from other people's pain, and he was certainly not about to start now.

Susan was gazing at the ground, but she looked up when she heard his footsteps. Her face was pale and drawn, but then, given the circumstances, that was hardly surprising.

'Are you all right, Mrs Harper,' he asked softly. 'You shouldn't be on your own, you know. Isn't there anyone who can look after you?'

'My mum and dad are here,' Susan said. 'They live in Stoke, but as soon as they heard the news, they drove straight up here. They're being so very, very kind. I know I should be grateful, but . . . but . . .'

'But you feel as if you're being *smothered* with all that kindness?' Flint suggested.

'Yes,' Susan said. 'Does that make me a bad person?'

'Of course it doesn't,' Flint said firmly.

'It's just that I needed a bit of time on my own, so I've got some space to think.'

Flint nodded gravely, then reached into his pocket and pulled out his bag of Jelly Babies.

'Would you like one of these?' he asked.

She didn't laugh at him as so many people had done before he'd broken himself of the habit of handing his sweets around.

Instead, she smiled gratefully, and said, 'Thank you.'

'I'd choose one of the red ones, if I were you,' Flint advised. 'They're the most delicious.'

Susan laughed. 'You sound like a connoisseur.'

'I am.'

'Of *Jelly Babies*!'

'Yes.'

She took his advice and chose a red one. She slipped it into her mouth and bit it in two.

'Don't swallow it immediately,' Flint cautioned. 'Chew it slowly – savour the taste.'

She did as she'd been instructed, and when she'd finished, she said, 'I think you're the kind of man I could talk to – the kind of man I could trust.'

'Is there something that you'd like to tell me?' Flint asked softly.

'Yes . . . no . . . I'm not sure.'

Susan shook her head in a gesture which could have been frustration or anger – Flint wasn't sure which.

'Getting it off your chest will make you feel much better, you know,' he said.

'Perhaps tomorrow – or maybe the day after,' she told him. 'I have to think about it.'

Then she stood up and walked quickly down the hill.

He could have tried to force her to say more, Flint thought, as he watched her, but that wouldn't have worked, because, for all her vulnerability, she had an inner toughness which would only grow stronger under pressure. So it was better – far better – to let her do things at her own speed.

Perhaps what she told him would help to catch her husband's murderer, and perhaps it wouldn't. But, at the very least, it would explain why she had lied about going to bed the night Bill Harper was killed.

It was half past seven in the evening when I reached the stone-built country inn on the edge of the Forest of Bowland, and decided to call it a day.

I left my Granada at the very back of the car park – which was just about as invisible as I could possibly make it – walked into reception and rang the bell on the desk.

I'd been hoping I'd be dealt with by a dozy indifferent kid, with his mind only half on the job, but the man who actually appeared was in his early forties and had dark intelligent eyes.

For a moment I simply froze, then, with a heartiness which sounded false even to me, I said, 'What a lovely place you have here.'

'That's very kind of you to say so, sir,' the man replied dryly. 'How can I be of service to you?'

'I'd like a room, if that's possible.'

'Have you booked?'

I shook my head. 'I didn't know how far I was going to get tonight, so I thought I'd leave it to the last minute.'

The man glanced down at the register. 'We do have one room free, but I'm afraid it has neither its own bathroom nor a television.'

How should I react to that? I wondered. How would I have reacted if I'd been my normal self, rather than a fugitive?

'Naturally, I would have preferred both those things,' I said, 'but I don't suppose it will do me any harm to go without them for one night.'

I sounded about as natural as a third-rate actor on a bad day, I told myself, but the man behind the counter didn't notice it – or, at least, *pretended* not to notice it.

'Just for the one night, is it, sir?' he asked.

'Yes, I've got to be in Manchester by lunchtime tomorrow,' I lied. 'I'm a sales rep.'

Should I have said that? Would I have said it if I'd actually *been* a sales rep?

I didn't know.

I hadn't got a bloody clue!

The man behind the desk slid a form across to me.

'If you wouldn't mind filling in this for me, sir,' he said. 'And how will you be paying?'

'Credit card,' I said, automatically.

But by the time I was reaching for my wallet, I'd already realized my mistake. Paying by credit card would be tantamount to ringing up the Cheshire police and telling them exactly where I was.

'On second thoughts,' I said hastily, 'I'm carrying more money around with me than I really feel comfortable with, so, if it's all the same to you, I'll pay with cash.'

'Whatever you wish, sir.'

He quoted the price of the room, and I handed over the money.

'Dinner is served until nine o'clock, sir,' he said. 'Would you like to book your table now?'

For all I knew, I'd been on the television as well as the radio. It was clear that the receptionist didn't recognize me, but if my photograph *had* been on TV, there might be people in the dining room who would.

'I've had a long day, and I'm rather tired,' I said. 'Would it be possible to have some sandwiches sent up to my room?'

'Certainly, sir. What kind?'

I shrugged. 'It doesn't matter – anything will do. And could you send up half a bottle of whisky, as well?'

For the first ten minutes that I sat in my room, I was half-expecting to hear a loud knock on my door and, on opening it, to find myself staring at a couple of policemen whom the receptionist had wisely called the moment I'd left. But when a knock did finally come, it was only a girl carrying a tray with my order on it.

I nibbled lethargically at the sandwiches and took a few sips of my whisky. I was exhausted, both mentally and physically, but I knew that if I went to bed right then, I wouldn't sleep.

How many villages had I visited that day? I wondered. To know for sure I would have to count the number of crosses on my map, but I couldn't summon up the effort.

Paul Taylor *had to be* somewhere close – that was the only thing which explained Marie's presence in the area. Tomorrow I would find the village where Lydia had been brought up, I promised myself. And as I made that promise, I shivered – almost as if someone had just walked over my grave.

TWENTY-FOUR

The inn where I'd spent the night was only just starting to wake up when I left the next morning and, at the first village store I visited, the owner yawned several times during the course of telling me that he didn't recognize the woman in the photograph, and he had never heard the name Hornby Smythe.

I headed south, using the back roads, whenever possible, to minimize the risk of being spotted by the police. In the next few hours, I visited more village stores, put more crosses on my map – and was still no closer to finding out where my sister-in-law had hidden her lover than I'd been when I left Cheshire the day before.

It was just after eleven that I drove into a village located mid-way between Darwen and Blackburn, and saw a pub called the Prince Albert. The sign outside advertised hot snacks, and my rumbling stomach advised me that it would be wise to take advantage of this opportunity.

Mine was the only car in the car park, but as I got out of it, I felt a prickle at the back of my neck, as if a malevolent presence had me under its gaze. I looked around and could see no one. It was just the heat of the sun on my neck, I told myself, or the sense of unease only natural in a man who knew he was being hunted by every police force in the country – but the feeling that I was being watched refused to go away.

I felt a little happier once I'd stepped inside the pub, which was empty, apart from the landlord and one solitary drinker.

The landlord was a bald man, with an open, honest face and thick builders' arms, and when he assured me that the meat and potato pie he heated up for me had been lovingly made on the premises, by his wife, I believed him.

'I used to be a window cleaner,' he said, as I was eating. 'That's how come I got the brass together to buy this place. And I tell you, standing behind a warm bar beats climbing up cold ladders in the middle of winter any day of the week.' He paused to light a cigarette. 'So what are you doing in these parts, if you don't mind me asking, sir?'

I told him my well-used story and pulled out my well-thumbed photographs. He examined the one of Lydia standing next to the new car which John had bought her for her birthday.

'Nice looking girl,' the landlord said. 'A bit skinny for my taste . . . sorry, no offence meant, sir.'

'None taken,' I assured him.

'Yes, she's a bit skinny – but very nice.'

Yet had Lydia *ever* been skinny, I wondered. Or had she just fooled us with her flair for costume?

'You don't happen to know her, do you?' I asked.

The landlord shook his head.

'But then that's not surprising,' he said. 'I'm a newcomer to the village, you see.'

'Really!' I said politely.

'That's right. I've only been here for six years, and in the eyes of the locals, that makes me no more than a day tripper.' He looked across at his other customer, an old man who was nursing the half pint of mild. 'Why don't you ask Bob over there about her?' he suggested. 'He's lived in the village all his life. In fact, he still lives in the house where he was born.'

'Thank you,' I said.

'One piece of advice, though,' the landlord said. 'He's got nothin' against talking to strangers, but you might find him a bit more welcoming if you took him a pint.'

I did as the landlord suggested, presented the old man with a drink, and asked if I might join him.

He nodded, as if he were glad of the company.

'I hear you were born in the village,' I said.

'I was that.'

'So you must have seen some changes in your time.'

The old man took off his cap and wiped the top of his shiny bald head with it.

'Seen some changes?' he repeated. 'By gum, I have that. When I was growing up, there was hardly any motor cars round here. It were all horses and carts in them days.'

'Do you know everyone who lives in the village?'

'Everybody as does now, and everybody who ever has.'

I slid the photographs across to him.

'What about her?' I asked, making it sound like a challenge.

Old Bob took a pair of ancient glasses out of his pocket and perched them on his nose. He examined the photograph of Lydia by her car, briefly glanced at the others, then returned to the first.

'Is that car hers?' he asked.

'Yes, it is.'

'Well, she 'as done well for herself, hasn't she?'

I felt my heart miss a beat.

'So you know her, do you?' I asked.

'Course I know her. That's Linda Smith.'

'Smythe,' I said. 'Lydia Hornby Smythe.'

'That might be what she's calling herself now, but that wasn't her name when she were living in the village.'

He was an old man. He could be mistaken.

'Do you know where she lives now?'

'Haven't heard a dickie bird about her since she left.'

'And when was that?'

The old man scratched his head. 'Let me see. That'd be about the time our Freddie had his hernia operation, so it'd be what – seven years ago now?'

The timing was right, and the coincidence of the names was eerie, but I was still not convinced.

'Does she have any friends in the village I could talk to?' I asked.

'There's a few lasses she used to knock around with before she got above herself, but they'll tell you the same as me – they've never heard from her. But don't take my word for it. Ask anybody. Ask our Clem.'

'Who's your Clem?'

'Me nephew. He's done well for himself, has Clem. He owns a couple of electrical shops – one in Blackburn and one in Darwen.'

'And why should I talk to him in particular.'

'Well, he used to go out with her, didn't he?' the old man asked, as if he were surprised I didn't already know. 'But I'll tell you somethin' – it weren't him that did the chasing – it were her. She chased him with no more shame than a dog goes after a bitch on heat.'

'Tell me more,' I said.

The old man looked down at his empty glass. 'Thirsty work, all this talking,' he said.

'Let me get you another one,' I said, standing up.

'Aye,' the old man agreed. 'I might find space for just one more.'

I had assumed, the previous evening, that since Marie was running a courier-cum-support service between my sister-in-law and Paul Taylor, she would either be spending the night in Lancashire or in Cheshire, but I was wrong – as I turned out to be wrong about so many other things. As I was nibbling lethargically at my sandwiches in the hotel room near the Forest of Bowland, Marie had been checking into a modest hotel in Bristol – and at about the time I was buying a second pint for Old Bob, she was parking her black Golf GTI in front of the almost-stately home outside Bath that belonged to Hugh Morgan.

Knowing them both as I do, I think I can pretty much reproduce the conversation that will have followed.

Morgan, who jealously guarded that private part of his world which existed beyond the cons, will have said something like, 'I don't know who you are, but I didn't invite you here, so you can just bugger off.'

And Marie, drawing on her cigarette – and she will have had

a cigarette in her hand, I'm sure of that – will have replied, 'Good afternoon, Mr Morgan. My name is Marie O'Hara, and I'm a private investigator.'

That, naturally enough, will have made Morgan uneasy, and his next question is likely to have been: 'Who are you working for?'

'I'm working for a family very dear to your heart – the Conroys.'

Morgan's eyes will have narrowed. 'You're not the one who Rob Conroy hired to check up on me, are you?'

'The very same.'

'Then what I said earlier goes double – bugger off right now.'

Marie will have taken another leisurely drag on her cigarette. 'I'm surprised at your attitude, because while a great many people have said some really unpleasant things about you, no one's ever accused you of being stupid.'

'And what's that supposed to mean?'

'I had this picture of you as a man who can smell out a deal a mile away,' Marie will no doubt have explained.

'What kind of deal?'

'There *is* only one kind of deal – the kind where you've got something I want, and I've got something *you* want. And what you want, Mr Morgan, is money.'

I returned to the table – and the expectant Bob – with both a pint of mild and a whisky chaser. The old man knocked back the whisky in a single gulp, then wiped his lips on the sleeve of his jacket.

'I were telling you about my nephew, Clem,' he said.

'So you were,' I agreed.

'He's a few years older than Linda, but he fell for her like he were a sixteen-year-old. There were talk at one time about them getting married.'

'So why didn't they?'

'She broke it off.'

'Why?'

'Clem wouldn't say. I'm not really sure that he knew himself, if truth be told.'

But I thought I did. I'd had a nagging suspicion for a long time that Lydia was a fortune hunter, and now I had the proof. She'd set her sights on Clem – a man who owned two electrical stores – and when she'd seen just how easy it was to get him, she'd decided to go for bigger game. And I was willing to bet that it had been no coincidence when she and John met at the summer fête – it had happened not by chance, but because she had *arranged* for it to happen.

I reined in my outrage and reminded myself that I wasn't there to learn about Lydia's murky past, but to find Paul Taylor.

I took his photograph out of my wallet and handed it to the old man. 'Does he look familiar?' I asked.

Bob squinted at the picture. 'Reminds me a bit of my cousin Charlie, when he were younger,' he said.

'This is a fairly recent photograph,' I said patiently. 'I was wondering if you'd seen him around the village in the last few days.'

The old man shook his head. 'There's been nobody like that round here, I can assure you.'

Of course he wouldn't have seen Paul Taylor, I thought. Someone on the run from the police wouldn't go parading himself up and down the village – he'd be in hiding.

But hiding where, exactly?

The old man had said that Lydia had not kept in touch with any of her old friends so . . .

The aunt's house! She would have left it to Lydia – her only close relative – in her will, and Lydia may have decided to keep it empty, rather than put it on the market. That would make a perfect bolthole.

'Where did Lyd . . . where did Linda's aunt live?' I asked.

'Her aunt?' old Bob repeated. 'Linda Smith never had no auntie. There was her, her mam and her dad. That was all.'

'Then who looked after her when her parents died?'

Bob chuckled. 'Died? Thelma and Chris Smith?' He turned his head towards the landlord, who was polishing glasses. 'This feller thinks Thelma and Chris Smith are dead, Harry,' he said.

'Well, if they are, it's news to me,' the landlord said.

'Have you still got that postcard they sent last Christmas?' Bob asked.

'Must be somewhere round here,' the landlord replied. 'I'll see if I can lay my hands on it.'

'Of course, it broke their hearts when Linda cut them off like she did,' Bob told me. 'They used to look right miserable, but over time, they come to terms with it. Chris used to say, "Well, as long as she's happy now, that's the main thing".'

The landlord stepped from behind the bar and walked over to the table.

'This is it,' he said, handing me a postcard.

On the front of the card were various views of a place called Torrevieja, in Spain.

On the back, next to the address, someone had written:

> *No snow for us this year. Best thing we ever did, moving here!*
> *A merry Christmas and a happy new year to all our old friends in the Prince Albert.*
> *Thelma and Chris*

So if they were still alive – if one hadn't been killed in a plane crash and the other drunk himself to death – why hadn't they been at Lydia's wedding? But that was obvious. Lydia had chosen to re-invent herself and didn't want anyone around who could give the lie to the new person she had become.

'What did Mr Smith do for a living before he retired?' I asked.

'Chris? He ran the garage. You'll like as not have seen it on the way into the village. It were a family business, really. His missus served the petrol, and him and Linda did the repairs.'

'She . . . she . . . did the repairs?'

'That's right,' the old man agreed. 'I never much liked her as a person, but I will say this for her: she was a belting little mechanic – better even than her old dad.'

I told myself at the time that, while it might seem sensible to talk to more people in the village, it was too much of a risk, because a man on the run from the police can't afford to stay in any one place for too long. Looking back, I think I was just making excuses for myself – and the real reason I felt the urge to get away as quickly as I could was that the moment I left the safe confines of the pub, I sensed the evil eye on me again.

It should have been a ten-minute drive from the village to the centre of Darwen, but I was so deep in thought that it took me nearer to twenty.

Why had Lydia pretended, for so long, that she knew nothing about cars? I asked myself. Was it because she had *always* planned to commit murder?

No, I didn't believe it was.

I thought about all the members of the aristocracy I had rubbed shoulders with during my brief university career. They *knew* they were God's chosen people, and that nothing could change that. So it was all right for them to get rolling drunk, to have the sexual morals of a mink – and to get their hands dirty messing around with the engines of old cars.

Ah, but it was different for some of the aspiring members of the middle class. They didn't have five hundred years of history to buoy them up. Their grandfathers had been miners, and carpenters and day labourers. And if they drank to excess, were promiscuous, or demonstrated any knowledge of how things worked, they were saying, in effect, that they were still part of the class they were claiming to have left behind.

Yes, Lydia had thought it would be demeaning to admit that she could fix engines, and the fact that no one thought she could had come in very useful when she needed to sabotage the BMW.

Except that she *couldn't have* sabotaged the BMW herself, could she – she was securely locked up in the health spa when that took place – but she could have shown Paul Taylor how to do it.

But again, I was faced with the unanswered – and seemingly unanswerable – question: why would Lydia and Paul have wanted to kill John, when they could have had all they'd wanted without running the risk of going to gaol?

Darwen library is made of dressed stone and capped by an impressive dome. It was built in 1908, when cotton was still king, and the mills sometimes worked round the clock to meet their orders, so in the modern, largely post-industrial town, it perhaps looks a little out of place.

Inside, it is like any other small town library, with bright displays, a children's corner – and an archive room which has all previous editions of the local paper on microfilm.

It was in the archive room that I spent the next hour. I went immediately to the date of Lydia's birth, and having found in the announcements section that Linda Smith had been born on exactly the same day, I scrolled through the papers to see what else I could find out about her.

The first thing I came across was a picture of a primary school nativity play in which she was the Virgin Mary. It was the sort of grimy black and white photograph that newspapers used to print before the technology improved, but it was clear enough for me to discern a difference between her and her classmates. The other children, dressed as shepherds and kings, were conscious of the camera and conscious of the fact that they were playing the game of dressing up. Linda – standing there holding a doll to represent the baby Jesus – was not playing games at all. It showed in her stance and the expression on her face that she *was* Mary.

I moved on, and found an article celebrating the fact that the Smiths' garage had won the paper's 'Small Business of the Year' competition. Linda and her parents are standing in front of the garage. Her mother is beaming, and her father is positively puffed up with pride, but the look on Linda's face says that she shouldn't have to do this – that it is all too humiliating.

I had seen enough. I left the library and started to make my way back to the quiet street where I had parked my car.

Things never worked out as you thought they would, I reflected as I walked. I had come to Lancashire to find Paul Taylor, and instead I had uncovered Lydia's past. But, in a way, that was just as good – because now I had a hold over her, Lydia would have no choice but to tell me where she was hiding Paul.

It was as I turned the corner that I saw the boy hotwiring my Granada. I broke into a run – or as much of a run as my gammy leg would let me – but I was still about thirty yards away when the engine burst into life, and the car shot forward.

I stood in the road, waving my arms to make him stop, but it soon became clear that he wasn't going to, and that if I stayed where I was, he would simply run me down.

I stepped quickly out of the way. As the car roared past, the boy turned to grin at me. He couldn't have been more than fourteen or fifteen, and from the glazed expression in his eyes, I could tell he was high on something.

The Granada had almost reached the end of the road when it exploded. A column of flame rose high into the air, and the vehicle veered crazily to the right, before hitting a lamppost and turning over.

By the time I reached the wreckage, it was clear that nothing could be done for the poor kid.

TWENTY-FIVE

The table in the interview room at Warrington police station was scarred with countless cigarette burns from countless interrogations, and the man sitting at the opposite end of it looked as if he'd like to burn holes in *me*.

'Do you know why you're here, rather than in some cop shop in Lancashire?' he demanded.

'I assume it's because you had something to do with it, Owen,' I said.

'Yes, that's right. You're here because – God knows why – I persuaded the Lancashire constabulary that I'd get more out of questioning you than they ever could. So don't go making a bloody liar out of me, Rob. Do you understand what I'm saying?'

'Yes, I understand.'

'Didn't you hear the messages on the news?' Owen asked angrily. 'All those appeals to contact the police? You should have done. God knows, I pulled all the strings I could to keep getting them repeated.'

'I heard them,' I admitted.

'So why the bloody hell didn't you come back?'

I couldn't tell him the truth – not if I were to have even the slightest chance of keeping Marie out of gaol.

'I was afraid to come back,' I lied. 'I thought you were going to arrest me for Bill Harper's murder.'

Owen slapped his forehead with the palm of his hand.

'Arrest you!' he said exasperatedly. 'What *do* you think *I* think you are – some kind of homicidal lunatic?' He broke off, as he realized the implications – given my mental history – of what he'd just said. 'I'm sorry, Rob,' he continued, contritely.

'It's all right,' I assured him. 'I stopped worrying about people looking oddly at me a long time ago.' I took a deep breath. 'If I hadn't gone to Darwen today, that boy would still be alive, you know.'

'Oh, for Christ's sake!' he exploded again. 'First it was Jill, then your brother, and now this little junkie in Lancashire! You didn't put the bomb in the car, and you didn't choose to steal it. You can't hold yourself responsible for everything that happens to everybody.'

'I know, but . . .' I began.

'What the bloody hell were you doing up in darkest Lancashire, anyway?' Flint asked.

'I was checking up on my sister-in-law,' I said, sailing as close to the truth as I dared.

'And did you learn something interesting about her?'

'Yes, I did.'

'Well, then, let's bloody hear it!'

I told him that Lydia had once been plain Linda, and had worked in her father's garage. I outlined how she had once been all set to marry a shop owner called Clem and had then decided that she could do better for herself. I had just finished my story when the phone rang.

Flint picked it up. 'Yes . . . yes . . . I see . . . Thank you.' He replaced the phone on its cradle. 'That was the forensics department of the Lancashire police. They've been examining what's left of your car, and though it's too early to draw any definite conclusions, they think the bomb was fixed so it would blow up when the car reached a certain speed. I wonder why the bomber didn't just fix it to the ignition, so it blew up when you turned the key.'

Because that would have meant me being killed in the village that held Lydia's deep dark secret, and with all the fuss that would cause, it would be a secret no more. Far better, then, that I should be killed on some fast road miles from there, and if that caused a multiple pile-up in which other people were killed, that was just the way it had to be.

A great sadness overwhelmed me as I realized that the only way I could continue to protect Marie was to steer Flint away from Lydia. But after what she'd done – and might do next – I no longer had that option.

'It was Lydia who planted the bomb,' I said.

'Your sister-in-law!' Flint said incredulously. 'I know you've just told me she's supposed to be a pretty good mechanic, but even so, why would she want to kill *you*?'

'You've seen her,' I said. 'You know how much she values her place in society.'

'Yes, but . . .'

'I'd learned the secret she's kept buried all these years, and she was terrified I'd tell all her friends.'

'She'd never try to kill you just for that,' Owen said.

'She's sacrificed her family and friends – everyone she grew up with – to her ambition. Do you realize just how much she must have hurt her parents by ruthlessly cutting them completely out of her life? Going from that to killing me isn't such a big step.'

'But how did she even know you'd be in Lancashire?'

'She didn't. But after our last couple of conversations, she must have guessed that I might be.'

'And so she drove all over the county, looking for your car, and when she found it she planted the bomb.'

I shook my head. 'She didn't have to go looking for me. I could have visited every village between here and Scotland for all she cared – as long as I stayed away from that particular one.'

'So what you're saying is that she was hanging around the village on the off-chance that you'd turn up?'

'She's put so much effort into leaving Linda behind and becoming Lydia that that would seem a very small thing to her,' I said.

'I still can't accept it,' Flint told me.

'Well, maybe I'm wrong,' I admitted. 'But if Lydia didn't do it, she'll have an alibi, won't she?'

It was early evening when Flint, accompanied by Sergeant Matthews, knocked on my sister-in-law's front door.

When Lydia answered, she was wearing a towelling robe. She didn't seem particularly worried they were there, Flint thought. If anything, she was merely displaying the irritation that important people feel when they're bothered by the petty details which everyone else is forced to deal with as a matter of course.

She noticed Flint looking at her robe. 'I've been out in the garden, catching the last rays of the afternoon sun,' she explained in a lazy drawl – and even in this she seemed to be pointing out that she was one of the leisured class, while he was definitely not.

'Catching the last rays of the afternoon sun,' Flint repeated. 'It's not quite like the old days, when the grieving widow shut herself off from the world for a couple of years, is it?'

Lydia's face hardened. 'I wasn't anticipating another visit from you, Mr Flint,' she said.

'I wasn't anticipating making one, Mrs Conroy,' Flint countered.

They all stood there in silence for perhaps ten seconds, then Lydia, realizing that Flint was not going to be the first to break, said, 'So why are you here? Have you got some more questions?'

'That's right, Mrs Conroy.'

'Well, be quick about asking them, because – to be honest with you – it's getting rather chilly standing here.'

'I think it might be better if we conducted our business inside, madam,' Flint said.

'All right,' Lydia said reluctantly, 'go through to the lounge – you should know where it is by now – while I get changed. You can pour yourselves a drink, if you want to.'

Once they were in the lounge, Matthews looked longingly at the drinks cabinet and then questioningly at Flint.

The chief inspector shook his head.

'She'd like that,' he said. 'It would be a case of her dispensing her bounty to the peasantry – and I'm not about to give her that satisfaction. Besides, I make it a rule never to accept drinks from people I might soon be arresting for murder and attempted murder.'

'Do you really think she planted that bomb, sir?' Matthews asked.

'I'm not sure what I think,' Flint confessed. 'When Rob Conroy first suggested it, I thought he was being paranoid, but we've learned a couple of things since then which possibly suggest that he's right.'

'She doesn't act guilty.'

'No,' Flint agreed. 'What she acts is *Lydia Conroy* – the lady of the manor. It's a role she's been working on for the last six years, and she's got it damn near perfect now.'

There was the sound of high heels clicking down the stairs, then Lydia entered the lounge. She was wearing a green shot-silk dress, which was just short enough to reveal a pair of brown knees.

'Have you been working on your tan all day, Mrs Conroy?' Flint asked, feeding her some rope with which she just might hang herself.

'No, I've only been in the garden for the last hour or so. The rest of the day, I've been out.' Lydia frowned. 'Don't you think it's about time you told me what this is all about, chief inspector?'

'Did you happen to listen to the radio or television news this afternoon?' Flint asked, ignoring the question.

'No, I didn't,' Lydia replied – and the slight flicker of her eyes, when she spoke, told Flint that she was lying.

'So you won't have heard there's been a car bomb in Darwen, Lancashire?'

'No, I hadn't heard. How terrible!'

'The car bomb went off near the library. Do you happen to know Darwen at all, Mrs Conroy?'

He could almost see inside her head, as her brain weighed up the choices she had.

'Yes, I used to live somewhere quite close to Darwen – though it was a long time ago,' she said finally.

'The car that was blown up was a Ford Granada.'

'Yes?'

'In fact, it was your brother-in-law's Ford Granada.'

Lydia put her hand to her mouth. 'Oh my God, it can't be true!' she gasped. 'But it is true, isn't it? Poor, poor Rob!'

'I'm sorry, madam, I seem to have expressed myself very badly,' Flint said. 'The car was blown up – it was a right bloody mess by all accounts – but Rob wasn't hurt.'

'But it said on the . . .' Lydia began, before she realized she was about to make a very big mistake and clamped her mouth firmly shut.

'It said on the *what*, madam?'

Lydia shook her head. 'Forget it.'

'Ah, but, you see, I can't just forget it,' Flint told her. 'What you were going to say was that on the news it said that a man had been killed in the explosion. And that's quite true – a man was – but he wasn't your brother-in-law.' Flint's voice hardened. 'Why did you lie just now about having heard about it?'

Lydia raked the fingers of her right hand through her hair.

'I'm so confused,' she said. 'First you upset me by telling me Rob is dead, now you say he isn't. If you ask me, you're handling the whole situation very badly indeed.'

'Nice recovery,' Flint said admiringly. 'But we both know that you've made a slip there's no going back on.'

'I have no idea what you're talking about,' Lydia said.

'Of course you haven't,' Flint said contemptuously. 'Bombs are becoming a real problem these days, and that's because there's so much information available on how to build them that anyone with a bit of technological knowledge can put one together.' He paused. 'You have some knowledge of technology, don't you, Mrs Conroy?'

'Are you accusing *me* of planting a bomb?' Lydia asked, outraged.

'You had two committee meetings yesterday, and three today,' Flint said. 'You cancelled them all.'

'Yes, I wasn't feeling well.'

'Sorry to hear that,' Flint said. 'The thing is, when I'm not feeling well, I go to bed. But not you, it seems. The neighbours have told us that on both days you left early in the morning and didn't come back until the evening. Where did you go, Mrs Conroy?'

'How dare you talk to my neighbours?' Lydia demanded.

'In case you've forgotten, I'm conducting an investigation into the death of your husband and the attempted murder of your brother-in-law, both of which I happen to think are more important than your social sensibilities,' Flint growled. 'So I'll ask you again – where did you go, Mrs Conroy?'

'Yesterday, I went to the Lake District,' Lydia said, in a tone which was flat and almost emotionless.

Flint sighed. He'd reached this stage in dozens of other cases and recognized it for exactly what it was – the point at which the suspect stops trying to pretend innocence, and instead challenges him to prove guilt.

'And where did you go today?' he asked.

'Today I visited the Yorkshire Dales.'

'Any particular reason for choosing those two places?'

'Fresh air helps me to clear my head.'

'I would have thought you'd get enough fresh air without even leaving the village,' Flint said.

'Then perhaps it was fresh *scenery* I was looking for.'

'They're both longish journeys, wouldn't you say – at least a couple of hours in each direction?'

'I suppose so, but I wasn't looking at my watch.'

'Still, when you've got a car as comfortable as the Volvo, you can pretty much drive for ever,' Flint said. He paused. 'Except you didn't take the Volvo, did you? You took the little Renault that you normally use just as a run-around. Now why was that?'

'It's more economical,' Lydia said.

Flint made a show of looking round the room. 'Yes, I can see you set great store on being economical,' he said. 'But I don't think you did it to save money – I think you did it because the Renault is much less conspicuous than the Volvo would have been.' He paused again. 'Did you stop at any point to buy petrol?'

'Why should that matter?'

'Because if you stopped for fuel and *if* you paid for it with a credit card, then you'll be able to prove that you actually were where you said you were.'

'I bought some petrol at a service station on the M6, on my way up to the Lakes,' Lydia said.

'Or on your way up to central Lancashire – to the village you were brought up in.'

'I hated the Darwen area,' Lydia said. 'I couldn't wait to get away from it, and there's no way I'd ever go back.'

'I think you did go back,' Flint told her. 'I think you waited to see if Rob turned up, and when he did, you planted a bomb in the engine of his Granada.'

'And I suppose you're going to say that I also messed with the brakes on my husband's car,' Lydia said.

Flint shook his head. 'How could I? You've got a watertight alibi for the night before the crash.'

Lydia smiled. 'That's right, I have, haven't I? So are you going to arrest me for trying to kill my drippy brother-in-law?'

'No,' Flint said, 'nor for *actually* killing the joyrider. But I am going to ask your permission to search this house.'

'And if I refuse?'

'You have the right, but I should warn you that if you choose to exercise that right, I have ample grounds for obtaining a search warrant.'

'If you want to search, then search,' Lydia said defiantly.

And Flint knew then that he would find nothing to tie her in with the crime.

It was a strange sensation to be spending the night in a house that was less than half a mile away from the home of the woman who had tried to kill me only a few hours earlier, but Owen Flint had seen to it that the Cheshire police posted guards outside, and I didn't think even Lydia would be crazy enough to tackle a couple of six-foot policemen.

I had just poured myself a stiff drink before going to bed, when the phone rang. I almost ignored it, but there was a persistence about the ringing which made me slam down my drink on the coffee table and snatch up the receiver.

'Yes?' I said irritably.

The voice which answered me made my stomach churn.

'Is that you Rob?' it asked, excitedly.

'Marie? Where are you?'

'I'm in Bristol.'

'Why are you there?'

'I'm looking for Paul Taylor, of course. That's what your sister-in-law hired me to do. Surely you must have guessed that.'

How easy it was for her to hurt me, I thought – even from a distance, down an impersonal telephone line.

'Don't lie to me, Marie,' I said bitterly.

'Lie to you? What are you talking about?'

'You weren't looking for Paul Taylor. You've known where he was all along.'

'What makes you say that?' Marie asked.

There was so much evident surprise in her voice that, for a moment, I almost believed her. Then I reminded myself of what I actually knew – of what a brush with cold, hard reality had taught me.

'You've been up in Lancashire,' I told her. 'And the only possible reason for that would be to visit Paul.'

There was another pause at the other end of the line, then Marie said, 'How do you know that? Have you been up to Lancashire yourself?'

'Yes, *I* was looking for Paul – I mean *really* looking for him. I thought Lydia might have hidden him somewhere near her old home.'

'I was working on the same theory,' Marie said.

How could she lie to me like that? I wondered. How could she lie, and lie and keep on lying?

'You're contradicting yourself,' I said harshly. 'One second you're telling me that Lydia hired you to find Paul Taylor, the next you're saying she knew where he was all along. That doesn't make any sense at all.'

'It does if you think about it,' Marie said quietly. 'The way I had it figured out at the time I agreed to take the case, was that she *was* hiding him, and she wanted to be sure he couldn't be found. And what better way to test how safe he was than to hire someone like me to try and track him down?'

It was plausible – but then Marie could always sound plausible.

'You say that's how you had it figured out at the time you took the case,' I said. 'But you sound as if you don't think that's true anymore?'

'That's right – I don't.'

'Why have you changed your mind?'

'Because now that I *have* found him, it's obvious that Lydia had nothing to do with his disappearance.'

'You've found him?' I said sceptically. 'Every police force in the country is looking for him, and *you've* found him?'

'That's right,' Marie agreed. 'Listen, Rob, can you lay your hands on ten thousand pounds in a hurry?'

'I suppose so,' I said, remembering that my father always kept a fair amount of working capital in his safe. 'But what do you want it for?'

'I want it because it's the modern-day equivalent of thirty pieces of silver. For ten thousand pounds, I can buy a man who'll take me to where Paul Taylor's hiding.'

'Shouldn't you tell the police what you've got?'

'That wouldn't work. The moment they went to see him, my man would deny he knew anything, and they'd never be able to prove he did.'

'And what about your client?' I asked. 'Where does she fit into all this? She could raise the money easily.'

'I know she could. But . . . but the fact is, I really don't want to get her involved.'

'I'd have thought she was pretty much involved already,' I said.

'Can't you just trust me on this?' Marie pleaded. 'Instead of asking all these questions, can't you just say, "Marie, I'll get the money and meet you on Temple Meads Station at three o'clock tomorrow afternoon"?'

Despite everything I knew, and everything I suspected, I still couldn't resist her.

'Marie, I'll get the money and meet you on Temple Meads Station at three o'clock tomorrow afternoon,' I repeated dutifully.

'You're a sweetheart,' Marie gushed. 'I love you.' She paused again. 'I meant that, you know. I really *do* love you.'

And then the line went dead.

TWENTY-SIX

When Owen Flint arrived in the village next morning, I was already on my way to Bristol. If he'd known that, he would have disapproved, and might even have tried to stop me. But he didn't know, and by the time the police car in which he was a passenger was halfway up the High Street, he'd seen something which banished all thoughts of me completely from his mind.

What he saw, as the car drew level with the post office/general store, was a woman – a tiny, distant figure – standing next to the stocks in front of the church.

'Drive on,' he said to Matthews, who was already indicating that he was about to pull over.

'But I thought you wanted to stop at the shop, sir,' the sergeant said.

'Well, I don't,' Flint snapped.

'You know what you're like if you don't get your morning's supply of sugar, sir,' Matthews cautioned.

'What I want you to do, sergeant,' Flint said, 'is to drive to the church, stop to let me out – and then bugger off for at least an hour.'

Matthews shrugged. 'You're the boss,' he said.

'Big of you to notice,' Flint replied.

Matthews pulled up by the pump house, and Flint got out of the car.

Susan Harper did not move an inch, but the chief inspector could feel her gaze boring into him.

When he was close enough to hear her words, she forced a smile to her face and said, 'Have you got any sweets, mister?' in what she obviously hoped was a comic voice.

Flint smiled back at her.

'Sorry, I ate the last of my emergency supplies at half past four this morning, and I haven't had time to buy any more yet,' he said. His expression altered – becoming both more serious and more concerned. 'What is it you want to get off your chest, Mrs Harper?' he asked gently.

'I feel like such a hypocrite,' Susan Harper told him. 'My husband's dead. I should be drowning in a sea of grief, but the fact is, I'm not.'

'You can't judge yourself by the way you've seen other people behave when they've lost a loved one,' Flint said, sympathetically. 'We all react to death in different ways.'

'You don't understand,' Susan Harper countered. 'It's not a question of not grieving enough – I'm not grieving at all. It's like I'd heard that someone I hardly knew had died.'

'Maybe that's just what it is,' Flint suggested. 'Maybe he *was* someone you hardly knew.'

'I was sure *you'd* understand,' Susan said gratefully.

'It really wasn't a very happy marriage, was it?'

Susan shook her head.

'I thought I was in love with him when we got married. And maybe I was. But it certainly didn't last very long. I don't think . . . I don't think there was much there to love. The only thing Bill really cared about was getting on in business, and he'd have done *anything* to achieve his aim.' She brushed a stray strand of hair out of her eyes. 'I'm rambling on, aren't I?'

'No, not at all,' Flint assured her. 'Just tell me the whole thing in your way, and at your own speed.'

'I was a virgin when I married Bill. Isn't that a strange thing to be in this day and age?'

'It's more common than you might think,' Flint told her, though he had no idea whether that was true or not.

'Anyway, Bill was the only man I'd ever been with, and I'd honestly never thought of being unfaithful to him, even after we'd stopped sleeping together regularly. And then I . . . then I . . .'

'Met a man,' Flint prompted.

Susan Harper looked down at the ground. 'That's right,' she mumbled.

'And was that man Philip Conroy?'

'How . . . how did you know that?' Susan gasped.

Who else would it be, given that she was virtually a prisoner in the world that was Conroy Enterprises? Flint thought.

'It was just a lucky guess,' he said aloud. 'Where did you first get to know him?'

'At a party. We were always going round to parties at a Conroy house, or having them round to ours. Philip was nice to me – attentive.' A sad smile came to her face. 'He used to call me his Sweet Little Enid. Isn't that odd, when my name's Susan?'

'Very odd,' Flint said.

And he was thinking, you really are a complete bastard, aren't you, Philip Conroy?

'From then on, one thing just seemed to lead on to another,' Susan Harper continued. 'He said he loved me, you know – he told me that just before he took me to bed for the first time. But he didn't really love me at all, and when the novelty wore off, he said it would be better all round if we broke up.'

'Did Bill know anything about what was going on?' Flint asked.

Susan laughed bitterly. 'No, Bill never found out about the affair. But, do you know, even if he had, I don't think he'd have minded. Philip's one of the bosses, and if Bill was allowing him to have me, it would be sort of like bringing an apple for the teacher.'

'Does what you're telling me have some sort of bearing on your husband's death?' Flint probed.

'I think so. I missed Philip, you see, even though I'd finally realized what he was like. So when Bill was out swimming, the night that he was killed, I went to Philip's house.'

'And why did you do that?'

Susan Harper raised her head again and looked Flint squarely in the eyes.

'I went to beg him to take me back.'

'And is that what happened? You saw him, and you asked him to take you back?'

'No. When I got there, his house was in darkness, so I thought he must have gone to bed. I had my own key. I opened the front door and I went up to his bedroom. He wasn't there. I couldn't stay long, because I knew I'd have to be at home by the time Bill returned from his swim. I was halfway down the lane when I heard footsteps crunching on the cinder track behind me. It was obvious what had happened. Someone had come up the fields from the main road.'

Flint nodded. 'Go on,' he said encouragingly.

'I turned around. I saw no more than a dark shape, but I could tell from the way he moved that it was Philip.'

'He didn't see you?'

'No, I was standing against a hedge.'

'Why didn't you speak to him? After all, that's why you went there in the first place.'

'I'd screwed up all the courage I had simply to go and see him – and when he wasn't at home, that courage just melted away. I'm not sure I'd have been brave enough to talk to him if he'd come back to his house before I left, but out on the lane, it was just impossible. I was terrified of what he might say to me, you see.'

And the little sod would probably have said a mouthful, Flint thought – because his kind didn't care *who* they hurt.

'What happened next?' he asked.

'He got out his keys and opened his front door. Then he seemed to change his mind. He closed the door again and crossed the lane to his garden gate.'

'Go on.'

'He went into the garden. I heard him open the shed door – it's got a squeak – and then I tiptoed away.' Susan Harper paused for a second. 'It seems very strange to be betraying the man you love for the sake of the husband you don't.'

'Neither of them were worthy of you,' Flint said.

'I know,' Susan Harper agreed. 'But that still doesn't make it any easier.'

As the train pulled into Temple Meads station, I saw Marie standing on the platform, waiting for me. She was wearing one of her smart, aggressive, business outfits – a dark suit with white piping – and her beautiful red hair, instead of cascading over her shoulders, was pinned tightly back.

I stepped off the train and walked towards her. I longed to throw my arms around her and hug her to me. But I didn't. We never touched – except accidentally – and even after what she'd said on the phone the previous evening, I still felt constrained to let her make the first move.

'Have you got the money?' she asked, speaking in just the same crisp tone as she'd adopted when she'd given me her report on her investigation into Hugh Morgan's affairs, back in Oxford.

'It's good to see you,' I replied.

The irony was wasted on her. 'It's good to see you, too,' she said, without any trace of warmth at all. 'Have you got the money?'

I tapped my inside jacket pocket. 'It's here.'

'The full ten thousand?' she asked anxiously.

'The full ten thousand,' I assured her.

'Right,' Marie said. 'Let's go to the buffet, and I can brief you on developments so far.'

It was almost as if I'd dreamed the last part of that phone call, I thought, as I followed her past students with rucksacks, women in expensive country suits who were only in town to shop, and dossers who held out their hands for spare change and kept one eye open for the police.

'*I love you,*' she'd said. '*I meant that, you know. I really do love you.*'

How could she have spoken those words only a few hours ago, and yet be so cold now?

'You still don't understand what's going on, do you, you bloody fool!' jeered a nagging voice at the back of my mind. 'She needed money for the next phase of her operation, and what better way to ensure you came through with it than by telling you what she knows you've always wanted to hear?'

I didn't believe it! I *wouldn't* believe it!

And yet the thought had come from inside my own head, so there had to be at least a part of me which accepted it as a strong possibility.

We reached the buffet. Marie, without asking me what I wanted, ordered two coffees, and took them over to the smoking section. As soon as she'd set the tray on the table, she took out her cigarettes and lit up.

I sat down opposite her. 'You know Bill Harper's been murdered, don't you?' I asked.

Marie nodded. 'I heard about it on the radio. But it's got nothing to do with this case.'

'The police seem to think it might have.'

'The police are wrong,' Marie said, waving her cigarette like a dismissive magic wand. 'Paul Taylor's probably the one who killed your brother, and he's never left Bristol since the crash.'

'You sound very sure of yourself.'

'It's my job to be sure of myself.' Marie smiled, but it was a complacent smile, rather than an affectionate one. 'Do you want to know how I found Paul Taylor when the combined might of several police forces failed?'

'Why not,' I said, though there were many things in my tormented mind that I would rather have talked about.

'As you know, I started my search in Lancashire, but the moment I found out that on the day of the crash, Paul had gone into a bank in Bristol and withdrawn twenty thousand from the company account—'

'He'd done *what*?' I interrupted.

'He withdrew twenty thousand pounds from the company account. Didn't you know?'

'No, I didn't know,' I admitted, 'but more to the point, how did *you* know?'

'If you get two publishers together, they'll talk about nothing but publishing,' Marie said. 'Isn't that right?'

'Yes, I suppose it is.'

'In the same way, two coppers will talk about nothing but police work. And if they're doing that talking in a pub, and you've positioned yourself so you're quite close to them, you'll find you can learn all kinds of interesting things – especially when one of them has a mouth as big as Detective Sergeant Matthews has.'

'But even if Paul Taylor drew out the money in Bristol, how could you assume that he was still—'

'I checked up on Taylor's background. He's led a completely conventional life. He was brought up in a nice suburb, attended a good secondary school, and chose a sensible business course at university. He's never shown any real spirit of adventure in his entire life – and he's never been in trouble with the police.'

'So?'

'His picture has been in all the papers, there've been reports about him on the television, and the police have been manning a hotline round the clock,' Marie continued. 'If they'd been looking for you, rather than Paul, they'd have had you within a couple of days. But Paul is still missing. How do you explain that?'

'Perhaps he's gone abroad,' I suggested.

'Not him,' Marie said. 'He's scared enough being on the run in this country. Abroad, he'd be absolutely terrified.'

'So what did he do?'

'To stay hidden, he needed help – the sort of help which wasn't too scrupulous, and possibly had criminal connections. The problem was that nice, straight Paul didn't know anyone like that – except that he did!'

'Who?'

'Was your father part of the team negotiating the purchase of Western Haulage?

'Yes, Grandfather insisted on it, because he wanted all the directors to be behind the deal.'

'And Paul would have gone with your father?'

'Of course.'

'So he'll have met Hugh Morgan then, and even if your uncle couldn't see that he was a villain, Paul could.'

'Oh, Uncle Tony could see he was a villain, all right,' I said, 'but since the honest partners were prepared to sell the company cheap, he didn't really care.'

'So Paul was in Bristol with his pockets full of money, blood on his hands, and nowhere to run to,' Marie said. 'He had no choice but to turn to Hugh Morgan – and once I'd realized that, the rest was easy.'

'What did you do?'

'I went to see Morgan and gave him some guff about there being a substantial reward for information which would lead me to Paul Taylor. At that point, I still wasn't one hundred per cent sure I'd got it right, but as soon as I mentioned the money, his eyes lit up, and I knew I was spot on.'

'He admitted it?' I asked amazed. 'Just like that?'

Marie snorted. 'Of course it wasn't just like that. What he said was that he wasn't sure, but he might know a man who knew a man who might be able to get the address where Paul was hiding. He didn't want any money himself for providing this information, but the other two men would probably want ten thousand pounds each. I told him that for that kind of money I could find plenty of men who knew men, and he said that in that case, maybe it could be fixed for ten grand between them.'

'Why is he so willing to sell Paul out?'

'My guess is that Taylor's now paid him all the money he could lay his hands on, so there's no point in running the risk of hiding him any longer. So, given that Morgan was planning to withdraw his protection anyway, the extra ten thousand is something of a bonus.' She lit a second cigarette from the stub of her first. 'By the way, he wanted *you* to know that he was involved in this. He was most insistent on that.'

He would have been, I thought. He'd promised to get his revenge and now he had – first by impeding the murder inquiry for quite some time, and then by squeezing money out of me.

'The reason you asked me for the money, rather than going to Lydia, is that you don't trust her,' I said. 'Is that right?'

'Yes.'

'And when did this lack of trust begin?'

'It was there right at the start. She either wanted Paul to be found or to make certain he couldn't be found – and whichever it was, that meant she was tied in with the murders in some way.'

'So even though you didn't trust her, you still agreed to work for her?'

Anger flashed in Marie's eyes. 'I had no choice but to work for her,' she said. '*I'm* not rich, like you Conroys. If I was going to carry out my investigation properly, I needed someone to pick up my expenses, and Lydia's offer was like a gift from heaven.'

'Let me see if I've got this straight,' I said. 'You were already intending to try and find Paul Taylor, even before Lydia hired you?'

The anger in her eyes was suddenly replaced by defensiveness. 'That's right,' she agreed.

'Why?'

She shrugged. 'It's an interesting case.'

'An interesting case?' I repeated 'Tell me, Marie, what *makes* it so interesting – the fact that it involved my family?'

'Perhaps.'

Lydia had been right – about this matter at least. Marie had always shown an unnatural interest in the Conroys.

Even during that first meal we had together in the little Italian restaurant in Oxford – the very night we met – she'd been pumping me for information. I could see that now.

But *why* had she done it? Though Lydia claimed that *she* knew the reason behind it, I was as much in the dark as I'd ever been.

'Just what kind of game are you playing, Marie?' I asked.

'Game?' she echoed, as if she had absolutely no idea what I was talking about. 'No game! Someone tried to kill you, remember?'

'Of course I remember.'

'And that really matters to me,' Marie said. 'Doesn't it matter to you, Rob? Don't you want to find out who was responsible for three members of your family dying unnecessarily?'

It was an evasion, and I knew it, but what else could I say but, 'Of course it matters to me.'

Marie stubbed her cigarette out forcefully in the ashtray. 'Then can I suggest that instead of questioning me like this, we get on with the job we've both come down here to do?'

'Will you ever tell me what's going on inside your head?' I pleaded. 'Will you ever let me see what you're really feeling?'

'Perhaps when this is over,' she said. 'Maybe then, I'll finally be able to let myself come clean.'

TWENTY-SEVEN

There were uniformed officers in every room of the house – going through drawers, tapping the backs of cupboards, and lifting floorboards. The man who had instituted the search stood next to the picture window in the lounge, looking down across the fields to the mere, while the man whose home was being subjected to such detailed scrutiny paced agitatedly up and down behind him.

'This is totally outrageous,' my cousin Philip said.

Owen Flint turned round to face him.

'The magistrate who signed the search warrant didn't seem to think it was too unreasonable,' he said mildly.

'Why would I have murdered Bill Harper?' Philip demanded. 'I promoted him. I gave him a status in the company equal to my own.'

'You've made the point before,' Flint reminded him. 'But the promotion was business – the murder might well have been an affair of the heart.'

Philip laughed. 'An affair of the heart? Whatever can you mean by that, Mr Flint?'

'You chucked Susan Harper, but then you discovered – much to your surprise – that you really were in love with her. And you had to have her at any cost – which is why you killed her husband.'

'Do you think that Bill would have objected if I'd used my droit de seigneur to take his little Enid off him – because I don't,' Philip said. 'And far from falling in love with her, if it hadn't been for the convenience of her happening to live in the village, I probably wouldn't have bothered with her at all.'

You really are a little shit, aren't you? Flint thought.

'Susan's nothing but a vindictive little bitch!' Philip said, with sudden venom, 'and if it's the last thing I do, I'll find a way to pay her back for this.'

'I wouldn't think you were exactly in a position to be making threats, sir,' Flint said. 'Besides, look at it this way – Susan Harper's testimony may have made you the number one suspect for the murder of Bill Harper, but at least it's got you completely off the hook for the murders of your father, uncle and cousin, because she's your alibi for the night before the crash, isn't she?'

'Yes, she is,' Philip agreed. 'With Bill away in Bristol and Swansea, it was the ideal opportunity for us to spend some time together. But she's totally wrong about the other thing. It wasn't me she saw coming up the fields and entering this house.'

'Who was it then? A burglar? A passing tramp who just happened to have your door key? The Mad Hatter?'

'I don't know,' Philip said angrily. 'You're the police – you find out who it was.'

A uniformed constable entered the room, carrying an iron bar in a plastic evidence bag.

'We found this buried in the garden, sir,' he said.

Flint turned to Philip with a pitying expression on his face. 'You look surprised we've found it so quickly,' he said. 'Haven't you ever heard of metal detectors?'

'Anyone could have put it there,' Philip said frantically. 'All they had to do was open the gate and dig a hole. I can see what's happening here. I'm being framed, aren't I? I'm being set up for something I didn't do.'

'If you didn't kill Bill Harper, then you've got nothing to fear,' Flint told him. 'But let's just say you killed him, and then buried the murder weapon. Can you be sure – absolutely sure – that one of your neighbours, out for a late-night stroll, perhaps, didn't see you at it?'

Philip's head jerked back, as if he'd been slapped.

'Are you saying that you've got a witness?' he asked shakily.

'I'm saying there's a *possibility* of a witness,' Flint said, noncommittally.

Panic flooded Philip's eyes. 'Even if I did bury it – and I'm not saying that I did – it's just an iron bar,' he said. 'There's absolutely no proof that it's the murder weapon.'

Flint shook his head. 'You think that, just because you cleaned it, you'll have got rid of all the traces,' he said. 'If you do, you're wrong, boyo – terribly, terribly wrong. The lads in forensics will have come up with enough material to fill a small book by tomorrow. And there'll be other things. We'll find your footsteps leading down to the mere – and we'll be able to tell when you made them. We'll find soil samples on your shoes. There may even be some bloodstains on your clothes.'

'He didn't blee . . .' Philip began.

'No, he didn't, did he?' Flint said. 'So that's one little pointer we can't use. But like I said, there'll be enough others.'

'Am I being arrested?' Philip asked, now on the verge of hysteria.

'Not till we've done a few tests,' Flint told him. 'But if I were in your shoes, I wouldn't go making any long-term plans.'

The tests would turn out to be positive, he was sure of that. So they'd have both the means and opportunity to help them make their case. The only problem was, he still had no idea – absolutely no bloody idea at all – *why* Philip should have wanted to kill Bill Harper.

Marie stubbed out the third cigarette she'd smoked since we entered the buffet, and glanced down at her watch.

'It's time to make a move,' she said. 'Give me the money.'

I placed the brown envelope on the table between us. I was expecting her to put it in her handbag, but she merely grabbed it, and then stood up.

'Let's go,' she said.

We made our way across the station, towards the main exit. Marie still had the envelope in her hand, and I found myself looking around nervously for signs of pickpockets and muggers.

'When will the exchange be made?' I asked.

'Soon,' Marie replied, unhelpfully.

We were almost at the street. A newspaper seller was shouting out the day's headlines, and one of his customers took a sudden step backwards and banged into Marie.

'I'm terribly sorry,' the man said. 'I can't think what could have made me so incredibly clumsy.'

'No harm done,' Marie said.

The man stepped clear of her. 'Are you sure you're all right?'

'Positive.'

'Well, in that case, I've got a train to catch.'

The man hurried away, but not before I'd noticed the corner of a brown envelope sticking out of the corner of his newspaper.

I turned my attention to Marie. She was studying a single sheet of cheap writing paper.

'This is the address,' she said.

'But how do you know it's the *right* one?' I asked. 'That bastard Morgan could have written down his granny's address, for all you know, and still have taken the money.'

'When you cut through all the morality crap, he's simply a businessman making a deal,' Marie said. 'Why would he bother to double-cross me – and possibly store up trouble for himself later on – when it's just as easy to tell me the truth?'

'If he's not double-crossing you, he's double-crossing Paul Taylor,' I pointed out.

Marie snorted. 'There's nothing I can do about that – because you simply can't protect people like Paul Taylor. They're *born* to be double-crossed.'

I'd always realized we came from different worlds, but now – when I was already feeling out of my depth, and in danger of drowning, while she was as calm as if she'd never left the paddling pool – I began to see just how different our worlds were.

We left the station and turned right. Marie's Golf was parked on a double yellow line, but – with the luck of the Irish – she hadn't been ticketed.

'There's an A to Z of Bristol on the passenger seat,' she said. 'Look up Alexander Terrace.'

We left the city centre behind us and were soon passing through an area of grim terraced houses, most of which seemed to have been abandoned.

'It's not very salubrious, is it?' I said.

'Did you really expect Hugh Morgan to book a desperate fugitive like Paul Taylor a room in the Ritz?' Marie asked.

I read a street sign, and then checked my map again. 'Alexander Terrace is the next street on the left,' I said. 'As far as I can work out, number seventeen will be about halfway down it.'

Marie indicated, but instead of turning, as I'd expected her to, she merely pulled into the curb.

'No point in advertising the fact that we're here,' she said.

We walked down the street. Many of the houses were boarded up, and even those still occupied looked as if they would crumble to red brick dust with the slightest encouragement. There was an alley running along the side of number eleven and Marie came to a halt there.

'Go up to number seventeen, and knock on the front door,' she told me. 'Make sure you knock *very loudly*.'

'And where will you be?'

She looked at me as if I was a slow pupil she really despaired of teaching *anything*.

'I'll be round the back, of course,' she said.

As I walked up the street, my heart was pounding at what felt like double the usual rate, and I was suddenly as cold as if I'd plunged into icy water. It was possible, I told myself, that we were only a few minutes away from finding out why three of my family had died – and though there was a part of me which desperately wanted to know the answer, there was also a corner of my being which feared that perhaps the truth might be so horrendous that it would be better left hidden.

I reached number seventeen. The brickwork was eroded. The black paint on the front door was peeling. The faded curtains at the front window were tightly drawn. I didn't know how much Paul Taylor was paying for his hiding place, but whatever it was, he was being cheated.

I knocked loudly on the front door and saw the curtains twitch. I knocked again. There was the sound of running footsteps in the hall. I bent down and opened the letterbox.

'Be sensible, Paul,' I shouted. 'You know you're going to have to talk to me sometime.'

The footsteps were getting fainter. I knocked a third time and wondered whether it was as easy to break down doors in real life as it always seemed to be in the Hollywood movies.

There were more footsteps – two sets – and the door swung open. Paul Taylor was standing there, bent forward. Behind him was Marie, with his arm in a lock. He looked like nothing so much as a terrified child, and I found it almost impossible to believe that this man, this pathetic wretch who Marie had rendered completely helpless, could be a killer – even a long-distance one.

'You've no right to do this to me,' Paul gasped.

'No right!' Marie said harshly. 'You're a fugitive from justice, sunshine. It's *you* who doesn't have any rights!'

'If Marie releases you, do you promise not to try and make a break for it again?' I asked.

Paul looked up at me with eyes which were filled with defeat. 'What would be the point?' he said. 'I've nowhere left to run to.'

'Why don't you let him go?' I suggested.

'You come inside and close the door behind you first,' Marie told me, maneuvering Paul a little further back down the hallway.

Once I was in the passage, Marie let go of her captive's arm. Paul reached up with his left hand and massaged his shoulder.

'You hurt me!' he complained.

'It's your own fault – you shouldn't have struggled so much,' Marie said indifferently.

'Shall we go into the lounge?' I asked.

'If that's what you want to call it,' Paul said bitterly.

When he led us into the room, I saw exactly what he meant. Apart from a three-piece suite which must have been old when my grandfather started making furniture, the room was bare.

'Welcome to my humble home,' Paul said, the bitterness still very much in evidence in his voice. 'How did you find me?'

'How do you *think* we found you?' Marie asked.

'Did Hugh Morgan sell me out?'

'Of course,' Marie said. 'And he did it without a second's hesitation. He doesn't give a toss about you. Nobody does. Nobody wants to help you, either – except for us. And even our help is dependent on how cooperative you are.'

Paul sank heavily on to the sofa. A cloud of dust rose around him.

'I suppose I should have expected it from Morgan,' he said. 'I had nothing left to give him. Perhaps I should have gone while I still had a little bit of money, but where would I have gone *to*?'

He looked tired, I thought, very, very tired. And much older than the last time I'd seen him.

'Did you kill my brother?' I asked.

He shook his head wearily. It was the gesture of a man who, having failed in his one brief dash for freedom, had finally given up hope and no longer cared what happened to him.

'Say it!' I demanded. 'Tell me you didn't kill my brother.'

'I didn't kill John. I didn't kill any of them.'

'Then who did?'

'Lydia.'

'You're lying to me!' I said angrily. 'Maybe she was behind it all, but Lydia was in the Middleton Health Spa the night the car was tampered with. According to Chief Inspector Flint, she couldn't have got out without being noticed. Besides, she called room service in the middle of the night, like she'd done all the other nights she'd stayed there.'

Paul shook his head again. 'She called them all the other nights, but *that* night it was me.'

'You're saying you could imitate her voice well enough to fool a woman who'd probably heard it fifty times before?'

'No, I couldn't,' Paul agreed. 'But I didn't need to. She'd left a tape with two messages on it. I played the first one – ordering the coffee – over the phone. And I played the second one from the bathroom, when room service arrived. Lydia said that was where she normally was when the coffee arrived, so it wouldn't arouse any suspicion. And as for issuing orders, and then not waiting for a reply, she'd been doing that all week. I tell you, she planned it all out very carefully.'

Marie lit a cigarette. 'Go back to the beginning,' she ordered him.

'You mean, when we first met?'

'No, you bloody idiot!' Marie said harshly. 'I'm not interested in the whole of your nasty little affair. Just go back to the beginning of your visit to the Middleton Spa.'

Paul Taylor bowed his head. 'It was Lydia who arranged it. She said we needed some time away, in order to talk things through, and I agreed because I didn't want a scene.'

'*You* didn't want a scene?' I said. 'Lydia said that was what *she* was afraid of.'

'Why should I have made a scene?' Paul protested. 'I was the one who was dropping *her.*'

'I don't believe you,' I said. 'Lydia told me she was dropping you because she felt guilty about having betrayed her husband – but why would you want to drop her?'

'I wanted to end it because I'd realized I was in love with someone else,' Paul said.

'Who?' I asked.

A look of total astonishment – which I'll swear he couldn't have faked – filled Paul's face.

'Don't you know?' he asked.

'No, I don't,' I told him.

And then – in a flash – all the odd facts and unexplained events which had been floating around my head came together, and I *did* know.

'Oh God, no!' I moaned.

'When exactly did you make your first visit to the spa?' Marie asked crisply.

'It was two days before the crash. That's when I told her I was finishing with her.'

'How did she take it?'

'She was hysterical. She said she was going to kill herself.'

'What did you do?'

'I left.'

'You didn't think there was a chance she *might* kill herself?'

'Not for a second. Lydia is as hard as nails. There's nothing soft or vulnerable about her – and that's why I could never make myself love her, however hard I tried.'

'You went back to the spa the next day – the day before the crash,' Marie said. 'Why?'

'She phoned me and said that if I'd just do one little thing for her, she'd let me go without any more trouble.'

'And did she say that one little thing was to pretend to be her for the night?' Marie asked.

'Not on the phone – she didn't explain it until we were up in her room and she'd shown me the tape recorder.'

'Did she tell you *why* she wanted you to pretend to be her?'

'No.'

'And you didn't ask her?'

'I did ask her, yes, but all she'd say was that it was very important and she'd explain everything when she returned. I suppose the truth is that I wanted her off my back so badly that I'd have agreed to almost anything she asked – however crazy it seemed to me. Anyway, she took my car, and left just after dinner, before the gates were closed.'

'And *did she* explain everything to you when she got back?' Marie asked.

'Oh yes,' Paul said, shaking his head in horror.

'So tell us about it.'

'She said beforehand she couldn't return until about ten o'clock next morning, when she'd be able to slip in unnoticed

in the middle of the traffic which was coming in to use the spa
facilities. So until she got back, she said, I was to put a "Do
not disturb" notice on the door, and stay in the room.'

'And what did she do when she returned?'

'She turned on the news channel on the television.'

Marie nodded, as if that had been what she'd expected him
to say.

'Did she explain why she'd developed this sudden interest
in the news?'

'No, she just said that I should just shut up and watch. So
that's what we did – sitting side by side. There was some inter-
national news first – a report on an earthquake somewhere, I
think – and then the report on the crash in South Wales. There
were pictures of the car. It looked a bloody mess. The police
hadn't released the names of the victims at that point, but they
did say there'd been five people in the car, and three of them
were dead. Lydia said, "Good, John's bound to have been one
of the fatalities, because he'll have been the driver." I didn't
know what she was talking about, so she explained it to me.
She told me how she'd got into the garage, what she'd done to
the hydraulics, and how she'd cut through the brake cable.
"Most people would have made a mess of it," she said, "but I
knew just how far to cut so it would give way at the right time."
You should have seen her eyes. They were mad – completely
mad!'

'What happened next?' Marie asked.

'I still couldn't accept it. I told her she couldn't seriously
expect me to believe that she'd deliberately set out to kill five
people. She said that of course she hadn't – that the only one
she'd been interested in killing was John. She hadn't even known
there'd *be* five people in the car – there certainly shouldn't have
been.' Paul Taylor shuddered. 'As if her not knowing there'd
be five of them made it better – as if she was only responsible
for the death of the man she *wanted* to kill.'

'Go on,' Marie told him.

'She said John's death made her a very rich woman, and that
now she'd got her hands on the money, I'd want to stay with
her. I told her she was insane, and that I was going to the police.
And her eyes turned colder than I'd ever have believed anybody's

could be. "You'd better not do that," she said. She looked down at her handbag, which was on her knee. "I've got a gun in here".'

'Had she?' Marie asked.

'Yes, she had.'

'And did she point it at you?'

'No, I think she thought she'd done enough by letting me know she had it. But there were other things she did threaten me with.'

'Like what?'

'She pointed out that, after what I'd done for her the previous night, the police were bound to suspect I was involved in the murders. And even if they didn't, I still wouldn't be safe, because a rich woman like her could easily ensure that I had a nasty accident.'

'Did you believe her?' Marie said.

'Oh God, yes!' Paul said. 'She killed three people without turning a hair. She wasn't going to worry about having one more murdered.' He gulped. 'A second later, the coldness melted away, and she was stroking my hair. "We can't get married right away," she said. "But when a little time's passed, it will be perfectly acceptable. And once we're married, we'll have a wonderful life. I'm a very important person in the village, you know. Everyone looks up to me." He shook his head. 'I think that's really why she did it. Not so she could have me – although she *did* want me. Not for the money – though that was nice too. The main reason she killed John Conroy was in order to keep her position in the village.'

'What did you say to her?'

'I was half out of my mind with fear. If I'd told her I wasn't going along with her scheme, she'd probably have killed me, right then and there. So I said I was sorry I'd been acting strangely, and it must just have been the shock. If only she'd told me beforehand, I said, I'd have been prepared. But now I could see how clever she'd been, and we *would* have a wonderful life together.'

'And she bought it?' Marie asked skeptically.

'She must have done, or – I swear to you – she'd never have let me walk out of there.'

'What excuse did you give for leaving?'

'I said it wouldn't look good if I was there when the police arrived to tell her that her husband was dead, so I'd go straight back up to Cheshire, and wait for her there.'

'But, in fact, you went to the bank to draw out twenty thousand pounds, and then you went to see Hugh Morgan?'

'He was the only person I could think of – because Lydia was right, you see. I couldn't go to the police, could I?'

'Maybe not then,' Marie said. Her voice was more ragged and emotional than it had been earlier, and I understood, for the first time, that she'd been making a tremendous effort to keep control of herself. 'No, maybe not then.'

'When else could I have gone?' Paul asked miserably.

I think he realized he'd made a mistake the moment the words were out of his mouth – realized it even before Marie grabbed him by the lapels of his jacket and hauled him to his feet.

Though he was taller than she was, he somehow seemed to look weak and puny when contrasted with her towering rage.

'When else could you have gone?' she demanded. 'You could have gone when she first put forward her crazy plan. It should have been obvious why she needed an alibi – even to you. You could have prevented a tragedy if only you hadn't been so gutless!'

'If I'd known . . .' Paul protested.

In one effortless movement, Marie released his lapels and delivered two whip-crack open-handed slaps which sent him reeling back on to the sofa.

Paul put his arms up to protect his face, but Marie had already flung herself on him, and was screaming, 'Bastard! Bastard!' and trying to claw his face away.

'Marie!' I shouted, but I don't think she even heard me.

I grabbed her from behind and pulled her clear. She struggled for perhaps a second or two, then went limp and started to cry. I guided her over to one of the decrepit chairs, and gently lowered her into it. She buried her head in her hands and began to weep in earnest.

'What is it, Marie?' I asked softly. 'Whatever made you lose control like that?'

'I don't want to talk about it,' she said, between sobs. 'I . . . don't . . . want . . . to talk . . . about it.'

TWENTY-EIGHT

I t was almost incredible, as I watched the way that Marie handled the Bristol rush hour traffic with such skill and expertise, to think that only an hour earlier, she'd been a blubbering wreck, but when she spoke now, her voice, still thick with the tears she'd shed, brought it all back.

'What exactly is the deal that you've made with the police?' she asked.

'The Bristol police won't announce they've got Paul Taylor in custody until tomorrow morning, and Owen Flint won't arrest Lydia until I'm there to cushion Grandmother against the shock.'

'And that's why you're going back to Cheshire, is it – to cushion your grandmother against the shock?'

'Yes.'

'But it's not the only reason, is it, Rob?'

'No,' I agreed reluctantly.

'So what other reason do you have?'

'I want to talk to Lydia, too.'

'But why – for God's sake? What's the point in putting yourself through all that when there's no need to?'

'There *is* a need to,' I said. 'I have to see for myself whether or not the woman who killed my father and brother really is a monster.'

'Let me answer that question for you, right now,' Marie said. 'If she'd killed for love – or even money – then perhaps you could understand what makes her mind tick. But you heard what Paul's told you. She killed to avoid a scandal! And that's simply not human.'

'I still have to see for myself,' I said.

Marie sighed. 'Yes, I suppose you do.'

We had arrived at Temple Meads station, and Marie pulled up close to the main entrance.

'Come back to Cheshire with me,' I pleaded.

'I can't do that,' she said. 'Not in the shape I'm in.'

'We're *both* in bad shape,' I argued – though I still had no idea why the encounter with Paul Taylor should have had such an effect on her. 'Couldn't we try to get through this thing together?'

'I don't work that way, Rob,' Marie told me. 'I have to sort things out on my own.'

'If you really loved me, like you said you did . . .'

She raised a hand to cut me off. 'Please, not now, Rob. It's not the right time.'

'It's never the right time for you,' I said angrily. 'And it never will *be* the right time.'

She looked down at her watch. 'If you don't go right away, you'll miss your train.'

'To hell with my train!'

'Your grandmother needs you. And you've only got a few hours to get her used to the idea that her two sons and one of her grandsons were killed by a member of the family.'

I reached for the door handle. 'So what will you do now?' I asked. 'Go back to Oxford?'

'Perhaps. I haven't made my mind up yet.'

'And when will I see you again?' I asked imploringly. 'I really need to know.'

Marie shrugged her shoulders. 'Soon.'

'What does that mean?'

'A couple of weeks. Maybe a little longer.'

'And what if I need to contact you in the meantime?'

She lit a cigarette. 'You won't be able to.'

There was so much to say, and yet, with Marie's secrets like a huge barrier between us, there was nothing to say at all. I slammed the car door and watched her drive away.

And as I stood there, I remembered the day, so many years ago now, when I had stood outside another railway station and watched my darling Jill go away – forever.

It was early evening as I walked up the High Street, and in the distance I could hear the birds singing their last serenade of the day. As I passed the neat Georgian houses of my childhood, I tried to analyse my confused feelings as best I could. There was hatred, of course, for the woman who had killed my brother and my father. And there was bitterness, too. But above all, I thought, I was still plagued by a feeling of total incredulity – I simply still couldn't believe that Lydia had killed for the reasons which logic and fact told me must have driven her.

As I turned on to Smithy Lane, I remembered the night John had tried to tell me the truth, and I'd been so wrapped up in my own misery that I hadn't been listening. But would it have made any difference if I had heard his confession – would I have been able to alter the chain of events?

I didn't think so. By then, the chain had been so strongly forged that only a truly drastic occurrence – the death of either Paul or Lydia – could have broken one of its steely links.

I walked up the path to Lydia's front door and knocked. It was the housekeeper who answered my knock.

'I'd like to see my sister-in-law, please,' I said.

The housekeeper sniffed. 'I'll see if Mrs Conroy is in.'

She retreated down the hallway, returning perhaps a minute later.

'Follow me,' she said.

She led me into the garden where I'd first met Bill Harper. Lydia was sitting at an expensive wrought-iron table, a cocktail in her hand. She was wearing a simple, yet chic, kingfisher blue dress, and around her neck there was a single row of expensive pearls. She looked every inch the part she had always wanted to play.

She did not get up to greet me.

'The only reason I've agreed to see you at all is to tell you how displeased I am with you,' she said coldly.

'Displeased with me?' I echoed.

'Certainly. The police have been through everything in my house – peering in my cupboards, running their big, sweaty hands over my precious things. Well, I blame you and your grubby little chief inspector friend for that. And he, at least, will be made to pay for it. I've already rung the chief constable – who happens to be a personal friend of mine.'

'And what did he say?' I asked.

'As a matter of fact, he wasn't available at the time I called, but I made his people promise me that he'll ring back as soon as he can.'

'He won't ring you back, Lydia,' I told her. 'And the *reason* he won't be returning your call is because he knows it's all over for you.'

'What do you mean – all over?' Lydia demanded haughtily. 'You're not making any sense at all.'

'I talked to Paul Taylor this afternoon.'

Her eyes, which had only been angry and superior up to that point, suddenly hardened – and I got a sense of what Paul Taylor must have felt that morning of the crash.

'So you talked to Paul, did you?' she said. 'And what did he have to say for himself?'

'He said that while he stayed in your room at the health spa, you drove to Bristol and sabotaged the brakes on the BMW.'

She laughed. 'The poor pathetic fool! Everyone knows I couldn't tell one end of an engine from another.'

'Yes, you've gone to great pains to establish that over the years,' I said, 'but I've been up to Lancashire, remember. I know about Linda Smith, who was an even better mechanic than her father.'

Lydia paled.

I think that until that moment, she'd almost forgotten about my journey to her old home – even though she'd tried to kill me for making it.

And why should she have remembered it? What had happened there, had happened in a distant place which was connected with a past she had almost convinced herself had never existed. So maybe Linda Smith *had* planted a bomb – that had absolutely nothing at all to do with Lydia Hornby Smythe.

But now here I was, suggesting that it was Linda who was real, and Lydia who was the fake – and the idea terrified her.

'Have you . . . have you told anyone in the village that I – that Linda – used to be a grease monkey?' she asked.

'No,' I said, 'but I've told the police.'

'Do you mean that grubby little Welshman?'

'Yes.'

'That's all right then,' Lydia said dismissively. 'He doesn't count for anything round here.'

'Did you really plan to marry Paul Taylor – or did you just

say it to keep him quiet until you got the chance to kill him, too?' I asked.

'I should have shot him in that hotel room,' Lydia said. 'I should have shot him and claimed he was trying to rape me. People would have understood. I would have been a heroine.'

Poor Paul!

She'd had to seduce him, if only to stave off the inevitable.

And he had gone along with it, because his conventional upbringing compelled him to do everything he possibly could to try to convince himself that he was really a heterosexual.

'I think I know why you had to kill them when you did,' I said. 'It was because you could see that Grandfather was dying, and you were afraid that the second he was decently buried, John would go through with his plan to resign and move to Greece.'

'He had no consideration for me,' Lydia said bitterly. 'No thought at all of the position I hold here.'

Images of John's wedding day flooded my mind.

Dialogue ran through my brain as clearly and unfalteringly as if I was listening to a tape through headphones.

John, sitting hunched on my bed, as if all the cares in the world were pressing down on his powerful shoulders.

'I think this whole thing is a mistake.'

'What makes you say that?'

'I just don't think it's going to work.'

'But you must have a reason. Has Lydia done something or said something which has led you to believe . . .'

'It's not about Lydia. *It's about me.'*

My father, sitting at the breakfast table, looking uncomfortable when I'd asked him what he knew about Lydia.

'Not a great deal.'

'And haven't you even tried to find out?'

'John's an adult.'

'But even so . . .'

'. . . and therefore perfectly capable of taking his own decisions. Besides . . .'

'Besides what?'

'I'm so relieved that John is getting married at all.'

And then, of course, there had been Philip at the reception, leaving the girl he was with in order to boast to me.

'I've only just met her, but I'll have her before the night is out. Probably have more luck than your brother John will.'

'And just what do you mean by that?'

'You don't know, do you? You really don't know.'

'Know what? Is this something to do with Lydia?'

'Well, bugger me. And I always thought you were the smartest out of the three of us.'

But all that had been as nothing compared to the way I'd misread the signs during the last few weeks of my brother's life.

'When John said he was in love, I thought he meant he was in love with *you*,' I told Lydia. 'He talked about "us" when he mentioned moving to his Greek island, but you weren't part of that "us", were you, Lydia?'

'I could have given him everything, if only he'd worked with me,' Lydia said. 'He could have been *Sir* John in a few years – and I would have been Lady Conroy. But he was prepared to sacrifice all of that – just to follow his animal instincts.'

'He fell in love,' I said, 'something I don't think you've ever experienced. To you, John was never any more than a ticket to getting what you really wanted. And you knew what he was like, even then, didn't you? That's why you wore clothes which disguised your figure, and had your hair cut so short – all so you'd look boyish for him.'

'You'd been a great disappointment to the family,' Lydia said, taking obvious pleasure from knowing how much she was probably hurting me. 'You were the one who was expected to get married, because you were the one best able to bring the next generation of Conroys into the world. When it became obvious you wouldn't do it, John took the responsibility on himself – even though that was the last thing he wanted personally. Shall I tell you what he was like in bed?'

'No, that isn't necessary,' I said.

'He couldn't get it up, however hard he tried – and each time he failed, he'd cry like a baby, and say he was so sorry. As if I cared! As if sex ever really mattered to me!'

'And the strange thing is that, in his way, I think John really did love you,' I said. 'But it was nothing like the love he came to feel for his new partner. Paul might have been weak, and sometimes even unfaithful, but that didn't matter to John – because he knew he'd found the real thing.'

What a complicated life the three of them had led, each of them knowing what was going on, yet none of them being able to admit it – John because of what it might have done to Grandfather, Lydia because . . .

'Can you imagine what it would have done to my position here in the village if I'd allowed the two of them to go off together?' my sister-in-law asked. 'I'd have been nothing but a laughing stock. Everything I've worked for all these years would have been taken from me overnight. It simply wouldn't have been fair.'

Yes, as the abandoned wife – a woman who had not only lost her husband, but had lost him to *another man* – she would have been nothing but a joke to all those people she sat on committees with. But being a widow was quite a different matter – there was a certain cachet in being a widow.

'The police will be here in a few minutes,' I said. 'You'd better get ready for them.'

'The police?' Lydia repeated. 'You mean that nasty little Welshman? Why would he come here?'

'To arrest you.'

Lydia threw back her head and laughed. 'Arrest *me*? It's true he's searched my house, but do you seriously think he'd be *allowed* to arrest *me*? I told you before, the chief constable is a personal friend of mine. The Lord Lieutenant of the county has drunk cocktails in this very garden.'

She was still laughing as I stood up and walked away.

Owen Flint was waiting in the lane outside with two constables.

'Are you glad you talked to her?' he asked.

'Yes, I think I am,' I said. 'Hate's a very destructive emotion to carry around with you, and it's hard to hate someone who lives so much in a fantasy world that she's lost both her sense of responsibility and any feelings of guilt.'

Owen popped a sweet into his mouth.

'Half an hour ago, I arrested your cousin Philip for the murder of Bill Harper,' he said. 'The forensics are absolutely rock solid. Do you have any idea why he did it?'

'No,' I replied. 'But whatever reason he gives you, you can be sure of one thing – as far as he's concerned, it won't be *his* fault that Bill's dead.'

TWENTY-NINE

Marie was not in Oxford. I knew that for a fact – not simply because she never answered her phone, but because, since my return from Cheshire, I had spent two more long nights in a rented car outside her flat. And she never appeared.

As I sat there, on the third night of my vigil, watching her front door through tired, prickly eyes, I was haunted by memories of a phone call I had received an emotional lifetime earlier – the one that Jill's father had made to me.

It wouldn't be Marie's father who made it this time, of course. It couldn't be, since he had recently died. But perhaps some other caring relative from the other side of the water would think it a kindness to ring me.

'Mr Conroy?' the call would go.

'Yes, that's me.'

'I'm Marie O'Hara's cousin, Siobhan.'

'Yes?'

'We've never met, but she's told me so much about you that it's almost like you were one of the family.'

And all the time she was talking, I'd be thinking, 'Why doesn't she get on with it? Why doesn't she say what she's got to say?'

Finally, she would. *'I'm afraid there's been an accident. Marie's . . . well, there's no easy way of putting it . . . Marie's dead.'*

Yes, that was how it would happen.

And it would happen because I hadn't been there with her

– just as Jill's accident had happened because I hadn't been there with *her*!

I told myself I was thinking like the lunatic I had once officially been – that I couldn't have saved Jill then any more than I could save Marie now – but it didn't help. I was obsessed with the longing to protect her, yet I had no idea of how to even *find* her.

If only she'd ring me!

If only she'd tell me where she was!

But she didn't ring, and it wasn't until the end of my third night's watch that I realized what I was going to have to do if I was ever to have a chance of finding out where she'd gone.

It was eleven thirty in the morning. Andy McBride and I sat in the bar of the Bulldog, on St Aldate's. I was sipping lethargically at my now tepid coffee. Andy was looking moodily into his glass of orange juice. Neither of us had spoken a word for several minutes.

It was Andy who finally broke the silence. 'You'll never manage it on your own,' he said.

'I'll *have to* do it alone,' I told him, 'because I'm not prepared to take you along and run the risk of you going back to prison.'

Andy shrugged. 'Och, I'm noo stranger to a prison cell. There'd be nae hardship there for me.' He grinned. 'An' think of what great publicity it'd be for ma new book.'

'No,' I said firmly. 'Just tell me how it's done, and I'll do it on my own.'

'Tell me all I need to know aboot becoming a publisher,' Andy said. 'You've got five minutes.'

'I couldn't possibly begin to explain . . .'

'Exactly – an' no more could I explain housebreaking in five minutes. It's a skilled job we're talkin' aboot here, and you wouldna have a snowball in hell's chance on your own.' He put his hand on my shoulder. 'Let me do this, Rob – please.'

There was a begging look in his eyes I simply couldn't resist.

'All right,' I agreed.

Andy drained his orange juice 'Well, if we're gonna do it, we'd best get it over wi'.'

'Now?' I said, shocked. 'Hadn't we better wait for darkness?'

Andy gave me the same professional look of pity that Marie had given me outside the crumbling terraced house in Bristol, where we found Paul Taylor.

'I've always worked in daylight,' he said. 'The more folk there are aroond, the less chance there is you'll be noticed.'

'Don't we need some tools?' I asked.

'Like what?' Andy asked, grinning again.

'I don't know,' I said helplessly. 'Skeleton keys or something.'

Andy reached in his pocket and produced a bunch of odd-shaped keys.

'Like these?' he asked.

'Where did you get them from?'

'I borrowed them from an "acquaintance".'

'And how long have you been carrying them around with you?'

'Ever since you told me that Marie had'na come back to Oxford.'

Either by luck or judgement, the first key Andy tried opened the front door of the house on the Banbury Road.

'Piece o' piss,' he said softly to me. 'You'd think a private detective like her would be more security conscious.'

Marie *had* taken more precautions with her own flat, and for two gut-wrenching minutes I stood in the corridor while Andy tried a series of keys on both the standard and the security locks.

And then we were in – right inside the place which, despite all the other things that Marie and I had shared over the previous two years, she had never allowed me to see.

At first sight, it was innocuous enough. The main room contained the kitchenette and the living area. There were three other doors leading off it, presumably to the bathroom and two bedrooms.

'The first ninety seconds you're in a place, you're as safe as hooses,' Andy whispered. 'Every minute after that, your risk doubles.'

I looked around me – two armchairs, a television, a filing cabinet and a large table with Marie's computer on it.

'Check through the filing cabinet and I'll see what's on the table,' I told Andy.

'It'd be a big help if we knew what we was lookin' for,' the Scot said.

But the problem was, we didn't know. I could only hope that we came across a memo she'd written to herself, a set of directions she'd taken down over the phone, or a sketch map of a place she intended to visit – something, *anything* which might tell me where my Marie had gone.

I sifted through the papers on the table. There were reports for clients, receipts for petrol, bills for restaurants outside the Oxford area – and an envelope with a Limerick postmark which dated it as having been sent only a few days earlier.

I took the single sheet of paper out of the envelope.

My dearest Marie, it began.

I quickly scanned the rest of the text. The writer said that everyone was fine and missing her, that the dog had had puppies, that the milk yield was up from the previous month, and that preparations were well underway for the annual fête.

At the bottom of the letter were the words: *I'm always thinking about you. Your ever-loving Dad.*

Her dad!

'My father's died,' she'd told me. 'We weren't very close, but I still feel guilty.'

Lies, all lies!

Her father was alive, and from the tone of the letter, they had a very affectionate relationship.

How many other falsehoods had she fed me? I wondered, despairingly. How little of what she'd said to me had ever been true?

Had she been smiling when, over the phone, she said she loved me – almost amazed at how easy it was to fool me?

'Not much in there,' Andy said, sliding the filing cabinet drawer closed. 'She dunna seem to be much of a woman for paperwork.'

'No,' I said dully. 'I don't think she is.'

But holding that letter in my hand, I asked myself if I really knew anything about her.

'Time tae check oot the rest o' the place,' Andy said.

I nodded and, almost in a trance, walked to the nearest of the doors which led off the living room. I turned the handle, but it was locked.

'Now tha's what I call a gud piece o' work,' Andy said, gazing admiringly at the lock. 'You go an' check the other rooms, while I work out a way ta get this booger open.'

The bathroom was neat, tidy and totally devoid of any clues. Marie's bedroom told me nothing, either. I did note that some of her outfits were missing, but that just said she'd gone away – which I knew already.

I was checking under the bed when Andy appeared in the doorway.

'I think you'd better come an' see what I've found,' he said gravely.

And suddenly I was very, very afraid.

'It's not . . . she's not . . .' I managed to gasp.

'I've nae found her body, if that's what you're worried about,' Andy assured me, 'but you'd still better prepare yourself for a shock.'

In trepidation, I crossed the living room again, and forced myself to enter the second bedroom. It was smaller than the one I'd just been in, and there was no furniture at all. Instead, corkboard filled every inch of wall – and to that corkboard were pinned a large number of newspaper articles, photographs and documents.

I examined the closest ones. There was an article from one of the Northwich papers which carried a picture of my Uncle Tony at a charity function. Next to that were two photographs of him, both obviously taken with a long-distance lens.

I moved on. There were copies of articles he had written for a haulage trade magazine, and any number of pictures of him out with his various girlfriends.

The whole room was nothing but a museum – *a shrine* – to my uncle.

'Does this mean wha' I think it means?' Andy asked.

Unable to find the words to answer him, I merely nodded.

I had learned the bitter truth at last, I thought, as I felt a hard iron band tightening across my chest. I finally understood why she had been waiting outside St John's College that night. And I knew now why she had lost all control in that dilapidated house in Bristol and attacked Paul Taylor so viciously.

I'd no idea where she had first met my uncle – perhaps at some kind of security conference, perhaps in a pub – but that didn't really matter.

What *did* matter was that she had become just another one of the long string of mistresses that my uncle had had since Aunt Jane left him. He had got bored with her in the end, of course – he always got bored with his concubines – but, unlike all the others, she had not been able to let go.

And the bitter truth now facing me was that Marie had never been interested in me at all – I only existed for her because of my connection with him.

The room was starting to spin before my eyes, and there was a strong taste of bile rising in my gullet. Holding on to the wall for support, I made my way across the lounge to the bathroom. Once there, I leant over the toilet bowl – and was violently sick.

The first double brandy I'd knocked back in the Bulldog had helped to settle my stomach. The second had done a little to ease the aching in my soul – but not a great deal.

'I'll be around for as long as you want me to be, Rob,' Andy McBride said, from across the table. 'You know that, don't you?'

'I know it,' I said, 'and I'm very grateful.'

'Och, it's nothin' ta be grateful aboot,' Andy replied. 'I owe you. When I needed it, how many months did *you* stick to *me* like glue?'

'Several?' I speculated.

'For ten months, two weeks an' three days you never left my side while there was still a chance of me gettin' my hands on a drink. An' if ye need the favour returning, you only need to ask.'

'That won't be necessary,' I said.

But even as I was speaking, I was looking down at my empty brandy glass and thirsting for a refill.

'I've been through it all maself, Rob,' Andy said softly. 'I can recognize the symptoms creepin' up when I see them.'

One more drink, and I would call a halt, I promised myself.

'If you don't mind, I'd like to be alone now,' I told Andy.

The Scot shook his head. 'You don't want to be alone at all. It's just that given your choice of company, you'd prefer the bottle to me.'

'It's not that at all. I just need a little quiet time to think things through,' I protested.

Andy nodded gravely. 'Aye, well, you canna help a man if he dusna even want to help himself. I'll be awa' noo, but if you want me, you know where you can find me.'

I watched him leave the pub, his shoulders stooped as if the failure had been his, not mine. I thought of calling him back, but instead, I ordered myself another double brandy.

Less than an hour ago, I had had hope, I thought. Not much hope – but at least enough to keep me afloat. But now I had seen Marie's shrine to my uncle, and all of that was gone.

My mobile phone rang irritatingly in my pocket. I decided to ignore it, but when I pulled it out to hit the off button, I saw that the screen display said my caller was Owen Flint, so, with a sigh, I pressed "answer".

'Where are you?' Owen asked.

'Oxford.'

'That's a pity. I was rather hoping you'd still be in the Cheshire area.' He paused. 'Listen, I know you've been doing quite a lot of running around recently, but I'd really appreciate it if you'd come up here one last time.'

'What's the problem?'

'The problem is your cousin Philip. He's admitted to the killing – even filled us in on some details we'd probably never have uncovered on our own. What he won't tell us is *why* he killed Bill Harper.'

I was tired and dispirited, and I didn't want to be having this conversation. 'Does it really matter *why*?' I asked.

'Juries are usually a bit unhappy when we can't give them a motive,' Flint replied.

'From the way you've been talking, I'd have thought you'd got a rock solid case, even if Philip denies the whole thing.'

'You're right,' Flint admitted. 'We don't need a motive. But I *want* one – for my own personal satisfaction.'

'Why are you telling me all this, Owen?' I asked.

'Because Philip won't talk to me – but he says he's quite willing to answer any questions *you* might have.'

'Did he say why?'

'He says it wouldn't be fair to let you spend the rest of your life not knowing what a bloody moron you've been.'

Yes, I thought, that sounded like Philip. 'I'll catch the next train up,' I said. 'I should be with you sometime in the late afternoon.'

Why wouldn't I?

It was only appropriate that I should oversee the last tragic act in the Fall of the House of Conroy.

And when I'd done my duty, I would walk down to the mere, and listen to wind-driven waves gently caressing the shore. But I wouldn't just stop there on the shore – I'd keep on walking until the water covered my head, and there was no more pain.

THIRTY

The walls of the interview room in the detention centre were painted brown up to chest level, and cream from there to the ceiling. The only furniture was an institutional metal table and two metal chairs. I was sitting at one end of the table, and facing me, at the other end, was my cousin Philip. By the door, a bored-looking prison officer was chain-smoking.

'Why did you come?' Philip asked. 'Was it because that bastard Flint asked you to – or because you yourself were curious to know why I killed Bill?'

'It was probably a little of both,' I admitted. 'But the main reason I'm here is to see if I can do anything to help.'

'Do anything to help?' Philip repeated. 'Why should you want to do anything to help me?'

'Perhaps it's because you're one of the few blood relatives I've got left,' I said.

And because I'd finally come round to accepting what both my Grandmother and Grandfather had told me was true – that whatever Philip had turned into, he wasn't entirely to blame.

Philip smirked. 'Let's see if you're quite so willing to help when you've heard what I've got to say. Now where should I begin? Shall I start by telling you what happened that night down by the mere?'

'If that's the way you want to do it.'

'I was sitting at home, thinking about how much I hated Bill Harper, when it suddenly occurred to me that this was the time of night when he usually took his swim in the mere.'

'Why did you hate him?' I asked. 'Was it because you were in love with Susan?'

Philip shot me a suspicious look. 'How did you know I was having it off with her?'

'Owen Flint told me.'

'Of course,' Philip said. 'You're old "chums" from your Oxford days, aren't you? No, I didn't kill him because I wanted his Enid.'

'Then why . . .?'

'I'll come to that later,' Philip said, with the arrogance of a man who knows he has complete control over the direction the conversation will take and is relishing the power that gives him. 'I was sitting there, and I suddenly thought to myself, "Why not just get rid of all your problems in one fell swoop?" I went to the garage and picked up the iron bar. I knew what I was doing was dangerous, but I just couldn't resist it. He made it so easy for me, you see. He knew I wanted him dead, yet he still went swimming in the mere at night. Alone! It was almost as if he *wanted* me to kill him.'

Or as if he never imagined for a second that you'd have the guts to go through with it, I thought.

But I held my peace.

'I walked along the stream until I reached the mere,' Philip continued. 'There was a full moon, and I could see him swimming through the water as if he hadn't got a care in the world. I found where he'd left his clothes, and hid close to them. When he got out of the mere, I crept up behind him and hit him over the head. It was a doddle.'

'What you still haven't told me is *why* you killed him,' I reminded Philip.

'That's where I'm over a barrel,' my cousin said bitterly. 'If I give you my reasons for killing him, then I might as well not have done it at all – but if I *don't* give you my reasons, I'll never get the police to reduce the charge from murder to manslaughter. Do you see what I mean?'

'Not really,' I admitted. 'You're going to have to be much more specific if I'm to make any sense out of it.'

Philip sighed, as if he didn't want to have to deal with the idiot child sitting opposite him, but accepted that it was necessary.

'I killed him because he was blackmailing me,' he said.

'Blackmailing you?'

'Of course! Why else do you think I would have made him joint managing director? It wasn't because I was fond of him. I didn't like him at all, and the way he brown-nosed to my father made me sick. So was it because I trusted him? Not a chance in hell of that. He wasn't loyal – he just knew how to pick the winning side. And that's why he came to me instead of you – because he was certain that he could get more from me.'

'You mean, he could have blackmailed me, too?'

Philip shook his head. 'No, it was quite a different matter with you. But he could still have given you everything you wanted.'

'I've already got everything I want,' I said.

Except for a grandfather, father and brother I would never see again – and not forgetting the woman I still loved, despite the fact that I was now convinced that she'd only been using me.

'You've got everything you want!' Philip repeated contemptuously. 'You've always been the goody-two-shoes of the family, haven't you? It's all come so easily to you.'

'Yes, incredibly easy,' I said, 'as long as you're prepared to overlook the fact that the woman I was going to marry was killed in a horrific accident, and I had a complete mental breakdown that lasted for nearly two years.'

'It's not my fault you went soft on one of your Enids,' my cousin said. 'If you'd been through what I've been through, you might have a reason to feel sorry for yourself.'

'I never said *you'd* had it easy.'

'You didn't have to put up with your father bringing his tarts into your home at every hour of the night. You've never known what it was like to want a mother's shoulder to cry on – and to know there was no shoulder there for you.'

'Philip, I . . .'

'I used to walk past your house some nights and see you all through the window – sitting around the table. God, how I envied you. I promised myself, back then, that one day *I'd* be the one in the privileged position – that I'd find a way to make you all dance to *my* tune.'

'You can't make up for your own childhood unhappiness by bringing misery to other people now that you've grown up,' I said.

'Maybe I can't,' Philip agreed. 'But I was prepared to give it a damn good try. Do you want to know the first thing which came into my head when I heard the details of the crash?'

'If you want to tell me, I'm willing to listen.'

'I thought, "I'm sorry John died. I'm sorry because, if he hadn't, I would have been his boss. I would have had the power over him." Does that shock you?'

'No,' I admitted. 'But it makes me very sad.'

Philip's lip curled contemptuously. 'I don't want any sympathy from you,' he said.

'So what do you want?'

'I want you to know that, for at least a little while, I had you completely fooled.'

It was a hollow sort of victory, but I supposed it was all he had left to hang on to.

'How did you have me fooled?' I asked.

'You remember what happened after that old idiot of a solicitor had read us Grandfather's will? I was just telling you how I was going to take over Cormorant Publishing and make it into something you would despise, when the phone rang. It was Bill Harper.'

'I remember.'

'Do you also remember what he asked you?'

'He asked me if you were there.'

'And what else?'

'I think he asked me if the will had been read.'

Philip nodded his head. 'That's right. The bastard knew just the right psychological moment to break his dirty little secret.'

'What secret?'

Philip shook his head in disgust. 'You still don't get it, do you? I'd have worked it out long before now.'

'I'm not very good at working things out,' I admitted. 'I didn't work out what was going on with John. I had no idea . . .'

'This isn't about John,' Philip said angrily. 'It's about *me*.'

'I'm sorry,' I said.

'Now where was I? Oh yes. Didn't it bother you, Rob, that immediately after I'd talked to Bill Harper, I offered to give you full independence to run your company the way you wanted to?'

'You explained to me that the threat of a strike in the furniture factory had made you realize running the other businesses would be a full time job, without interfering in Cormorant Publishing,' I said.

Philip's lip twisted again. 'And you actually believed me?'

'Yes,' I admitted. 'But perhaps that was because I *wanted* to believe you.'

'You didn't even bother to check up on whether there really *was* a chance of a strike?'

'No, I didn't.'

'You're a fool,' my cousin told me. 'The real reason I gave you *carte blanche* with Cormorant was because, after what that bastard Harper had told me, I had to do something to keep you quiet.'

'Quiet about what? I didn't know any secrets that might harm you.'

Another sigh of exasperation. 'All right, perhaps what I really mean is, I wanted to stop you making a noise.'

'I still don't understand.'

'I wanted to make sure that you didn't contest Grandfather's will, you cretin.'

'But how could I have contested it? It seemed to me that it was really very straightforward.'

'Spell out the terms for me,' my cousin said.

'You know them as well as I do.'

'Spell them out anyway.'

'Why?'

'Because if you don't, this interview is over.'

'You inherited the voting shares from your father because my father was dead, but if he hadn't been, they would have gone to him.'

'And who would have inherited them when he died?'

'I would.'

'And when you'd gone?'

'If I had a son over thirty-five, they'd go to him.'

'So control of the company would have been lost to my side of the family forever.'

'I suppose so, although it's always possible if I didn't have a son . . .'

'Did Bill Harper come to your hospital room after the crash and tell you what had happened?' my cousin asked.

I pictured him standing in the doorway, eagerly reluctant (or perhaps reluctantly eager) to give me the details – and I shuddered at the thought of it.

'Yes, I can see from the way you're reacting that he did,' Philip said. 'I thought he might have done. Harper wasn't the kind of man to launch his campaign before he'd done the essential groundwork. And since you're an important – albeit stupid – player in the game, giving you his version of the truth would be an essential part of that groundwork.'

'What game? What groundwork?'

'Oh, for God's sake!' Philip said. 'Listen, if Harper could have seen an advantage in telling you what actually happened, he'd have done so. But since he could gain more personally by lying, that's what he did. Now do you see?'

'No.'

'Who died first – according to Harper?'

'John.'

'And then?'

'My father.'

'And finally?'

'Uncle Tony.'

'Well, it wasn't like that at all. John probably did die first – a good liar always sticks as close to the truth as he can – but it was *your* father who asked Harper to get *my* father out of the car.'

Finally, I saw what he was getting at.

'But Uncle Tony was already dead?' I asked.

'Exactly. As the solicitor told us, Grandfather died about an hour before the crash, which meant that, though he never knew it, my father had had effective control for that hour. But then he died as well, and control went to Uncle Edward. True, he only had it for a minute or so – maybe even less – but that doesn't matter, because when Edward died, control passed to you.'

'So that's what Bill had on you,' I gasped.

'One word out of place from Harper, and I would have lost the company to you,' Philip said. 'I would have given him almost anything to keep quiet – but the only thing he would settle for was joint control. I thought I could live with it at first . . . but I couldn't. And that night, after I'd had a couple of drinks, I knew what I had to do. And I'm not ashamed of having done it – only of getting caught.'

'There was no need to do it,' I said. 'You could have continued running the company, even if I did own the controlling stock. I told you I was only ever interested in Cormorant Publishing, and it was the truth.'

'If only I could believe that,' Philip said wistfully.

Our world views were a million miles apart, and I was never going to convince him that I really didn't want Conroy Enterprises.

'I'll get you the best team of lawyers that money can buy,' I told my cousin. 'Don't worry about how much it costs. The company will foot the bill.'

'Of course it will,' Philip replied. 'The company will take care of me. The company will take care of you. It's always taken care of *all of us*, hasn't it?'

And at that moment, I think he really hated the company more than he had ever hated anything before.

THIRTY-ONE

Usk was about to fall, and I was standing in the church-yard, looking down at my family's gravestones. Behind me, I could hear the click-click of a woman's high heels on the flagstone path, but I didn't turn to see who it was – my business was not with the living but with the dead.

The gravestones still had a stark newness which made them look like intruders, but after one or two harsh winters, they would blend in with the sombre setting of the rest of the place. That was the way things were – the way things had to be. The graves would age – and the images of those they contained would gradually begin to fade in the minds of those still living.

'Life goes on, Grandfather,' I said to the nearest grave. 'However much we think it couldn't possibly, it still goes on.'

'Yes, it does, doesn't it?' said a voice which I instantly – and achingly – recognized.

I turned around. Marie was standing a few feet away from me. She was wearing a green dress which matched her eyes perfectly, and even though I fought it, I found my heart beating a little faster.

'Have you come to see him?' I asked bitterly, pointing at Uncle Tony's grave.

She shook her head. 'No, I've come to see you, just as I promised that I would in Bristol.' She took a packet of cigarettes out of her pocket, flipped open the top, then closed it again. 'Best not to smoke in a churchyard,' she said. 'Anyway, I'm trying to give them up.'

'I've been telling you to do that for a long time,' I said.

There was something wooden and unnatural about our conversation – but that hardly came as a surprise. Now that I'd discovered the truth about her and my uncle – now she no longer had a need to use me – we really had nothing much to say to each other anymore.

'You're angry,' Marie said.

'Don't I have a right to be?'

'I suppose so. But perhaps when you've heard what I have to say, you won't feel *quite* so hostile towards me.'

It was almost like my conversation with Philip – but in reverse – I thought.

'I'm listening,' I told her.

She looked around the churchyard.

'Not here,' she said. 'Let's go somewhere with a bit more life in it – somewhere I don't feel guilty about smoking a bloody cigarette.

We walked up the avenue of yew trees. Swallows were circling the church tower, and in the grass, tiny insects chirped urgent, incomprehensible messages. A small furry creature scuttled quickly across the path, then disappeared behind an ancient gravestone, and I was reminded of the day that John, Philip and I killed the shrew.

Marie and I passed through the lychgate and crossed the road to the George and Dragon.

'I'll go and get the drinks, you take a seat,' Marie said, pointing to one of the wooden benches in front of the pub.

I sat down and looked across at my grandfather's house. I thought of how much the old man had meant to me, and how the chain of command he'd set up to hold Conroy Enterprises together had caused so much damage.

Marie returned with the drinks – a pint for me, an Irish whiskey for herself. She placed them on the table between us.

'You said you'd come up here to give me an explanation,' I reminded her.

She lit a cigarette and puffed nervously on it. 'This isn't going to be easy,' she said. 'I've told so many lies in the past . . .'

'I know you have.'

'. . . but you have to believe that everything I'm going to tell you now is the truth.'

'Go on,' I said, noncommittally, still not sure whether or not she had stopped playing games – still not sure if she hadn't worked out one final way in which she could use me.

'I wasn't lying when I said I was brought up in Ireland, but I wasn't giving you the full picture either, which is that I was actually *born* in England. I told you I was adopted, didn't I?'

'Yes. The first time we met. Was *that* true?'

'Completely. It was true about my having a happy childhood, too. I knew I was adopted, but it never bothered me. Why should it have, when I had the kindest, most loving parents anyone could have wished for?'

'You were lucky,' I said, thinking of how my cousin Philip had talked about his own childhood, and even of my own parents, who had been kind but distant.

'Yes, I was lucky,' Marie agreed. 'But though it didn't bother me, I did start to get curious when I was in my teens. I'd catch myself wondering who my real parents were, and why they'd given me up.'

'That's only natural.'

'So when I was eighteen, just before I went to Trinity College, I decided to find out.'

'And what did you discover?'

'My real mother had been dead for a number of years by that time.'

'An illness?'

Marie shook her head, and her hair swirled around her shoulders. 'She committed suicide. An overdose.'

'And your father?'

'He was still alive. My first thought was to go and see him, but I somehow couldn't bring myself to do it.'

'Why was that?'

'I think it had something to do with the fact that he probably didn't even know I existed.'

'How's that possible?' I asked.

'I'd done all the background research by then,' Marie told me. 'I knew my real mother had left my real father early in her pregnancy. There's no evidence that he made any effort to find her after she'd run out on him, and I think that if he'd known she was bearing his child, there would have been. Anyway, she carried me to full term, but, because I'd have interfered with her career, she gave me up for adoption.'

'What was her career?'

Marie looked me straight in the eyes. 'She was an actress,' she said. 'Not a very good one, by all accounts, but a very eager one. Most people seem to think that it was her failure to make a name for herself that led to her suicide.'

She reached into her handbag and placed an old photograph on the table in front of me. It was of a tall, almost stately woman, standing in front of the village church. She had auburn hair which spilled in curls over her shoulders and was smoking a cigarette. I had seen the photograph before – in family albums. And so had Lydia – but unlike me, she had made the connection! And that was why Marie's interest in the family had been no mystery to her!

'Are you saying . . .?' I gasped.

'That I'm Tony Conroy's daughter, and Philip Conroy's sister? Yes, that's what I'm saying.'

'So when we met at St John's College . . .'

'It was no accident. I knew exactly who you were. I'd been following you for a couple of days before I made my move.'

'But why?'

Marie shrugged awkwardly. 'Again, I'm not entirely sure. I imagine that I thought that, if I got to know the family through what you told me, it might eventually make it easier for me to approach my father.'

'And did it seem like it was getting easier?'

'Yes, it did, but it also got more complicated, because I couldn't approach him without explaining it all to you, first – and you'd think I'd only been using you.'

'You *had* only been using me,' I said, trying not to sound too bitter, and failing miserably.

'Maybe I was, at first,' Marie admitted, 'but it wasn't long before you really started to matter to me. I'd finally made up my mind to talk to you as soon as you got back from Bristol, and then I was going to see my father.' She took a deep breath. 'But I'd left it too late, hadn't I?'

'You mustn't blame yourself,' I said, as I felt my battered emotions swing from self-pity to empathy for her. 'You couldn't have known.'

Marie reached up, and angrily brushed a tear away from her eye.

'I felt as if, through my own cowardice, I'd cheated him out of something he was entitled to,' Marie told me. 'Maybe he wouldn't have cared about having a daughter one way or the other – but now I'll never know.'

'That's when you decided to find his killer?'

'Yes. It was the least I could do for him. The *only* thing I could do by then. And when Lydia offered to retain me, it seemed like it was meant to be.'

'But you didn't trust her?'

Marie shook her head again. 'I didn't know that she only wanted Paul Taylor found so that she could kill him before he had a chance to speak to the police – but I sensed that something was wrong.'

I thought back to our impersonal meeting on Temple Meads station. I'd been devastated that she'd been more concerned about the money than she'd been about me – but that only seemed natural now that I understood she had been hunting down the man she thought was her father's killer.

And it was natural, too, that her cool, professional shell should crack after she'd heard from Paul Taylor how easy it would have been for him to prevent the murders.

'You said I mattered to you, didn't you?' I asked.

'I did. You *do* matter to me.'

'Then why wouldn't you go to bed with me? I know you wanted to.'

'I did – I can't tell you just how much I wanted to – but I couldn't allow it to happen.'

'Why not?'

Marie sighed and lit another cigarette. 'I've had love affairs before, and though I've always tried to be a good Catholic, I've taken precautions. But contraceptives sometimes fail, and if they'd failed me, I would have had the baby because I couldn't – I just couldn't – deny that baby the chance to live.'

I needed to make sure I had at least one thing clear before I went any further.

'That night you phoned me from Bristol, you told me you loved me,' I said.

'I should never have told you that.'

'Why – because it wasn't true?'

'No – because it wasn't *fair* to you.'

I still wasn't getting it.

'If we love each other, then why don't we just get married?' I asked. 'And if you get pregnant, then that's great – because we'll both love having children.'

Marie suddenly looked sadder than I'd ever seen her. 'For God's sake, Rob, we're cousins – and sometimes cousins just aren't biologically compatible,' she said. 'I might give birth to a child who was chronically disabled – who knew nothing but pain for his or her whole life. I can't risk that.'

I reached across the table and took her hand in mine. 'But surely there are tests we can take to find out whether or not we're compatible,' I said.

'There are.'

'Then why don't we take one?'

Marie pulled her hand away and shook her head.

'I'm not brave enough for that. It would be like committing ourselves to living happily ever after – when there's a very good chance that we wouldn't be able to.'

'If the test turns out badly, I could have a vasectomy,' I said, though even as I said the words, the thought of not having children was tearing a hole in my heart.

Marie shook her head again – sadly and mournfully. 'I want children, Rob. It would destroy me not to have them – and I think it would do the same to you.' A single tear ran down her cheek. 'I'll always love you – I want you to know that – but this just has to be goodbye.'

A voice from my past drifted – unsummoned and totally unexpectedly – into my mind.

Jill – my darling Jill – standing on Warrington station and talking about the Conroys.

'*The family's too closed in,*' she said. '*It feeds on itself, and that can't be healthy.*'

I had tried to break away, but Jill's death and Grandfather's offer had dragged me back in. And now the curse of the Conroys was being visited on me again – because the woman I had fallen in love with had turned out to be one of them.

If only Aunt Jane had not run away, I thought, self-pityingly. She and Uncle Tony might have had a miserable life together, but at least I'd have known who was who – at least fate wouldn't have been in any position to spring this huge booby trap on me.

I thought back to the night, long ago, when Uncle Tony had discovered that Aunt Jane had left him. Uncle Tony, my father and my mother were all standing in the hall. John, like the obedient son he had always been, had gone to his room as instructed, but I had stayed at the top of the stairs listening to every word which was being said below.

'*When did this happen?*' my mother had asked, after Uncle Tony had told her that Aunt Jane had left him.

'*This morning,*' my uncle replied. '*At least it was probably this morning.*'

'*Aren't you sure? Surely if she hadn't been there, you'd have known.*'

'*She doesn't usually get up until noon.*'

'*But even so . . .*'

'*And ever since we stopped sleeping together – which is nearly a year ago – we've had separate bedrooms.*'

They'd had separate bedrooms for nearly a year!

That could only mean one thing!

'Listen, Marie, I don't think her acting career was the only reason your mother ran away from home,' I said excitedly. 'Maybe it wasn't the reason at all.'

'Then why did she leave?'

'She left because whoever your natural father was, it certainly wasn't Uncle Tony.'

'You're sure?'

'I'm positive.'

I reached across the wooden table and took Marie's hand again, and this time she did not pull away from me.

'Taking the tests isn't going to be a problem,' I said. 'We'll pass with flying colours – because you're only Philip's half-sister and there's not a drop of Conroy blood in you.'

EPILOGUE

Shortly before his death, my gentle, sensitive brother John told me that when you have someone to love, business suddenly doesn't seem as important any more. Back then, I could never even have begun to imagine how right he was – but I understand it well enough now.

These days, my business activity is restricted to an occasional trip to Manchester. There, I sign papers relating to several companies I own – and thanks to Grandfather's legalistic machinations, am never allowed to sell. I do not run these companies – even my grandfather's complex and devious mind couldn't come up with a way to make me do that! – and though they earn me considerable dividends, most of this money goes straight into the Conroy Foundation for Good Works. This is not, I should point out, because I have suddenly become saintly, but simply because my needs are few.

When I'm in England, I take the opportunity to visit my cousin Philip. He has already served a fair chunk of his sentence and, with good behaviour, should be out of gaol in two or three years. When he's released, I will probably offer him an executive post in Conroy Enterprises, but I don't think he will accept it – he seems to have lost his taste for power.

I have tried to see Lydia on a few occasions, too, but the nurses who watch over her have told me she is far too busy writing letters of advice to committees she once chaired – letters which always go unanswered.

None of that matters. It is part of my old life. The village of my childhood is like another planet, and even Oxford has started to seem unreal. These days, I spend most of my time on the small Greek island which my brother first discovered.

It's a good life – a peaceful life. When we want fish, I walk down to the market and buy it fresh from the sea. When I feel like cheese, I milk one of the goats which wander around in the olive grove which came as a part of the

ramshackle villa I bought and am slowly – painstakingly –
renovating myself.

We are not quite cut off from our old life here. Occasionally,
a thin-faced, sweet-guzzling chief inspector from South Wales
will spend part of his annual leave with us. And once in a while
– and always unexpectedly – we will be visited by an eminent
Scottish author who is currently both dazzling his students at
Harvard with his brilliance, and totally confusing them with his
thick Glaswegian accent.

My son and daughter both attend the local school, though I
make time to give them the lessons which will enable them to
return to England one day, should they choose to.

I myself will never return. Though life on the island is in
many ways simple, it is also whole and complete. I can stand
on the harbour wall looking out at the vast blue sea – which,
in reality, isn't vast at all – and feel the centuries of history and
civilisation vibrating beneath my feet. I can climb to the highest
point on the island and make myself at one with the gods who
ruled long before the holy mystic of Palestine entered Jerusalem
on an ass.

I have a small sailing boat now, and once every few months,
my wife and I will leave the children in the care of my frail
grandmother and her sturdy nurse Jo Torlopp (now happily
married to a barrel-chested Greek fisherman), and sail away to
other magic islands. Marie says that I'm a natural sailor, but
my once hard-boiled private eye has so lost her judgement that
she seems to think, in the face of overwhelming evidence to
the contrary, that I'm good at everything I do.

I love my life here, and am living it for myself and my family,
but there is a sense, too, in which I try to live out my brother
John's dreams for him.

I feel I owe him that much.